Helen Baxter

SALLY SCARTH

NAOMI JACOB

has also written

Power
Jacob Ussher
Rock and Sand
Young Emmanuel
The Beloved Physician
The Man Who Found Himself
"Seen Unknown . . ."
That Wild Lie
The Plough
Roots
Props
Poor Straws
Groping
The Loaded Stick
Four Generations
"Honour Come Back"

The Founder of the House
Barren Metal
Timepiece
Fade Out
The Lenient God
No Easy Way
Straws in Amber
This Porcelain Clay
They Left the Land
Under New Management
The Cap of Youth
Leopards and Spots
Private Gollantz
White Wool
Susan Crowther
Honour's a Mistress

ONE-ACT PLAYS

The Dawn   Mary of Delight

AUTOBIOGRAPHY AND BIOGRAPHY

Me : A Chronicle About Other People

"Our Marie" (Marie Lloyd)   Me Again
More About Me   Me in Wartime

GENERAL

Me in the Kitchen

SALLY SCARTH

NAOMI JACOB

44th Thousand

HUTCHINSON & CO. (Publishers) LTD

London   New York   Melbourne   Sydney   Cape Town

To Jane and Harding Cartwright, with
my love, and the admiration which has
grown with the years.

MICKY.

Sirmione,

Italia.

Printed in Great Britain by
William Brendon and Son, Ltd.
The Mayflower Press (late of Plymouth)
at Bushey Mill Lane
Watford, Herts.

BOOK ONE

CHAPTER ONE

The matron interviewed Mrs. Hardcastle in her private room. The room was cold, the floor covered with oilcloth polished until it reflected the legs of the table and the long expanse of chiffonier. Matron liked the room, thought of it with pride, and when she made her rounds of the wards and the paupers' quarters, sometimes murmured, for she was a religious woman, "My days have been cast in pleasant places, thanks be to the Almighty!" Mrs. Ellen Hardcastle, housekeeper at Stallingford Manor, eyed the room with distaste in her expression. A poor kind of room, she reflected, comparing it with her own comfortable sitting-room at the Manor. The furniture was cheap, it was lacking in character, "leave alone comfort". There were few photographs, and those of people who were obviously of little or no importance in the scheme of things. She thought of her own room, with the shining and excellently blackleaded grate, the chenille table-cloth, the canary in the gilt cage which hopped from perch to perch so energetically. She remembered her collection of photographs, not ordinary photographs either, which stood on the bookcase, on the mantelshelf and on the "what-not". There was the house-party of last year, when "H.R.H." himself had been present, there was one, small but infinitely precious, signed in a sprawling, sloping hand, "Victoria R." There were others of her ladyship sitting in a basket chair with her big Persian cat, Pasha, on her knee. His lordship, her ladyship—bless them both—taken on their wedding day. Oh no, her own room was a very different affair from this!

The matron, wearing bombazine and a queer tight-fitting white cap with a goffered frill, sat with her hands folded on her lap. She was thin to the point of emaciation. Her lips closed like a trap, and her eyes were small and desperately active.

Mrs. Hardcastle thought, 'It's a blessing as I found out about poor Lizzie's bairn! Not much of a place fur bairns this, or my name's not Ellen Hardcastle!'

The matron smoothed down her bombazine skirt, and spoke. "The guardians have considered the case of Sarah—er—Hardcastle, and as you are prepared to assume responsibility for her they see no reason why they should refuse to allow you to take the child."

Mrs. Hardcastle ejaculated, "Refuse!" adding a second later: "Pah!"

The matron disregarded both ejaculations, and continued, "I feel it only right to warn you that Sarah—er—Hardcastle is not one of our best girls. She is self-willed——"

"Character! I like it!" Mrs. Hardcastle flung out.

"She is inclined to be fussy over her clothes, her food——"

"Likes things nice, I'll be bound!"

In short, the matron was casting aside all attempts to be even moderately pleasant. "Sarah is anything but the kind of girl we consider likely to do well in service."

In service! Speaking to Ellen Hardcastle as if Stallingford Manor could be compared to the house of Mrs. Richards, the grocer's wife, where a "general" was kept, and treated like some slave!

Mrs. Hardcastle bridled. She, too, smoothed down her skirt, conscious that it was of rich, heavy silk, not bombazine. Mrs. Hardcastle moved her shoulders under the well-made mantle and fingered her velvet bonnet-strings. Real velvet too, none of your cotton-backed rubbish.

"There is service—and service, ma'am," she said coldly. "My niece is going to no ordinary place, let that be understood, if you please. Stallingford Manor is something different from the tradesmen's houses in the town. I should like to see Sarah, if you please."

"Certainly." The matron rose. "There will be papers to sign, of course."

Mrs. Hardcastle began to peel off her over-tight black kid glove. "I'll sign 'em."

A moment later Sarah Hardcastle, daughter of Mrs. Hardcastle's sister—for the "Mrs." was merely a courtesy title given to all respectable housekeepers—entered the room. She was twelve years old, tall for her age, with no claims to good looks except her fine wide-apart grey eyes and her good skin. Her hair was scraped back from a bony forehead, and plastered close to her head. She wore a shapeless cotton dress, and an apron. Her feet were encased in heavy black shoes, her hands were red and roughened from hard work.

The matron said, "Ah, Sarah Hardcastle!"

Sarah gave a quick, almost epileptic bob, and muttered, "Yes'm."

"This is your aunt, Mrs. Hardcastle, Sarah——"

Sarah cast one terrified glance at the tall, stout lady, who was so magnificently dressed that for one wild moment the child had thought that she must be Queen Victoria, then bobbed again, saying breathlessly, "Yes'm."

Mrs. Hardcastle held out her hand. "Come here, child."

Sarah hesitated, her aunt thought that she shivered, then made a kind of plunge forward, and reached her aunt's side. She stood there, her red hands clasped before her, staring wildly at the figure in black silk, who looked exactly like some of the ladies who came visiting the inmates of the workhouse at Christmas and walked round, apparently creatures from another world.

"I am your aunt, Ellen Hardcastle," the lady said. "I have only lately heard that you were in"—she sniffed suddenly and disdainfully—"this place. Had I known, you'd have been out of it long since. Only through the kindness of his lordship did I hear. I've come to take you away."

Sarah clenched her hands still more tightly, then licking her lips, said in a hoarse voice, "Ter t'prison?"

"Prison?" Mrs. Hardcastle shot a quick glance at the matron. "Prison? Who'd be sending bairns like you to prison for any favour? Not likely! I'm taking you to Stallingford Manor, where there's the chance of your life awaiting for you. Can you sew nicely?"

Again that wild look in the child's eyes. "Aye—that's aboot all Ah can do! Ah'm a reit good sewer, Ah am."

The matron interposed, "Oh yes, Sarah sews very nicely indeed."

Mrs. Hardcastle disregarded the interruption. "Can you read and write?"

The child nodded the sleek dark head. "Aye, a bit o' baith. Not sooch a lot though."

"Well, you'll pick it up! You're to have seven pounds a year. Think of that—seven pounds!"

"Pounds o' what? Beef?"

"Nay," her aunt laughed, a fat, rolling sound which was like something comfortable, like really good plum duff, or newly baked bread, or the smell of freshly ironed linen, "nay, beef! Money, my dear, money. An' you're going to be a good girl, and a hard-working girl and"—Mrs. Hardcastle fumbled for the right phrase—"do your duty in that state of life ter which it shall please God—and his lordship—to call you."

Sarah stood listening. Not that she understood half of what the two women said. She heard her aunt say, "Nay, she'd no right to be here at all, and wouldn't have been if people had taken the trouble to look around and find out a bit about the child!"

She watched the matron pinch her lips together, saw her bring out papers to which Mrs. Hardcastle put her signature, writing less easily than one might have expected from such a grand lady. There was another short conversation about clothes.

"Nay, thank you," Mrs. Hardcastle said, "I want none on 'em. Not that seeing what his lordship pays i' rates and taxes we've not a right to 'em, if so be as we eether wanted or needed 'em. We don't, praise be! Sarah 'ul come with me to John Jackson's an' I shall get all that's needed." She paused, then said again, "Aye, all that's needed, if you please!"

Sarah was told to get her hat and cloak, and ran like the wind to find them. She was going away, leaving this horrible place where she had been—it seemed for years and years. She hated it, with its smell of dirty clothes, greasy food, and newly scrubbed boards. She had always hated it, ever since the day when her mother had been buried and a stout man with a scarlet face and a "cheese-cutter cap" had led her from the graveside, saying in a voice which sounded as if it had been well soused in beer, "Now, move along! No 'enging beck. Now yer're a little pauper yer mun learn ter step out! Do as yer told. Speak when yer spoken to. Do as yer bid!" He had talked loudly to another man who walked beside them, saying, "Ah dean't hold wi' it! You an' me an' decent folks havin' ter pay ter keep bastard brats i' luxury!"

The other man had chuckled. "Not soa mooch bloody luxury if yer arst me, mate."

The scarlet-faced man returned, with some heat, "An' why should theer be, tell me thet? Did Ah arst thet they cum inter t'world? Noa! Did you? Noa? Then tell me wheer is the reit as we has ter pay fur 'em? Blasted paupers!"

It was all different. Life with her mother hadn't always been easy. Plenty of times they had scarcely enough to eat, and sometimes her mother cried dreadfully. Once they had slept under a hedge, and another time in a barn near a farmhouse. Sometimes they spent the night in a workhouse—casuals—and her mother had to pull dirty old rope into little pieces. Sarah had hated the nights they spent as casuals. Hated the filth, and the smell, and the way people spoke to you—as if you were dogs or worse. Once, when her mother's fingers were sore with picking at the rope, she had taken a hairpin out of her hair, bent it into a kind of hook, and had begun to tear the tarred rope with it. Sarah could still remember the tone in which a man spoke to her !

"Now then, whatcher think yer doin'? Lazy bitch! Had yer night's lodging fur you an' yer brat an' doan't wanter pay fur it. Afraid o' spoiling yer fingers, eh? Think that——"

She never heard what else he said because her mother sprang to her feet screaming, telling him to shut his foul mouth and keep it shut. There had been trouble of some kind, and a tall man in a good suit of clothes had come and talked to her mother. She could remember that he said again and again, "Now, what's this? What's this?" Then he had stooped down and shoved his face close to her mother's and laughed, saying, "Got to pay fur stopping here fur the neit, you know that?" Then, laughing : "Like ter pay—and leave the okum alone? Easier, after all?" She had hoped that her mother would pay, and let them get out of the place on to the high road again. Instead she had turned back to the pile of tarred rope and begun to pick it to pieces again, saying nothing at all.

The summer days were pleasant enough, Sarah remembered. Long straight roads, with fields on either side. Sometimes they stopped at one of the fields, and her mother helped to rake hay, or bind corn, and even sometimes pick potatoes. Men always stared at her mother, smiled and laughed. Once, a big farmer, in breeches and fine cloth leggings, said, "Tha's ovver bonnie fur this life, ma wench. Thee'll find nobbut trouble waitin' fur thee, wi' that faace."

Her mother said, "Nay, mister, Ah shan't find mor'n what Ah've gotten already."

Then at last they'd come to Stallingford, and her mother had fallen down in the street and said, "Nay, it's not a bit of use, it 'ul have ter be t'House."

Someone had helped her to the workhouse, and they had been admitted, and her mother had been put to bed. Sarah had been put with a lot of other children, who smelt nasty and were always scratching their heads or their bodies. She had never had any good clothes, she had slept "rough", but somehow the air and the fresh wind and the sun and rain prevented her clothes from smelling, and her hair had always been clean. One night, when they had slept in a lodging-house, Sarah had found a small dark-brown insect crawling about on her leg. Her mother had cried, and said, "Nay, that's aboot t'finish, that is, when ma bairn gets bugs on her !"

She had cried for her mother, and someone said, "Nay, it's not a bit o' use crying, thee muther's deid. Happen Matron here 'ul gie thee t'lend o' a bit o' crape fur thee hat fur t'funeral."

Now as she hurried back down the long stone-flagged corridor, with her bonnet in her hand and her "charity bairn's" cape over her arm, Sarah thought of the funeral. They had let her see her mother lying dead, in a long narrow coffin, painted black. The coffin was filled with wood shavings packed closely round her mother's body, and scattered over it. Her mother's eyes weren't quite shut, you could see the blue shining through the half-open lids. An old woman with no teeth who stood near said, "Poor thing, us oughter ha' hed pennies fur 'um."

She had wanted to touch her mother's hands, because she had always loved to hold them. They were hidden under the shavings, and when she tried to push the shavings aside to get to them, someone said, "Nay, mind t'bairn, dostha want her ter see her muther naked ! Nay, gie ovver, luv. Kiss thee muther an' let be."

Then the funeral, and the man with the scarlet face—later she was to find that his name was Mr. Heggles—and he was a beadle. She never knew what a beadle was. When the children dared they called after him, "Bettle, bettle." She had just stayed on and on in the workhouse, until one day someone said that she was twelve, and would go out to service. She had gone with five other girls—Clara Bates, Mary Sanders, Polly Gives, and Ellen Mason—before a room filled with gentlemen. One gentleman said to Matron, "And these are the girls, eh, Matron ? They do you great credit, I'm sure."

Matron had smiled and bowed her head, and said, "Thank you. I try to do my duty, I'm sure, sir."

One man with a long white beard had made a booming noise which turned out to be: "We're sure of that, sure of that, Matron !"

The little girls had stood in a line. Sarah had been terribly afraid, because all the gentlemen were very grandly dressed, and one of them had a piece of round glass in his eye, and when he turned it caught the light and shone like a lamp. Matron read out the names of the girls, and when it came to Sarah's name the man with the glass in his eye said, "Er—ah—one moment—just one moment——"

Matron said, "Yes, m'lord, yes ?"

He leant back in his chair, a bigger chair than the rest of the gentlemen had, and taking the glass from his eye rubbed it with a very large, white handkerchief.

"What's that name ?" he asked. "Sarah—er—ah—what ? Hardcastle ? D'ye say Hardcastle ?"

"Yes, m'lord, Hardcastle—Sarah."

He put out a hand—like his handkerchief it was very large and white—saying, "C'm here, little girl. That's right—no need to be afraid."

"She's not afraid, m'lord," Matron said. "I've never known child less——"

He stared at her. "Did I speak to you ?"

"No, m'lord, no, of course not."

"Kindly remain silent. Now tell me—er—Sarah. Have you any other names ? Yes, yes, Hardcastle, but anything else ?"

She had swallowed hard, because in spite of what Matron had said she was frightened.

"Yes, sir—Sarah Ellen Hardcastle. I am twelve years old, sir. My mother left me here in the care of Matron and other kind people. I am very grateful, sir, for all that has been done for me——"

The big man moved in his chair, and said to the man next to him, who had a face as red as Beadle Heggles, "Good Lord ! Who, tell me, Carter, teaches them this infernal rubbish ! What d'we want 'em to be ? Cringing slaves or decent God-fearing men and women ? That's parrot talk !" Then to the matron, "D'you teach them this—balderdash ?"

"Well, m'lord, it's usual—I mean to say——"

"Pah !" he retorted, as if he had suddenly tasted something nasty. "Pah ! Let's have no more of it. Gratitude's one thing—being a lickspittle's another." He turned back to Sarah. "Sarah Ellen Hardcastle," he said, "d'you know where your mother came from, eh ?"

Sarah said, "She told me as me grand-da had a farm——"

"Ah, a farm !" He shot a glance at the man next to him. "The plot thickens ! Now, Sarah, I can see that you're clever, eh ? That's right—er—clever. Can—you—remember—where this farm was ! Ah ! Now think !" He spoke very slowly, saying every word as if it were terribly important. The other children were staring, all the gentlemen were leaning forward in their chairs watching her.

"Naay," she said, "Ah dean't reitly mind, sir."

"Was it Stallingford?"

"No, sir. It weer—were—summat like—me mammy did tell me. It weer—summat like——"

"Take your time," the gentleman said easily, grandly, as if all the day belonged to him.

"Summat like Polly—Polly—Polly wat. Nay, yon's not reit."

The gentleman smiled. "Pretty Polly Perkins?"

"Nay," she had forgotten to say "sir" and was wrinkling her brows with the effort to remember. "One time we passed it—me an' me mammy—she tell'd ma: 'Yon's wheer thee grand-da lives. Name o' it's—Polly——' Nay, Ah've fergot agean."

"Pollithwaite?" said the gentleman.

Sarah almost shouted, "Aye, mister, yon's it! Tha's gotten it reit."

The whole room seemed filled with sound, with laughter, full-throated, coming from men who were not afraid to laugh, who held positions where no one dared tell them to hold their mirth back. One small, thin man, who when he laughed sounded like a hen that had just laid an egg, beat his fist on the table before him.

"Hach—tach!" he went, his face twisted, his eyes full of tears. "Tha's gotten it reit! B' Gad, Stallingford—you'll find that 'ul take a bit of living down!"

The man called Stallingford smiled, tolerantly amused. "I shall be content not to live it down, Mortley! Not a bad comment to have made concerning one. Well, Sarah"—he looked at her, his eyes twinkling—"we've found it, then! Pollithwaite." He glanced round at the rest of the gentlemen as if he were going to prove to them how clever he was. "Tha's tould us all as we mum knaw, choose how! Ah'll tell thee what—tha's din thesen a reit guid turn t'daay, sitha."

She had forgotten to be frightened, and smiled back at him. "Eh," she said, "Ah din nout ondly tell thee t'naame on me grand-da's farm. Ah war hard set ter think on it."

Again they laughed, and the gentleman began to speak to his friends, talking behind his hand; she caught the words. "Hard-castle—died last year—last back end," he said, and smiled because he was talking dialect. "My housekeeper—a good body if ever there was one . . . sister—we-e-ell, flighty. Hence . . ." He waved his hand towards where Sarah stood. He beckoned to Matron, and she went forward and stood close to the table. His smiles had gone now ; somehow Sarah felt that he didn't care such a lot about Matron. He spoke quietly and very quickly, and she kept saying, "Yes, m'lord", and "No, m'lord".

They must have all been feeling very good-tempered that day, for after they had listened to where it was proposed to send the other small girls, they felt in their pockets and passed money up to the tall, smiling man, who could speak like other folks as well as like what the gentry did. He sorted out the money, and then called out the names of the children.

"Clara Bates—there you are, m'dear. Be good, be truthful and you'll be happy. Then, Mary Sanders—take that. Work hard and be a credit to us all." He looked at his list again. "Polly Gives, Ellen Mason—a little present for you both—serve God, honour the Queen, and you'll have nothing to worry about." And at last, "Now, Sarah Ellen Hardcastle, you'll stay here until someone comes to take you away. Make the best of your life, not the worst. Be truthful, and—good. Er—ah—stand fast against temptation, and—er—God bless you."

He leant back as if it had been something of an effort to find the right thing to say to each child, then sat suddenly upright as if someone had pulled a string. "Er—Matron—I want that money spent—and I am sure these gentlemen agree—in buying something for these children—er—before they go out to—er— domestic service. Let us have the bills here for inspection at the next guardians' meeting, please. Thank you. Good morning, children."

ii

Sarah went with this new and magnificent aunt to Jackson's. Clothes were bought for her, neat and hard-wearing, but finer than anything she had ever seen.

"What's them ?" she asked, pointing to some garments.

"Nightgowns, my dear, to wear in bed."

"Eh ! We allus weer our shifts at t'House."

"S-sh ! No call to mention that place !"

Driving back to where her aunt lived, in a dog-cart, where Sarah hung on the back seat terrified that she might be flung into the road at any moment, she heard Mrs. Hardcastle talking to the man who drove the fine horse with the shining coat, and the glittering harness.

"Just like his lordship to send you, Mr. Walters. He knew that I should feel it, going to that place. Very considerate of him, I'm sure. I should have been sadly set about if Herbert or William had driven me in, I'm sure. Never had such a thing in our family—never. My father was a hard man, Mr. Walters; a just man, but hard."

Mr. Walters replied, "Aye, just men oft'times is hard, Mrs. Hardcastle."

"And when poor Sally—well, you've heard the story—did what she did—he wouldn't have her indoors again. Not was it ever so! I knew nothing of it, while I went home and asked where Sally was. My Da said, 'Ellen,' he said, 'never mention her name. She's no daughter of mine!' I was heartbroken. I did my best—tried every way to get track of her, but it was no use. Ah, poor girl, it was a sad end."

"I don't doubt," Mr. Walters said heavily, "as the poor thing weer not ondly sining but sined ageanst. Let them as is without sin and cettera."

"I've always said so," Mrs. Hardcastle agreed, "never were truer words spoken."

He flirted his whip over the broad back of the mare, causing her to leap forward so that Sarah was almost flung into the road. Hearing her little cry of astonishment, Mr. Walters turned a smiling face and nodded to her.

"Hang on, luvey," he said, "if it's ondly bi the skin of your teeth!"

"Have my teeth got skin on them?"

He chuckled. "Nay, not that I knows on, they've not."

The whole thing was like a dream. In front under the seat were parcels and packets, each one holding clothes for her, for Sarah Hardcastle. She was wearing a little print frock and a hat of dark blue straw with a dark blue ribbon. The workhouse clothes had been left at the shop. Her aunt had said grandly, "Send them back to where they belong, if you please, Mr. Jackson. We want none of them! It's all been a mistake, and thanks to his lordship we've been enabled to put it right."

Mr. Jackson raised his eyebrows, bent his head on its long neck and listened while her aunt talked at length, speaking very softly, never stopping, scarcely giving Mr. Jackson time to ejaculate, "Tch, tech", or "Tut, tut," at the proper intervals.

Sarah had known that they were speaking about her, wondered vaguely if they were saying that she was good or bad, pretty or ugly, clever or stupid. Not that it mattered very much, no one spoke harshly to her, no one caught her ear in hard fingers and tweaked it, no one shouted, "Sarah 'Ardcastle—I'll give you summat ter remember, see if I don't." She wriggled on her slippery seat when she thought of the various occasions when she had received "something to remember". Aye, but Matron could lay it on !

The trap turned, swayed through gates, with pillars on either side. On the top of the pillars were animals—lions, Sarah thought, holding shields. Mr. Walters saluted a lady who stood at the gates with his whip, and Mrs. Hardcastle called, "Good afternoon, Mrs. Collet, good afternoon !" They went under trees, two rows of them, tall, flinging dark shadows over the road. Between the trees Sarah could see grass and once she espied a rabbit scuttling away, showing only a flash of white as it disappeared into the earth.

"Eh, yon's a rabbit !" she cried.

"That's right, luvey," Mr. Walters agreed. "Poor Willie Porter is fair worried to knaw what ter do wi' em. They're all over the place."

Her aunt laughed. "Mr. Porter's always worried over something, poor man !"

Then she saw the house. A house with—so it seemed—hundreds and hundreds of windows, with pillars, and wide steps, with a great terrace before it, and long stretches of smooth grass, where some people were sitting in chairs having some kind of a meal. She'd heard of a picnic—that must be a picnic. Mr. Walters drove round the side of the house, into a great yard paved with flags. He called in a commanding voice, "Here, some of you ! Look lively now. Help Mrs. Hardcastle down with her parcels."

Young men, wearing striped waistcoats, with long black sleeves, ran forward. One of them lifted Sarah down and said, "Had a nice ride, missie, Ah be bound."

Her aunt took her hand and led her to a door through which they passed. They walked down a long corridor, and her aunt opened a door and went into the most beautiful room Sarah had ever seen. It was large, and the floor was covered with a bright carpet, patterned with flowers of all kinds. The grate shone brightly, and where the fire would be in winter stood a splendid plant—a fern, Sarah thought. There were easy chairs, on one of which a large yellow cat was lying, while a canary chirped in a

B

gilt cage which hung in the window.   There were pictures on the walls, and photographs in frames standing on tables and shelves.

Mrs. Hardcastle stood looking round, as if to make sure that nothing had disappeared in her absence.   She stooped and patted the big cat.   "There you are, Tommy—and how's my Dickie— tweet, tweet, Dickie !   Sarah, take off your hat, and we'll have some tea.   Just ring that bell there."

"Waffor ?" Sarah asked.   "Is the others cuming ?"

"Others, no !   That's for Alice.   Oh, Alice—I'll have tea, if you please.   This is my little niece, Sarah.   Yes, come to learn to be useful—and good, we hope."

Alice, tall, with a red face which seemed to have been polished, said, "Oh, certain to be good, I'd think bi the looks of her, Mrs. Hardcastle."

"We shall see," Mrs. Hardcastle replied darkly.   "Toast— no, too hot for toast, Alice.   Bread-and-butter—yes, and a pot of my strawberry jam.   And the seed cake—yes."

A wonderful tea, laid out on a shining white cloth, cups with flowers round them, and bread-and-butter cut thin so's you scarcely knew you were eating anything at all.   Only there was plenty of it, and you could eat as much as you liked, so the thinness didn't matter.   Sarah sighed, "Eh, it's a luvely plaace, this is.   Is it yourn ?"

"You'll have to try to talk nicely, Sarah," her aunt admon- ished.   "We can't have that common talk here, my dear.   No, of course, this house isn't mine.   I'm the housekeeper."

"Whose house is it, then ?"

"The most Noble the Earl of Stallingford," her aunt told her, rolling the words out as if she loved them.   "The Most Noble the Earl and Countess of Stallingford.   And there is his photo- graph !   That one there, in uniform.   A fine figure of a gentle- man !   And her ladyship is just as——"

Sarah screamed suddenly, "Eh, but Ah knaws him.   He talked ter me at t'House, he did.   Talked just like wot Ah do an' all."

"What are you talking about !   His lordship is the chairman of the guardians.   He saw you, and knew who you were——"

"Not while Ah told him he didn't ?   He kep' saying what was me grand-da's farm called ?   Ah couldn't mind, he kep' on saying this an' that.   Eh, reit comic he weer."

She felt elated at the sight of the man who had talked to her, she kept looking at his picture, admiring the way he stood, the

way his head was thrown back a little, as if he were not afraid of
anything in the world. He wasn't smiling in the picture, but you
felt that he might at any minute. He wasn't like an ordinary
man, he was like God.

Mrs. Hardcastle said, "Well, well, I know nothing of this.
Tell me what his lordship said. Just see if you can remember!"

Remember! Could she ever forget? His smile, the glass
which he put in his eye and then took out and polished on that
immense white handkerchief. His voice when he had spoken as
she did, his dancing eyes when he had looked round to see if all
the other gentlemen understood the joke. The change when he
had spoken to Matron—and Sarah had known that he didn't like
her. Remember! She told her story, her aunt listened, smiling
and nodding her head, saying sometimes, "Now, now, you're
making that bit up!"

"Nay, Ah niver am! It's gospil! He said . . ." and on she
went again.

The story ended, her aunt leant back in her chair. "I never
did! Why it's as good as a play! Think of his lordship joking
away like that! And Sir Trafford Mortley too! Just ring that
bell again, Sarah, I'd like Mr. Blachlet to hear this. Ah, Alice,
just take my compliments to Mr. Blachlet, if you please, and say
that I should be glad if he could spare a minute to step along
here."

Mr. Blachlet stepped along and was offered a glass of sherry.
He was tall and stout, wearing a coat which showed a great deal
of white shirt-front, his manner was dignified and tinged with
condescension.

He bowed slightly. "Most kind of you, Mrs. Hardcastle,
most kind. And this is the little wanderer of whom you told
me. How do you do, my little girl? Now, you wanted to see
me, Mrs. Hardcastle? Was it about Maude? I am very much
afraid that Maude is going to cause trouble in the still-room—if I
may say so—very much afraid."

"It's not about Maude, though I'm afraid you're right. We'll
talk about that later. I want you to hear about his lordship.
You'll be surprised!"

"Nothing," said Mr. Blachlet, sipping sherry with appreciation, "could surprise me where his lordship was concerned—
always provided that it was good, essentially good."

"Listen to this! Sarah, tell Mr. Blachlet."

Again she told the story, thrilling with pride to speak of the

man with the glass in his eye.   She remembered every word, even
the interruption by the other gentleman, but always she kept her
hero in the centre of the stage.

The story ended, her aunt said in triumph, "And what, Mr.
Blachlet, do you think of that ?"

"I think—thank you, perhaps another half glass—I think
that it would take a gentleman like his lordship to behave in such
a manner under such circumstances." He turned to Sarah.
"My dear child, remember all your life what you owe to his lordship and to her ladyship for allowing your good aunt to bring
you here.   Nothing which you could do for them, no work which
you could accomplish, could ever wipe out the debt which you
owe them.   Your own wishes, your own desires, your own life if
needs be, should be at their disposal.   You understand that ?"

Sarah nodded, then looked again at the photograph.   "Aye,
that's reit.   Ah'd do aut fur him !   Ah'd die fur him if so be as
he wished it."

CHAPTER TWO

THERE were times when Sarah Hardcastle used to pinch herself, during the weeks which followed, to make certain that she was not dreaming. It never occurred to her—or for that matter to anyone else—that no child of twelve had a right to be earning its living, assuming duties, rising early, and being allowed time for exercise as a favour not as a right. Having spent the past six years of her life in "t'Union", realizing the fact that she possessed no rights as a pauper, that she was fed and clothed merely through a merciful Providence represented on earth by a committee of gentlemen known as the Guardians, she regarded Stallingford Manor as a place which was considerably more comfortable than Heaven. Heaven, the conditions of life there, the character of its inhabitants, had all been carefully explained to the infant paupers by the workhouse chaplain, the Rev. Samuel Proctor. Until now the thought of Heaven had seemed desperately unattractive, though Mr. Proctor had made it clear that the likelihood of any of the small paupers reaching Heaven was remote in the extreme. Hell, he assured them, with yawning fires were already being banked up in readiness for them, and, it appeared, they were only likely to escape on condition that they realized what worms they were, and, as worms, squirmed on their metaphorical small bellies to Matron, the master, himself and Heggles.

Sarah confided in a whisper to one of her companions, "Ah'd as leaf gan ter hell, it 'ud be grand an' warm onny road."

The other child, being bred in a world where tale-carrying was one means of gaining favour, reported to Matron that Sarah Hardcastle said she wished to go to hell. Sarah Hardcastle was accordingly dealt with in the only fashion which the matron considered suitable for pauper children.

Sarah had been cold, hungry—for workhouse food was of the poorest possible quality, and the quantity was strictly limited—unwanted and perpetually punished ; she had slept in a dormitory with twenty-four other children, all insufficiently washed. She had worn clothes which were ingenious in their ugliness, and she had suffered from the knowledge that everyone she passed in the streets knew her for a pauper, and either pitied or scorned her.   To find herself sleeping in a bedroom occupied only by the rosy-cheeked Alice, with not only white blankets but white sheets on the beds, to hear that she was to take a bath every Saturday night, and then go straight to bed, to realize that meals were served with something almost approaching dignity, and that the said meals were not only eatable but very pleasant, seemed incredible to her.

She came to look forward to those meals, with the frank greediness of a healthy child.   She loved the big servants' hall, where her aunt sat at one end of the long table and Mr. Blachlet at the other.   She liked to let her eyes go slowly up and down, noting the various faces, ready to smile back when someone smiled and nodded at her.   It was astonishing how kind all these well-dressed people were to her.   Mr. Blachlet would nod and smile, saying, "Ah, good morning, little girl," and she learnt to reply, "Good morning, sir."   On the other hand, there was, it seemed, no occasion to call either Mr. Black or Mr. Thorpe—sir. You merely said, "Good morning, Mr. Black," or "Good morning, Mr. Thorpe."   You said "sir" to Mr. Lingley, because he was his lordship's own private servant, and Sarah, watching him, felt a little shiver of excitement to think that he actually spoke with his lordship every day, handed him his coat, fastened his boots and pressed his trousers.   She wished that she might have been a boy, and learnt to be a valet !   Miss Cecile—her ladyship's maid —was called "Mamzel", which appeared to be a kind of dignified pet name.   She was tall and slim, with dark flashing eyes, and Sarah formed the opinion that Mr. Lingley liked her very much indeed.   Then there was Mrs. Bishop, who had been nurse to Lord Victor and Lady Gwendoline.   They were too old to need a nurse now, Mrs. Hardcastle told Sarah, because his lordship— "his young lordship that is, of course, is rising eighteen an' Lady Gwendoline is fifteen.   But the family is that fond of Mrs. Bishop that she stays on, just as if there were still children in the house". It appeared that Mrs. Bishop, who was enormously stout, spent her time mending linen, making chair-covers and curtains, and preparing new underclothes for Lord Victor and Lady Gwendoline.

Sarah was curious regarding these children, the girl only three years older than herself.   She had caught sight of her walking in the gardens, with a short stout lady dressed in a very tight plaid skirt and a short jacket of bottle green.   The lady's name, Sarah was told, was "Frawline". She was a governess and was teaching Lady Gwendoline to speak German. It seemed that it was very necessary to speak German because the Queen liked it.

His young lordship was at a school called Eton. Sarah wondered if it was so called on account of the excellent quality of the food. It seemed that something of the wonder of his lordship hung about his young lordship, for Mr. Blachlet said, "A chip of the old block, and not such a small chip either, believe me!" While Mr. Lingley declared that he was possessed of real taste in clothes and cravats. "Small wonder that he likes to get into something different after that everlasting topper and tail coat!"

Mrs. Bishop wheezed, "He's a dear kind boy, as his sister is a dear little lady. I shall never say any different, nor couldn't if I tried, unless I liked to tell lies, which I never have done from earliest childhood."

It was Mrs. Bishop who inquired about Sarah's abilities as a seamstress, who set her a fine towel to darn and was so delighted at the result that she asked if Sarah might not come into the nurseries and really learn how to sew.

"For believe me, Mrs. Hardcastle, with them both growing up, with his lordship wanting new shirts—not to mention other things—almost every month, it seems, with her little ladyship wanting—and rightly—the very latest style in underclothes—my hands are full. To say nothing of her ladyship's tea-gowns and morning gowns, all with lace in rows and rows, and all of the finest. Mamzel is a great help to me—but it's in the designing, not in the making. There's a new dress for Lady Gwendoline"— Mrs. Bishop sighed deeply—"the latest! Dark blue with bands of satin, yes, the same colour round the skirt. There is a second skirt of that—if you please!—looped up at both sides and the back finished off with a round bow—if you know what I mean— no ends. The bodice tight, finished with bands of satin, as the skirt, and a bow of real lace, more of a 'jabot'—that's Mamzel's word—at the neck. Elegant, but oh, the work on those bands! I'd be glad of another pair of hands, indeed I should."

So Sarah went to the nursery, and learnt to rub cold cream on her hands at night so that they should be kept soft and nice and not "catch" on the satin. She learnt to make the finest tucks in the finest cambric, to sew on frills without crushing them. She learnt to press clothes, to sponge away marks, fruit-

stains, and the mud from dogs' paws ; she learnt to take the
bones out of heavy corsets, to wash, iron the garments themselves
and neatly insert the steel and whalebone once more, button-
holing the ends of the steels.   She watched Lady Gwendoline
standing, it seemed for hours, while Mrs. Bishop and Mamzel
circled round her, pinning here, snipping there, muttering to each
other with their mouths filled with pins.

Mrs. Bishop said, "I've gotten a new helper, Lady Gwendoline
—Sarah Hardcastle."

Lady Gwendoline, tall and slim for her age, without that heavy
bulkiness which comes to so many girls of fifteen, nodded to
Sarah, so that her long fair hair swung backwards and forwards,
as if blown by a gentle breeze.

"I hope that you like being here," she said.   "You must be
very good with our dearest Bish, mustn't she, Bish dear ?"

"She's a very good, hard-working little girl, I will say that."

Sarah bobbed and blushed, and thought how lovely Lady
Gwendoline smelt, and how her hair shone, and how bright her
eyes were, and what beautiful shoes and stockings she wore.
She hadn't seemed to mind a bit taking off her dress in front of
Mrs. Bishop, Mamzel and Sarah, just slipped it off and stood in
her petticoat and bodice—all threaded with ribbon—as if it was
the most natural thing in the world.

One day her ladyship came, and as she entered the nursery
Sarah's heart gave a leap in her young flat chest, because for one
brief moment she thought that his lordship might come too, and
she longed to see him again.   Her ladyship was alone ; she didn't
walk, she sort of floated into the room wearing a dress which
looked like a long coat, made of dark green cloth with lighter
stripes, fastened with big silver buttons, and trimmed with some
soft fur of a lightish brown.   It was difficult to understand what
she said at first ; she didn't speak like ordinary people.   Her
first remark sounded like, "Harr arr yearah, Bish dearah ?
Gwendoline tells mah herah dress is chawrming.   So clevarah of
yearah—and Cecile too."   After a time you got used to it, and
understood almost at once what she meant to say.

She was very tall, her daughter was like her, a small edition of
her mother, Sarah would have thought had she known what
"edition" meant, which she didn't.

Mrs. Bishop said, "I've done my best, m'lady, so has Mamzel,
I will say.   And this, m'lady, is the little girl, Mrs. Hardcastle's
niece.   The girl his lordship was so good as to take an interest

in. She's doing very nicely. Sarah, show her ladyship that initial you've embroidered on Lady Gwendoline's nightgown. It's nicely done, I think, m'lady."

Her ladyship took the garment which Sarah held out to her, she examined the elaborate initial attentively, then handed it back to Sarah. Sarah bobbed and said, "Thank you, your ladyship, ma'am——"

"I hope that yourah happy hereah," she said. "She looks pale to me, Bish dearah. Bettah see that she gets out enough. You know how particulah his lordship is about fresh airah. How old are you ?"

Sarah bobbed again and said, "Twelve past, m'lady, please."

Adelaide Stallingford stared at her, then spoke to Mrs. Bishop. "Poor little thing ! Only three yearahs youngah than Gwendoline. Don't let her bob up and down like that, this isn't an—er"—she had been going to say something else, Sarah felt, and at the last minute changed the word in her mind—"er—institution. Well, be happy, Sarah. If you can't be happy with Mrs. Bishop you'll never be happy anywhereah. Good-bye, Bish." She went, leaving a trail of scent behind her, some soft perfume which, Sarah felt, could never have been used by anyone else. She sighed, and said to Mrs. Bishop, "Eeh ! She's luverly, isn't she ?"

"In thought, mind an' deed," Mrs. Bishop said heavily. "A —lady ! In every sense of the word, as his lordship is a—gentleman."

After that she was sent out every afternoon for an hour to walk in the park. "Not," Mrs. Bishop said, "in the gardens, remember. Kitchen garden, well, yes—but not the flower gardens."

It was wonderful to walk in the park, to watch the rabbits scurrying about, to follow the little beck that ran through the deep grass, its smooth flow interrupted here and there with small artificial waterfalls. The great trees flung great fans of shade, and beneath their branches the air felt suddenly, almost frighteningly cool. Sarah turned and looked back at the great house, which seemed to her like some fairy palace, basking in the soft afternoon sunshine. Such a house ! With its many windows, its flights of stone steps, its lawns—they looked as if they were made of smooth, fine velvet, and the flower-beds which glowed like jewels.

She could see the fountain playing in what they called the "Italian garden", the tall jets of water catching the sunlight, and falling like diamond rain into the marble basin. The yew hedges cut into strange shapes, birds, peacocks, stairs and turrets looked so thickly dark in contrast to the glittering water and the bright green of the grass. As she watched, and it seemed to her that the whole panorama was spread out for her especial benefit, she saw two peacocks walk along the terrace. Not dark and sinister like the peacocks of the yew hedge, but glittering, fantastic creatures, with small proud heads, and a strutting walk which seemed to be part of their character. She sighed, it was all too beautiful.

"And I live here," she said softly. "This is where he brought me, outo' yon horrible plaace ter this !"

The sound of the clock in the stable yard reached her, a quarter past three. She had still half an hour before she need be back to make tea for herself and Mrs. Bishop. Half an hour in which she could do anything she liked ! The very thought was luxury. She turned away from staring at the house, and began to walk through the long grass towards the beck. It was pleasant to sit there, to take off her stockings and dabble her toes in the running water. Then she saw him. He was walking towards her, swinging a stick.

It was nearly two months since she had come to Stallingford, and this was the first time she had seen him. For a moment she stood transfixed, watching him. How easily he moved, how splendid he looked in that short, light jacket, and that small hat perched on one side of his head. He held a cigar in one hand and the smell of it reached her as she stood there. Ought she to hurry away, should she fling herself down in the long grass and hide until he had passed ? Or should she walk forward, and merely avert her eyes or stand and give a particularly deep "bob" ? Just as she was standing there, perplexed, he turned, looked over his shoulder and whistled. A dog came bounding towards him, a great dun-coloured creature, which, Sarah knew, was his lordship's own special dog. "Agamemnon" he was called, and the name had caused considerable speculation in the servants' hall. Mr. Blachlet gave it as his opinion that the dog was named after some Eastern potentate met by his lordship on some of his travels. Mr. Lingley said, on the contrary, the gentleman—Agamemnon—was a well-known traveller himself, a kind of Christopher Columbus. There were various opinions, but everyone was agreed that the dog was a magnificent creature and of great value, also that he was devoted to his lordship.

Now the dog passed his master and came rushing forward towards Sarah. She had never seen such a dog, she had known very few, except those who used to fly out from farm gates when she and her mother passed, barking and growling. She stood petrified, certain in her own mind that she was going to be torn in pieces. The dog checked his rush, and came forward, sniffing her skirts and her feet. She clasped her hands, praying that if this were death, she might die without making any noise and disturbing his lordship. At least that would in part atone for an early and probably painful death.

"Nay, dog," she whispered, for his name was beyond her, "nay, dog, dean't eat ma !"

Then his lordship called, "Hi ! Agamemnon, now, sir ! Come here !" and a second later : "All right, little girl, he won't hurt you. Hi—Agamemnon—d'you hear me, sir ?"

The dog left her and galloped back to his master. Again his lordship called, "That's all right ! No harm done." He was quite close to her now, she could see his yellow moustache, his long fair beard—like gold, spun gold in the sunshine. "What are you doing wandering about in my park ?"

He was laughing, his voice sounded as if he teased her. "Don't you know this is private ground ?"

She raised her eyes, and to her horror found that they were full of tears. She didn't know why, she wasn't unhappy. How could she be when he spoke so kindly to her ? She swallowed hard, and said, "Ah was told to cum. Mrs. Bishop told me ter cum, sir—m'lord."

"Mrs. Bishop up at the house d'you mean ? What have you to do with Mrs. Bishop ?"

"Ah work with her, m'lord. Ma name's Sarah Hardcastle, m'lord."

"Ah, Sarah Hardcastle !" He laughed as if proud of himself for having remembered. "Of course ! *Sarah*—er—*Ellen* Hardcastle. You see—Ah've gotten it reit agean, eh ? Oh, I know all about you. And so you're wandering about the park, eh ? What's this I hear"—he assumed a frown, though his eyes still danced "what's this I hear about a certain Sarah—er—Ellen Hardcastle who gives an excellent imitation of—Lord Stallingford ?"

She was too terrified to see the light in his eyes, she saw only the frown, and felt the blood drain away from her heart. He would send her away. "Who is this wretched pauper child," he would say, "who dares to imitate me? Take her away, send her back to the House where she came from!"

It never occurred to her to say, "The others asked me to. I only did it to show your wonderfulness. I wanted them to know how splendid you were. I didn't understand that I ought not to have done it." She knew now what the Rev. Mr. Proctor meant when he told them that when they faced the pains of hell their tongues would cleave to the roofs of their mouths!

She stood there, her whole body stiff with fright, then with a supreme effort she said, "Your lordship—Ah niver meant—Ah ondly—Nay, m'lord, gie me a reit thrashing, beat me, but dean't —oh, dear lordship, send me away. Ah'll niver do it agean. Ah tak' me Bible oath as Ah'll niver—beat me, as hard as you like— harder'n what——"

He was stretching out his hand, he was going to take her at her word and beat her. Catch her by the neck of her dress and swing that stick which he carried so that it came down again and again on her back. It would be like the days when Matron was angry—yet, no, it could never be like that, because here was his lordship a just god, who had been mocked! He had a right to avenge himself, he had a right to mete out punishment, he held the power of life and death in his hands! She had offended him, and in his mercy he was only going to beat her, not fling her into the outer darkness of the workhouse.

He said, "Come here, why are you shaking so? What is this about being beaten? I don't want to beat you, I don't want to send you away. Were you beaten in the workhouse? Often? What for? You poor little child, no one is going to send you away. I was—er—amused. Do you understand, amused? I laughed at the idea of your imitation. Blachlet says it is delightful. I must hear it—you must tell it to me, this imitation."

She covered her face with her hands. "Oh, m'lord, no, never, Ah'll niver do it agean, not for no one. I couldn't! It weer reit down bad of me, Ah just didn't understand. If Ah had Ah'd niver have done it, nowt 'ud have made me—nowt."

He was standing with his hand on her shoulder, looking down, still smiling, but his eyes looked strange. He began to talk as if he had forgotten that she was there.

"Beaten—those wretched bairns. That thin-lipped, horse-faced woman. And the man—just the same with the boys! Psh! I've been taking too much on trust, we all have—Carter, and Mortley and the rest of us. Call ourselves Guardians—of what, of whom? Sit in that confounded committee room, and listen to the matron's plausibility, watch the master washing his hands with invisible soap. No, no, my boy, this will not do—most certainly—this will not do." His hand grew heavier on Sarah's shoulder, she wished that he could throw all his weight on her, wished that he might be tired and that her strength could help him to walk more easily.

He said, "Walk back to the house with me, Sarah. I want to hear a great deal about this workhouse where you once lived—where," he said very quickly and firmly, "you're never going to live again. Never—er—you know what never means, eh? Now tell me——"

They walked back together, his hand still on her shoulder, the great dog striding beside them, sometimes pushing his muzzle against his master's hand. He asked questions of Sarah, this wonderful lord. His voice was very gentle and kindly, yet whatever she told him he made no comment.

"The food, Sarah—it was good—er—eh? Nice food, well cooked?"

"Sometimes, m'lord—not allus."

"You could always eat it though, if you were hungry?"

"Not allus, m'lord—we weer allus hungry, but even soa, yer stummick just turned at it."

"Ah! But in winter time you were nice and warm in bed, eh?"

"Eh!" She shivered at the thought of it. "Eh, it weer cold! We uster chrad twa an' three on us in one bed, lying reit cheek bi chowl. T' place weer reit ram allus wi' bairns' bodies. It weer ovver cold ter wesh mooch."

"Still, they were kind—er—to you. You were never ill-treated, eh?"

"Nay, when we weer bad Ah reckon as we had ter be punished." He heard the queer acceptance of the pauper in her tone. "Sometimes it weer just a clout she'd gie us, but when she weer chollus minded she'd clawt yer or tak' t' stick ter yer."

"Clawt?" he said. "Clawt? I don't know that one, Sarah. What does it mean?"

She made a little gesture with her hand, the fingers turned in, as if she clawed something. "Like t' road cats goes on," she said. "Scrattin' wi' claws."

"Ah! I see . . ."

He asked no more questions, but walked on in silence, his hand still resting on her shoulder. Sarah thought that to walk with God, as Adam did, must be like this. She felt secure, as if she had been buffeted in a rough sea and reached firm, dry land again. They reached the gate which led to the kitchen garden. Stallingford stopped.

"Listen, Sarah," he said. "I never want you to pity yourself. Never pity yourself—eh? What has happened is over and done with. Like a bad dream—eh?—a nightmare, yes? Over, morning's come. Don't look back—look forward, and don't be afraid. Bad to be afraid. Weakens one. There, run along to Mrs. Bishop, and if you're late tell her that I kept you talking. I shouldn't wonder if I came along to the nursery one day—asked you to put a button on my glove—or something like that, eh? See that you do it nicely for me. There—good-bye, Sarah. Remember—don't look back. Forward—that's the word—forward."

He turned and walked away, the dog trotting at his heels. Sarah disobeyed him, she couldn't help it. She turned back to watch him go—so tall, so straight, so beautiful.

"Eh—m'lord," she whispered, "Ah'll be reit good—allus."

ii

The weeks passed, they were busy making a new dress for Lady Gwendoline. Blue silk, paler than forget-me-nots. It was to be worn at "Lord's"—though what Lord no one seemed to know very clearly. Her ladyship had been to London. She, too, was buying a new dress; Mamzel talked about it at great length in the servants' hall, waving her hands and bunching up her fingers, laying them against her lips as if she were blowing kisses to everyone. Whatever was going to happen—and Sarah could never make out very clearly—his young lordship was in something called the team, and he was going to run. Everyone seemed to think that he was going to do something wonderful—run or make someone else run, it was difficult to understand.

Mr. Blachlet said, "Ah, a great sportsman in the making, Lord Victor. He'll want a match here, I don't doubt. I suppose we can get a side together?"

"William and Herbert," Mr. Lingley said, "Porter, Mr. Walters—though he's on the heavy side—you, Black, and you,

Thorpe, myself—I used to wield a pretty neat bat—you, Mr. Blachlet, his lordship, I don't doubt, and Lord Victor. Porter told me that young Mellet isn't bad. They think a lot of him down in the village—and probably there'll be friends of his lordship's staying here. Oh, we can manage a Stallingford eleven all right."

"The coach is going the day after tomorrow—taking the journey in easy stages," Mrs. Hardcastle told them, "her lady-ship was telling me this morning. The family are going to drive to Darlington, and then on by train. You're going, Mr. Lingley ?"

"I'm going, Mrs. Hardcastle." He laughed. "A gentleman must have his gentleman's gentleman ! Yes, you'll be without Mr. Blachlet and myself, minus Walters and Mamzel here. I may decide to take Thorpe, with your permission, Mr. Blachlet. Lord Victor 'ul need someone. Flannels, blazers and so forth—then his rig-out for later ! Plenty to do, too much for one pair of hands."

Sarah listened. Flannels, blazers, what did it all mean ? Where were these people going ? Why was it all so important ? Later she asked Mrs. Bishop. It appeared that they were going to watch his young lordship and his friends at school play a game of cricket against other young gentlemen who went to another school. Sarah remembered she had seen some of the men down in the village playing this game, cricket. She had thought that it was just a game, but it appeared from what Mrs. Bishop said that the whole future of England depended upon which of these schools won.

She said, "It's the nashional game, Sarah. Like what hunting's the nashional sport. Foreigners can't play it, no more than they can ride. No more they can't shoot, except it's pigeons. A poor business, I've heard his lordship say !"

Sarah almost whispered, "Does his lordship shoot well ?" and then blushed that she should have even put such a question. Of course he shot well !

"A very fine shot indeed, his lordship," Mrs. Bishop said. "There is some who maintains that Sir Trafford Mortley is a better, but—folks 'ul say anything if it suits them."

Sarah wondered how Sir Trafford Mortley could sleep at nights, knowing that people made such preposterous assertions ! Mrs. Bishop's soft comfortable voice flowed on. There were those who said that some mysterious gentlemen called "H.R.H." was the best shot in England ; there again Mrs. Bishop had her own opinion without wishing to be disloyal. It was certain that "H.R.H." wasn't the horseman that his lordship was, though she had heard it said that he rode with courage and never looked for gaps.

Little Sarah Hardcastle sat there on a low chair, listening, comprehending rather less than half that was said to her. She heard stories of "the Family", with ramifications, and allusions to cousins and first and second cousins. She heard long-dead Lord Stallingfords referred to as if they had left this world only a week ago. "That was when most of the silver went," Mrs. Bishop drooned on. "Sir Francis—the Earldom came with the Restoration. Sir Francis was all for the King. Times were difficult while that bad old Cromwell was doing his wickedness, for no Stallingford could ever bear to go about with a long face. Not likely! Then, of course, when the King came into his own, young Sir Roderick—the only Roderick there has ever been—was sent for and made Earl. Gratitude that was, of course. In the days of the Regent, that's Her present Majesty's uncle, the Earl was most kind—most kind to the Regent. Helped him in many ways. That was the Earl who was the patron of Tom Cribb. Yes, a great Corinthian. It's interesting to know that—or so I've heard—no king can be crowned unless the Earl of Stallingford is present. He carries a silver—no, gold surely—yes, gold salver."

So it went on, snatches of stories, bits of information, muddled and confused but all relating to "the Family". The Family were endowed with power which had in reality never been theirs. They had been in the forefront of every battle, "from the very first they were against Luther. His lordship at that time is known to have said, 'Who will get rid of this troublesome priest for me?'" They had embraced the Protestant faith only when they felt that it was for the good of England. "Always very attached to England—their lordships."

The long room was very quiet, the windows opening on to the garden let in the scents and sounds of the summer evening. The birds were singing their last song to the day which was dying, the scent of the flowers seemed to flow into the room, heavy with the dew of evening. The stout old nurse sat there, her big capable hands folded on her lap, telling stories of the men she had known, the women she had loved and their forebears. Little Sarah felt her eyes growing heavy, she had been up at six, and she knew that sleep was waiting to claim her. Yet she could not bear to

ask if she might go to bed. All these stories were about him,
about his grandfathers and great-grandfathers. Anything which
concerned him even remotely was important—more, it was a
privilege to know these things. Tomorrow she would make some
excuse to pass through the long gallery and take quick glances
at Sir Roderick and Sir Francis, at the first Earl and that Earl
who had been so kind to the Regent. She would remember
everything that Mrs. Bishop had said, she would look at the
painted faces closely—if hurriedly—to make sure that some of
these men looked something like the greatest and most noble of
them all—his lordship.

She felt her head nod, knew that her eyes were unbearably
heavy, when the miracle happened. The door opened, and her
ladyship's voice said, "Herah we are, Bish, coming to say good-
bye. We're off early tomorrow. What message shall I take to
Victor for you?"

Then, behind her ladyship, his lordship entered. They were
both dressed for the evening. Sarah had never seen him dressed
so before, and the severe black and white showed up his fair hair
and beard, making them look more like gold than ever. He
came forward, standing with his hands in his pockets, saying,
"Yes, what message for Victor?"

Mrs. Bishop was on her feet, but he pushed her back into her
chair, saying, "No, no—sit down—now what's the message?"

"Oh, m'lord!" She was laughing with pleasure. "A message for Lord Victor? Well, if you'd be so kind, say Bish says
that he's going to carry his bat! And, if I might add, m'lady,
not to drink iced drinks when he's hot."

"Carry his bat, eh? Tall order, Bish—still, he'll do his best."
Then he saw Sarah, and said, "Hello, Adelaide, here's my little
protegée! How are you, Sarah Ellen Hardcastle? D'you
know, Bish, Agamemnon tried to eat her the other day? Indeed
he did. Now, what message do you want to send to the hero of
the Eton Eleven, eh?"

Her ladyship said, "Stallingford, don't tease her! How he
loves to plague people, doesn't he, Bish?"

"No, no, that's all right! Sarah understands me! Don't
try to pretend that she's frightened of me!" He slapped his
thigh and laughed. "D'you see any green in my eye? Now,
Sarah!"

She gave her queer little bob. "My duty to his lordship,
m'lord."

"Ve-e-ry nicely said, b'Gad! Sentiments do you credit, Sarah!"

Just as if she had not been present, her ladyship said to Mrs. Bishop, "She seems a nice little girl, Bish."

"Quite a good, obedient little girl," Mrs. Bishop returned. "I have nothing to complain of regarding her, m'lady."

"That's very nice to hearah! Poor child. I think it's time she was in bed, though. Good-bye, Bish, and we'll bring your Victor home in triumph!"

"'Pon my word—that's a nice play on words! Victor the Victorious! Good-bye, Bish, and behave nicely while I'm away. Good-bye, Sarah—er—she's too young to be called Sarah. Sally—that's better, eh, what?—Sally—good night, Sally."

Mrs. Bishop said, "Quick, open the door for her ladyship!"

Sarah ran to the door, swung it open and dropped her curtsey. Her ladyship smiled down at her, and his lordship just brushed her cheek with his fingers as he passed through.

Going back to fold up her sewing, Mrs. Bishop beamed at her. "Well—if them's his lordship's orders, 'Sally' it must be, I suppose. Now, my dear, off to bed with you."

That night Sally went to sleep with the same words running through her head, again and again. "He says that I'm to be called 'Sally'. He says that I'm to be called 'Sally'."

CHAPTER THREE

SARAH, looking back in years to come, never knew how the years passed. Her existence was completely tranquil. True, she toiled and spun—or occupied herself with what corresponded to these—but she took no thought for the morrow, she never speculated as to what she should eat or drink, or wherewith she should be clothed. That her work was hard never entered into her consciousness. It never occurred to her that her bedroom was plain and without ornament ; she never considered that, beyond her clothes, she had no personal belongings whatever. Her wages were paid to her aunt, and her aunt proceeded to replenish Sarah's wardrobe as she thought fit. The girl had no voice in choosing anything. It never struck her that it might have been pleasant to visit the emporium of Mr. John Jackson alone ; to have, in a limited way, run amock, and have selected things which might have some small claim to being either beautiful or colourful.

By the time she had reached her fifteenth birthday, since she left the workhouse, Sarah Hardcastle had never been further than Stallingford, she had never heard any music other than that which was played in the church on Sundays, and the only times she had attended any form of entertainment had been when she had been allowed to go to the parish hall to listen to a concert given by more or less—usually less—gifted amateurs.

At fifteen, she had grown tall, good food and sufficient rest having conspired to fill out her childishly bony frame, and give her an air of health. She was strong, her skin was always good, and her large, intelligent grey eyes were beautiful. The slightly prominent forehead which had been so apparent when she was younger had lost its uneven appearance, it was broad and not too high. Her nose was nondescript, but her mouth was well-shaped and her chin round and firm. Her figure was still without curves, giving her a boyish appearance.

She could write sufficiently to make up order lists for her aunt, she could read the weekly paper, but she did so without much ease or any great pleasure. Her sewing was beautiful, she could embroider exquisitely, and Mrs. Bishop stated that sheets mended

or darned by Sally were more worth looking at than those which
were still new and perfect. Mamzel, only too happy to pass on
work to other people, could trust her ladyship's silk stockings to
Sally ; it was Sally who had discovered what marvels in the way
of restoring dropped stitches could be worked by means of a
crochet hook ; it was Sally who learnt from old Mother Craddock
in the village how to mend fine gloves ; it was Sally who made
friends with Mrs. Zackerly, who came from Bedfordshire, and
was taught half a dozen lace stitches which were invaluable in
repairing her ladyship's fichus and jabots.

She had made a place for herself at Stallingford, though what
exactly that place was no one could have stated precisely. Ellen
Hardcastle was growing old, and rheumatism had found a victim
in her. She was happy enough to allow Sally to help in the housekeeper's room, to allow her to make out lists and check linen.
Mrs. Bishop, wheezing more than ever, with eyes which were
failing, was content to leave most of the mending to Sally. The
girl was never idle, and yet had you asked her she would have
replied that she did nothing—"Nothing that's really anything, as
you might say."

She rose at six, and made tea for Mrs. Bishop, she had her
own breakfast in the servants' hall, and went immediately to her
aunt's room to act as clerk, dispenser and half a dozen other
things as well. Later she went back to the nursery, and began
her sewing and mending. So the whole day slipped past, and yet
at night, when she went to her room, she often wondered what
she had done, and how it could be worth anyone's while to keep
her.

Even after three years the shadow of the "House" still
lingered. Not that she was afraid that she might be sent back
there. His lordship had promised. "Never," he had said, and
what he said he meant, she knew that. But sometimes at night
she would wake and imagine that she were back, sleeping in a
huge room which stank of small unwashed bodies, or that she was
trying to eat the greasy, heavy food, or waiting for Matron in
that terrible little room, waiting to be punished. It was then,
when she came out of her dreams, and found herself in her own
bed—with Alice snoring loudly in the bed not two yards away—
that her heart almost burst with love and gratitude to those
people who had brought her out of the house of bondage into
what was—veritably—a Promised Land.

Her waking dreams were always of them—of Lord Stallingford and her ladyship, of the golden-haired Lady Gwendoline, or of Lord Victor. She was not a creature possessed of any great imagination, but such as it was it ran on the lines of how she might repay the goodness of the family to her. She dreamed that his lordship might lose something of great value, and she—Sally—might find it after great difficulties and dangers. She dreamed that one evening before a great dinner-party, Mamzel might be taken ill. Not seriously ill, but some malady which should incapacitate her for a few hours. Her ladyship's hair must be done, her ladyship must be dressed. Mamzel would say, "No one can do it, except ziss Sallie. She can do eet so vell." Sally would go, would work miracles with her ladyship's hair, and when it was finished her ladyship would say, "You've done my hair—ah—beautifully, Sally. Even bettah than Cecile." Lady Gwendoline—there Sally's ideas grew vague, but it was certain that Gwendoline must be in some peril from which Sally could save her. And Lord Victor—he too must be placed in some dreadful danger, and Sally—at the risk of her own life—must protect him.

Impossible, romantic dreams, the dreams of a child, but under them all lay something which was not impossible, not purely romantic, and which was not childish. Under them all lay that deep devotion which Sally nurtured and cherished. To her the Family were beings apart. It seemed impossible that they should suffer as did ordinary mortals—from toothache, stomach-ache, colic or colds in the head. Even to imagine such a thing seemed like treason. To catch a glimpse of any of them was to make the sun shine for her on the darkest day. For months she might see none of them, for they were often away. They went to London, when it appeared that his lordship had to make laws for the whole of England ; they went to the South of France because they wanted the sunshine ; they went to Scotland because it was necessary that they should kill birds—kill them, it appeared, by the hundred. They even went to places in some country of which she was never very certain, to take what was called a cure—a cure for what, she never knew. When they went to London some of the servants went with them. Lingley and Mr. Blachlet, Mr. Wilkins, who took the horses, and sometimes Thorpe and Brown went as well. Mrs. Bishop used to go, but for the last year she had stayed at home.

"It's too much for me," she said. "I'd not wonder if they took you next year, Sally."

"To Lunnon, Mrs. Bishop ?"

"Yes, where else ? The Lunnon house has to be run some-how. Aye—and if I know anything about south-country servants—it is run *somehow*, and that's all it is !"

Both Mrs. Bishop and Mrs. Hardcastle were very bitter about south-country servants. It appeared that they were, "in the main", capable of all kinds of wickedness, not to say complete villainy.

"That chef," Mrs. Hardcastle said, "with a Frenchified name ! I seen him, Mrs. Bishop, and the moment as I set eyes on him—I knew ! A bad 'un if ever there was one, with his nasty messes and his gallons of cream. Half of it goes back to the dairy, I'll be bound, and the money is popped into 'mongsewer's' pocket ! Oh, the tales as Mr. Lingley has told me ! D'you mean to tell me that our Mrs. Rawlins can't do all that he can do, and do it far better ? Look at that glazed boar's head she sent up last year, look at her raised pies, her birds in aspic—her sauces ! Why, they do say that when his Royal Highness said that he'd come for a few days' shooting, he laughed —speaking to m'lord—and said, 'On condition that Phoebe's still there !' Always calls her 'Phoebe', does H.R.H. Very affable to her on more than one occasion. I did hear that he hinted that we might let her go to him. His lordship laughed— very friendly with H.R.H. he is, of course. He said, 'The Rembrandt, the'—nay there, I've forgotten the name of the Italian gentleman who did that drawing in the long corridor—'the Queen Anne silver, the family diamonds, sir, they're yours when you want them, but—Phoebe . . .' H.R.H. said, 'Ha ! Her value is above rubies, eh ?' Very clever retort, eh, Mrs. Bishop ?"

Little Sally Hardcastle sat and listened, heard great names bandied about, learnt that his lordship was said to have the finest beard in England, not even excepting the "Red Earl's", learnt how the Queen liked this politician and "couldn't abear" another. Heard how this Duke always had his own bed taken about with him wherever he went, and how another never took anything for breakfast except six raw eggs broken into a crystal goblet. She heard of the beauty of the Princess of Wales, of the nation's anxiety at her illness, of how devoted "he" had been. "Actually having his writing-table moved into her room, Mrs. Hardcastle, so her ladyship told me, so's he could be near her."

"Which," Mrs. Hardcastle returned, "might or might not be a

kindness to a sick woman, for woman she is, princess or not, after all."

She heard of the "Alexandra limp" and marvelled that people could be so "daft" as to imitate a sick woman and think it clever or smart. But they were strange folk these gentry, Sally mused, attaching so much importance to small things, and disregarding matters which seemed to be of real gravity. She heard stories of scandals in high places, noted that the people connected with them were greeted with effusion, and even appeared to have become more popular through the publicity given to their escapades.

"The list for the rooms has come down," her aunt said to her one morning. "Better go through it, Sally, and see who's to have which room."

Sally read through the list written on the crested paper in her ladyship's delicate flowing handwriting.

". . . Sir George Fairlie——"

"What, again?" her aunt exclaimed. "Well, let's hope that he's bringing his own man with him. Poor Thorpe was hard put to last time, with him never going to bed sober, and wanting brandies-and-sodas at seven in the morning! Where's Lady Millicent?"

Sally consulted the list. "The Blenheim. How did you know she was coming, Aunt?"

Mrs. Hardcastle sniffed. "Sir George is coming, isn't he?"

"Yes, Aunt. I read out his name——"

"Oh"—irritably—"don't ask questions, child. You'll know when you're older."

People of a different world, with different ideas, and rules of conduct. What might be permitted, even condoned, among them would mean dismissal and disgrace to servants. That was the only explanation—they were different, and Sally accepted that fact. She lived so much among older people that she came to have her own means of amusement. She walked alone, and during those walks she loved to take out what she thought of as her own album. Mrs. Hardcastle had two beautiful albums, filled with photographs of the Family, and grand people who had stayed at Stallingford. It was delightful to look through them—"make certain that your hands are clean first, Sally"—and see what Lord Victor looked like at the age of five, and how Lady Gwendoline had appeared to the world when she was three. But her own album was better!

She could mentally look at which picture she liked, no need to wash your hands, or sit upright at a table. Under the trees in the park ; along by the beck, on the bank of the long narrow artificial lake, where the proud swans floated up and down, and the little waterhens were so busy darting backwards and forwards among the reeds ; even in church on Sunday, when the curate—for the rector, the Rev. the Hon. Cyril Stamford, preached only in the mornings when the Family were at home —was longer-winded than usual, Sally could look at her pictures.

The first was always of his lordship. That day he had met her in the park, when she thought that Agamemnon was going to eat her, when he had said that she should never be beaten again, and never sent back to t'House. Her ladyship, when she had sent for Sally and said, "I want you to go into the woods and get some violets for me, Sally. Look about and bring me a really large bunch—purple and white. They're for my aunt"—only she said, "my aurnt"—" she's very fond of wild violets." When Sally came back with a great bunch, her ladyship said, "Chawrming, quite chawrming ! Now, can you ask Mrs. Hardcastle to pack them nicely for me ? Plenty of soft damp paper—and make them look nice." But Sally had packed the flowers, and Mrs. Hardcastle had taken them to her ladyship.

Another picture of Lady Gwendoline, standing in the nursery, sulky and cross, saying to Sally, "Where's Bish ? Gone out ? Whereah ? Oh, to her sister's ! I want that petticoat with the wide frill. Kate's got a dozen thereah and not one of them the right one."

Sally had said, "I'll get it, m'lady. It's all ready, just wants a stitch here and there."

"Thank goodness ! Life's an awful bore, isn't it, Sally, when you can nevah find the clothes you really want and people are so stupid ?"

Sally, who had never had any difficulty in finding her clothes, because she never had more than three of anything, said, "Oh, it is indeed, m'lady, it is indeed."

Lady Gwendoline had waited while Sally put the last stitches in the petticoat, saying, when Sally assured her that she'd bring it in a minute, "No, I'll take it. I'd like to stay here—ah—and talk to you, Sally. You're awfully understanding, really."

"Thank you, m'lady."

She had talked about her studies and how thankful she was that "Frawline" had gone, and how she hated speaking German, and how much nicer French was. She had said that she supposed that she'd be presented very soon, and be decked up in feathers and things.

Sally thought that it sounded like some kind of torture, and said, "Dear, dear, think of that," but Gwendoline went on without listening. She said "and then" she supposed she'd get married, and that really it was Victor's place to be married first. "The heir and all that"—and did Sally remember when Sir Harry Cormick came last year and brought his son, Terrance Cormick? Didn't Sally think that he was nice-looking? And the Cormicks were as poor as church mice, and wasn't it a shame, and did Sally think that it mattered?

"Well, it's nicer for everyone to have money, isn't it, m'lady?" Sally said.

"We've got plenty! Oh, is it done, Sally? Come along to my room and I'll give you some things——"

"To mend, m'lady?"

"No, silly—for you, for being nice and understanding."

"Oh, but—wouldn't her ladyship be angry? I mean—they'd not be—well, not be right for me, m'lady, would they?"

"Sally, how too utterahbly silly! I can do what I like with my own things, can't I? Much bettah for you to have them than for them to go to the decayed gentlewomen or the refuge Come on, Sally."

So Sally went to her room. A lovely room with long windows overlooking the park and the Italian gardens, and full of beautiful furniture covered with chintz. Lady Gwendoline had called for Kate, and said, "Oh, look hereah, Kate, I want some things for Sally. Open those drawers, will you?" She had dragged things from the drawers: black silk stockings. "You mended them, Sally, it's only right that you should have them"—and nightgowns—"they're frightfully old-fashioned now, you mustn't mind that!"—and two petticoats, only Sally said, "I'll take the lace off of them, m'lady. It's reel lace, and worth a mint."

"Really? Oh, well, give the lace to Bish and keep the petticoat." She was talking all the time, pulling things from drawers and wardrobes, flinging them on the bed, commenting on them as she did so. "I used to like that—I'm tired of it. Remember, Sally, I wore that when Mr. Cormick was hereah." She laughed, a friendly kind of laugh, which made Sally feel that she had liked Mr. Cormick very much indeed. "That dark dress would fit you, wouldn't it ? Oh, of course it would—take it." On and on, until at last she stopped and said, as if she were tired of the whole thing, "There, take them away, Sally !" Just as Sally was leaving the room, her arms filled with clothes, Lady Gwendoline said, "Oh, have some sweets—hereah, take the box. It's only half finished. Yes, take it."

Of course she had told Mrs. Bishop about the clothes, and Mrs. Bishop had consulted with Mrs. Hardcastle. They agreed that it was all right.

"After all, Mamzel gets her ladyship's things, an' Kate 'ud never fit these. She'd look like an overgrown maypole—ondly that she's fat. I really don't see why not."

Mrs. Bishop had agreed, nodding her head and wheezing. "It's quite right. Sally's a good girl, and they think a lot on her. Oh yes, no need to blush, Sally, I know, for I've been told."

Wonderful to be "thought a lot on" by the Family. One didn't deserve such praise. And a last picture, for she had heard the stable clock chime the half hour, and only fifteen minutes' freedom remained. Lord Victor . . . He had come first to the nursery three years ago, after that famous match when he had made fifty-four runs not out. He rushed into the nursery, shouting, "Hello, Bish—fifty-four not out. How's that, Umpire ?"

He was seventeen, Sally knew that. Not very tall, and fair like his father. He moved his hands a great deal when he talked and often broke off, leaving a sentence unfinished.

Mrs. Bishop said, "Now, I am reely pleased, pleased *and* proud, m'lord."

He said, "Not bad, eh, really, honestly not bad—for me ! Oh, it was a great match, I can tell you. Fearful excitement ! Great match for us, horrible match for them. Beaten hollow. Absolutely hollow. I say, Bish, where's the rocking-horse ? You've not let them do away with my rocking-horse, have you ? Can't do that ! Old and trusted animal, must be looked after in his old age. That's only fair. . . . In the attics . . . Can't allow that, must have him down again. *Ingratus non est.* That means I'm not an ungrateful cove—or I fancy it does. Hello, Bish, who's the little girl ? New importation ?"

"That's Sally Hardcastle, m'lord. Mrs. Hardcastle's niece."

Sally bobbed and blushed. He smiled, nodding his head. "Oh, Sally Hardcastle. It's a pleasant name, Bish—Sally Hardcastle, isn't it ? How old are you, Sally Hardcastle ?"

"Rising thirteen, m'lord."

"When you have a birthday, tell me, and I'll send you a present. What shall it be, Bish ? What's a nice present for a nice little girl ? Think quick, Bish, because I've got to go. Tommie Beyforth and John Summers are waiting for me."

Mrs. Bishop said, "That's for you to say, m'lord. It's most kind, most kind. When is your birthday, Sally, tell his lordship."

"It's—it's—the twelfth of August, please, m'lord."

"I say—take care someone doesn't mistake you for a bird and shoot you ! Nice little grouse. I always think that the singular of grouse should be grice, Bish. Well, little Miss Grouse, what would you like ? Quick—one—two—three !"

She drew a deep breath. "I'd like—I'd like a little workbox, please, m'lord."

He was half-way to the door, still laughing. "A workbox—a huge, tremendous, massive workbox for August the Twelfth. The glorious twelfth and a glorious workbox ! Good-bye, Bish ; good-bye, Sally Hardcastle."

And it had come ! Sent from London, because he was going to shoot birds with some friends, and wasn't at home when the woods and the fields were resounding with the sound of guns. But he had remembered, and there it was—it stood on the table in her bedroom now. Shining dark wood, lined with red satin all puckered and frilled. With needles, and silks and a bodkin, scissors and everything that anyone could want. It was over-whelming. Mrs. Bishop said, "Well, that's a very great condescension, I'm sure. To think of his lordship remembering ! Of course, they all remember my birthday, and many's the handsome presents they've given me—that's different. I've been here over thirty years. Thirty I said, did I ? Nay, it 'ul be forty next back end. Well, you must be a proud girl today, I'm sure."

"Oh, I am, Mrs. Bishop."

"I should just think so."

She wondered how he had remembered, wondered if he had made a little note in that small red book which he carried in his pocket. He had remembered—that was what really mattered. He had gone to a shop—the address was Bond Street, her aunt said the best street in London—he had chosen a workbox for her. It was unthinkable.

As a matter of fact, Victor Stallingford had said to his aunt

Mrs. Powers, who adored him and whose heir he was reputed to be, "Most beloved of aunts, do something for me. I've promised a workbox to a little girl for her birthday. August the twelfth. Her name is Sally Hardcastle. Nice, isn't it ? Buy it and send it for me, will you ? A big one, y'know, full of needles and pins and ink and knitting needles and scissors and rubbish."

His aunt twinkled at him.. "A change from your usual presents, Vic ! Last time it was—garters ! Unless my memory betrays me, you bad boy !"

He waved his hands as if he swept away all his past follies. "Years and years ago. I'm a changed man ! She's a servant— oh, I don't know exactly—sewing-maid. Anyway, she's only thirteen, and—birthdays are momentous occasions, aren't they, Aunt Catherine ?"

Then the clock struck and Sally knew that she must race for home or be late. She closed her mental album and ran.

ii

Her sixteenth birthday dawned. She got up quickly, for the house was full of people and help was needed everywhere. Gentlemen had come bringing their servants, their cases of guns and in some cases their wives—though these were less important than the guns, so Lord Victor had told Mrs. Bishop the night before. He had come into the nursery before dinner, magnificent in a tail-coat and white tie, his hair looking very curly and the smallest possible golden moustache beginning to show on his top lip. He stayed for only a few minutes, and talked very fast about nothing.

"D'you realize that I've grown up, Bish ? I didn't, I swear, until they began to look at me with grave eyes and talk to me seriously. Now—look at this party ! You've seen 'em ? My mother says, 'It's a young people's shoot'; my father says, 'We've chosen young folk particularly for you, Victor.' I don't want young people, Bish. Lady Alice Chalfont and Miss Ann Matters. I don't like Alice Chalfont and I don't like Ann Matters. I like you better, Bish dear—you and Sally. Hello, Sally—your birthday tomorrow ! Look how I remember things ! How's the workbox ? No, Bish, I shall marry you—or Sally. What a lark. My dear father and mother, I wish to announce my approaching marriage with Mrs. Bishop or"—

smiling and adding very quickly—"Miss Sarah Hardcastle! Whew, Bish, what a lark!"

Mrs. Bishop shook her head half reprovingly. "My lord—really! What things to say!"

There were to be great doings for his birthday—his coming of age. The servants were to present him with a loving-cup, the tenants with a huge silver salver. There was to be dancing on the lawn for his lordship's guests, and dancing in the servants' hall the following night for the lesser folk. Fireworks, Mr. Porter said, adding gloomily, "An' when it's all ower, a bonnie sight ma gardens 'ul be! Varry weel, junketing an' sichlike; but mind ye, Mistress Harrdcastle, it's meself as min pit things tae reits when awe's ower."

"Make those under-gardeners of yours do the work, Mr. Porter," she said.

"Mak'!" he echoed. "Ye mun say mak', wumman, fur it's mak'in' they need. They're naethin' but a feckless lot!"

There was a discussion over the amount that each servant would and could give. Mr. Blachlet took charge of the financial side of the present; he produced a long roll of paper and said, at the end of the servants' supper, "I myself feel it incumbent to head the list—or rather head it in conjunction with Mrs. Hardcastle, Mrs. Bishop and Mrs. Rawlins. I trust this meets with the approval of all."

Sally felt her heart miss a beat. What could she give, what had she to give? Her wages were paid to her aunt, she had never possessed more than sixpence at one time in her life. Unthinkable to offer to give sixpence to his lordship's birthday present. It might have been different had he not once given her that magnificent workbox. But having given it to her, she felt mean, unworthy. In her aunt's room she stood, longing to ask, "What am I to do? What am I to do?"

Her aunt, sitting monumental in her armchair, said, "There's this question of his lordship's present, Sally. How much would you like to give? As one of the younger servants there's no call for you to give as much as, f'rinstance, me or Mr. Blachlet. On the other hand, I feel as you owe something to the Family, and—it's for you to say what you'd like it to be."

"But, Aunt—I mean, I can't give anything!" Her voice was childish in its desperation. "I've got no money."

"No money! What's the child talking about? O' course you've got money. What d'you suppose happens to your wages, m'dear ? They're put away for you regular. Four years—aye, how time flies—since you came here." Her broad face became reflective. "Aye, four years. A poor little scrap of a thing you were too—wi' your hair scraped back off your face and your hands red as beets. They've had some changes at that horrible place where I found you since then. It appears that his lordship went raving and raging down and he and the rest of the gentlemen sent yon hard-faced creature packing. Oh, things are very different there now, so I hear—very different. How his lordship discovered—what he did discover—I can't say, but seemly he had all the facts at his finger-tips. Food, beds, washing, clothes, cleanliness and what not. There's a new master an' a new matron there now. His lordship said to them, I'm told, when they came, 'You're new, and new brooms sweep clean they say. See to it that they continue to sweep clean, or you may find that I can wield a broom pretty effectively myself.' But—about this subscription. Open that desk and hand me your bankbook. Yes, there it is. You've got—let's see—twelve pounds three shillings and fourpence in. Think o' that !"

Sally did think about it, and felt staggered. Twelve pounds three shillings and fourpence ! It seemed almost wrong that she should have amassed such wealth, and still have had clothes bought for her.

She said, "Oh, Aunt—I'd like to give it all, please."

"All ! Nay, luvey, I like your spirit, but that 'ul never do ! Mr. Blachlet and me, and Mrs. Bishop an' Mrs. Rawlins is only giving five pounds apiece. It 'ud never do for you to give it all ! Seeing as how the Family have always taken such an interest in you, shall we say—thirty shillings ? And very handsome, too, I will say. Yes, thirty shillings 'ud do nicely."

Good temper seemed to permeate the whole house. People were lending one another things to wear at the servants' ball. Mamzel was giving advice as to how dresses might be transformed into suitable confections. Mrs. Rawlins had a new silk dress, of course, so had Aunt Hardcastle—magnificent, restrained and grand. Mamzel said, "Now what about zees leetle Sallee—she moost 'ave somesin ver' nice. 'Er firrst ball, a grreat occass-i-on."

Sally twisted her fingers and looked appealingly at Alice. Alice nodded.

"She gotten a luverly dress as Lady Gwendoline give her. Blew it is—good as noo. It could be made ovver ter soot Sally, Ah reckon, Mamzel."

"Eet vill be my espec-i-al care, leetle Sallie. Go—brring eet to me, qvickly."

Alice, giving her great boisterous laugh, said, "Ah'm teaching her ter dance. Reit light she is on her feet an' all. Nowt lumpy abart ower Sally, Ah'll saay."

Mr. Blachlet gave it as his opinion that in order to do credit to the Family the whole staff might well spend a few quiet hours in practising steps. "I used to be no mean performer," he announced, "and from what I remember of the last time Mrs. Hardcastle and I trod a measure, she still possesses a toe which is not only fantastic but light. I trust that I may engage myself for a dance with you, Mrs. Hardcastle. Nothing like being in time, eh? A quadrille, may I beg?"

She replied, "It's yours, Mr. Blachlet, I'm sure."

It wasn't true, Sally told herself. It couldn't be true. The great ball when the superior tenants and the gentry disported themselves, with a band sent all the way from York to supply the music. When her ladyship wore her diamonds, and Lady Gwendoline floated round looking like something from another world, too lovely to belong to the earth. Only his young lordship looked sulky and displeased. He had made such a beautiful speech to the tenants, calling them his "good friends", assuring them that he only hoped that one day they might love him half so well as they loved his father and mother. He had spoken of England's greatness, of the army and the navy, of the nation's gratitude to "One who is the only Ruler of Princes", for the recovery of the Prince of Wales. He had made them laugh by saying that however good, however attentive, Drs. Jenner, Gull and Clayton had been, he hoped that the Prince might have no further use for any of them! He had admired the great silver salver, he had held the loving-cup in his hands and smiled with pleasure when Mr. Blachlet said, "Never was a loving-cup, my lord, more filled to the very brim, indeed pressed down and running over with the commodity from which it takes its name."

Now his laughter seemed to have died, and he danced scarcely speaking, doing his duty as if it held no joy for him. Sally went to bed that night—or rather that morning, for the sky was beginning to be streaked with scarlet and orange when the ball ended—feeling that there had been one dark place in the glorious day—his lordship's sullen face.

The next night he was changed. He was all smiles. He made a speech, not a serious one this time, but bringing in the names of most of the servants, referring to them affectionately, recalling some incident of his childhood, and reducing everyone to laughter when he said, "I was fourteen when I borrowed first from Blachlet. Five shillings I think it was, eh, Blachlet ?"

"That's correct, m'lord."

"By the way, Blachlet, did I ever pay it back ?"

"You did not, m'lord—but hope springs eternal in the human breast !"

"Will you be a sport, and take half a crown at a time ?"

That was when the Earl called out, "Take what you can, Blachlet, when you can get it. I know my son. Having come of age won't change him !"

They danced—with the same band from York to provide the music. Mr. Blachlet danced with her ladyship, and very dignified and correct he looked, the Earl took out Mrs. Hardcastle, and when the dance was over said, "By Jove, you're too good for me, Hardcastle, far too good." Lady Gwendoline danced with Mr. Lingley, and his young lordship with Mamzel.

One of the under-gardeners, William Scarth, asked Sally to dance with him, and, half afraid, she consented. He said, "Tha's reit light on thee feet, Miss Sally. Ah could dance wi' thee aw' neit long an' never tire." He was a nice-looking young man, and smelt strongly of household soap and some kind of hairgrease. He breathed hard, and held her very stiffly, but she enjoyed it. When the dance was over he took her back to her place next to her aunt and whispered, if a hoarse rumble could be called a whisper, "Ah like nowt better'n to tak' a walk wi' thee, Miss Sally, sum Sunder. It's reit luvely threw t'woods."

The Earl and Countess were going, they smiled at everyone, said how pleasant it had been, and after a few moments their daughter followed them. Only his young lordship stayed, dancing every dance and obviously enjoying himself. He came over to where Sally sat with her aunt, bowed before Mrs. Hardcastle and said, "And now, am I to have the treat of the evening, Hardcastle ?" She was tired, Sally knew that—knew, too, that her feet ached.

She smiled gallantly, saying, "It's most kind of you, m'lord, most kind. Ondly——"

"Only"—he bent lower still and spoke very softly—"only all you women are alike. You wear beautiful shoes—those are really charming—and—they are just a leetle bit tight. Now admit it !"

"Well, p'raps, m'lord."

"I knew it. Sally, dance this with me. A polka. Great fun."

His head was above her, but he kept whispering softly as they danced.

"I've been waiting to dance with you. You look so pretty, Sally. You are pretty, only I never knew it before. You dance beautifully—far better than Alice Chalfont and Ann Matters. They're like loads of lead. Heavy and dull—oh, so dull, Sally ! Can't we get out of here and dance on the lawn ? No, I suppose that wouldn't do. What a bore it is to remember what is done and what isn't done. Always the nicest things mustn't be done. It's ending—I must go. I've to be off early in the morning. Don't forget me, Sally."

Then, when he took her back to Aunt Hardcastle, he spoke quite differently.

"She dances very nicely, your niece. Thank you, Sally. Good night, good night, all of you. It's been a splendacious evening."

For a moment he stood framed by the big doorway, laughing and waving his hand, then he was gone.

BOOK TWO

CHAPTER ONE

EVERYONE speculated as to whom Lady Gwendoline would marry. Everyone speculated as to whom Lord Victor would marry. Heads were shaken and lips pursed over the time both of them took to make up their minds. True, there was some excuse for Victor ; he was working hard, passing examinations, and finally going to Paris and the Embassy. Sally asked Mr. Blachlet what he was, this profession which he had taken up—what did it mean ?

"His lordship is a diplomat," Blachlet told her. "Lord Victor—that is, Lord Leister, only one finds it difficult to forget his childish—er—nom de plume, as it were—is attached to the Embassy in Paris."

"What is a diplomat ?" Sally asked.

"A diplomat is one who deals with and understands diplomacy," he told her.

She frowned ; it was puzzling. She hazarded, "Politics, Mr. Blachlet ?"

"Of a kind," he admitted.

"Would you call Mr. Gladstone a diplomat ?"

Blachlet raised his bushy brows. "I should call that gentleman many things, Sally, but assuredly never a diplomat !"

"Mr. Disraeli, then ?"

"Ah ! That's a bird of another colour, Sally—a very different pair of sleeves, as you might say. They tell me that Her Majesty is very partial to Mr. Disraeli—very."

And Sally went back to the nursery still undecided as to what a diplomat was, and what were the duties that kept Victor in Paris.

Sally was alone in the nursery now. Mrs. Bishop kept to her room, where she sat wheezing and coughing, only waiting for the various members of the family to pay her visits. She never asked about the linen or the sewing, and yet when orders were given to Sally she always felt that it was only right to say, "Yes, m'lady, I'll tell Mrs. Bishop."

Once, when his lordship came to speak about having some

stocks copied from the one which he carried in his hand, she repeated her phrase, "Yes, m'lord, I'll tell Mrs. Bishop."

He laughed. "But you can do it, Sally. Not too difficult for you, is it ? Just copy this exactly. Must be exact, y'know. I got this in Vienna years ago ; never had another I liked so well. Very wide blade, y'see. That's the blade, Sally. Must be wide— or so I think. That's where I differ from old Thomas Brewer in town. I told him that if he couldn't manage to make stocks to my pattern, then I'd have 'em made here. Think you can do it, Sally ?"

"Oh yes, m'lord." She turned the long length of white piqué in her hands. "I'll tell Mrs. Bishop."

That was when he looked at her queerly, half frowning, then said, "Loyal little soul, you are. It's a fine thing—loyalty, Sally. I don't believe that one can cultivate it, it's got to be a natural product. Indigenous to the soil. All right, Sally."

"Thank you, m'lord."

She scarcely knew what he meant. Why had he said that she was loyal ? What did he mean by "indigenous to the soil" ? He seemed to like using difficult and puzzling words. Not that she hadn't picked up a lot of words during the last few years. Her speech, though it still held the broad vowels of the north country, had grown easier. She might use dialect words—often did—because to her they seemed so much more apt than others, but unconsciously she used them as if they were placed in inverted commas.

She might not be strikingly intelligent, but she was quick to learn and ready to adapt herself. She "liked things nice", and her bedroom—occupied by her alone since Alice married Harry Mellet the joiner—was always a miracle of neatness. Her ladyship said once to Mrs. Hardcastle, "What a very pleasant young woman Sally has grown into !"

"Thank you, m'lady. Yes"—with slight deprecation—"she's a good girl, I will say that."

"She has such"—Adelaide Stallingford hesitated—"such nice ways. You never knew, did you, Hardcastle, who her father was?"

"No, m'lady. I've heard this and heard that—but I'm not one to listen to gossip, and at best that's all it was. My cousin Lizzie said that my poor sister was—well, very friendly with a young gentleman from the Oxford University. But, after all, that's nothing but talk. It was a sad blow to me ; nothing of the kind in our family before, m'lady."

"No." Then reflectively: "It might have been. She's very quick to learn."

"Sally's never axed, m'lady, and I've never thought wise to tell her anything of this talk. One doesn't want to put ideas into her head."

"No, indeed; very wise."

She was a pleasant young woman; everyone agreed about that. Not that she couldn't flare up and show temper now and again, not that she'd stand "putting on", for all her good nature, and kept herself to herself, too! One newly arrived young footman, good-looking and well-spoken, had tried to make himself too pleasant to Sally Hardcastle, and everyone in the servants' hall knew that he had his face slapped for his pains. Young Willie Scarth, the under-gardener, was the fellow she favoured most. She often went walking with him on Sunday afternoons, and always spoke highly of him, though the majority of people regarded him as very slow, if honest and hard-working. Sally had gone to tea with his old mother more than once, and returning had told her aunt what a nice old lady she was.

"It's not a big cottage," Sally admitted, "and it seems a bit cramped after the big rooms here, but it's neat, and everything that will shine—shines."

"And young Scarth," Mrs. Hardcastle asked—"what about him?"

Sally considered. "He's nice too, Aunt. He's very interested in his work, and likes to talk about it. Tells me about flowers and how they like to grow, and what kind of soil they like."

Mrs. Hardcastle sniffed. "Sounds dullish to me. Yer're not falling in love with him by any chance, are you, Sally? Under-gardener—well, you might do worse, but you might do a lot better."

Sally blushed. "There's nothing like that about it. We're just friends."

She did like young Scarth, with his shining face, like the red side of an apple, his nice clear eyes, and his short blunt nose. She liked his hands, too—big, broad hands, clumsy-looking and yet capable of making the most entrancing little nosegays of lad's love, forget-me-nots, scented geranium and a bit of syringa. His voice was deep; he spoke slowly, as if he chose each word carefully, unwilling to waste a single one. It might sound dull to Aunt Hardcastle, his talk about flowers, but Sally liked it. She found it soothing. There were times when she grew a little weary of the incessant chatter in the servants' hall, the speculations concerning Lady Gwendoline, the forecasts as to whom Lord Leister would marry, and the endless stories concerning the Royal Family. William Scarth appeared to know little about these great folks, and showed little or no interest in them either.

Together they would walk through the Stallingford woods, and his deep, slow voice fell pleasantly on Sally's ears.

"Maybe theer's a many as thinks plants is all alike," he'd say—"joost summat as graws outer t'ghrand, but Ah knaws diff'rent from that, Miss Sally. Plants has keracters saame as what folks have. Some on 'em's kindly, well doing, asking nowt —like some herbs—parsley, f'example. Pervided as you've gotten a 'green thumb'—it 'ul graw onnywheer. Ondly you min have a 'green thumb'. Noo, parsnips—not that Ah ever care a lot fur 'em mesen—yon min dig an' drill, an' work t' soil afore they'll do aut fer you. Some plants an' roots is natur'ly healthy, others is ready ter catch anything as is going. Onions, f'example, an' leeks. Ah'm no hand wi' leeks."

Or he would tell her about the birds, using queer dialect words which she could not understand. The animals, too, in the fields, for these he had strange names.

"Luke, Miss Sally—yon's t' fust gimmer," when he meant the little ewe lamb, staggering about after its mother, or, "Nay, that's nowt, nobbut a bite fra' a cleg. Naster'n what a humble bee's sting is, Ah'll tell ye." He called a bat a flittermouse, and Sally thought how much prettier it sounded than the usual word. He told her, as he came through the yard of the home farm, where he had been on an errand for Mr. Porter, how "yon wicked old steg cum afther ma ter gie ma a reit nip on t'leg."

He laughed when she said, "But, Mr. Scarth, what is a steg? I've never clapped eyes on one."

"Aye, boot you have, monny a time, Miss Sally—a steg's yon wicked old gander."

She thought some of his words beautiful, and liked his voice, when he spoke softly and almost lovingly about the birds.

"T' spring's a nice like time, Miss Sally," he said, "when t' birds have maade their nests—eh, an' clever they are an' awer— and i'le barhollies is cheeping an' chirping awaay wanting food. Theer's sum bonny birds here an' herabouts—goldies, an' lairocks —why"—in answer to her question—"them as clim reit oop in t' sky singing their hearts out—aye, larks an' hay chats—them wi' white throats—an' devil screamers—them as yer can tell

t'weather bi. When they fly low—thee mun luke art fur rain.
An' piets—they saay as if yer see won it's bad look, but think on,
Miss Sally, when tha see won there's almaist certain ter be anuther
cloase bi, if so be as folks 'ul be a bit patient. Joost bide a bit,
an' t'other piet 'ul be alang afore many minutes have gone bi."

He never tried to kiss her, only took her hand when he left
her and said, "That's bin a reit pleasure ter ma, maybe thee'll
cum oot agean nex' Sunder, if soa be as it's fine."

Then one Sunday he told her that it was "Carling Sunday",
when every right-thinking Yorkshire housewife cooked peas in
butter ; not green peas, but the dried brown peas, he said. As
they walked through the wood he kept stepping off the path to
pick her bits of palms—though she had always known them as
catkins—because next Sunday would be Palm Sunday. He
said, quite suddenly, "Ah dean't knaw as it's struck thee, Miss
Sally, as thee an' me's bin walking oot a goodish while now. Ah
dean't knaw if tha's axed thesen t' reason why Ah like ter goa
walking wi' thee—but Ah'll tell thee. Ah'm—why, Ah'm reit
fond o' thee—reit fond. Theer's not anuther young girl as Ah
care aut fer, barring thee."

She said, "I'm glad that you like me, Mr Scarth."

"Couldn't tha say—Willum ?" he asked.

She laughed. "Well, then—William."

He grinned contentedly. "Tha says it reit well put *in*, like
t' road gentry talks."

"Do I ? I suppose that I've learnt to talk that way up at the
Manor. I didn't always, I can tell you. I spoke right broad
when I first came here."

"Aye," he nodded, "Ah heard summat concerning it. Varry
sad like. But—Sally—Ah'm not doing soa badly ; theer's ondly
me muther an' me, an t' cottage is reit nice—enoof ruum fur—me
muther an' me an'—my wife. If soa be as Ah had one. Hast
aut ter saay ter it, Sally ?"

His fresh-coloured, healthy face was drawn with anxiety ; he
stood twisting his big hands together, alternately watching her
face and then looking down as if he sought inspiration from the
toes of his heavy, meticulously clean boots. Sally looked at him.

The idea of marriage had never really occurred to her seriously.
She knew that he liked her, she knew that she liked him—but was
that enough to make you wish to spend the rest of your life with
a man ? He was nice, he was kind, too, and thoughtful for her
comfort always. She knew that Mr. Porter thought well of him,

trusted him, and gave him a certain amount of responsibility. She had heard the old Scotsman say more than once, "Aye, yon Scarth'll go farr, or I'm nae judge o' men. Trrustworrthy, that's wha' he is."

Kind, thoughtful, trustworthy, a good son, a good worker—she let her mind dwell for a second on all these qualities, and again she thought, 'But is that enough ?'

William said, "Hast tha got nowt ter saay ter ma, Sally luv ?"

"Why, yes"—she flushed—"it's a great honour, William. I'm glad that you think so well of me, but . . . I don't think that I want to marry anyone, not as yet. I've never thought of—of loving you somehow."

"Maybe tha could mak' a stairt," he suggested hopefully.

"I don't know . . . I can't say . . . Oh, I'm sounding unkind. I don't mean to——"

He said quietly, "Naay, tak' thee time—saay what's i' thee heart, Sally luv."

She spoke quickly, almost desperately. "I've never thought of marrying anyone, you see. Seems as if I'd always been at the Manor—as if I'd always be there in the future. To go away, live somewhere else—well, it's strange, William."

In the depths of her consciousness was the thought, 'I don't want to leave them——'

And a second later, because she was honest, even with herself, she modified the thought so that it came, "I don't want to go away and never see him again."

She said, still talking hurriedly, half breathlessly, "You see, they've been very good to me. I couldn't leave them not—well, all on a sudden. It 'ud not be right."

They stood at the end of the woods, where the trees thinned a little, with the afternoon sun sinking behind them, making the silver birch trunks gleam suddenly, softly, warmly rose. The early evening was quiet ; at intervals the chirp of a bird broke the silence, or some small animal scurried through the bracken on its way to home and safety. Before them stretched the soft green of the long meadowgrass, with its sudden unexpected dashes of white where the meadowsweet and cow-parsley swung heavy in the still air. Beyond the green came the low, hand-built stone wall which separated the good land from the moor. The moor not yet dressed in its royal purple, but already glowing warmly with a soft violet hue, among which the yellow gorse glimmered like purest gold. The wide expanse rose slowly, gradually, as if it might have stretched away to meet the horizon where the blue sky began and have lost itself in infinity.

William Scarth stood watching Sally intently. His rather stiff, solid figure in its Sunday suit might have been cut out of wood. William had learnt to stand perfectly still when he was watching the movements and habits of the birds and wild creatures which he loved, when the slightest movement could send them flying to their nests or diving down to their holes in the earth. He felt that, somehow, he was watching a shy wild creature now, as his eyes rested on Sally Hardcastle. He must be patient; she must not be frightened or dismayed. He could wait until she chose to speak.

'Onct she's flaid,' he thought, 'Ah shall loose her fur good an' all. Ah mun bide.' She was not looking at him; her eyes were turned towards the moor; those eyes which were usually so calm and untroubled had changed. She was puzzled, she did not understand herself. She liked William; she supposed that every girl wanted a home of her own, a home and bairns. She remembered, when Alice had married, she had been able to speak of nothing and no one except Harry for months. It had been, "my Harry this", and "my Harry that", until it had seemed to Sally that for Alice the world held only one person, and that the young joiner with the red hair and the pleasant freckled face.

"How d'you know when you're in love, Alice ?" Sally had asked.

Alice's rosy face had shone as if someone had put a light against it.

"How do yer knaw ?" she asked, her hands clasped suddenly. "Eh—once it cums theer's no missing it, Sally. It's—it's that strong, it fair lifts yer off of yer feet. It's summat as is stronger nor what you are. It maks yer luke at other chaps an' wunder what other lassies can see in 'em. Beside yer own chap t'others luke kinder waffly like. Almaist silly, if yer knaw what Ah mean. Yer feel as if onny other chap barring yer own soa mooch as laid a finger on yer arm ye'd be fit ter kill him. Theer's ondly one chap in t' world—and he's yourn, and yer his. That's what luv's like, s'near as what Ah can tell yer, Sally."

Sally, remembering, thought of William. She had no need to turn her head to look at him, she knew his features, the set of his shoulders, his big, broad-palmed hands, his hair, which, despite the scented grease which he used, was always ready to become unruly. Could she feel like that about William ? Could

she ever feel like that about him? Did she feel that all other
men were—kinder waffly compared with him? Could he ever
be the only chap in the world?

Could William ever say ridiculous things to her, silly things
which managed somehow or other to sound like music, the
loveliest music in the world? "You look so pretty, Sally. You
are pretty, only I never knew it before. . . . Can't we get out of
here and dance on the lawn? . . . Don't forget me, Sally." If
William asked her to sew a button on his glove—always supposing
that he ever wore gloves—would her heart beat so fast that the
pounding of it would make her hands shake, and her fingers
uncertain? When she passed William in the kitchen garden,
when she saw him coming down the long narrow path, would
she feel half-frightened because she had to pass so near him?
Would the whole garden seem to blaze with sunlight the moment
she caught sight of him? Anyway, was it love that made you
feel these things? She didn't know. Yet here was William
waiting for his answer, standing so patiently and still. He was
like one of those rocks that rose out of the moor in odd places—
immovable, unchangeable.

She moved, and turning her head met his eyes watching her
gravely.

"I'm sorry, William—I just don't know what to say," she
said.

He sighed. "Ah see. Just tell me, Sally luv, is theer sum
other chap as tha likes better'n me?"

She felt a sense of panic. Had he guessed what was in her
mind? It wasn't possible.

"No, oh no—there isn't anyone else, really there isn't."

"Why, then, Ah mun be patient, Ah reckon," he said. "Ah'll
just tell thee this, chucky, Ah wait fur thee, Ah tak' thee wheniver
yer minded. It dean't matter when, Ah can wait. Just cum
ter me an' saay, 'William, Ah figure as it's all reit,' an' Ah'll have
uz axed at chetch as soon as Ah can get down ter t'parson. Ah
tak' me dying oath on that, an' Ah'm not a chap as taks oaths
wi'out thinking on what Ah'm daeing. That's all, Sally
lass."

"Thank you, William," she said, "it's very nice of you. I'm
grateful to you for liking me so well."

For the first time he laughed. "Like—naay, Ah dean't like
thee—Ah luv thee, better'n what Ah do mesen, choose how.
We'd best be getting back, Sally."

ii

It was that same night that Mrs. Bishop told her that "they" were taking her to London with them. Her ladyship had watched Sally, it appeared, and as Lady Gwendoline liked her, Sally was to go up to town and attend her young ladyship.

"Mind you," Mrs. Bishop admonished, "it's a gert honour an' privilege. To have the looking after of her young ladyship—and everything. To live in that grand house in Belgrave Square, and see the sights—some of 'em, at least. You're a lucky girl, Sally."

So Sally went to London, with Mr. Lingley and Mamzel. They travelled together in a third-class carriage, while the Family sat in luxury in a first-class reserved one. At Darlington the stationmaster came forward and talked—deferentially but with a certain jocularity—to his lordship. When the train came in he showed them to their carriage, and stood chatting until the train moved out of the station. When the train steamed into York, Sally said breathlessly, "Oh, is this London?"

Mr. Lingley was very kind, and pointed out the towers of the Minster, and explained that London was far larger and, he added, considerably dirtier. Mamzel yawned, saying that she hated train journeys and always got a headache. After that she leant back in her corner, closed her eyes and slept. Mr. Lingley brought out a sporting paper and a book which appeared to be a favourite of his called *Ruff's Guide to the Turf*; he proceeded to make elaborate calculations on the backs of envelopes, and scarcely vouchsafed a glance at the passing landscape. Sally sat entranced. She was going to London, there was to be a ball for Lady Gwendoline, it was rumoured that "H.R.H." would be there and the Princess. Mamzel hinted that it might be possible to get a glimpse of them.

"For me," she said, "eet is nossing, so ver' many times 'ave I seen zem. But forr you, Sallee—it vill be a grreat ex-per-i-ence. She is beautiful, 'e is a fine figure of a man. Pairhaps a leetle 'eavy, but—ver' att-rac-teeve. You shall see 'im."

How strange that Mr. Lingley should be so little moved at the idea of going to London. He merely raised his eyes when they stopped at a station and said its name in a bored voice. True, at York he had got out and hurried along to his lordship's carriage, he did the same at Doncaster and Grantham, only to return and bury himself in *Ruff's Guide*.

Sally sat staring at the landscape. How it changed. There were wide rivers, green fields with neat hedges, towns where there seemed to be nothing but tall chimney-stacks, and smoke hanging over everything. She saw villages and wondered if each had its particular family living at some manor or hall, she saw lonely cottages and wondered if the people who lived in them were happy and contented. Sometimes there were children standing at level crossings who waved as the train passed. She liked that and waved back to them, feeling less lonely. She longed to be able to lean out and cry, "Children—look at me, I'm going to London !"

London itself was a disappointment, there was no saying or thinking anything else. The huge station was dirty, people pushed and shoved, porters uttered loud and strange cries as they propelled their barrow-loads of luggage. The air seemed to be heavy, charged with something which smelt strongly and unpleasantly. Mr. Lingley, very superior with his knowledge and experience, said, "This is London, Sally. They tell country yokels that the streets are paved with gold, and the silly fools believe it."

His lordship, wearing a long travelling-coat almost touching his heels, nodded as he passed, saying, "Ah, Sally—your first visit to London, eh ?"

She said, "Yes, m'lord." Because she had learnt that very often when "they" asked questions they didn't expect an answer. They just spoke out of politeness and kindness. Her ladyship said, "Cecile, get the luggage along as quickly as you can. We're late, and I've got to dress." Mamzel jabbered off some French very quickly, and her ladyship answered in the same language. It must be queer to talk several languages easily, Sally thought. Almost like being different people, because she didn't suppose for a moment that French thoughts were the same as English ones. Lady Gwendoline touched Sally's arm, and said, "Come here, Sally—listen." She spoke very softly, scarcely looking at Sally as she spoke. "Listen, when you get to the house, see if there's a letter for you. If there is, bring it to me immediately, will you ? Oh, not if it's from someone you know, of course. But if it's in a handwriting—you've never seen before. Bring it immediately, Sally."

Sally blinked her eyes and said, "Yes, m'lady, of course—yes."

All the way to Belgrave Square she sat thinking, "A letter for me, and I'm to take it to her—what's it all about ? Eh, I hope nothing's wrong. It's a worry ! Maybe it's a joke. I hope it's a joke—I'd not like anything wrong to happen to her. What on earth 'ud I do ?''

There was a letter. There were two letters—one sent from Stallingford. It must have been written and posted the night before. It was from William. He wrote :

Dear Sally,
*To mind you **that there**'s one in Yorkshire as thinks of you and wishes you well. Don't forget me in London.*
Your loving William.

The other was written on thick cream paper, in handwriting which was very black and splashed all over the envelope. Sally carried it up to Lady Gwendoline's room, and said, "Would this be it, m'lady ?''

Gwendoline almost snatched it from her. "Yes—that's right. Sally, don't tell anyone. It's—it's all nothing. Nothing that matters really.'' Then she ripped the envelope open and stood reading the letter, while her foot kept tapping impatiently on the carpet. She sighed, folded the sheet, and suddenly looked at Sally and laughed.

"Oh, life's difficult, Sally. Only I won't allow it to be difficult. It's got to come right for me. It's *got to* !''

Sally said, "Yes, m'lady. I'm sure it will. It's bound to.''

They stood looking at each other, the girl of twenty-one, fair, exquisitely dressed, polished and accustomed to having everything on which she set her mind ; the girl of nineteen, with her grave eyes and smooth straight hair, her clear skin, and her erect figure—the girl who had never possessed anything, who had never been particularly considered or consulted about anything, who had worked since she was twelve years old, and counted herself fortunate in having been allowed to do so.

Gwendoline said, "There's plenty of time, isn't there ? I'd like some tea, I think. Ring for it, and—tell them to bring two cups. You'd like a cup, wouldn't you ?''

"It's very kind of your ladyship—very kind.''

Somehow, while she drank her tea, Gwendoline began to confide in Sally Hardcastle.

"Sally, I've always liked you. You're so understanding. I want someone to talk to. I can't talk to—the other girls I know.

They're all jealous, or narrow-minded, or not interested, because all they think of is how they can contrive to marry Leister! Sally, you've got to help me. He's wonderful, the most wonderful person in the whole world. He's just as good as we are. They say that his grandfather was—King of England. He's— he's racketed a good deal, until he met me. Now he wants to be—different. He's changed, he says so. He's older than I am—I don't believe that matters, Sally. I'd rather have a husband who was older than I was. He's thirty-five. That's not old, is it ?''

"Not what you'd call—old, m'lady," Sally said.

"He's so handsome, so amusing. Different from the men I meet ; he's travelled all over the world. Africa, India—yes, even Russia."

"Just look at that !" Sally cried, wondering why on earth people wanted to go to these outlandish places.

"He's dining here tonight. I shall have to pretend that I don't care, that I like young Tommy Cavannah much better, and all the time I shall be wondering how and when and where I can speak to him alone. Oh, Sally—you don't know what it's like to love anyone as I love him !"

"No, m'lady, I don't expect I do."

"Of course you don't !" Gwendoline laughed, and seemed suddenly younger, more approachable. "Of course you don't, because no two people ever loved each other as we do. He says that we're like all the great lovers of the world rolled into—us. Romeo and Juliet, Helen and Paris, Abélard and Héloïse, Dante and Beatrice."

"Just fancy that, m'lady—all those people !" She glanced at the little gilt clock which ticked so fussily on the mantelpiece. "I should think you'd better begin to dress, m'lady."

"Yes—of course. And, Sally, if any more letters come— bring them to me at once, won't you ? *At once*—don't keep me waiting for a second, will you ?"

In a moment she was different. There were no more confidences. It was, "Give me that, Sally," and, "Fasten that, Sally"—you went back to just being a machine. In her heart Sally found the latter position less embarrassing than the first. Only once, when she twisted before the long pier glass did Lady Gwendoline slip back to her first attitude. "I think that I look nice, Sally, eh ?"

"Lovely, m'lady. Lovely—that dress becomes you so well."

She smiled. "I want to look—very nice tonight."

"Oh, you do, m'lady. Indeed you do."

Down the stairs she went, her dress with its ruchings and flounces whispering and rustling as she swept along. Sally sighed. It must be wonderful to be so lovely, to know that the man you loved adored you, to feel that you were—like all those people with unusual names whoever they might have been.

Then someone said, "Hello, Sally! Fancy finding you here!" Adding more softly, "You're the first really nice thing I've seen since I came over this morning. How are you?"—his lordship, wearing that severe black and white which suited him so well; his hair shone where the light from the big chandelier caught it, his eyes were dancing. Sally drew a long breath, drew it almost as if she shivered.

"Good evening, m'lord."

He bent nearer. "Is that all you've got to say to me?" He mimicked her gently. "Good evening, m'lord? Nothing else? Oh, Sally, Sally! Can't you say that it's nice to see me, that you think I look well, or ill, or hideous or delightful?"

"I am very glad to see you looking so well, m'lord," she said primly, wishing that her heart would hammer less violently against her stays.

Leister laughed. She thought that it was the most beautiful music she had ever heard.

"Model Sally," he said, then added, "I believe that the real meaning of 'model' is an—imitation. Is that what you are? An imitation of a real person? Wouldn't you like to be quite real, Sally. Will you be—one day? Oh, I wish that I could come and talk to you. I'm going to hate this stupid dinner-party—lots of people I don't like. Silly young women, and I must talk to them. An American, who is rolling in money, and wears queer clothes, and"—he gave an affected shiver—"Hallard! I wonder what you'd think of Master Hallard? I'd trust your judgment. There, I must go. Stand there, where you are now, Sally, and when we go into the dining-room I'll look up. Smile at me, give me courage to sustain me through this awful, dull, dreary dinner! Good-bye—remember, smile!"

She stood where he left her, her hand pressed against her side; once she sighed. 'That's what it's like, then,' she thought, 'there's only him in the whole world. Him and me. I'd like to—die now. Just standing here, watching him go down the stairs. He said that I was to wait and watch for him going in to dinner. He said that he'd look up. I can't bear it, I don't believe. It's like all the joy and all the pain in the world being given to me to hold. It's—it's too much.'

She was standing there when Mamzel came along the corridor following her ladyship. Lady Stallingford nodded. "Ah, Sally—waiting to see my daughter go in to dinner ? I hope that you've managed all those intricate hooks on her new dress, and that she does you credit !''

"Oh, her ladyship looks beautiful, m'lady, beautiful.''

Mamzel and Sally stood together, and they saw Mr. Blachlet cross the hall. Mamzel whispered, " 'E is a fine figure of a man, ziss Blachlet, no ?'' Heard his voice, very round and mellow, announce, "Dinner is served, m'lady.'' Again Mamzel whispered, "Now ve shell see, eh ?'' Her ladyship, with a short, stout man who wore glasses with gold rims, his lordship with a tall pretty girl. "Zees ees 'oo zey veel wish Leister to marry—Lady 'Eleen Fairlees.'' Lady Gwendoline with a tall dark man with curly hair who bent over her when he spoke, two more men, two more women, and Victor Leister and another girl. As he crossed the hall, he spoke to his partner, and raising his hand pointed to some picture which hung on the stairs. She looked, nodded and said something ; again he looked up and smiled.

Mamzel whispered, " 'E shows to 'er zees old picture—painted by Sair Lely.''

Sally, her hand still pressed against her heart, said, "Of course—ves ''

CHAPTER TWO

IT was exciting to be in London, exciting but not always very pleasant, and sometimes worrying—when Lady Gwendoline decided that she wished to walk in the Park, and Sally was ordered to accompany her, for instance. They walked through streets, entered the park by some huge gates, to Sally the whole place seemed crowded in the extreme. People were riding, cantering and galloping. "Rotten Row," said Gwendoline. "I ride there sometimes." A long line of ladies and gentlemen stood at the rails, and from time to time one of the riders drew up and spoke to a friend. Again Gwendoline glancing at them said, "I believe my brother's riding this morning. We'll go along here, Sally, I hate the crowd."

She walked briskly, as if she had some definite purpose. They left the riders behind, they were in quiet walks now, and Sally stared round, admiring the flowers, but thinking that the grass looked dingy after Stallingford. She felt as if she were two separate individuals on that morning. One, Sally Hardcastle, who walked demurely beside her young mistress, the other—Sally could not give her a name, but she was certainly not Sally Hardcastle—leant with those well-dressed ladies and gentlemen, on the rails watching the riders—no, watching for one rider only. He came cantering past, saw her, swung off his hat, and pulled up near to where she stood. "Hello, Sally! Here's a lovely morning!" People watched, listened and wondered who Lord Leister talked to. "Sally," he had said—who was this mysterious Sally?

Gwendoline said impatiently, "Oh, Sally, don't go wool-gathering! I've spoken to you twice. Listen—here's someone I know. Just walk behind—I'll call you when I want you."

Sally started. "Yes, m'lady."

He was tall—yes, she had seen that last night—tall and dark, with a moustache which fell curving over his lips. Sally thought, 'I wonder what his mouth's like!' He was wonderfully well dressed, his frock coat fitted without a wrinkle, his top hat, which he swung in his hand, shone and glistened, his gloves were grey, the exact shade of his spats. He gave the impression of having devoted a great deal of care to his toilet, and of having succeeded in turning himself out perfectly.

His voice was almost too finely modulated. "Ah, Lady Gwendoline—this is a piece of good fortune ! May I walk with you ? Enchanted !" He bent his head and said something so softly that Sally could not hear. Gwendoline laughed, and said, "You're really dreadful." They walked on, and a few moments later Gwendoline turned : "Sally—we're going to sit down, over there, among the trees. Go and watch the horses if you like, be back in twenty minutes."

"Go and watch the horses !"

Sally, in her neat little jacket, with the small inconspicuous basque, her skirt with a very limited flounce at the back, and her dark straw hat with its twist of ribbon made her way to the Row. She wandered along, on the fringe of the well-dressed crowd, her eyes searching among the riders. What beautiful women ; what splendid horses ; how fine the men looked, so elegant, sitting their horses so easily, chatting and talking to their companions ! Everyone seemed to know everyone else, Sally thought. Some of the men scarcely had their hats on their heads at all, so frequently did they salute and bow to the ladies who watched. There was a gap among the watchers, and almost fearfully she pressed forward. She felt afraid among all these elegant people. Suppose someone should turn and stare at her, wondering what a lady's-maid was doing there ! 'Nay,' Sally thought, 'I'd die of shame. Aunt Hardcastle would have something to say at me pushing myself forward among my betters !'

It seemed that he was level with her before she realized his presence. She even heard his laugh, rather high and very gay. He was riding with an elderly man, with a purple face and white side-whiskers. Leister rode with one hand on his hip, and to Sally he seemed the embodiment of all that was graceful and gallant. His eyes were restless, his glances darted here and there. She felt a sense of panic lest he should see her, lest his eyes should meet hers. She tried to look away, to assume tremendous interest in a young woman who was having some difficulty with a restive little mare—but she realized that it was impossible. Try as she would her gaze went back to that slim figure on the big bay horse.

He saw her. She caught the sudden glance of astonishment. For a second he seemed unable to believe his eyes, then his smile widened, and he swept off his hat and bowed as he might have bowed to some duchess. Then, turning back to his purple-faced companion, he began to talk eagerly, and so was lost among the crowd of riders.

A woman standing near Sally said to the man with her, "That was Lord Leister, wasn't it ?"

"Yes. Victor Leister, riding with old Telford. Did he bow to you, Mercia ?" ·

"No, my dear. I wondered for whom that very elegant greeting was intended."

Sally longed to say, "It was for me, madam. I'm his sister's maid, and that's how he greets a servant. That just shows you what he is, shows you how courteous he is, how thoughtful, how good."

She turned and walked back to where Gwendoline sat under the trees with Archibald Hallard. Gwendoline was flushed, Sally fancied that she had been crying. Her companion was leaning forward, his hands clasped, talking earnestly. Sally thought she heard him say, "It's bound to be all right . . . once I get free of these damned Jews—they hang round a man's neck." Walking home, Gwendoline was friendly and expansive again.

"Isn't he a splendid figure, Sally ?" she asked. "It makes me so angry when I remember that Papa and Mama don't like him. They're unjust to him. They don't know him. I do. He's always been treated badly by his father. Never been given a chance. No need to tell anyone that I saw him this morning, Sally. It's a secret between us, eh, Sally ?"

Sally said, "Yes, m'lady", and "Really, m'lady ?" at intervals and wished that her heart didn't feel so intolerably heavy about it all. Hateful to deceive his lordship—the man who had saved her from the House—dreadful to deceive her ladyship who was so kindly and pleasant, horrible to deceive his young lordship—that worst of all !

It did not seem that life at the big house in Belgrave Square went as smoothly as at home. There were long discussions in Lady Gwendoline's sitting-room, when her ladyship said, "Gwendoline, my dearest child, do be wise—Mr. Vanderholt is such an admirable match, and such a nice man. One could trust him anywhere, with anything."

"Mama, he's so dull. Dull and old !"

"Then young Cavannah ! What a delightful young man. Handsome, of the highest character. Everyone likes him, and the Prime Minister told your father the other day that he had great hopes for him, great hopes."

"But I don't *like* Tommie Cavannah, Mama!"

Her ladyship, snapping her fan so sharply that Sally feared that she might break the fine ivory sticks : "Oh, how can you be so obstinate !"

His lordship came and talked, standing there on the hearth-rug with his splendid beard flowing down like a golden cascade over his white-shirt front, saying, "Just a moment, Sally. I'll call you presently," and before she had gone into the bedroom and closed the door beginning to talk very loudly and angrily. Impossible not to hear some of the things he said, impossible not to gather one's own conclusions as to what he spoke about. ". . . Head over ears in debt . . . every Jew in London . . . I've no intention of paying off his debts . . . not one penny from me—or your dear mother . . ." Then, still more loudly: "Remember, Gwendoline, not one penny . . . racing debts . . . card debts . . . and"—a long pause—"women ! You force me to speak plainly . . . Young Cavannah . . . horse of a different colour . . . hard-working—and devoted. Spoke to me in a most manly fashion . . . respect . . ." And so the heavy, angry voice went on, sometimes scarcely more than a rumble, then rising with indignation to a high key, taking on a louder tone.

Gwendoline cried, and when his lordship had gone, wrote a long letter and gave it to Sally to post.

"They don't understand," she wailed, "they don't even try to understand. I won't give him up, nothing shall make me, nothing."

Even his young lordship was depressed. He came into his sister's sitting-room one evening, when the others had gone to some ball, and sat down, his hands on his knees.

'Just,' Sally thought, 'as William Scarth might sit !'

He said, "I'm off tomorrow, Sally. Back to Paree—Gay Paree which isn't nearly so gay as it's painted, believe me. I don't want to go. I'm worried, disturbed. Oh, I saw you in the Row the other morning. I couldn't believe my eyes. I was riding with old Telford."

She nodded. "Yes, an old gentleman with a red face."

He nodded. "That's it—old Telford, the hope of every young diplomat. They say that he can pull more strings than any man in Europe. I looked, thought, 'That's mighty like my Sally.

Mighty like! Can't be, though; it's not possible.' But it was possible—it was Sally." He laughed as if his depression had vanished. "Did I bow with proper respect? I hoped that I did. I wanted to shout, 'Hello, Sally!' only that wouldn't have been respectful. Do you forget all about me the minute my back's turned? I wonder. I expect so. Don't tell me that you'll forget me and remember that unpleasant, black-haired piece of iniquity Archie Hallard!" He shook his head. "I don't like him, don't like him at all." He wrinkled his nose as if he smelt something unpleasant. "Not pretty the stories one hears about him, not at all pretty. A bad fellow."

She said, "I've only seen him, m'lord."

"I don't mind your seeing him, but I don't want him to see you, Sally. Once he clapped his nasty eyes on you, there's no saying what might happen. What should I do? Insult him, make him challenge me to a duel! Whew! That would set Mayfair talking! Nice talking to you, I can say what I like. No need to be serious and grave and weighty. You don't say much, do you, Sally? I like saying your name—Sally, Sally, Sally. Nice name, and it belongs to a nice person. Think of me tomorrow, won't you? I'm not a very good sailor. Then the next day I shall be the correct young but so promising under-secretary. Why don't you write to me when I'm away?"

"I'd not know what to say, m'lord."

He stood up, and standing before her, laid his hands on her shoulders. "I wonder what I want you to say. Wonder if I want you to say anything at all? I don't know. I'm in a muddle, m'dear, and that's the truth. If ever—remember—if ever you were in any trouble—any trouble—or if ever"—he was speaking very slowly now—"you want me—come to me. Look, here's my address in Paris. I wonder if you'd ever come to Paris. It would be fun to show you Paris. Your eyes would get very round and dark, wouldn't they? Little restaurants, lovely food. You like good food, don't you?"

She moved a little uneasily under the touch of his hands on her shoulders.

"Yes, m'lord, I like good food."

He laughed, flinging back his head. "You're just a little parrot, Sally. You repeat only what I say to you. Can't you be original?—or maybe I shouldn't like it if you were. I must go—I shan't see you tomorrow. Give me a kiss, Sally."

She started back, twisting herself free of his hands. "Oh no, m'lord, please, no. I couldn't do that. It wouldn't be right."

"Not even if I told you that—I wanted you to kiss me—really, truly, sincerely ?"

"Please—I couldn't."

"Then I could !" He caught her to him, kissed her lightly on either cheek, then held her at arm's length, smiling and saying, "Not so very terrible, was it ? There"—seeing the distress on her face—"there, don't be upset, Sally. They were friendly kisses—really and honestly friendly. I like you so much—you're one of the world's pleasant people. Be happy, m'dear, and—write to me in Paris. Sally's first letter to her friend Leister."

"Good-bye, m'lord," she stammered, "I don't mean to be silly. I'd—do anything in the world for you—anything."

He stood with his hands in his pockets, watching her gravely, looking suddenly very like his father.

"I believe you," he said, "or for my father, or my mother or my sister, eh ?"

"Of course—of course, m'lord."

"Umph ! Queer how distasteful it is to share anything—even devotion—with one's family. There, you're making me serious again. That won't do ! Good night, Sally, good night."

He was gone, and she stood staring at the closed door, as if she half expected him to come back to her ; then slowly she sat down on the nearest chair, covered her face with her hands and began to cry.

ii

His lordship and her ladyship were going away. Only, Mr. Blachlet said, for a couple of nights, then they were returning for the ball, Lady Gwendoline's ball. His young lordship might get back from Paris or he might not, it was difficult to say. Very intent on his work, Lord Leister, possessing, Mr. Blachlet didn't doubt, a very distinguished future ahead of him. It was unfortunate that Lady Gwendoline had suffered so terribly from toothache, and that her dentist demanded so many visits to save a particular tooth. Sally listened, and felt again doubts as to the intensity of Lady Gwendoline's suffering. True, she went to the dentist—Sally saw her go in ; but Sally was always instructed not to wait. Lady Gwendoline preferred to return home in a four-wheeler when the dentist had finished his work.

"I hope that he didn't hurt you very much, m'lady?" Sally ventured.

"Oh, I hate dentists; but they're necessary, I suppose."

She was unwilling to talk much these days, always writing letters and tearing them up, only to begin another. Long letters they were, in her sprawling, rather unformed handwriting. Obediently Sally took them to the pillar-box at the corner of the Square. She was irritable, never satisfied with her dresses, her hair, her shoes. She alternated between wild gaiety and acute depression; more than once Sally had found her in tears.

One evening she was going out alone, her aunt, Mrs. Powers, was to chaperon her. She laughed as she dressed. "He'll be there, Sally. He swore that somehow he'd contrive to get an invitation. The Mercies are old-fashioned, stuffy people. They'll be delighted to entertain him"—again she laughed—"the son of a king! What rubbish it all is. Oh, I'm so happy. Do I look nice, Sally, really very nice?"

When she had gone, Sally sat down to mend stockings, she loved the smooth silk, liked to feel it against the backs of her hands. It was one of her small conceits that she could mend stockings so that the darn never showed. As she darned, she thought. Paris, what was Paris like? Would the day ever come when she should go there? Yet, after all, she didn't want to go—except to see that one person. He had said that it would be fun to show her Paris, that her eyes would grow large and round. What had he meant about not liking to share devotion with the rest of his family? What nonsense he talked, and yet what a delight it was to listen to him. "You're a pleasant person," he had said. "I like you very, very much."

'Eh, ma luv,' Sally thought, thinking in the broad comfortable dialect which always seemed so friendly and warm, even to think, 'theer's nowt Ah'd not do fur thee. Ah'd dee fur thee if it 'ud gie thee onny extra ease.'

The door opened and his lordship came in. He looked very tall, impressive, and his face was very serious. He stood for a moment as if uncertain what he wanted to say, then with a little movement of his shoulders, as if squaring them preparatory to lifting some burden, he said, "Sally, I want to talk to you."

"Yes, m'lord."

"Her ladyship knows that I have come to talk to you. She knows what I am going to say. She approves. Now, I know

that your position is difficult. I have my own ideas as to what
has been—transpiring—yes—that is, happening. Difficult for
you to know exactly where your duty lies. Difficult to—what
shall I say?—to carry tales, and yet difficult not to do so. I'm
sure that you follow me, Sally. Yes?"

"Well, m'lord, in a manner of speaking I do, and yet I scarcely
do, if you know what I mean. There's been nothing—well,
nothing wrong, as you might say."

"Wrong—umph! We-e-ell, except that surely disobedience is
wrong? Children, obey your parents. Honour thy father and
thy mother—eh, yes? I'm not asking you to tell me anything.
I don't look for miracles. If you're told to go home—well, home
you've got to go. Luckily, Burton—Mr. Burton in Wimpole
Street, y'know——"

"The dentist, m'lord?"

"Ex-actly, the dentist. He happens to be a very sound
fellow, good fellow, yes—a man of good ideas. He—communicated with me. Quite true, there is work for him to do. Needs
doing. M'daughter's teeth are, it appears, in a bad way.
Burton's idea is—little and often. Ten minutes today, another
ten tomorrow. Better for the patient. So—there you are.
Now listen attentively, Sally. Her ladyship and I are going
away for two days. Must go. Long-standing engagement.
Can't disappoint people—Royalty present. Almost a command.
I could have asked my sister to stay here. No authority, though.
Too easy. Likes her own comfort. Nice woman, but indolent.
Could have spoken to Blachlet"—he shuddered—"not pretty.
Shabby sort of thing to do. Nasty. Giving a girl away to a
man. Good fellow, Blachlet, very good, but—well"—for the first
time he smiled—"we preferred to trust you, Sally. On duty,
Sally. Watchdog, guarding the place, guarding your mistress.
Don't leave her, Sally. Never mind if she resents it—set your
teeth, and grin and bear it. Park, dentist, shopping—theatre—
well, even there. Sit in the pit, watch. Not congenial work, I
know that—don't like asking you, but—trustworthy, that's what
we feel you to be. May need money—cabs, seats in a theatre—if
such a thing happens, which I trust it won't—here y'are." He
pulled out a gold sovereign purse. "Hold out your hand. Five,
seven, eight, nine—ten. Now—for emergencies. Always provide for emergencies." His hand went to another pocket, he
pulled out a pocket-book. "Five, and another. That's twenty.
Ought to be enough. That's on the safe side." He drew a

SALLY SCARTH 75

long breath. "Ah, glad that's over. I don't like it—I know that you don't like it either. Got to be done. Eventual happiness. Not a nice man, Sally—unpleasant fellow. Knows that I don't approve, knows it perfectly well. So that's all arranged, Sally, eh?"

"I'll do my best, m'lord. I only hope that you don't think I've not been behaving rightly. I didn't quite know—oh, I'm not making excuses, only—it was difficult."

He patted her arm with his big, white hand. "I understand, m'dear. Ought to have—er—er—confided in you sooner. My fault entirely. Do your best, your very best."

"I will indeed, m'lord."

"Then good night. We shall not be ungrateful. Good night, and thank you."

"Thank *you*, m'lord."

iii

It all seemed to begin the minute that the Earl and Countess drove away from the house. Lady Gwendoline had come home very late—or very early, whichever way one looked at it. As Sally undressed her she sighed and laughed softly, then suddenly swung round and laid her head on Sally's shoulder, saying, "Oh, Sally, Sally—I don't know if I'm happy or desperately miserable. It's all so difficult. But—it's going to be all right. If you're playing against someone, and you're sure of your own play—force their hands."

Sally thought, 'That's not her talking. That's something she's learnt from someone.'

In the morning her ladyship came into the bedroom. Lady Gwendoline was making a pretence at eating breakfast, just breaking up toast in her fingers and sipping tea.

She said, "Oh, Mama—have you come to say good-bye?"

Lady Stallingford said, half reprovingly, "There is a saying about the mountain and Mahomet, if you remember. Did you have a nice time last night? Your aunt brought you home? That's right. We shall be back on Thursday morning, I hope. In time to make any last arrangements for your party. Miss Halsey has everything in hand. She's really invaluable to me, that girl. Such a nice girl, too." Then, and Sally wasn't certain if she were laughing or quite serious, "Be good while Papa and I are away, Gwen."

"Of course, Mama.   Have a nice time."

"Look after my daughter, Sally."

"Yes, m'lady, of course I will."

And as she said it she had a queer sense of uneasiness, of impending worry.   The door had scarcely closed when Lady Gwendoline sat upright in bed saying, "Sally, take this tray.   I'm going to get up.   Is my bath ready ?   Listen, I want you to pack a couple of bags for me.   The large ones.   I'm going to stay with my aunt, Mrs. Powers, until Mama and Papa come back.   She likes young people, and it's so dull here with only Miss Halsey to talk to.   There's always lots of fun at Mrs. Powers'.   Pack the pale blue and the rose—I'll carry my jewel-case."

"Will you be taking me, m'lady ?"

"No—no—I can't very well.   My aunt's house is small, and she has masses and armies of servants.   One of them will look after me.   Take a holiday, Sally.   I'm sure you'll enjoy seeing something of London.   Pack the walking-dress—the maroon with the dark green, and some morning-gowns.   The one with the Mechlin lace—I want to wear my nicest things."

Sally's heart was beating fast.   She would have given anything in the world to say, "You're not going to your aunt's.   I know it and so do you.   You're going somewhere with that man, and you shan't, I've got to prevent you.   I promised."   For a moment, as she took out the fine underclothes, with their minute tucks and exquisite lace, as she lifted up the beautiful shining silk stockings and prepared to pack them in the bags, she wondered what she could do.   She might ask Mr. Lingley—but no, she remembered that Mr. Lingley had gone with his lordship.   Mongsewer—she couldn't speak to him, and his lordship had been against anyone speaking to Blachlet.   She must manage somehow alone.   Must—she had promised that she would.

When Lady Gwendoline emerged from the bathroom, Sally said tentatively, "I could come round, m'lady, every morning and evening, you'll not be so—well, so used to a strange maid."

"Oh no, that's all right, Sally.   After all"—there was the faintest possible pause—"after all, it's only for two or three days."

Someone brought a note ; Sally took it.   His writing !   It was evidently quite short, for her ladyship read it in a second, her face flushed.   Sally fancied that her hand shook a little.   "Tell them to wait for an answer, Sally.   I'll write it now.   It's from my aunt."

It seemed to be impossible that she should really have left the room and forgotten to take the letter with her! There it was, lying on the dressing-table, while Lady Gwendoline wrote a reply in the sitting-room next door. Sally hesitated. What was it that Gwendoline had said about "forcing someone's hand"? Something to do with a game—well, this was a game that she had promised to play, and play it she would!

Moving quickly and quietly, she looked down at the opened letter. No need even to touch it, she felt that she couldn't have borne to touch it. Big bold writing, she could read it without stooping down.

. . . *the Lord Warden, Dover. I daren't travel down with you. I'll come down late tonight. Then tomorrow, my dearest, Paris and freedom. I send you all my love and . . .*

Here the writing continued over the page, and Sally did not think it necessary to read more. The Lord Warden, Dover. Who was he, what was a warden? Where precisely was Dover? Was this Lord Warden perhaps someone who arranged weddings, or issued tickets for people going abroad? Surely this gentleman with the resounding title must be a person of importance, of good standing; or was he possibly one of Mr. Hallard's friends? A gentleman, but not a nice gentleman, not a proper person for her young ladyship to mix with. And he—Hallard—was coming down late tonight. Was he? She straightened her shoulders. Sally Hardcastle would be there to meet him, never mind what her ladyship planned to do. Sally Hardcastle would get to Dover if she had to crawl there on her hands and knees. She'd find this Lord Warden, and if he tried any nastiness she'd give him a piece of her mind, lord or not!

"Were you going immediately, m'lady, to Mrs. Powers?" Sally asked.

Gwen gave her the note. "Give that to the messenger. No, I shan't go round until eleven. In time for luncheon. I believe she's got a party—young people."

"Oh, very nice, m'lady."

"It's always fun at my aunt's!"

Dreadful how easily lies came when once you began! Here was Lady Gwendoline telling one after another, just fumbling for a word now and then, but cool as could be. Oh, dear! Sally hurried with the packing, thinking, thinking, and the more she thought the less clear things seemed. The packing finished, she left her mistress still busily scrawling letters and made her way down to the servants' hall. Lady Gwendoline had said, "I shall want a four-wheeler just before eleven o'clock, Sally."

Mr. Blachlet was reading *The Times*. He said that no other paper was worth reading. He looked at her over the top of it as she entered. "Ah, good morning, Sally. Looking fresh as the proverbial flowers in spring."

She nodded. "I've been busy, Mr. Blachlet. Packing for her ladyship. She's going to stay with Mrs. Powers while his lordship and her ladyship are away."

Blachlet lowered the paper. "Lady Gwen is ? First that I've heard about it. Did her ladyship know ?"

"Why, of course, Mr. Blachlet. She was in talking to Lady Gwen this morning before she went. Saying that it would be nice for her, because Mrs. Powers' so gay, fills her house with young people. She's not taking me, because Mrs. Powers has so many servants of her own. It's only for a couple of days, after all."

She thought, 'And it's not only other folks as can lie, Sally Hardcastle. You're doing pretty well at it yourself, choose how !'

"True, quite true. Just like her ladyship to think of it. Give us all more time to work at the preparations for the ball. My word, it's going to be a splendid affair."

Sally nodded. "Yes ; it must be nice to be rich, mustn't it ?"

Blachlet was taking things easy that morning—more, he was not unwilling to sit and talk with Sally. The girl was improving, growing attractive. Nice girl, always ready to listen and not interrupt. Tolerantly he asked, "And I wonder what you'd do, Sally, if you were rich."

Her brain was working quickly—what would she do ? Should she say, "Stay with Lord Warden, but I don't know where he lives", or should she say, "Dover—and then on to France. Do you get tickets from Lord Warden ?"

She considered. "I'd like to travel, I think—yes, travel. France. I'd like to go to France, wouldn't you ?"

"My dear, I've been many times. In my youth I was in the service of a gentleman there. An Englishman who preferred Paris to London. Beautiful house on the Champs Élysées."

"Is Dover a nice place ?" How bald and outspoken it sounded !

"Ah, Dover enters your mind because of France and Paris, eh ? The place where one embarks for La Belle France, as they call it. Dover—well, it's not a bad place. I've stayed there with his lordship on more than one occasion."

"Does his lordship know Lord Warden ?" Sally asked.

"Know Lord Warden ? Ah," Blachlet laughed, "you mean *the* Lord Warden, Sally. Yes, we've stayed there several times, his lordship and I. Very pleasant hotel too. Very pleasant."

An hotel ! Lady Gwen was going to meet this man at an hotel. Lady Gwen, who never moved without a maid, or went to any entertainment without a chaperon. There was something terribly wrong here. Sally had heard of scandals, but they had been connected either with gentlemen or ladies who were much older than Lady Gwen. She had heard her aunt speak with disparagement of "young ladies who were too on-coming". "No gentleman," she had said, "would wish to marry a young lady who'd not conducted herself right. No matter who she might be." "She ruined herself when she behaved so wicked with young Mr. Tracey"—how had she behaved wickedly ? Sally wondered. She had seen the girl in question, she had been pretty, and she certainly had no baby Sally understood that the usual wages of wickedness, or badness, or low-living, was that you had a baby—a bastard baby. She was one herself, she knew that, and look where she'd been found—in the House !

She had read books—not many, but sufficient to give her certain information about these villains who led young girls away and deserted them. That was without doubt what this man was planning to do. "Ruin lies before her"—"she is betrayed by her perfidious lover"—"deserted and abandoned". People would point at her, whisper behind their hands, not ask her to house-parties or dances. She would be "scorned" and— what would his lordship and her ladyship feel about it ? His young lordship too, with his brilliant future and his diplomatic career ? This might even harm him in the eyes of old gentlemen with purple faces and white side-whiskers. They might shrug their shoulders and wonder why "Leister hadn't taken better care of his sister". He'd said, "If ever you wanted me, if ever you were in any trouble, come to me." He had given her the address, his address in Paris. Well, now she was in trouble, and it wasn't any good going to Paris to tell him all about it, there wasn't time. How could she send for him ? There wasn't time for a letter—there wasn't time for anything except a telegram

Could you send telegrams to foreign parts ? Paris was a foreign part, she knew that. She might ask Blachlet—but no, she'd asked him enough questions.

She sprang to her feet. "Eh, I'd forgotten, I've to get her ladyship some ribbon !"

Blachlet smiled. "Letting your wits go wool-gathering, eh, Sally. Well, run along."

Out in the street, she asked people to direct her. How stupid they were.

"Post-orfice, miss ? Thet's rite. Fust onner rite, seccon' the lef'. Then, if it 'ad teef it 'ud bite yer."

What a fashion to talk ! She found it, and walking to the counter said to a depressed-looking young man who wore steel-rimmed glasses, "I want to send a telegram to France."

He glanced up, jerked his head to the right, and said, "Yerse—over ther—et thet desk."

A stout woman was writing busily on a telegraph form. Sally looked over her shoulder to see how it was done, then extracting her precious card, wrote the address in her uncertain childish hand. Then added :

Please come at once to the Lord Warden Hotel at Dover. It is very important. I cannot tell you why now, but it is. Come as soon, please, as you get this, I beg you to. I must see you and your mother and father are away.

Sally.

Then she crossed out her name and added, *I am in great trubble. Sally.*

Offering it to the young man, he read it, added up the words, and named a sum which staggered Sally.

"Nay," she said, lapsing into her Yorkshire because she was startled. "Nay, yon's an awful lot for that."

He said, "Well, you could make it a lot shorter'n what it is. Those 'ands' and so on."

"Nay, leave it," she said, "send it like that." She thought, 'After all, it's his lordship and not me as is paying for it. I daresant risk him not understanding what I mean.'

She walked back to Belgrave Square, went up to her mistress's room, looked for mislaid gloves, for lost handkerchiefs, and finally, swallowing hard, said, "Would you mind, m'lady, if, when you left for your aunt's, I went off for the day ? I've got a cousin

who lives near the Tower of London"—she knew the Tower of
London, knew that there were houses round it, this mythical
cousin might live in one of them—"she'd like me to spend the
day."

Gwendoline was gracious. "Of course not, Sally. Go, and
have a nice time. Look, here's a sovereign, get a present for
your cousin."

Then, a four-wheeler ordered, and luggage brought down, and
Sally's heart pounding hard, wondering if she'd be able to catch
the address. She had her own little handbag ready, so small
that it would attract no attention. Lady Gwendoline said,
"That's right, Sally, my aunt's in Hartingford Street—number
seven."

She drove away, Sally gazed wildly round the square, then
dashed madly towards another cab coming towards her.

"Quick, mister," she said, feeling like the heroine—or the
villain—in a novel, "go after that cab there, follow it. It's going
to a station. I'll give you twice your fare if you don't lose him.
My mistress is in it, and she's forgotten her handbag."

He stared down at her. "Git in," he said, "Oi'll not loose
'im. Best 'orse i' Lunnon between vese sharfts."

CHAPTER THREE

It was almost too easy driving through London with the other cab in sight. Once or twice Sally thought that they had lost it, but it always appeared again when the traffic divided. They came to a big station, and Sally asked, "How much is the fare from Belgrave Square, please?"

"The fare?" the red-faced cabby exclaimed. "Yer promised me double if I kep' 'im in sight."

In an instant Sally ceased to be a young servant rather frightened, she was a Yorkshire girl, and she "up and let him have as good as he gave".

"All right, mister. What Ah said, that Ah'll do. Ondly just have the civility an' sense to tell me what the fare is, so's Ah can double it."

"The fare's five bob," he told her grudgingly.

"That it never is!" she returned smartly. "It's never more'n three shillings. There's six for you, and get along!" She slapped the six shillings into his palm, picked up her bag and ran into the big dark station. There was her ladyship at a booking office, getting a ticket. Sally slipped behind a barrow-load of luggage, and when Gwendoline moved away she went forward and took the place which she had vacated.

"Return ticket for Dover, please."

"First clarse?" A man peered at her through the small opening. "I say, first clarse?"

"I heard you! No, third."

"Next window."

There were other people at the next window, a fat woman looked over her shoulder and demanded, "'Oo yer shovin'?"

"You, Ah expect," Sally said.

"Whaffor?"

"Because a chap's shoving behind me, that's why!" In her turn she spoke to the man behind her, "Gie ovver, do! We'll get on no faster for pushing and shoving." She was nervous at the delay, afraid that the train might go and leave her stranded. At last she had the precious ticket, at last a porter told her where to find the train, and walking slowly along the platform she saw her mistress, leaning back in the corner-seat of a compartment, holding a book in front of her face. Sally entered a third-class carriage immediately behind Lady Gwendoline's compartment. The adventure had begun.

It seemed to take hours to get to Dover. Sally stared out of the window, and decided that the country was flat and dull; it looked good enough land, but there was a lot of bog about, and the cottages were the queerest she had ever seen, with one side of the roof about half a mile long. Strange-looking houses like small towers stood near the farms. She wondered what they were; longed to ask a woman in the other corner, and then her courage failed her. Better keep quiet, and how often had her aunt warned her, "Never talk to strangers, Sally, you never know where it leads to." She wished that she had eaten more break-fast, or bought a bun at the station. There was a queer sinking feeling in her inside. She tried to forget it by thinking what she would say to his lordship. With the thought of him, her heart beat faster. Tonight she would see him, speak to him, hear him say "Sally". She had never thought much of her name until he said it, then she knew how pretty it was. She would have to tell him everything, about what the Earl had said, about reading his sister's letter—would he frown and think that a very dishonest thing to have done? she wondered. She'd tell him that she hated doing it. 'Ondly I didn't know what else to do, m'lord'. How-ever would he get rid of "that Hallard"? She had no clear ideas, except that she felt certain that he would get rid of him, and do it all very quickly and quietly and effectively. Then they'd all come back to London, and she would get him to make some explanation for her to Mr. Blachlet. Vaguely she wondered if they'd all get back that night or have to wait for the next morn-ing. She'd never stayed in an hotel. Then she saw the sea, and flinging caution to the winds asked the woman in the other corner, "Excuse me, m'am, is that the sea?"

"That's the English Channel."

"Not the sea?"

"The English Channel is the sea! Have you never seen it before?"

"Never, m'am. It looks—wild."

"It's calm today—thank goodness. I'm crossing to France. I'm a poor sailor."

She didn't look the least like a sailor, rich or poor, Sally thought. She looked like an ordinary elderly woman. Perhaps in France they had women as sailors.

"Is this Dover we're getting to now?" Sally asked.

"This is Dover. Don't let the porters rob you. They're all thieves!"

"Thank you, m'am, I won't."

When the train stopped Sally hung back. For the first time since they left London she felt uncomfortable, ashamed. There was her mistress talking to porters, forgetting how many bags she had, growing flustered and short-tempered, while Sally Hardcastle, who by rights ought to have been attending to that luggage and her mistress's comfort, stood hidden by an open carriage door, watching, doing nothing to help.

"Get a cab for me," Gwendoline said. "The Lord Warden."

Sally followed her at a distance, saw her get into the cab and drive away. She went on foot. No sense in getting there a minute after her ladyship, better walk in a few minutes later. She almost enjoyed her walk, the air smelt fresh, it had a real taste, she thought. The streets were busy, and some of the men walking along seemed to be foreigners and sailors. She noticed how the sailors moved, how they swayed a little, and wondered if they were poor sailors or comfortably off. She asked a great many people to direct her, because they talked a dialect she did not know, and it was possible to remember only the first part of what they said; but she found the hotel, and stood outside for a moment to try to get her ideas into some kind of order. She'd have to tell lies again, that was certain. She went in and found the hall empty. It looked enormous to her. In a glass-fronted office a young man sat with a big book open before him. She went forward, clutching her small bag. The young man looked up, cocked his head on one side implying a question. Sally's eyes were good, she went nearer, and saw that the book was a ledger containing the names of the guests in the hotel and the numbers of their rooms.

She said, "I might want a room for tonight, if you please. Could I have one?"

"A single room, madam?"

"Well—yes—that's right, a single room."

Peering at the book she saw the last entry, "Mrs. Hallard—No. 21".

Mrs. Hallard! That was a nice thing! To enter her name as Mrs. Hallard when she was nothing of the kind. That was the sort of badness this man was trying to teach her. Sally longed to say, "That's all wrong. That lady is the Earl of Stallingford's daughter, that's who she is!"

She licked her lips. "It's this way," she said. "I'm maid to Lady Gwendoline Leister. We're waiting for her brother, Lord Leister, who's coming from Paris. Anyway, I've to wait here while they come. I might have to stay all night. Maybe we shall all stay all night. It's better to have rooms booked, isn't it?"

The clerk smiled. "Well, it's difficult to reserve them for you—when it's not certain if you're staying or not. I mean I might have other people asking for rooms, you see."

"That's right," she agreed, "fair's fair all the world over. When will the train be here from Paris?"

"The boat?" He still smiled, one couldn't help smiling at her. She was so neat and fresh-looking, with really beautiful eyes, and a mouth which looked very soft and sweet. Not a pretty girl, exactly, and yet attractive. He thought, 'I bet these maids see something of life, knocking round with the nobs!'

She said, "Look at that! I meant the boat, of course."

"There's one in about five o'clock."

"Tonight . . . Eh, that's late. Well——"

A waiter came up and standing at her elbow said to the young man in the desk, "Luncheon to be taken up to Number twenty-one. Small bottle of 'thirty-six."

"Right."

That was a relief, anyway, she was lunching in her room. No chance of her coming down and finding Sally Hardcastle eating in the dining-room. Or ought she to ask if there were a special dining-room for ladies' maids?

She said tentatively, "I'd like some luncheon—it's a long way from London."

"The dining-room's through there," he leant forward, pointing. "Hope you'll enjoy it. You're rather late."

"And if Lord Leister should come sooner than what you think, will you let him know immediately that I'm here? Hardcastle is the name, Sarah Hardcastle."

All her life Sally was to be able to forget worries for the time being. Once she had done everything possible, her distress and anxiety remained in abeyance until the moment came when she must of necessity face them again. Now she had done all that was possible. She had got to Dover, she knew that her mistress was eating a solitary lunch with a small bottle of 'thirty-six, whatever that might be, in her own room. His lordship was on his way, and nothing more could be done until his arrival. So Sally ordered cold beef and pickles, a small glass of draught beer and some crusty bread with butter and cheese. She watched other people eating their late luncheons, she speculated about them, wondering who they were and where they were going. That little man who was so fussy, and sent the waiter back twice with his beef after turning it over and over on his plate with the fork. She thought, 'Eh, I'll bet he's not easy to live with, yon one !'

The stout lady, with enough Whitby jet in the way of ear-rings, brooches, chains and bracelets to stock a shop didn't look easy either. Her face was fat and still contrived to look pinched and cold. She had a tall, angular woman with her. A daughter, Sally decided. Their voices rose and fell, the one deep and authoritative, the other obedient and submissive. A tall man with a grave face sat alone at another table, he never raised his eyes from the book he was reading, and yet instinctively Sally felt that if he did they would be nice, kind eyes.

There were two young people at a table in one of the windows. They didn't seem to mind what they ate, they were so busy talking and laughing softly. Once or twice they glanced round the room, and she thought that they sent their happiness twink-ling over to everyone. They'd so much that they weren't able, as it might be, to use it all themselves. Some of it overflowed and reached other people. Even the somewhat melancholy waiters looked less gloomy when they spoke to the young couple. Sally decided that it was very interesting to have luncheon alone in an hotel.

"Coffee, miss—will you take coffee ?"

She started, she had been so absorbed in the young couple, wondering what it felt like to be sitting and talking laughing with the person you loved best.

She blinked her nice grey eyes, as if forcing herself back to reality, then smiled at the waiter. "Well, d'you know I believe that I will—yes."

She thought, 'I'm having a right do, I am. I wonder if it's wrong to be eating heartily like this with that other trouble hanging over us all. Well, there's nothing to be done about it as yet, and I shall be better able to face things if I've had something to eat and drink.'

The waiter was at her side again, bending over her and saying, "Coffee, miss—and there's a gentleman asking for you."

"For me?" She half started from her chair, then looking towards the door saw Leister standing there, swinging his hat in his hand. He motioned to her to remain where she was and came forward. How swiftly he moved, how slim he looked, his eyes were smiling, and yet she felt that anxiety lay behind the smile. He stopped the waiter, and she heard him say, "Something to eat. Yes—I know that I'm late. Anything cold—and be quick."

Then in another half dozen quick steps he was at her side.

"Sally—it's true, it's not a hoax! No, sit still, don't move. Let me sit down and look at you. Really, really you, Sally, come all the way from London. But you said you were in trouble. Has someone been damnable to you? That fat Blachlet, or that long-faced Lingley—what is it, Sally? Tell me, don't be afraid. My dear—I'm so glad to see you. It's all going to be wonderful. I've been thinking and wondering, I've been miserable and uncertain, and now, seeing you here—like this—I know. It's all crystal clear. Tell me, quickly. Oh, you must wonder how I got here so quickly. I wasn't in Paris. No, I was in Calais. Some dreadful pompous potentate of sorts was arriving there, and I was sent, among others, to see that he got into the right train and didn't lose his papers and his temper, and so perhaps fling England into war! My friend—Henri Lassalle— oh, you'll love Henri, but not more than you love me, Sally— opened the telegram and sent it on to me—presto! I left the fat potentate, and told other people to pat his hand and give him apples to eat and papers to read and rushed for the boat—and, what's more important, caught it. Oh, it's going to be such fun—not in Paris, we'll go out to the forest among the painters and live simply and beautifully. But, Sally, tell me. I talk too much. I can't help it. I've got to tell you everything. Now, I will listen, I won't speak again."

She stared at him, her cheeks flushed at first, then slowly losing their colour, so that now they were white; her eyes seemed to have grown larger in her face, her lips were not quite steady.

Leister said, "Sally—Sally, what is it?"

"I don't know, m'lord——"

"Oh, my dear, can't you call me by my proper name!"

"No, m'lord—summat's wrong somewhere. I don't understand. I didn't send for you——"

"But you did ! I've read your telegram twenty times, it's here in my pocket !"

"Yes—yes." She was clasping and unclasping her hands. "I sent it, but it wasn't for me as I sent it. I mean—it's got nothing to do with me, as if it could have ! It was to ask you to come and help me. You said if ever I was in trouble I was to send to you. But—oh, m'lord—it wasn't me sending for you to come to me."

The waiter said, "Will that be as you like it, sir ?"

Leister said, "Put it down, yes—all right. Bring me a brandy —a double brandy."

"Yes, sir."

He slid his hand over the table-cloth so that his fingers touched hers.

"Listen," he said, "I don't understand. There's something very wrong somewhere. You've got to explain. You love me, I'll swear that, I saw it in your face when I came in. I love you, Sally—I've really loved you ever since—oh, years and years ago. You're not going to tell me that you've been playing a game. I don't think that I'd ever, ever forgive you. Explain, Sally."

Catching her breath, as if she sobbed softly, she said, "M'lord —just give me time. Don't hurry me. I'll tell you."

He nodded. "Yes, I'll be quiet. Now—tell me."

Slowly and carefully, because she didn't feel that any of this was real, because her mind was so confused by what he had said, by the tone of his voice, by the gladness and excitement in it, and she dared not speak too quickly for fear she should miss some vital point, she told the whole story. As she spoke she felt that the man who had come into the dining-room a short time before was vanishing slowly under her eyes. His smile died, his eyes ceased to dance, his lips grew harder and older-looking. When he spoke his words were very clipped, his questions direct.

"Hallard—you're certain it's Archie Hallard ? When did this letter come ? You are quite sure that you read it correctly? You told them at the office that you were expecting me—and my sister. Um—yes, I see. Very well, we'll see it through."

Then he began to eat, and sip his brandy ; to eat very quickly, as if he didn't care whether he tasted what he ate or not. Only once he laid down his knife and fork and looking directly into her eyes, said, "And so the telegram had really nothing to do with me ?"

"No, m'lord—not in that way. It couldn't have had——"

"Tell me one thing—swear that you're speaking the truth—swear it on anything you think the world of——"

She thought, 'There's only you that I do think the world on, you are my world.'

"Yes, m'lord—I swear I'll speak truthfully."

He spoke so softly that she could scarcely catch the words. "You do love me, Sally ?"

"Yes, m'lord—I do—love you."

"Then we'll deal with this unpleasant business first——"

She walked out, following him, keeping a few steps behind as she had been taught to do when with any of the family. At the office he nodded to the clerk, nodded as if he were there on a holiday, without a care in the world. He had thrown his long, light, travelling-coat over his arm, he still swung his hat in his hand.

"I'm afraid that my sister's maid here"—he indicated Sally with his hand—"isn't used to travelling very much, and she's got things rather—well, rather mixed. My sister came down this morning, she drove down, and her maid came by train. It appears that my sister is here now."

The clerk raised inquiring eyebrows. "The name would be, sir ?"

"Leister — Lord Leister. My sister — Lady Gwendoline Leister. Number"—then turning to Sally, he asked—"what number did you say ?"

"I thought, m'lord—twenty-one."

"The name in which that room is taken is Mrs. Hallard, sir."

"No, no !" His tone was amused, tolerant. "That's plainly impossible. Mrs. Hallard is a very old lady—she must be eighty if she's a day. The lady in twenty-one, she isn't eighty, is she ? No, of course not." He spun round and faced Sally directly. "What a queer trick that is of my sister's—I have never known the time when she didn't muddle names ! I remember once, because she was reading a letter from Clarice Preston—and a waiter asked her what fish she'd have, she said, 'Clarice Preston—well grilled.' We've always laughed about it. It's a form of absentmindedness. I had an aunt exactly the same. However"—he faced back to the clerk—"it appears to be a general mix up—what the Italians call a *fritto misto* ! Could you get me a cigar, by the way ? Something good."

"Certainly, your lordship." He turned to the shelves behind

him and Leister flashed one understanding look at Sally, as if he
said, "We're managing splendidly !"

"I'm very fond of a brand called—Donna Malana. Got
them ?"

"I'll look, I'm not certain."

Leister leant forward, with one quick twist he had spun the
big book with its lists of names and rooms round, picked up a pen
and changed the name "Hallard" to "Hallarton-Wyse", then
round it went again.

"Never mind, give me something else. Ah, these are quite
good. Yes, this will do." He had the cigar in his fingers, and
twisted up a slip of paper into a spill. The clerk offered a match.

"Yes, that's better—thank you. The spill—one good turn
deserves another—light your next smoke with it." He gave the
bit of twisted paper to the clerk.

Sally thought, 'It's a very crackly bit of paper—sounds like a
bank-note."

"And now," said Leister, "we might go and find this absent-
minded sister of mine."

They mounted the stairs together, neither of them speaking.
Only at the door of the room did he catch Sally's hand for a
second, saying, "I've not forgotten, only this must be settled
first. You meant what you said, Sally ?"

"You must forget it," she whispered, "I ought never to of
said it, only you made me swear. It's just silliness, m'lord—no
good could come of it. Not good——"

"S-sh"—he laid his finger very lightly on her lips—"don't say
these things. Now will you wait outside for a few minutes ?"

He went into the room, and Sally sat down on a stiff velvet-
seated chair which stood in the corridor. She felt desperately
tired, confused, and uncertain of herself. 'If only I could have a
good cry,' she thought, 'I'd feel more like myself again !'

Leister's face, his voice, his dancing eyes—she could hear and
see them still. He had thought that she had sent for him—for
herself. Incredible ! That she, Sally Hardcastle, could have
imagined such a thing. She had thought at first that he was
making fun, only when he began to speak of Paris, saying that
she'd love his friend, Henri Someone or Other, told her that they'd
live in a forest, had she realized that he was serious, that he really
wanted her to come away with him. He loved her—he said that
he'd loved her for years. But lords didn't fall in love with their
sister's maids, with girls who had no fathers, who had tramped the

roads, and finally gone to the House. They didn't even make love to these girls, though Sir George Cormick's son Lancelot had—so the gossips said—got one of the housemaids into trouble at Bosmere. He hadn't taken her away to Paris to live in a forest. Sir George had paid a lot of money to young Briggs, who kept the grocer's shop at Hallingly; he'd married the girl and enlarged his shop. Made it, people said, almost like a London shop ! But Lancelot Cormick—even though his father was knighted—wasn't like Lord Leister. He was just a sporting gentleman, caring for nothing except horses and dogs and racing and such like. He wasn't a young gentleman with a great future.

Sally sighed as she sat there with folded hands. He had said that he loved her. That at least was something that no one could ever take from her. More—he had meant it. Even now, when he had left her at the door, his eyes grave, his face so handsome and serious, he had remembered. It wasn't just something he'd said in' jest. She wondered when she had first known that she loved him. Somehow it seemed to her that her first devotion to his father—the man who had saved her from the House—had all centred itself in his lordship. It was as if her devotion had been too great to be—well, belonging to her. She'd loved the Earl as one might love a great but distant god. Then, his lordship had been different. He had made her feel that, after all, they were made of flesh and blood like each other. They were both human beings. He had laughed and joked—oh, never in any way that he shouldn't, but he had been—friendly. Right from the time when he came in after the Eton and Harrow match to talk to Mrs. Bishop. He said that he loved her—he'd proved it. He hadn't come to Dover to help his sister, he had come because he thought that Sally Hardcastle had sent for him. It was like a miracle. If nothing else ever happened to her, life would have been worth living just for that knowledge.

'All the same,' Sally thought, 'nothing's going to happen, like living in forests, and making a lot of talk that 'ull do him harm in his work. I'd never do that, never.'

She wasn't really unhappy, she was a little stunned, and once or twice the thought crossed her mind that if only she could have been born—gentry, if only she could have had schooling, and money for clothes and a nice house—what then ? If he could have come and said that he had spoken to her father, and that her father approved, and when could they be married. . . .

She gave her shoulders a little shake. 'Sally Hardcastle, give

over, do, thinking so soft and daft like. Surely—when he's told
you that he loves you—that's something as never comes to girls
like you? You don't suppose, do you, you great silly, that
Cormick told that housemaid that he loved her? Would he
have come racing all the way over the sea in a boat for her? Of
course he'd never!'

The door opened and Leister came out. His face was still
very pale. He looked, Sally thought, very tired, dispirited.

"How is she, m'lord?"

He shook his head. "It's terribly difficult, Sally. She says
that she's of age, that no one can stop her. She isn't quite of age,
but she will be in two days' time. He's a bad fellow, you see, we
all know that. Head over ears in debt in the hands of the Jews.
There was some scandal or other in the regiment. Not a man
that other men like, Sally. He thinks that there is money—he
thinks that once he has compromised my sister, my father will"—
he fumbled for a word then—"pay him to marry her. He won't.
I know my father—so do you. Kind, just, generous, and good—
yes, good; but when he says 'no' he means it. He'd face a
scandal, but he wouldn't face being blackmailed into saving his
face."

Sally said, "I heard his lordship—one evening—talking that
way to her. I couldn't help hearing. I'd never known him so
angry, never."

Leister nodded. "I know. What would her life be, Sally?
They could never live in England. They'd tag round the
Continent, mixing with the wrong kind of people, the gaming-
table loafers. The second-rate. He'd be unfaithful. They say
that he's never yet contrived to treat a woman decently. That's
the life my sister—my father's daughter—is contemplating for
the sake of this blackguard! He came to the house once—that
was owing to a misunderstanding. He isn't the type of fellow
that my father tolerates. My aunt met him. She's a darling,
but she's got no judgment at all. What the devil am I to do?"

Sally stood pinching her lower lip between her thumb and
forefinger. She wished that she could be wise, that she could
help him. Why was she so slow-witted, why couldn't she have
some brilliant flash of imagination, intuition? Her face cleared a
little, though the little puckered frown still showed between her
level eyebrows.

"You say that he's in debt, m'lord? Mightn't he—if he was
told that there wouldn't be a penny-piece otherwise—take a sum

of money and go ?   A bird in the hand's worth two in the bush.
It might be worth trying.   I've got some money his lordship
gave me.   Over twenty pounds."

His face split into a grin which was almost boyish, she saw his
white teeth flash for a second, then the youthfulness went, leaving
him serious once again.

"Bless you," he said, "he'd want something substantial.   But
it's worth trying.   I believe that it's an idea, Sally.   Couple of
thousand down, eh ?"

"I'd start lowish, m'lord, and maybe work up a bit.   That
kind always drives a hard bargain, I've heard my aunt say—with
tradesmen and such-like."

"He'd be flattered to find himself lumped with the Stallingford tradesmen !   Sally, we'll try it.   I think we'd better go
back to my sister.   Don't let her frighten you, dear."

"Oh no, m'lord."

Gwendoline was sitting near the window.   Sally wondered if
she were watching for Mr. Hallard to arrive.   She turned as they
entered, saying to Sally, "Oh, there you are—you little snake in
the grass !   You're not wanted here, my father's paid spies make
no appeal to me."

"That 'ul do, Gwen," Leister said.   "As a matter of fact
we've got a lot to thank Sally for.   Sally's played a good game,
and my father and mother have every right to be grateful to her.
They will be, too, if I know anything about them.   We should all
be in a pretty mess if it hadn't been for Sally."

"I don't want to hear Sally's praises being sung.   The whole
family seems to think Sally's something—extraordinary."

He nodded.   "If that's what they think, I'm not certain that
I don't applaud their good sense."

Sally said, "I'll just go and unpack your things for the night,
m'lady."

"If you hear us talking, remember to listen carefully.   You
may like to repeat it to my father !"

Suddenly furious, Leister said sharply, "Be quiet, Gwen !
That's disgraceful !"

"Perhaps you'd like to go into my bedroom with her, Victor."

Sally turned and fled into the bedroom ; she could hear their
voices, angry, undisciplined, dreadful.   They were saying terrible
things to each other, trying to hurt and wound.   She had never
believed that her mistress could say such things, make her voice
so shrill and coarse.   Leister's came so cold that Sally shivered.

If he should ever speak to her in that way! She laid out clothes for the night with hands that shook, but she did her work and felt better for doing it. There was no need to unpack everything, they would be going back to London in the morning—she was certain of that; but she wanted something to do, she wanted to work with her hands, to walk backwards and forwards from the bags to the wardrobe—she wanted to open and close drawers, to fill them with beautifully made clothes, some of which she had embroidered herself. In the midst of all this unreality, ordinary things—laying out clothes, unfolding skirts and shaking out their folds—seemed the best method of keeping sane.

She laid down a pile of fine linen, someone was walking very quickly down the corridor, someone had knocked on the door of the room next door, and Leister's voice called to them to come in. She laid her hand on her heart. Supposing Hallard grew angry, suppose that he killed his lordship, suppose—suppose—suppose? . . .

"Leister!" She heard the new voice cry, and heard his lordship say very quietly:

"Entirely at your service!"

"This is unconscionable!"

"It might have been——"

Then a jumble of sound, three people speaking at once, her mistress sobbing; Hallard's voice soothing her, and then Leister's, slow and careful, expressionless.

On and on the murmur continued. Sometimes Gwen cried, "That's not true!" or "Don't listen to him, Archie!"

"My sister," Leister's voice rang out suddenly, "has not got one penny of her own." Later: "My father can do exactly as he pleases, except what must go to the estate and its upkeep." Then the low voices again, they were arguing, discussing terms; Gwen was sobbing. Sally felt desperately sorry for her. How dreadful it all was. At last Hallard's voice alone, expostulating, Sally thought that he was making some kind of explanation to Gwen. A door opened, heavy steps retreated down the corridor, the bedroom door burst open and Gwen Leister rushed in crying, "I'll never forgive you, Victor, never! Get out of my sight, Sally—I loathe you all! I've you to thank for this—you little gutter brat!"

CHAPTER FOUR

VICTOR LEISTER sat on the edge of his bed, his hands deep in his trousers pockets, his good-looking face clouded and distressed. He had dined with Sally Hardcastle, and he had tried to tell her all that was in his mind. When he had first fallen in love with her he didn't know. Perhaps he had slipped into love unconsciously on one of those visits to the nursery at Stallingford. He had forgotten, it had all come so gradually and so unavoidably. "Something I couldn't get away from, Sally. It had me caught and held fast—it was too late then to do anything except admit— that I love you."

She listened, scarcely speaking, and he felt that in some queer inexplicable way she was far wiser than he. She faced life with greater certainty, she had knowledge—where she had obtained it he didn't know. Of course, he knew her history vaguely. He had heard his mother say, "Poor little thing, that's why she's so genuinely devoted to your father. She looks on him as a kind of saviour." She was a workhouse child, a "fatherless bairn", with very little education, no talents—unless her beautiful darning could be counted as one. She wasn't even startlingly pretty. Her one real beauty was those big serene grey eyes. Her skin—that was lovely, soft and smooth, clear and cool. Put her next to his sister, Gwendoline, and not a soul would look at Sally. There was nothing obviously lovely about her. She was just—Sally.

He was a very average young man, sufficiently clever, sufficiently intellectual, sufficiently good to look at. His life had been no better and no worse than the lives of other young men of fashion. He had indulged in expensive flirtations with lesser actresses in burlesques. He had sent them flowers, garters with imitation diamond buckles, flowers ; he had invited them to supper, offered them champagne, embraced them with more fervour than dignity—and forgotten all about them. He had indulged in a short affair with a girl in a tobacconist's at Oxford. There had been a terrible rumpus, his father had read him a lecture, and—that had ended the matter. This was different.

All he knew was that during the last year or so he had longed to get back to Stallingford, and had been half afraid, half ashamed, to admit, even to himself, the exact reason. He knew that he had come to take back presents for Bishop, silly little things that gave him an excuse to run up to the nursery almost immediately after his arrival. "Must go and take Bish her present !" He had raced up the stairs, knowing in his heart that what he really meant was, "I must catch a glimpse of Sally."

Two years ago he had found a change in her. She had ceased to be the little girl who helped Bish ; she had grown, her figure had formed, her whole carriage had improved. Her smooth hair seemed to have caught something of the sunlight in it, and he had left the nursery feeling queerly disturbed and yet conscious that she had always interested him, and that what had happened now was merely that—his eyes had opened. He had seen her, clearly, for the first time. He remembered how that night as he dressed, he had said to his reflection in the mirror, "Victor, it behoves you to be very careful, my boy."

He had been careful. He had never said anything to her that the whole world might not have heard. She had never shown that his presence embarrassed her. That was one of the marvels about her—her calm acceptance. Other maids might flutter a little if he spoke to them, reply breathlessly, "Yes—m'lord—oh yes." Sally always spoke quietly, and looking back he wondered if they had ever had a conversation together. He had talked ! He loved talking ! She had merely assented to what he said, or thrown out some non-committal phrase or other. "How very pleasant, m'lord", or "Fancy that, m'lord".

He knew so little about her. Not what colours she liked, what books she had read, what were her favourite dishes, if she were religious—nothing. Only that she was Sally Hardcastle, his sister's maid.

That dance in the servants' hall, when she had looked so pretty, wearing a blue silk dress. She had almost sparkled because she was enjoying it so much. He had watched her dancing with some oaf, his hair smothered in bear's grease, and felt his heart contract. Was she in love with the fellow ? "Walking out" ? He had thought then, 'I should hate her to marry anyone—hate it—hate it ! She really belongs to me !' Then he had danced with her, and she had been—as he had known she would be—light and utterly delightful. She smelt of lavender—of scented geranium—of lad's love. Which, he didn't know, he knew only that it was a scent which was soft and sweet, real, simple and good.

In London he had kissed her. Taken her in his arms, and pressed his lips to her soft cheeks. She hadn't either swooned or cried out, she had not struggled ; and afterwards she had been composed and quiet. On the journey back to Paris, Leister had been unable to forget her. Henri—who had been educated in England—noticed how absorbed he was.

"Victor, you have fallen in love ! I know it. You are sad, and yet there is a light in your eyes. Tell me—let me help you. I am romantic, and love makes an instant appeal to me."

He had been sulky at first, had told Henri that he imagined a lot of rubbish, that he thought love was the beginning and end of the universe. Henri replied that this was precisely what love was, and only fools thought otherwise. Why, then, did poets—some of the wisest of men—concern themselves almost exclusively with love ? Slowly, because Henri was his best friend, and blessed with sensibility, Victor told him. Henri listened gravely, sympathetically.

"And there you have the story !" Victor ended.

Henri sighed. "And so you feel better—*rien ne pése tant qu'un secret.*"

"What shall I do ?"

Henri shrugged. He both shrugged and sighed a good deal, but he had a heart of gold.

"You will do what you want. If I were sufficiently cynical I should say that this is the only rule for life. You really love her, this Sallee ?"

"Damn it, I don't only know that I'm *in love*, I know, too, that I *love* her. I'm always thinking of her, comparing other women with her—to their disadvantage. I tell you that I can't live without her."

"And yet it will be sufficiently difficult to live with her ! And yet—why should it be ? Here in France these things can be arranged—with care and a little discretion. Not in Paris, for even under-secretaries live in that fierce light which beats upon embassies. In—in—the forest, ah !"

They had talked very late about Sally, they had dined together and still discussed her. Victor said, and meant it, that the one difficulty would be his marriage. He must marry, it was necessary. He was an only son. He explained that the thought of any woman except Sally nauseated him. Henri said, "It is always like that !"

They had continued to talk of her, the idea of her and her lowly position made an instant appeal to Henri and his romantic nature. When Victor left for Calais where he was to assist in welcoming and attending to a stout Eastern potentate with the unpleasant habit of spitting chewed betel-nut all over everything within a two-yard radius, Henri said, "Courage ! You must go over for the ball given by your family, and—bring back Sallee."

The telegram had reached him in Calais. At first he had imagined it to be a joke of Henri's and had felt angry and insulted, then realization had come that indeed it was from Sally. He had thrown engagements to the winds, told young Forster and Charlie Merton to take his place, and left for Dover. To find this turmoil and Sally taking charge and doing wonders and never losing her head, and actually dining alone off cold beef. Somehow that cold beef seemed so solid—reliable sort of stuff, just what Sally would choose.

At dinner, while Gwen lay in her room and sobbed and raved and shouted furious and insulting words, he told Sally all this, and she stared at him with wide grey eyes, looking now faintly shadowed with fatigue. She spoke very little. Yes, she admitted that she loved him, she did not attempt to disguise the fact that he was the whole of her world. She said so quite frankly and openly, without confusion.

"Then tomorrow," he said, "you shall stay here. I'll take my sister back to town, and come back to Dover for you. Then we'll go to Paris together—and be happy. It's all so easy, no one can stop us, no one need know. A cottage in the forest, dinners at little restaurants, time to laugh, and talk, and read—d'you like reading, Sally ?"

"Well, I've never had a lot of time, but—oh, I do like it."

"Music too, pictures—everything. Oh, my dear, dear Sally— what a good life it's going to be !"

"But—not go home at all—I mean, me not to go home at all ?" she asked.

"There's no need. It would only lead to complications— questions—difficulties."

"I couldn't go off like that, m'lord. Not when you think why I came to Dover in the first place. It would be—oh, it would be dishonest. I came to Dover to stop her ladyship—well, doing something foolish, and I couldn't end by going off myself.

No, I'd want to give my notice in properly. What I did after-wards would be my own business."

He sulked a little, said that it was obvious that she didn't love him as he loved her ; and for the first time she smiled and spoke to him as if they were equals, saying, "Now, you know as well as what I do, that's not true !"

"Do I ? It doesn't look like it to me——"

"Then maybe it's because you're tired and your eyes are getting sleepy, like the bairns' do when it's near bedtime." She smiled, her eyes very tender. "Eh, you like your own way, don't you ?"—with a little sigh, "An' the dear knows I'd like to give it to you in everything."

After dinner she went back to being his sister's maid and said primly, "If you'll excuse me I'll just go and see if her ladyship wants anything else, m'lord."

He had met her coming out of his sister's room. Gwen was quieter, it appeared, but she wanted Sally to sleep on the sofa in the sitting-room because she was nervous. Nervous and utterly wretched. Leister had scowled and muttered, and Sally said that after all she was his sister's maid, and there was a very good sofa there, and she'd be as right as rain.

"But I thought——" he began, and then stopped, and said almost violently, "oh, very well. Good night !"—and had turned away. He might even have gone directly to his room, if Sally had not said very softly :

"Nay, don't go like that. I can't bear it."

He caught her hands, and said, "Sally, Sally, forgive me. My nerves are all on edge. I'll be glad, thankful, when it's over and we can be together."

"So 'ul I—you know I will, I don't need to tell you."

He took her in his arms, held her tightly to him, kissing her hair, her cheeks, her lips. Very soft, smooth lips they were. She laughed, that little happy chuckling laugh which he had heard so seldom.

"Nay, have done !" She spoke as she might have done to a child, chiding it gently. "Who knows who might come along ! Good night, and God bless you."

Now in his own room, it was queer how that "good night and God bless you" had worried him. Had he made it clear that he wanted her to come to him as his mistress ? Did she understand what he meant ? It would be quite like Sally to imagine that— love or not—he wanted her to clean his house and mend his socks.

He would have to talk to her, to explain that he would settle
money on her, so that in the event of his marriage—and that
must come sooner or later—she would be independent. He was
tired, his nerves stretched like fiddle-strings. He wanted to
sleep—he had wanted to sleep with his arms round Sally, and he
felt cheated and robbed of what was undoubtedly his. "Good
night and God bless you." His frown deepened. That was her
attitude. "The dear knows," she had said, "I'd like to give it
to you in everything," when she told him that he liked his own
way. His welfare, his safety, his advancement, his future.
Those things would count with her always. If someone "got at
her", told her that a scandal might harm him—what then ? "I'd
kill anyone who came between us," he said softly, "kill them."

ii

The following morning Sally was his sister's maid once more.
To his "Good morning, Sally," she returned, "Good morning,
m'lord. I was to tell you that everything is packed, and that
her ladyship would like to speak to you before we leave."

At first he thought that she was play-acting for him, and
smiling, said, "Very nicely done, darling."

The startled look on her face disillusioned him. "No,
please—we must be careful. Really we must. It's not—it's not
that I've forgotten anything. I've not. I couldn't—only we
must mind what we say and do."

He nodded. "Yes, I suppose so. How horrible it all is !
Don't doubt me, Sally."

"I could never do that."

On the train to London she travelled alone in a third-class
carriage, while he sat with his sister. Gwendoline Leister had
somewhat recovered. She was undoubtedly very frightened,
very apprehensive as to what might be awaiting her at home.
Her brother said, "Leave it all to me. Admit that you were a
frightful fool, that you played with fire—and, luckily, didn't get
burnt."

"It's so horrible that Sally knows. I shall never like her
again, Victor, never."

He frowned. "It would have been a good deal more horrible
if Sally hadn't known. Get it into your head, my dear sister,
that you owe Sally a good deal. She won't talk, she isn't the
talking kind. As for not liking her—that's infernal nonsense."

Gwendoline was indignant. "What, when she read my letters! You think that's trustworthy!"

"Desperate diseases," he returned; "don't be a fool, Gwen."

Sally, in her third-class compartment, sat with her hands folded, not allowing herself to speculate as to what might happen. It was enough that she and Leister understood each other. She had no illusions, she knew that he proposed to take her away and—live with her. Like the books said—live in sin. Somehow, in this case, it didn't seem like sin. She had heard of kings and princes living with ladies they couldn't marry, just because they were—what they were, kings and princes. Those ladies, she didn't doubt, were gentry, all except one she'd heard of who sold fruit in a theatre. She didn't suppose that if the king—always supposing that there was one—which there wasn't at the moment—came riding along, that he could marry anyone like Lady Gwendoline. He'd have to marry a princess—of the blood royal. She'd heard her aunt use that expression. Princess Louise had married the Marquis of Lorne, but it appeared that he was a Scot and for some reason Scotsmen were different. Then, his lordship—the man who said that he loved her, compared with her, he *was* a prince. He couldn't marry her, it wouldn't be right or fitting. Yet, since they loved each other, since he longed to have her with him, what else was there to be done? No, Sally found no flaws in her argument. It wasn't like some village girl going wrong with a man she could just as easily have married. Not a bit the same.

Once when the train stopped at a station he came running along the platform just to put his hand in at the window, take hers and say, "You're all right, Sally? Not too dreadfully lonely? I'm hating it all desperately! I wish you'd let us run away now—no, I do understand, I will be well-behaved. There, good bye, Sally, see you in London."

She felt that she had been away for years. At the station his lordship told her that he had telegraphed to Blachlet and that she was to behave as if nothing strange had happened. "Don't say anything to anyone, Sally," he said, "until we have seen my father."

She said, "No, m'lord, of course not!" But that "we" made her cheeks flush with pleasure. Afterwards she thought, 'You silly thing, you! He only meant Lady Gwen and he,' but even then some of the pleasure remained.

When the house door swung open, Blachlet was there in the

hall. "Good morning, m'lady, good morning, m'lord. Very pleasant to see you home again, m'lord, very pleasant."

"Pleasant to be home again," Leister said. "My sister persuaded me to come back for this ball, and—here I am ! When do you expect my father and mother, Blachlet ?"

"Tomorrow morning, m'lord. Her ladyship wishes to see to all the final arrangements. The last touches, as one might say. I think she'll be delighted with what has been done. Without exaggeration—everything looks wonderful, m'lady."

Lady Gwendoline said, "Really—how nice. Let me have my luggage upstairs at once, Blachlet. Get everything unpacked, Sally."

"Yes, m'lady."

Just as if they had never been away, as if she had never gone to Dover to meet Mr. Hallard, just as if everything was quite unchanged. It was queer at dinner in the servants' hall to realize that everyone longed to ask questions ; to see how Mr. Blachlet kept the ball rolling so that no one had a chance to say anything. Mongsewer twinkled his little boot-button eyes and said, "Eend so 'ees lorrdsheep come 'ome wance more ! Tell mee, did 'eaire ladysheep go to brring 'eem ?"

Sally said, "I couldn't say really, Mongsewer."

Mr. Blachlet shot an approving glance towards her and boomed, "The main thing is that his lordship is back. I happen to know that her ladyship—his mother—wished his presence very much indeed."

That night his lordship took his sister to a play, and invited Mr. Vanderholt to dine first and then accompany them. He was busy in the library all the afternoon, notes were sent here and there, Mongsewer was sent for and interviewed. He came out rubbing his hands and saying that he for one was never "catched 'opping" but prepared for every emergency. Finally it appeared that seven or eight people were dining, that his lordship had taken not one box but two. He had spoken most affably to everyone concerned, saying that he knew that it was dreadful of him, with the ball looming in the immediate distance, but that he had been "kept with my nose to the grindstone" and was longing for a little gaiety. "So," he ended, "on the assumption that to know all is to forgive all—I trust that I am excused."

Everyone agreed that his lordship really had the nicest ways. Blachlet said, "Ah, that's what diplomacy does for anyone with his intelligence. Polish, that's what it is, polish." Just before they left for the theatre, Leister came running up to the little sitting-room where Sally was sewing. He dashed in, holding a pair of gloves in his hand, saying, "Sally, could you mend them for me—they're my favourite pair?" Then, catching her hand, he drew her to him, whispering, "That's an excuse, an excuse to catch a glimpse of you. It's been a beastly day, I've never worked harder in my life. Getting people at short notice isn't easy. I'm trying to—establish something in people's minds. Trying to—engineer a coup. D'you know what that is? Of course you don't, and why on earth should you? What a blessing this stupid ball is coming so quickly. If I slip away during the evening, will you come and dance with me? Where? In the morning-room? Sally, kiss me, say good night. Tell me that you love me, that you're happy—and"—he bent his head listening, as he heard steps in the corridor—"and please mend my gloves, Sally."

She smiled at him, someone was outside the door, probably coming in for something her ladyship had forgotten. "Of course I'll mend them, m'lord"—and still smiling she lifted the gloves and pressed them against her lips for a second before the door opened.

It was done so quickly, without hurry, that Leister smiled with pleasure. That was his Sally, never fumbling, doing whatever she did neatly, beautifully, easily. A maid said, "Oh, I beg pardon—m'lord—Sally, her ladyship wants a lace handkerchief."

His lordship, still smiling, said, "I'm coming—I'll bring the handkerchief."

As the door closed he said, "She didn't see, Sally——"

"See?" Sally exclaimed, "that girl 'ud never see anything unless it was so close that it bit her. You must go—her ladyship doesn't like to be kept waiting."

iii

She had not seen him all day except to pass him on the stairs. The house was humming with excitement, an awning was being erected from the edge of the pavement to the front door, an awning with red carpet under it for the ladies and gentlemen to walk on. Plants were carried in by men in green baize aprons; they were placed on the stairs, on window-sills, everywhere.

Flowers too—in festoons, wreaths and great drooping bunches. Dressmakers came and went, men were admitted just to walk about and look at the flowers, they made notes in little books and went away again. Blachlet said, "The gentlemen of the Press." And—Lord and Lady Stallingford with their son and daughter remained closeted in her ladyship's boudoir. Sally had seen Lady Gwendoline go in, looking half frightened, half defiant. They seemed to have been there for hours. When she came back to her own room, she said to Sally, "You'd better go along there. They want to speak to you. Listen, Sally, I suppose that you did what you felt was right—I know this idea of loyalty you've got—but you can't expect me to like you very much for doing what you did, can you?"

Sally said, "Oh no, m'lady, I shouldn't like anyone myself who'd done—what I did. Only—I didn't know——"

Gwendoline shrugged her shoulders. "I dare say it will work out quite well in the end."

"I'm sure it will, m'lady," Sally returned, not knowing in the least what or who "it" might be.

In the boudoir the Earl stood at the window looking taller and more dignified than ever, her ladyship—she'd been crying—sat in a low brocade-covered chair near the little Empire desk, and Leister stood on the hearthrug and smiled at Sally as she entered.

Leister said, "Ah, here's Sally. My father and mother want to speak to you, Sally."

That was all he said, but his eyes met hers, and she thought, 'It's just as if he'd given me a kiss. He couldn't look that way if he didn't love me.' She said, "Yes, m'lord."

The Earl came forward and took her hand in his. When he spoke his voice sounded queer, different, almost shaking. "We—my wife and I—are deeply indebted to you, Sally. When I spoke to you a few days ago I never realized where the trust which I imposed—yes, imposed upon you would lead you. You've done very well. My son has told us. You have behaved with—with dignity. Good thing to have, Sally, dignity. Now, I do not need to tell you, the whole unfortunate business is at an end. Forget why you went to Dover, why you had to send that telegram to my son—you understand?"

Looking, Leister thought, shy for the first time, she answered, "I—have forgot, m'lord."

"It's—it's—a secret which you share with me and my family, Sally."

"I'd not wish to share it with anyone else, m'lord."

He said, and his voice was steadier now, "I believe that—believe it sincerely."

"Thank you, m'lord." She was turning to go, when Leister said :

"Oh, Papa, the rest."

"Ah ! Yes, of course. Yes. And this you are at liberty to tell everyone. My daughter is going to marry, very shortly, Mr. Henry Maddison Vanderholt. It was arranged last night. We—her ladyship and I, are very happy about it."

It was impossible not to hide her astonishment. She had seen Mr. Vanderholt ; little, rather bald, with glasses, and a very queer way of talking.

She said, "Oh, I'm very pleased to hear it, m'lord, I'm sure."

"The other—er—was a mistake."

"I was sure of that, m'lord."

He stared at her, pulling his long golden beard through his white fingers. "Umph !" he ejaculated.

Sally pulled out a little packet from her pocket and offered it to him. "It's what you gave me, m'lord. The money. I've written down what I spent on a piece of paper. It adds up right. I hope—I hope I didn't spend over-much."

He stared harder than ever, then said explosively, "Oh—take it—keep it——"

Leister said, "I don't think, Papa—Sally, give it to me, I'll see if you have added it up correctly. Thank you. Now, Mama—Papa and I have done our parts—we leave the rest to you, please."

Her ladyship held out a blue velvet case. As usual when she first began to speak, Sally could scarcely understand her. "Herarah, Sally—we wanterah give you something." Then her voice grew easier to understand. "My son said, and I am surah that he was right, that you'd rathah not have—er—money. This—it's a brooch—was once my mothah's. I was very, very fond of my mothah—and so I am giving it to you, Sally."

And her ladyship—never so friendly as his lordship—put out her hand and drew Sally to her and kissed her. She *was* crying, Sally could feel the tears on her cheeks.

She said, "Oh, m'lady—you oughtn't to—I mean—it's much too kind. I never did anything. It was his lordship—he did everything." She was almost crying herself.

It was Leister who snapped the emotional strain. "Sally—

this is audited and found to be absolutely correct. I congratulate you. I wish that I could make my own accounts balance so admirably."

"Thank you, m'lord. Will that be all, m'lady?"

"Yes, Sally, and—thank you."

Outside, Leister joined her as she stood for a moment to look at the brooch. He stood quite close to her, looking over her shoulder. "Like it, darling Sally?"

"It's—it's lovely. Too lovely for me."

"That's impossible! I'll give you better, one day."

She twisted her head round so that she could look at him. "I know now what a 'coo' is."

"A 'coo'? Oh yes—well, what is it?"

"An engagement! You said that you were trying to bring one off last night."

Sally saw his face twisted with laughter, then she turned and hurried back to her own quarters. 'I shall have a lot to learn,' she thought. 'But if I can make him laugh, I don't care how silly I am. What is a 'coo, then, I wonder?'

Night, and lights outside the house, carriages rolling up, ladies magnificent with their jewels, people here and there to whom everyone else bowed. Sally, in the corner of the little gallery which ran round the ballroom, stood and watched. The band entranced her, the rhythm of the music, the wail of the violins, the scent of the flowers, the splendid dresses. Lady Gwendoline smiling, and obviously thanking people who were offering her congratulations; Mr. Vanderholt, beaming at everyone, his glasses flashing as he moved. His lordship, tall and stately, dancing a good deal, but looking, Sally thought, as if more stately dances would have suited him better. Her ladyship talking to Royalty, looking just as good as they did, even better than some of them. And—Lord Leister. More than once he lifted his head and stared at the gallery, and she knew that he was trying to prove to her that he thought of her in the midst of all his gaiety, in the midst of all these grand people, while he mixed with men and women who were his equals.

Sally went to bed that night thinking how much she loved him. A queer sort of love, perhaps, which demanded so little and was willing to give so much. Possibly her early life, those days when she had tramped the roads, gone hungry, been buffeted about in the casual wards of workhouses, had taught her to be content with very little. She could remember her mother very

plainly, always willing to find something at which to laugh.
True, there were times when she sighed, when she sat with her
chin in her hand staring at nothing, times even when she cried
weakly, hopelessly. But small things made her smile, little
things gave her real pleasure.

"Nay," she had said to Sally very often, "maybe we've gotten
vary little, but there's others as have less nor what we have."

The small child trotting along by her side had asked, "What
'un we gotten, Muther ?"

"Why hunderds o' things. T' sky's blew, t' air's fresh, luke
yonder at yon funny li'le dog, wi' its tail carried soa proud !
That's enoof ter mak' yer laugh ! Sum folks is grizzly, but plenty
ithers is kindly, ready ter offer a bite or a sup o' milk fur thee,
ma chucky ! Nay, things might well be a lot worse."

That belief had clung to her. Things were never so bad but
what they might be worse. It would have been nice to have been
born Miss Sally Hardcastle of this or that big house and this or
that grand family. But she hadn't been, and so what was the
use of gurning and grizzling about it ? She had her health and
strength, she never ailed anything, her teeth were good and
sound, her hair was plentiful and her skin was clear. In addition
to all that the most wonderful man in the world said that he loved
her !

For the first time she thought of William Scarth, and remembered him with a kind of dismay. William loved her, he had
said so, and when she left Stallingford he would be hurt, his
good, sound, honest heart would ache.

'Poor Will'um,' she thought, 'but that's the road on it. One
man's meat is anuther man's poison. I wish that I needn't 'a
hurt Will'um all the same.'

CHAPTER FIVE

THE London festivities were over, and they were back at Stallingford. The wedding was to take place there, and Mr. Vanderholt wished to sail for New York as soon as possible. True, the Family kept rushing up and down to and from London, for there were dresses to be made, presents to buy, and a thousand things to do ; but Leister remained at Stallingford. He had applied for extra leave, so he told Sally, adding that it was honest enough, for his father needed him, and he was able to assume some of the responsibility.

"Though how," he said, "we shall get everyone into the minute church passes my comprehension. It's going to be the most dreadful pack !"

Sally said, "Some of them were saying that they wondered that the wedding wasn't at St. George's or St. Margaret's."

He glanced at her quickly. "You didn't wonder, did you, Sally ?"

"No," she said, "I just felt if it had been me I'd like to have a wedding among all my own folks. This is where you—belong, isn't it ? I mean you're like kings here, and this is your kingdom in a way of speaking."

"Yes, of course you'd understand, Sally."

He was graver, she thought, kinder than ever, but quiet. He never chattered now, as he used to do about anything and everything. There were times when he slipped up to her room, and stood holding her hand in his, watching her with serious, intent eyes.

"I'm a dull dog these days," he said. "I promise you once we've got away I shall be my ridiculous self again. Chattering sixteen to the dozen. You know I have a lot to think about, Sally."

"Eh, my dear, as if I didn't know it. I only wish that I could help you——"

"You do," he said, "you do, in a thousand ways."

"Nay, I doubt you just say that."

Then once he came to see her, and began to talk seriously. His voice sounded heavy. He fumbled a little for words. He said, "Sit down, Sally darling, I want to talk to you. They're all out, we shan't be disturbed. Sally—you do understand, don't you ?"

She smiled back at him. When he looked grave, worried, she felt that she was years older than he was, that she wanted to smooth away his frowns with her finger-tips and tell him not to worry.

She said, "Why, I don't know. I understand a lot of things——"

"What we're going to do, for instance ?"

"I know that we're going away, because we love each other, and because that's the only way we can be together. Yes, I understand all that."

He stood up and began to walk about the room. How easily he moved, never bumping into things as other folks did in a room, not making a sound, just pacing up and down with his hands clasped behind his back, stopping suddenly just in front of her.

"Sally—I don't need to ask—you're—you're a good girl ?"

It never occurred to her to resent his question. He was going to make himself responsible for her ; no one but a fool wanted to buy a pig in a poke.

"I've never been with any man i' my life," she said simply, "never."

He caught her hands and carried them to his lips. "Forgive me, I ought not to have asked that. Only—oh, Sally—I just had to *know*. I wish that I could tell you that I'd been—good in that way. I can't."

"There, there !" He was like her, child again. "Men's different."

"I wonder if they ought to be——"

"Nay, I couldn't say. It's enoof that they're not like women. Men don't get into the same kind of trouble as women do."

"And you realize that I want you to live with me—as if you were—my wife ?"

"Listen, my dear," she said, "I know what men and women are, an' what marriage means. I'm not 'fraid, I couldn't be with *you*. I once told you that I'd like to gi'e you everything in the world. I've nothing to give you—'cepting myself. That's yours ! Now, don't worry yourself. There's nothing to worry about—so long as we love each other."

"I know, I know ! There isn't, there can't be. Only—one

day, Sally mine, I shall have to marry. You realize that. I'm
an only son, there's the estate, the title—I shall have to. But
not for years and years—I swear that. Only that keeps coming
into my mind. Is it fair—to you?"

"One's always got to take the rough wi' the smooth," she
said, "and everything's got to be paid for. I shan't—I shan't
make a fuss, my dear. I tell you—I do understand."

"And children—suppose we have children—what then?"

"That 'ul be as God wishes," she replied calmly. "That's
summat that's beyond you or me."

He held her at arm's length. "Then," he said slowly, "you
think that God might be interested in us and our future—in spite
of everything?"

"I don't see why not," Sally told him, "when He concerns
Himself about sparrers and such like."

He had never been accustomed to restrain himself, to curb his
desires or rein in his passions, and yet with this girl he found
himself waiting as a man might have waited for his bride. Once
they had left Stallingford, once he had made himself responsible
for her, he would have no scruples. But here—even when he
thought of making physical demands on Sally Hardcastle, he felt
queerly ashamed and half shy. She wasn't the kind of girl to
take caresses lightly, she had too much dignity. There was
nothing of the full-blooded, rather animal country wench about
her.

Sally, for her part, went about her work as usual. Her heart
might be singing, but she never allowed her day-dreams to
interfere with her duties. She had talked to Aunt Hardcastle,
told her that once Lady Gwendoline was married she thought
that she herself might make a change. Aunt Hardcastle stared
at her blankly.

"Leave here, Sally! What-t-ever are you thinking about,
girl?"

"I've been here a long time," Sally returned. "I think that a
change might be good for me. Once her ladyship's gone—what
'ud I find to do? The mending, the linen maybe, but that's not
enough."

"I allus thought that you might take my place one day," her
aunt said heavily.

Sally laughed. "Nay, Aunt, I've not got your commanding
ways. I'd never be able to keep a big staff in order like you do.
I'm over soft."

"When did you think of going?"

"Not till after the wedding."

"Only ten days ahead!" There was dismay in her aunt's voice. "Nay, Sally, I don't know what I shall do wi'oot you, luv."

"None of us are so much worth that we can't be replaced! Nay, don't look so dowly, Aunt. Maybe one day I might come back."

Afterwards she wondered what on earth had made her say that. Come back—why should she come back?

ii

The wedding came. The house was crowded with visitors, the home farm had taken some of the single gentlemen, and the "Horse Shoe" in Stallingford the rest. Mr. Vanderholt stayed with his lordship's cousin over at Pagleworth and drove over, looking queer and a little out of place in his country clothes. Presents were laid out in the big billiard-room, and men came from London and wore the family livery, but everyone knew that they were detectives watching that no one got in and stole the jewels and silver. There was a reception, there were two huge dinner parties, there was dancing at night, and the house was in a continual state of turmoil. Ladies came with maids who were perpetually wanting a bit of this or a bit of that from Sally's store—buttons, tape, ribbons and so forth. Other ladies came without maids and needed constant attention. It was, "Just come to my room" for this or that the whole day long. Leister, meeting her on the stairs, frowned and said, "They're killing you with work. I loathe the lot of them, Sally." He grumbled that he never saw her, that she was always surrounded by a lot of gabbling women, all wanting, wanting, wanting. She smiled and said, "Nay, it 'ul soon be over."

And quite suddenly, so it seemed, it was over. Lady Gwendoline drove away with Mr. Vanderholt amid showers of rice and with a satin shoe tied on the back of the carriage. People swarmed to their rooms, and there was packing to be done, and inquiries to make concerning trains, and it seemed that the turmoil was worse than ever. Some people stayed, and there were smaller dinner-parties and a luncheon-party or two, but slowly the house began to subside into its ordinary routine.

Leister said, "Sally, it's intolerable. I can't bear it. I have to go back to Paris in four days' time. Come and meet me tonight. Where the garden runs down and joins the park. By the white gate. I'll be there at ten, darling. I must see you alone. I shall die of suppressed fury if I don't. You will, Sally, say that you will?"

"I'll be there."

Such a night, she thought, as she made her way through the kitchen garden she had met William there two days before. He had looked at her reproachfully, and said that he never set eyes on her these days.

"Nor anyone else, Will'um," she said, "I'm that thrang I've no time for anything."

"Maybe you'll have sided some of it away bi' Sunder?" he suggested.

"Nay, I don't know. Some of the guests may stay on a bit."

"Just fur a walk, Sally," he pleaded. "Not ower lang, just threw t' woods."

"I daren't promise, I daren't really."

"Why—wheniver you can, then. Ah'll wait on thee—tha knaws that, eh?"

William and his lordship. His lordship who was waiting for her now, down where the big elms stood, where the gardens ended and the rough grass of the park began. Standing there he would hear the ripple of the beck as it chattered over the stones, he would hear the sudden swish of the grass as some little wild animal scuttled for home, hear the sudden movement of a bird disturbed in its sleep, roused sufficiently to utter one chirp before it buried its head again under its wing.

She passed over the lawn, the clipped turf feeling cool and soft under her feet. She had scarcely sat down all day, and the dew-soaked grass was pleasant and refreshing. Since six that morning she had been at work, running here and there, answering questions, supplying wants, mending first one thing and then another. "Just a stitch here"—and "This bit of lace—that's right." She laughed softly. Silly to remember these things when she was going to meet him, when he was going to put his arms round her and tell her that he loved her!

How still everything was, and there a slim young moon came sailing along, bright and clean-looking. Like a sliver cut from a new sixpence. In the distance she heard Foss the stable dog bark suddenly, fancied that she heard "Hern the Huntsman", the

Earl's big bay, stamp in his stall. The dog down at the home farm had heard 'Foss' and was barking in reply. Now she could hear the sound of running water. She remembered how, years ago, she had liked to slip out and paddle her feet in the bed on summer afternoons. There never was such clear water, and yet, though so clear, it was tinged with the peat—faintly brown. Through the white gate, she thought, 'Eh, this sneck wants oiling, it's stiff,' and she stood in the park, glancing round.

Someone whispered, "Sally, Sally," and turning, she saw him leaning against one of the big elms. His face shone white in the moonlight ; she could see his teeth shimmering when he smiled, saw the whites of his eyes as he turned to look towards her. He was wearing a velvet smoking-jacket over his white shirt, it seemed to melt into the tree-trunk, so soft and dark it was.

"Sally !" He had taken her in his arms, and was whispering that she was tired.

"I didn't know just how tired until now," she said.

"Sit down here. Look, I'll put my coat down for you to sit on. No, of course I shan't catch cold. You fussing old woman, you !"

"Nay, it's only that you're so precious."

"Aren't you precious to me ? Sally—my Sally. There, lean against my shoulder. Are you comfortable ? Resting ? Happy ?"

She never knew how he changed or when, but suddenly he was talking very quickly, begging, pleading. Telling her how much he loved her, how much he wanted her, reminding her that she had said she wanted to give him everything.

"I do, luv, I do—only—not here——"

"Sally, the moon, the night—so still. No one in the whole world except you and me. The night that has been made for us—for no other people. In four days I must go—back to Paris. You'll come out to me there—I'll have everything ready. I can't leave you like this. I want—you to take away with me, to reassure me that you will come."

"Nay, I've promised. I won't break my word."

"Sally—be kind to me."

She sighed. "I can't refuse you anything, my dear—oh, my dear."

Walking back through the shadows, he held her hand and told her that he had been a fool when he imagined that he loved her. "I never loved you until now, Sally. Before it was a pale,

H

weak, feeble kind of thing.   Now it's real—strong—stronger than
I am."

Fondly she said, "My dear, you talk wild, don't you ?"

"Only the sober truth, Sally.   Tomorrow, darling ?   Tomorrow.   Oh, why are days so endless—why can't it be tomorrow
now, this minute ?   I'm hungry for you, darling."

"You're happy ?"

"Happy ?"   Leister laughed softly.   "I'm a king !"

In the darkness Sally nodded.   "Aye, I've always thought of
you that way."

"What—a king ?"

"Aye," she said again, "mine."

iii

The next night he was waiting for her.   He was as she had
known him first, before they went to Dover—talking rubbish,
speaking very quickly, rubbing his cheek softly against hers,
while she rejoiced in its masculine roughness, loving the faint
scent of eau-de-Cologne which hung about him.

"One day someone will ask you, 'Beautiful Sally, where did
you spend your honeymoon with that delightful and brilliant
husband of yours ?'   You'll say, 'Under the elms in Stallingford
Park—by the light of the moon, with the water playing lovely
music for us.'   Some day, when we're old, darling, we'll come
back and creep out here and recapture it over again.   We shall
keep on saying, 'Do you remember ?' or you will, because my
answer will always be the same, 'I could never forget'.   What
shall we do about those impertinent stars ?   What right have
they to come peeping at us !   They embarrass me.   Don't they
embarrass you ?   Abandoned Sally !   Do you know anything
about the stars, Sally ?   I only know 'Charles's Wain'."

She said, "We call it 't' wagon and 'osses'."

"'T' wagon and 'osses," he mimicked.   "I love your Yorkshire.
Talk it to me when we're alone, won't you ?   A foreign language
that you shall teach me.   Say something to me in your broadest
Yorkshire, Sally."

"Nay, fond head," she said.   "Gi'e t' lass a kiss, deean' be
freetened."

She was in his arms, when he whispered suddenly, "There's
someone coming.   Keep very still—don't move !"

A huge dog came lolloping through the grass—Agamemnon ! He padded softly towards them, sniffed Leister's coat and began to show every evidence of pleasure at the encounter. A voice called, "Come here, sir. Agamemnon, come here, sir." The dog rushed away. Sally heard Leister draw a deep breath of relief. "Thank heaven he's gone !" Then the big beast came back to them, circling round them, his tongue lolling, his tail waving.

The Earl was nearer now. He called, "Who is there ? D'you hear me ? Who is it ?"

Leister whispered, "When I stand up, run, run back to the house."

The voice came again, "Who is that ? Stand up at once !"

Very slowly, dreadfully slowly, it seemed to Sally, Leister rose. "It's I, Father."

"You ! Victor ! Good God ! Who is that with you ?"

Without turning, he said sharply, "Run, d'you hear me !"

For the moment the moon was hidden, heavy clouds had come banking up from the south, there would be rain by the morning. She could have run, left him, but something forbade her.

She said, "It's me—m'lord, Sally Hardcastle."

Better for his lordship to know that it was Sally Hardcastle, than to imagine that his son had been with some fly-bi-neit from the village. They had learnt that Sally Hardcastle could keep a still tongue in her head.

The Earl said, and to Sally his voice sounded cold, "Go back to the house, to bed. I'll speak to you in the morning."

"Yes, m'lord."

"No ! Stay here !" Leister said sharply. "I'll not allow her to be blamed, sir. The fault is entirely mine—no one else is to blame. I love her, she loves me. I'm taking her back to France in as short a time as possible. I want her to be with me, she's everything I want, everything."

"Are you crazy, Victor ? Sally—go back to the house."

"Sally, do as I tell you ! She'll walk back to the house with me, sir, and we'll talk this out. She can come away tomorrow. Nothing could make me happier. I refuse to allow her to be scolded or looked down on. I have all my plans made, and nothing shall alter them—nothing and no one."

"Very well." The Earl turned and, followed by the dog, went back through the little gate to the big house.

He was standing in the hall waiting for his son. Sally had refused to go in with Leister ; she slipped through the kitchen garden as she had always done. Worlds might totter, but Sally Hardcastle wasn't going to enter Stallingford through the front door.

Leister said, "Sally, don't be frightened. I'm quite, quite certain of myself. Wait for me, wait in your sewing-room. I'll come there to you. Don't be frightened——"

"Nay, it's no use of saying that," she said, "for I am—mortally."

"You know I love you ?"

"Yes—oh, I know that. It's *for* you, not *of* you or anyone else I'm frightened."

His father waited for him. Leister had never seen his face so austere. He felt that he scarcely knew that tall man with the fair beard and hard eyes. He did not speak, but motioned Leister to follow him into the library.

Only when he was seated at his huge desk, did he speak. "I thought better of you."

Leister said, "I'm in love with her, sir. Entirely and irrevocably. I've every intention of providing for her, of being good to her. She's everything I want, sufficient in every possible way. She understands the position, knows just what I feel for her. I have to leave in two days, and she will follow me."

"You think that an excuse ?"

"No, sir, merely an explanation."

"How long has this been going on ?"

"Do you mean how long have I been in love with her ?"

"If you call—that kind of thing—being in love, yes."

With sudden heat the younger man replied, "I do not call—that kind of thing—being in love ! I have been in love with her since she first came to London, I told her of my feelings when she followed my sister to Dover. Until two days ago we might have been any ordinary—engaged couple ! The fault that we—have altered that relationship is mine, and mine entirely."

"Let me understand you," Stallingford said ; "you mean that you actually propose to take this girl to Paris and install her as your mistress ?"

"I intend to take her to Paris, to live with her and do my utmost to take care of her. Not only do I intend to do so, I am going to do so."

"You must be mad !" The Earl rose and began to pace up and down the long room, with its heavy old furniture, its air of age-old dignity. There was nothing there which did not conform to all that was redolent of family pride and honourable ancestry. The walls were hung with small portraits, every one of them forming a link in the history of Stallingford's ancestors. The furniture was, it seemed, as historic as the portraits. It was all rather heavy, solid, and permanent. The desk, with its silver inkstand, its racks for pens, boxes for stamps and other impedimenta were all adaptations from old silver objects, transformed to a modern use. More than that, the room held something which was almost as tangible as its furniture, the whole atmosphere was heavy with security and stability. These people were not here today and gone tomorrow, they were as much part of the county as the Minster church twelve miles away, or the great elms that flung their shade in the park lands.

Leister stood with one hand resting on the desk, watching his father. He was pale, but his eyes were steady and his mouth determined.

"A madness," he said, "which would have been commendable had she been born in another sphere, I suppose."

"What silly sophistry!" his father retorted. "She is not born in another sphere, she is—what she is. Can you afford a scandal? Are you so established in your chosen profession that men will tolerate laxity from you? Can you risk flaunting her in Paris for all the world and his wife to see, and chatter over? You may be an under-secretary at the moment, but surely with your brains, education and position you aspire to something higher in the future?"

Leister took out his cigar-case with a mechanical movement; he held it up to his father as if asking his permission to smoke, then, taking one, he lit it carefully. Blowing out the match, he said with greater ease than he felt, "My aspirations at the moment are to be happy and to make Sally happy. That is their sum total."

"Then you should be ashamed of yourself! Where is she? Now—I mean."

"In her room."

His father walked to the great embroidered bell-pull and tugged it impatiently.

Leister watched, shrugged his shoulders and said, "She is as determined as I am."

"Ask Sally Hardcastle to come here," was his father's only comment on the statement.

The footman, unable to control his expression for a second, stared, then, recovering himself, said, "Yes, m'lord."

"And ask her to come as quickly as possible."

"Very good, m'lord."

Outside he whispered to his companion, "Something's up !"

Leister continued to smoke with as great an assumption of calm as possible, while his father paced up and down, frowning, tugging his beard, not attempting to conceal his agitation.

Sally came into the room. She looked as she always did, serene. Her hair was smooth, her face had lost some of its colour, and her eyes immediately turned to Leister.

He nodded. "Don't worry, Sally. My father wants to talk to you—to us. I'm not in the least afraid. We're neither of us afraid, are we, Sally ?"

"Why, no—m'lord, not afraid."

Stallingford ceased his pacing. "Sally, I shall not attempt to remind you that you owe my family a debt—you know it already."

"I should think that she paid that when she followed my sister to Dover," Leister said.

"I only want to ask you if it is true that you love my son ?"

"It's quite true, m'lord. He's more to me than anyone else in the world."

"Ah ! And so you propose to ruin him to prove your affection, eh ?"

"Ruin him, m'lord ! Ruin him !" She swung round to Leister. "Should I do that ?"

"Of course not ! How should you ruin me ? My life's my own. If the Embassy is so concerned with my private life—then the Diplomatic Service and everything connected with it can—go to the devil for all I care !"

She smiled. "You'd say that," she said, "you'd say that, anyway. But I want to know the truth." She turned to Stallingford. "Please explain to me," she said.

Queer what an odd dignity she had, the Earl thought. She showed neither fear nor over-assurance. Merely stood there, upright and calm, even capable of smiling at her lover, accepting his protestations as if she had been accustomed to receiving them all her life. This was a wench from a workhouse, a bastard, whose mother had tramped the roads !

"Listen, Sally," he said, "it may be that in modern life there is certain latitude accorded to young men of good family. But only a *certain* latitude. They cannot fly in the face of society, they cannot fling aside all their responsibilities. My son is heir to a great name, a great estate. He will one day be an hereditary legislator for his country. He will marry—marry some woman who can take her place beside him as one of the leaders of society. How would she accept the fact that he had kept a mistress in Paris for years ? He is, as you know, an under-secretary at the Embassy, but he will not always be that, he will rise in his profession—as his brains and his position entitle him to do. Her Majesty—God bless her—does not look kindly on irregular attachments——"

Leister said, "Isn't this all rather over-coloured ? I don't imagine that I shall ever occupy an ambassadorial chair !"

Without turning, Sally said, "Hush, my dear—hush, let me hear what his lordship is telling me. Yes, m'lord ?"

"It is inevitable that this connection would come to her ears. You may imagine that these things can be kept secret. You may behave in the most discreet manner—believe me, someone always discovers what is happening. People talk, other people listen, and—the whole thing is public property. My son will assure you that you are sufficient. You may be now, you may be for ten years, twenty—I don't know ; but one day he will find that he is left behind, that he is—nothing. Now and again the old whispers will reach him, and he will realize that you held him back, you ruined his career. Can you face that ?"

"Sally could and would face anything with me !"

"Nay, not anything that harmed you. I'd not face that," she said. "M'lord, will you swear to me, on your solemn oath, that you believe what you've said to be true ? That if his lordship lived with me—if I was his mistress—that it would hurt him, do him harm in this—I forget what it's called—Diplomatic business ?"

Stallingford hesitated for a moment. Her directness had disturbed him. He had always liked the girl, taken an interest in her, actually felt fond of her. Now he was fighting for his son. The moment of hesitation passed.

"I swear to you that I believe that this—association—might ruin his prospects."

"But other gentlemen do"—for the first time she stumbled over her words—"keep women."

"Passing follies, not more or less permanent relationships."

Leister said, "Observe, Sally dear, the high moral tone set by society. These relationships must be entirely unworthy, based on nothing but a passing attraction—and they may be permitted. Anything deep, real, sound—lovely—must be scrupulously crushed! Pah!"

She shook her head. "Nay, you fluster me with all those words. I didn't understand," she told Stallingford. "Maybe I ought to have done, but—well, I do love him, and he loves me. Oh yes, he does, m'lord. I was wrong to give in to him, I don't doubt that, but when you love anyone like I do his lordship—it's difficult. And we were going away so soon. I wouldn't harm him for all the world, I'd rather cut off my right hand."

"I knew that you would realize the gravity of this step once——"

"Sally, don't listen to him," Leister cried, "don't believe him. He doesn't know that these things are possible. You understand, or you did until he began to worry you with ponderous sentences and dreadful prognostications about the future. You are my future, Sally! You've promised—you've sworn that you loved me."

"So I do—too much to harm you, my dear love. Do you think that it's not going to break my heart? I feel now that it's killing me. To leave you! But nothing, not even you, 'ul make me stand in your light. Why, dear, I'd never forgive meself, never! No, you mun go back to France and make a great name and"—for the first time her voice shook—"let us all—me most of all—be proud of you. That's what's got to happen."

Leister did not address himself to her, he only watched her grave face, and to Sally it seemed that there was new courage and higher purpose in his eyes. He leant back against the big desk, his head up, and when he spoke his voice was full of pride.

"Now, and you pride yourself upon being a judge of character, perhaps you can glimpse something of what I've found in her! Have you ever met finer sentiments, greater selflessness, grander and more splendid nobility? You haven't, because these things in this quality, in these quantities, exist only in her. But I have my answer waiting for you! For you all, for the whole damnable organization that we call—our world! I won't live with her as my mistress, I won't try to hide her away in Barbizon! I'll marry her. My dear father, allow me to present you to the future Countess of Stallingford."

It was grandiloquent, it was flamboyant, but it was sincere, and standing there he flung back his head as if he defied the whole world, and gloried in doing it. Then, coming to where Sally stood, he took her hand, saying, "Dearest Sally, will you do me the honour of becoming my wife?"

His father made a sudden movement as if he would have separated them, and it was Sally who said, "Nay, don't disturb yourself, m'lord." To Leister she spoke very softly and gently. "My dear," and under the stress of her emotion she dropped back into the dialect which only that evening he had told her he loved, "Ah'll niver forget this not as long as Ah've breath in my body. Eh, my luv, my only luv—you're far ovver good to me. You mak' me fair 'shamed as Ah've nothing Ah can do to show my love fur you—'cepting one thing, and that's denying you everything you say you want. You knaw as Ah can't marry you. Seemly it will ruin you if I—live with you, and it's plain to me as it would ruin you a lot more if I married you. It's bin wunderful. I've nothing that Ah'm shamed of. I'm proud that you were t' first man Ah ever knew, the first man as ever made love to me, and—you'll allus be the only man in the world that has my whole heart. You must leave tomorrow—you'll see that he does, m'lord, won't you? And get back to Paris, and be happy and work hard."

Stallingford thought, 'She might be a mother sending her best loved child to school for the first time.'

He said, "Yes, Sally. He shall go tomorrow."

She looked at Leister, the tears were running down her cheeks, and she brushed them away with the back of her hand. "Nay, don't luke at me that road," she cried suddenly, "Ah've enoof to bear, wi'oot bearing your grief as well as my own. M'lord, this is the last time that I shall see him—maybe for years—an' then it 'ul all be different. Would you just leave me to talk to him alone?"

The Earl did not answer her for a moment. He looked at his son, at his white, pinched face, and noticed how he swayed backwards and forwards as if some physical pain gripped him. He looked at Sally, weeping silently, but in complete control of herself. She was holding out her hands to Leister, saying softly, "Cum here to me, my precious luv."

"Yes, Sally—I'll leave you. No one shall disturb you." Then, "I wish so earnestly that this need not have happened."

CHAPTER SIX

THE light came filtering in through the open windows. The sky was faintly coloured with the dawn, shot with pale orange, rose and blue. Birds were stirring, rustling about in the trees and bushes, cocks were crowing arrogantly, proudly, as if they were responsible for the birth of a new day. Sally Hardcastle lay on her bed, fully dressed, with her hands pressed over her eyes, thinking, 'Another day—why couldn't I have died in the night ? What's there to go on living for ? It's all over, and today he's going away.'

She had remained in the library with him, while he had pleaded and besought her to reconsider her decision. He had assured her that his father was wrong, that times had changed since he was young, people were more tolerant, broader-minded. His father, Leister said, had made a bogey, a thing of straw, rags and a turnip with a candle in for its head. He had frightened her with this scarecrow, but now that they were together, he said, didn't she realize the stupidity of it all ? Paris was waiting, life together, laughter, he would work far better with her by her side. He would come home to her, to spend long, lovely evenings. His life, which had been spent seeking amusement, sitting in first one café and then another, going from theatre to theatre, was ended. He wanted only to be with her, longed to make her proud of him.

He pleaded, begged, bullied, argued and raved by turns. He reproached her, saying that she had led him on, had taken his whole heart, his mind, his soul, only to fling them all back in his face at the first difficulty. He told her that she was a coward, that she was prudish and prim ; he invented incidents to prove that she had never really loved him, and she said scarcely a word, except to watch him with those big, clear grey eyes.

He had caught her in his arms, held her close and asked for forgiveness, saying, "I've been trying to hurt you, because I want you to share the pain I'm suffering—as I've wanted you to share everything with me."

"Nay, don't batter yourself to pieces, my luv," she said, "it's no use. I can't cum wi' you, neether you nor anyone else could make me. It's been like some lovely dream, an' now I'm waking agean. Well, it's something to have had such a dream."

"You'll ruin my life!" he cried wildly.

"Nay, yer life's your own. Only you can ruin it, and you've over-much pride to do that."

At last he had flung himself down on the big couch and covered his face with his hands, sobbing like a lost child. She had sat beside him, holding his hand until his sobs ceased and he slept. Then very gently she had slipped her hand from his, and leaving him sleeping had crept out and gone to her own room. All night she had lain awake watching the window, seeing the first signs of returning day ; her eyes dry, but with a pain at her heart which was almost unbearable. Today he would go away. His lordship had promised, and even Leister—impetuous as he was—would not risk a scandal by insisting upon seeing her. She must keep out of the way, she must not go near the Family's part of the house. Luckily, most of the guests were gone, and it would be sufficiently easy. They must manage without her. Perhaps, too, this morning, Leister might feel angry with her, might feel that she had betrayed him, and so might decide not to see her again. The thought, she reflected, ought to have hurt her, but she mused, 'Ah've got that much pain a little more or less doesn't matter, Ah don't notice it.'

She remembered last night. The library and his lordship talking, talking, talking. Leister, too—had a man ever looked so handsome as he did when he flung back his head and said that he was going to marry her ? How noble he had looked, how his voice had rung out, full of defiance and pride ! How could one help loving him ? "Dearest Sally, will you do me the honour of becoming my wife ?" Well, she had been his wife in a way. He had said that one day she would tell people that she spent her honeymoon under the big elms. She got up, took off her dark dress, washed, and brushed her hair, thinking all the time. She couldn't stay at Stallingford. Not that she was ashamed, but because it would be too difficult for everyone. Difficult for his lordship to remember that his son had asked her to become Lady Leister. Insupportable when Leister came home—and they were forced to meet. No, she must go—and where ? She must put Stallingford and all that belonged to it behind her—forget it all.

That was when she stood, suddenly rigid, with her hand pressed against her heart. Supposing that she couldn't leave it all behind ? What then ?

Sally Hardcastle had lived in the country all her life, and as a country girl knew all there was to know about the secrets of birth.

She had been taught in the church that "The wages of sin is death", and that had been interpreted in her mind as meaning that if you—were a bad girl—well, you had to pay for your badness. Not that she felt in her heart that she had been really bad. She had loved Leister, she still loved him, always would love him, but that didn't alter the fact that, sin or no sin, she had allowed him to make love to her, and she might possibly have to—take her wages. She remembered poor little Annie Piper, who'd been going to marry Fred Hartman who worked on the railway. He'd been killed by a runaway truck a fortnight before they were to be married. Annie had been "that way," she'd said to Aunt Hardcastle. "You see, Mrs. Hardcastle, Ah felt as Ah was his wife, an' he felt as he was my husband. It didn't seem wrong somehow—and now . . ."

Aunt Hardcastle had been sorry, even sympathetic, but she had reminded Annie that "There's many a slip twixt t'cup and lip, Annie. Look before you leap is a good thing to remember." Annie had said, "Yes, Mrs. Hardcastle, but it's ovver laate ter think o' them sayings now."

She'd thought of herself as Leister's wife—well, no, not his wife exactly, but as the next thing to it—as belonging to him, anyway. And now, just supposing that what happened to Annie Piper had happened to her ?

Sally stared at herself in the looking-glass. She was a bastard, and she might be the mother of another bastard. His lordship's son ! Her face stiffened, grew suddenly determined, she squared her shoulders, and her eyes narrowed a little.

"Nay, never mind what comes," she said softly, "I'll not have that happen to his child ! Maybe there won't be a child—as likely as not there won't—but I'll not risk it. I'll not leave it to chance, and have folks whispering about—my bairn and his !"

ii

On her way downstairs she passed Herbert, one of the footmen, looking sleepy and dull-eyed. She didn't like Herbert. She suspected that both he and Charles smuggled drink into their bedroom, that accounted for their silly looks in the early morning.

He said, "Hello, Sally. Were you being tongued for something or other that his lordship wanted you at that time o' night ?"

She remembered that it was Herbert who had come to her

room, wide-eyed, saying, "You're wanted at once in the library. What's up?"

She stared at him coldly. "Nice sight you look this morning, Herbert! Lucky for you that Mr. Blachlet isn't up so early, or he'd have summat to say to those eyes of yours! Not shaved neither, and your hair—like a last year's bird's nest! Last night"—she frowned—"it's like your impudence to ask. It's my business, but since you're so anxious to know, Lady Gwendoline's left some things she wants sending on at once, and only I know where to get hold of them. I hope you're satisfied."

Herbert's little eyes slanted at her. "Queer time o' night to send for you. I'd have thought that this morning would have done!"

"It would have done," she retorted smartly, "if I'd been you! As it is, the things are found and parcelled up and his lordship will take them to London this morning. I don't let the grass grow under my feet, Herbert, neither do I like work so much that I could lie down beside it, as you seem to."

Herbert scowled at her. "Grand quick tongue you've got, eh? Clever, aren't you?"

"Of course I am," she replied; "only just found out that? Too slow to walk last, aren't you, Herbert?"

She let herself out by the side door and walked into the kitchen garden. For a moment she stood breathing in the cool morning air. The rain which had fallen in the night had left everything smelling very sweetly. Sally stooped and picked a bit of southernwood, crushing it in her fingers, sniffing the scent appreciatively. She looked young, calm and without a care in the world, absorbed in her bit of sweet-smelling herb, enjoying the fresh air of the early morning. In reality her senses had never felt so keen, her nerves never so alert. She thought that on this summer morning everything was intensified for her. She heard everything, saw everything, the colours of the flowers had never been so bright, the song of the birds so clear. Her mind, too, was like the flowers: bright, like the air; clear, and like that small mouse which suddenly scurried across the path— intensely alive.

'I can't help but find a way out of it all,' she thought, 'on a morning like this. The whole world's been washed in the night —and my brain's been washed, too, seemly.'

The sound of heavy feet made her turn, and she saw William Scarth. She knew that her plan had been made ever since she stood in her own room, thinking. Only until now she had not admitted it even to herself.

She said, "Morning, Will'um."

"Mornin', Sally. Yer oot middlin' early, bean't yer?"

She nodded. "I like the morning air. Everything smells so nice, so fresh."

He tipped back his cap and scratched his head. "Aye, it's a reit bonny time, is t' marnin'. Ah allus think aboot what t' Buke says, 'Burden an' heat of the daay'. This is a lot better'n what middaay is, Sally. Sumetimes Ah thinks as maybe old age and reit youth is pleasanter'n—w'at middle age is. See how Ah mean, Sally?"

"Aye, I think I do."

He stared at her, his eyes full of devotion like a spaniel's. "Have yer thout onny mair aboot w'at Ah said ter yer, Sally luv? Aboot—uz?"

She laughed, surprised that she could laugh so easily and convincingly. "Why, yes—I suppose I have, Will'um. Only— I've bin that thrang, wi' the wedding and everything."

"W'at did yer think, Sally?" His tone was suddenly eager.

"Why—aboout us."

"Aye, but w'at aboot uz, chucky?"

"That I liked you very well, Will'um, and that I'd not mind sharing that nice cottage of yours. I suppose that's what I thought."

"Tha means as we'll get wed!" He was breathing hard, she could see the sweat standing on his forehead. "W'en, Sally, w'en? Tha'll not keep me waitin' ovver long?"

"When—eh, when? I'm sick an' tired of running after folks, and doing this and doing that. I want a house of my own and that's the truth. When—well, as soon as you've a mind. Will'um. It's not as if we've not known each other for a longish time, is it?"

He pulled out a blue-and-white spotted handkerchief, and wiped his face. "We'll be axed o' Sunder," he said. "Ah awaay an' speak ter t' passon at midday. Sally, Ah mun get on wi' me work —wilt tha meet me terneit? At t'end o' t'gardens—in t'park?"

Sally lifted her hand and crushed it against her mouth, then recovering herself said, "Eh, some fly or summat's bit me! They pinch, don't they? Nay, I'll meet you in the lane, round by the back of the home farm. Seven o'clock—no, I can't stop any more'n what you can. Good-bye, Will'um."

She went back to her work-room, and sat down heavily, feeling that every ounce of energy had been drained from her body and mind. She was numb, her mind was blank, she realized only one thing clearly, that she had promised to marry William Scarth in three weeks' time.

At breakfast Mr. Blachlet said, "I hear that his lordship is leaving us this morning, returning to Paris. The house will be very quiet—very quiet."

Sally, making a great effort, for the benefit of the still sulky Herbert, managed to say, "Oh, Mr. Blachlet, I'll give you a small parcel that his lordship is taking to London to deliver to Lady Gwendoline. It's quite small."

During the hours of the morning she sat sewing, only allowing her mind to turn back to Leister when she tied up the half dozen handkerchiefs which she had made and embroidered for him. Mechanically she looked at the monogram—the elaborate letter surmounted by the coronet which she had copied so carefully from one of his hair-brushes. She would give the packet to Blachlet to hand to him—he would understand.

The door opened suddenly and he came in. He wore his light travelling-coat, his face was white and there were deep shadows under his eyes. He stood watching her, without speaking, until she cried desperately, "Oh, don't look at me like that !"

"Like—what, Sally ?"

"As if I'd hurt you ! I didn't mean to, I couldn't do anything else."

"No," he said, speaking slowly and carefully, "I suppose not. We're both victims of this damnable system ! I've come to say good-bye, Sally. One thing—difficult—I've got to say it. If you were in any—trouble—through me, Sally—swear to let me know, and all the society laws, all the attacks from my father, all the rest of the stupidities that hedge us round shouldn't stop me coming back to marry you. I swear that on—on the love I have for you." He came nearer, caught her hands in his and said, "It's not too late now, Sally. Come away with me. Leave it all. Let's take our chance of being happy. Courage, Sally—come now, this instant."

"It's not possible, m'lord," she said. "And—I promised to marry William Scarth this morning."

He staggered back, she felt that she had struck him across the face. "My God—Sally !"

"It's—best, m'lord. I shall make him a very good wife."

She picked up the little parcel. "I made these for you ; I hope they'll be useful."

Leister said, his voice stupid and thick, "For me? How kind of you. Yes—thank you. Good-bye, Sally."

"Good-bye, my dear luv," she whispered. "I shall always luv you."

He twisted his face into a grin. "That won't help much! Good-bye, Sally—my Sally."

Later she told her aunt about William. Mrs. Hardcastle pursed her lips, indicated that she was disappointed. Sally defended him, saying what a good hard-working fellow he was.

"Hard-working I don't doubt, good—I don't doubt either, Sally—but an under-gardener! You might have done a lot better, my dear."

"Or a lot worse!" She laughed and felt that this wasn't Sally Hardcastle speaking at all. Sally Hardcastle wasn't there at all, she was on her way to London with Leister, they were going to Paris to be happy.

"When did you think of being married, Sally?" her aunt asked.

Here was the first difficult fence!

"In about three weeks' time. We're to be axed on Sunday." She tried to speak lightly.

"I' three weeks' time!" Mrs. Hardcastle sat stiffly upright. "Sally—what's the hurry, why i' three weeks' time? There's no—reason for it, is there?"

"Aunt! How can you! Why, yes, there's a reason—I want a house of my own, and I'm sick of sewing other folks' clothes and want a bit of time to make some for myself. That's the reason. I've been here for eight years—I want a change! He's a good fellow, and we're fond of each other. No sense in waiting, is there?"

"I s'pose not."

Everyone was very kind, but everyone made it quite clear that they thought she was throwing herself away on William Scarth. Mr. Porter said that indeed he was a good fellow, a wee bit on the slow side, but slow and sure was his motto, Mr. Porter didn't doubt.

"Nay doot he'll gan as far and maybe farther than chaps who seem quicker. The auld story o' the hare and the tortoise. Ma congratulations, Sally."

William was very happy. He smiled, he talked about what he was going to do to the cottage, told her of the little schemes he had for adding to her comfort. He was going to colour-wash the cottage in his spare time. "It 'ul tak' me fra' thee, Sally, but we've gotten all t' rest on ower lives ter spend tergether, an' Ah want it a reit li'le palice fur thee."

His mother was pleased, too, it seemed, and determined that they should begin their married life alone. She was moving herself and her leather-covered trunk to her married daughter's at York. William said that it would be strange without her, but that he didn't doubt it would all work out for the best in the long run.

Sally, listening to his slow, measured tones, watching his careful movements, his big hands which could be so skilful when he tied up plants or cut flowers, thought how easy it ought to be to love him, and how utterly impossible it was in reality. Respect, even affection—she felt those; but love, that queer something which changed the whole world, that had gone. Leister's voice had been music to her, his presence had been as if all the joy in the world had been concentrated and given to Sally Hardcastle. To be with him had been to live in a universe where the stars shone, the sun blazed, flowers bloomed and birds sang. An impossible, brilliant world—but one which Leister had made real, had made—theirs. She found herself continually insisting upon William's goodness. It had never occurred to her to speculate as to whether Leister were good or not. Again and again she assured herself that William was kind, thoughtful, attentive, clever with his hands, hard-working and so forth. She had never known or cared whether Leister possessed these attributes. She had known that he was handsome, gay, that he loved to chatter and make her laugh—and that she loved him. That had been all she wanted, or needed to know.

Mr. Blachlet, a few days later, smiling mysteriously, said, "Ah, Sally—his lordship wishes to speak to you. I do not allow myself to make prophecies, but I could make one with reasonable ease at the moment."

Breathlessly, because she had been taken off her guard, Sally said, "He knows—about me and William, Mr. Blachlet?"

"He does indeed, Sally, for I made the matter known to him myself, and most interested he was—most interested."

Into the big library again, and she fancied that she could still hear Leister sobbing, still hear him say, "Sally darling, will you do me the honour of becoming my wife?" It was like walking into a room where you had been with someone who had since died. Going back into a life which was over.

The Earl said, "Sally—er—sit down. Yes, sit down. I heard that you're going to marry young Scarth. Hard-working fellow. Porter thinks well of him. If there is anything you want doing to the cottage, let Mr. Haversley know—any small alteration. It's a nice cottage. . . ."

Sally thought, 'He's just marking time. This isn't what he wants to say really.'

He fumbled with some papers on his desk, then tapped with his fingers, and from time to time glanced at her as he felt that she might have something to say. She sat, silent, with her hands folded. She had known him since she was a child, admired, loved and been grateful to him. She had sworn that she would always do anything in her power to repay him for his goodness. Well, she had done what she could—she had safeguarded his daughter, and—given up his son. Not that she felt that she had done sufficient or wiped out the debt which she owed to him, but she was tired now, and wondering vaguely what he wanted to say, wished that it was all over and done with, hoped that no new demands were to be made of her.

With a queer, strange note of desperation in his voice he said, "Sally—has this—sudden determination anything to do with our interview here—a few nights ago? Were you—engaged to young Scarth then?"

"No, m'lord."

"It happened after you were convinced——"

She interrupted him. "After you convinced me, m'lord, that I mustn't think of going away with your son."

"Ah—I see."

There was another long pause. Sally did not move, and Stallingford sat twisting a paper-knife in his fingers. He had never found himself in a more difficult position. He knew of other families—never his, thank heaven—where this kind of thing —he even avoided putting his thoughts more clearly, so distasteful was the whole matter—happened. Some man was found to marry the girl, paid a substantial sum, and that ended the affair. True, there were villages where certain children bore a resemblance to the Lord of the Manor, children who were sniggered about a little, and whose parentage was an open secret. Money had wiped out any obligations. Then, as this was the accustomed procedure, why was he finding the whole matter so difficult? Why didn't he offer Sally Hardcastle a lump sum, while disclaiming any necessity for his generosity, and end it all?

Somehow he couldn't bring himself to do it. She had always had a queer dignity, this girl. She had never romped with the menservants, Blachlet spoke of her in the highest terms. She had behaved well over Gwendoline's silly affair—damned well. She had behaved well over this business with Leister. It might have been unpleasant—most unpleasant. The fellow was crazy about her. Even now Stallingford didn't like to look back on his last interview with his son.

"Well, sir, I'm going—and I hope that you are satisfied. You shook Sally's determination, obscured her clear sight and the real issue with words, words, words. You let her believe that I am some gifted potential ambassador. I'm nothing of the kind, and you know it as well as I do. I might have had almost perfect happiness with her. You prevented it. I find it very hard to forgive. Just one word more, sir—don't speak to me of marriage. When I find that—this has ceased to hurt intolerably—I will raise the subject. Not until. Good-bye."

Now, she didn't wail, she didn't threaten, she merely sat still and spoke when she was spoken to, except once, when she had actually interrupted him !

He sighed. He disliked difficult situations ; all his life he had prided himself upon doing "the right thing", doing it with charm and affability. He had never taken a great deal of trouble over anything. When he had found that something was wrong, well, he'd done his best to set it right as quickly as possible. Life had been easy, pleasant, and he had established himself as a good landlord and a kind master. He'd never been strikingly brilliant, he had never raised his voice in the House of Lords, and hoped that he never would. He had voted as he had been told, and not neglected his duty. More than once, when some young blackguard on the estate had got a girl into trouble, he had sent for him, and told him in good round terms exactly what he thought about him. "You're a damned scoundrel, let me tell you ! Taking advantage of a girl who trusted you ! Only one thing to do—marry her as soon as possible. I'll have no scandals at Stallingford, remember that !" The man had twisted his hat in his hands, shuffled his feet, and invariably said that of course he was willing to marry the girl and that he hoped his lordship would overlook the fault and that he'd do his best to behave properly in future.

"Make her a good husband," had been Stallingford's final injunction ; "see that she never regrets having married you !"

It never occurred to him that he might possibly not be doing the girl such a great service in insisting that "a damned scoundrel" married her. These marriages usually turned out pretty well in the end.

Now, he couldn't refer to his own son as a scoundrel, he couldn't insist on an immediate marriage, and here was the girl settling everything out of hand. Most disturbing. He said, "I take it that Scarth doesn't get anything much in the way of wages. It might be something of a change for you after living here for so long, eh ? Is there anything I can do ? I should like on behalf of myself and my wife to give you a—substantial—wedding present."

"Money ?" Sally said, "I don't think that I want money, thank you, m'lord. If you could use your influence to get William work somewhere else—like with Sir George Cope or Mr. Cormick—or some of those gentlemen—it would be very kind. He's very reliable." She paused for a moment, then continued, "If it wasn't too far away, perhaps——"

"You don't want to leave Stallingford ?" he asked quickly.

"There is my aunt, m'lord ; she's the only relation I've gotten."

"Quite. I understand. Very well, Sally. I'll see what can be done." He rose and held out his hand. "I wish—I mean this—that things had been easier, Sally."

"Yes, m'lord. Thank you, m'lord."

She took his hand and held it for a moment, then turned and walked out of the room.

iii

He had done it. William was offered the place as gardener with Sir George Cope at Wittingly, eight miles away. Not a large place, and he would have only one man and a boy working under him. Plenty of work at Wittingly, William said, but the wages were good, and Sir George was away best part of the year, gave you time to get on with things. There was no proper gardener's cottage, but a good one in the village, "just about t' best cottage i' t' plaace, s'far's Ah can see. Reit bonny lil' plaace, with a bit o' garden an' everything nice as nip. T' luck's cum ower waay, Sally luv."

It was a good cottage too, Sally thought, when she went over to see it. Old enough to be attractive, and not sufficiently old to be uncomfortable. There was a wide flagged path leading to the house, and a garden full of old-fashioned flowers, though Will'um shook his head over the rose trees and muttered that it was dreadful how some folks just "tuke all an' gaave nothin'.

Pickin' flowers, an' niver doin' a hand's turn ter feed t' bush oop
agean. Crewelty, Ah call it." The rooms were low but of a
good size, and there was plenty of light and air. Yes, it was a
good cottage. She bought furniture, not that she needed such a
lot, because William had all his mother's, and her ladyship gave
Sally some from the big attics at Stallingford—chairs and tables
and a four-poster bed. Linen and blankets too. She arranged
it all, never feeling for an instant that it was her own house.
There were times when she almost said to Wiliiam, "Eh, I do hope
as she likes it—that young woman you're going to marry,"
because it seemed so impossible that Sally Hardcastle was going
to leave Stallingford and live there at Wittingly.

She wondered if she were very wicked, deceiving William.
Ought she to tell him all about it, confess that she had known
another man, admit that she was not a virgin, not—what was
called—a good girl ? If she did, he would be certain to ask who
the man was, and she knew that she would rather have died than
confess the truth. Impossible to speak his lordship's name to
anyone—certainly not to William. No, if it were a sin, then she
would suffer for it, pay for it, and she'd not whine about it.
Debts had to be paid, and she'd pay this one. If there was a
child—there her imagination stopped short. She didn't know.
She might tell William, she might not. She knew that it was
considered a fearful crime to foist another man's bairn on to a
chap, to let him pay for its food and drink and clothing. Not
that she imagined that William would be unkind to any bairn ;
she didn't believe that he had it in him to be—but he'd want a
say in its upbringing, he'd want to make it a gardener if it were a
boy, and send it out to service if it were a girl. Well, right
enough, if she had a bairn by William ; but if she didn't, if she
knew that it was Leister's, then she wanted it to be hers, and hers
only. She'd bring it up, she'd say what it should be, how it
should earn its living ! 'It's all I shall have of his,' she thought,
'and it shall belong to me !'

William was content enough, it never struck him that she was
displaying little real interest in his plans for the garden and the
arrangement of the house. She worked well and swiftly, finding
it strange to be washing floors and helping to lift furniture. She
took it all as a matter of course, thought Aunt Hardcastle ; shook
her head over Sally's hands and said, "My dear, you'll have them
ruined for fine sewing !"

"I shan't be doing fine sewing," Sally said.

"More's the pity!"

Sally felt that she lived from day to day, never speculating as to what the next day might bring. Twenty-four hours had to be lived through, and another twenty-four would slip forward to be faced. She was not actively unhappy, she felt scarcely anything. Sometimes she would find herself wondering where Leister was, what he did, and if he ever thought of her; but she forced such thoughts away, and concentrated fiercely on something which demanded her whole attention.

Mr. Blachlet said, "Sally, my dear, you're working too hard. Rushing backwards and forwards to Wittingly. Oh, I know that her ladyship's very kind in sending the trap for you of an evening, no one could be kinder; but there are times when you get back here looking white and tired. Can't have our young bride looking anything but her best."

Her aunt said, "You're wasting your breath, Mr. Blachlet! Really headstrong she's become."

"Ah, but 'er 'ome ees of such in-ter-est," Mamzel sighed sentimentally, for somehow Mr. Lingley's interest in her had waned, and Mamzel was growing stout, and her moustache was growing more clearly defined than ever. "Eet is nat-ur-el she veesh to spend ver' mooch time zere! The dress—vich I mak' —veel be beautiful, Sallee."

The wedding day came. Sally rose early, and made a cup of tea as usual for old Mrs. Bishop, who never left her bedroom now, sitting there wrapped in shawls, vast and monumental. She wheezed, "Oh, Sally, you ought not to have bothered. On your wedding day too. I'm glad as you did, though, for I've something for you. Brides must have something blew, and I've got this locket for you, blew enamel, and gold. His lordship—his young lordship—give it to me when he went to school. There's a little picture of him when he was a baby inside. You can take that out and give it back to me. I tried, but my fingers are that stiff."

"Oh, Mrs. Bishop, how kind, and how bonny it is." She opened it and looked at the picture of a small child with tumbled curls. Leister—when he was a baby. "How old was he?"

"When he give me the locket? Oh, when that picture was taken? Nay, I forgot, about two or three. Can't you get it out, Sally?"

She fumbled with the glass. "I can't move it, Mrs. Bishop."

"Leave it where it is, then—I don't suppose that his lordship 'ud mind. He was always very fond o' you, Sally."

Sally kissed her. "Thank you for everything, Mrs. Bishop."

BOOK THREE

CHAPTER ONE

SALLY thought, 'The mornings are getting reight chilly,' as she walked down the garden with a brown earthenware dish filled with steaming mash for the hens. 'Poor things, they'll be glad o' this.' The garden itself was losing the full, colourful beauty of the summer. Here and there a rose still bloomed, but it had the air of having outstayed its welcome, of being a stranger among the Michaelmas daisies and the less bright blooms that belonged to autumn. On the low hills, which stretched away on the horizon, over the tall trees of the woods, a faint mist hung. The woods themselves were becoming gorgeous in copper, gold, rust and scarlet. A beautiful time, these early last months of the year, but tinged with something not devoid of regret. Sally, having put down her plate of hot food for the hens, folded her arms on the wooden gate at the end of the garden and stared out at the woods.

October. She had been married over two months, and still she had not become used to her new life. William was kind ; no woman could have wished for a better husband ; but he came from a class which looked to its womenfolk for certain things, and is not only disappointed but astonished if those things are not forthcoming. He himself was up and away to Wittingly House by half past six, taking with him his breakfast tied up in a clean checked handkerchief. Before he left he liked a "good cup o' tea" and a slice of bread and cold bacon. At ten minutes past twelve he was back for his dinner, eating with an appetite which was almost fierce in its intensity. At six he would come home once more, ready to take "a drink o' tea an' maybe a bite of caake", then off to dig in his own garden, unless there happened to be something which demanded his care and attention at the House. At half past eight he began to yawn ; by nine he was drowsy ; and before the church clock struck the half hour he was in bed and asleep.

Even on Sundays he walked down to the house, dressed in his decent suit of black, to potter about the gardens like an uneasy spirit, longing—Sally always felt—for Monday morning.

True, on Sunday afternoons he liked her to take a walk with him, and together they would wander through the woods or fields, while William's slow, quiet voice spoke of those matters concerning the countryside which held such fascination for him.

Thinking of these things, Sally moved impatiently. "Naay, what's wrong wi' me ?" she asked herself. "That's just how he is ! No more reason to expect him to change, nor what he has to expect me to change !" She gave her soft, intimate chuckle. "That's a point on it ! I've had to change, had to get used to a new life altogether. Oh, it's a good enough life. We've enough to eat, clothes to our backs, a roof over our heads, but—eh, it's all so small somehow."

It was small compared with the life which she had led at Stallingford, with its dignity—even the meals in the servants' hall had been served with some ceremony—the size of the rooms, the importance of the superior servants, the talk of the Family, of the guests, and of the various entertainments. True, she had always worked sufficiently hard at Stallingford, but it was her own work which she did, and no one else's. Here, all the work was her work, from making beds to peeling potatoes, from mending William's socks to feeding the hens. Before she had been a specialist ; now she was a handyman !

She found it difficult to share a room with William, to wake in the early morning to see his clothes flung over the back of a chair, to see his brush and comb lying on the dressing-table beside her own. She had never known how men made their brushes and combs so dirty.

"Naay, this comb wants a good dipping in soda-water !" she exclaimed, holding it at arm's length. "It's fair silted up wi' fluff or something. How d'you ever get it this road ?"

William had blinked his eyes and said, "Eh, Ah niver see a comb as didn't get that road, Sally. That's nowt."

"You'll see this one as wean't get this way agean," she replied. "I'll see to it." It irked her that William should imagine that a shave every other day was sufficient. She had been used to Blachlet, and Lingley, to the footmen, with their smooth chins and meticulously brushed hair ; William's face, with its bristles of reddish gold hair, offended her. She disliked the feeling of it when he kissed her, and once, when a sudden fit of irritation seized her, had said so.

"I can't stand it, Will'um. It hurts ; you don't seem to understand that," she said.

"Eh ?" he grinned. "Ah thout as moast wimmen liked it ! Ah've allus heard as they did."

"You've heard wrong as far as I'm concerned, then !"

He tipped back his cap and scratched his head. "Aye, seemly. Yer a queer 'un, Sally."

She even found it difficult to keep clean in a cottage. Privacy was something which had never entered into William's life. He washed—sluiced down—at the sink in the back kitchen, standing there in his trousers and socks, his big, square torso white with lather.

He puffed and blew, scrubbed and soaped. It did not affect him in the least if she walked in ; to him it was right and natural that she should do so. It was just as right and natural that when Sally carried a huge jug of boiling water upstairs, and, stripping, began to wash from head to foot in the basin—"dab washing" she called it—he should enter the bedroom if he wanted anything. That, she remembered, had been their first real quarrel. She had been standing stripped naked, delighting in the hot water, the smooth feeling of soapsuds, when he entered. Catching up a towel, she had flung it round her, demanding furiously, "What's this for ? Didn't you know as I was washing me ?"

"Why, aye." He stood staring at her. "What's t' matter ? Ah wanted a clean handkerchief."

"Can't you wait while I'm finished ?"

He had flushed under his tan, and she had seen his eyes flash with annoyance.

"Dean't speak ter me that road, ower Sally ! Ah've a reit ter cum in if Ah've a mind. It's ma room as well as yourn ; you're ma wife, bean't yer ? Ah seen yer wi' little or nowt on afore this, an' Ah dean't doubt as Ah'll see thee ageän. Have sense, woman !"

"If I've much more o' this," she flashed back, "it 'ul be your room fur good an' all, an' mine 'ul be t'other side o' t' landing. Am Ah niver to have a minute alone ?"

He had strode over to the chest of drawers, opened one, selected a handkerchief with care, and without speaking had walked out again, banging the door behind him. A moment later her sense of humour had asserted itself. Of course it was silly—right-down silly, if you looked at it as Will'um did. You slept with a man, let him have his will of you, and then got all vexed because he caught you stripped, washing. Only if you didn't look at it as he did, you felt there was a difference. Like

ofttimes in bed a man 'ud say things that in broad daylight you'd
smack his face for voicing.

She finished washing, cleared away the jug and basin, folded
the towel, dressed, and sighed as she did so.

"I suppose we all swaller camels an' choke ourselves wi'
gnats! Only some on us 'ud rather get choked wi' camels than
be irritated wi' gnats. I'm one on 'em."

Yet when she went downstairs there was Will'um putting
some flowers in a yellow vase on the tea-table, whistling—and he
whistled prettier nor anyone she'd ever heard—and looking up,
smiling, to say, "Nay, Sally lass—Ah'm reit sorry as Ah vexed
yer. Yer mun fergive ma. Ah'm a gert rumbustious kinder
chap, choose how."

"Nay," she said, "it's me that's just daft like."

Now, standing at the gate, while the hens fought and quarrelled
over the mash, she looked at her hands. Two months' work had
roughened them; they'd be no use for real fine sewing, for
embroidery—for embroidering initials—coronets, and entwined
letters—V and L. That was over; those days would never come
back. She'd lost other things too. The ability to speak nicely,
to choose her words with care. He—she caught her breath when
she thought of him—had liked to hear her speak dialect. He had
thought it so pretty, soft and—dear, he said. Now she spoke
very little else. It was difficult when Will'um spoke dialect
always. Made it seem that you were trying to be superior.
Aunt Hardcastle, coming over to take tea with her, had remarked
on it.

"Sally luv, no need to lose all your nice ways o' speaking!
Just now when you said to William, 'Hap it oop fur Aunt ter tak'
back hoame', I could scarcely believe me ears."

Sally had shrugged her shoulders and said, "Nay, it's easier
ter talk like Will'um does."

Aunt Hardcastle returned smartly, "Rubbish! No easier to
say 'hap' than what it is to say 'wrap' or even 'lap'. Talk sense,
Sally luv."

Not that Sally really minded her hands growing rough, or
getting up very early, or cleaning and cooking. There was a
certain satisfaction in having a home of your own, in deciding
what you'd eat, and when you'd do this or that. It gave you a
feeling of independence to be your own mistress. It was her
pride to manage well on what William gave her. Thirty shillings
he got, and vegetables. The cottage was five shillings a week—

the best cottage in the village. He gave her a pound, and kept
ten shillings. Not that he spent the ten shillings that he kept.
He had a money-box, a child's thing made of pottery, and it was
his delight to weigh it in his hand and say that it was getting
heavier every week. He loved to drop coins into it slowly, and
to listen to them rattling down among the sixpences and shillings.

He was a good lad, was Will'um. Smoked very little, and
never knocked his pipe out on her clean hearth. Liked a drink
of beer, but a pint was all he ever took with his supper, and often
he'd make her have a glass with him. He was kind, clean, hard-
working—he would be considered a model husband, an ideal
mate.

'That's what I'd think—it's what I do think,' Sally mused, 'if
I wasn't for ever looking back ovver my shoulder at—what's over
and done with. It's my own fault !'

Now she wanted to get things straight, that was why she was
hanging about at the gate instead of getting on with her house-
work and making the potato pie for William's dinner. Tonight
she'd got to tell him, there was no avoiding it any longer. She'd
deceived him when she married him, though she hadn't *known*
herself, not for certain. Now she'd got to add to her deception,
and allow him to think that the child she was carrying was his.
It wasn't his—she was certain of that—as certain as anyone
could be of anything. It might be, just possibly, but—"Pigs
might fly," Sally murmured, "but they're unlikely sort of birds !"
In her own mind, she felt with certainty that she had been
"three weeks gone" when she married William. Now—after
two months' married life, she must make him believe that she
had been pregnant for only two months.

'It's easy to say what I ought, and what I ought not, it's a lot
harder to do things than to make rules about 'em,' she mused.
'One lie breeds anuther, that's a fact.' She sighed, turned and
picked up the bowl, pecked clean by the hens. 'Nay, I don't like
lying. It's hateful ! Only it's not just *my* lie as you might say.
I've got to lie for—him.'

All that morning she tried to plan what she would say, there
were moments when she even wondered if she should tell William
the truth. Admit that she had been with a man before she
married him, that the child, while it might just conceivably be
his, was far more likely to be—the other chap's. If William
turned her out, well, she could earn her own living, for a time
anyway—and afterwards ? That was what frightened her—

afterwards. Not to have enough to feed the child, maybe to have to go on the tramp as her mother had done, to sleep rough, to take refuge in the casual wards, to be ordered about, mocked at, bullied. The child to be a "workhouse brat", a pauper, to be torn from her, dragged up in an institution! Nay, it didn't bear thinking about.

She wasn't robbing William of anything. She might have other bairns—and he'd be the father. This one—well, children didn't cost so much to keep, and she was working harder now than she'd ever worked at Stallingford. She cooked, cleaned, baked, sewed for William, surely the child's keep might be regarded as her wages? It wasn't as if they were gentry, with land and houses, silver and pictures to go to the eldest son. That 'ud be different. William Scarth's son wouldn't inherit anything much except his name.

She swung round to the chest of drawers on the top of which stood the little swing mirror, and resting her hands on the polished mahogany, she stared at her reflection.

"Sally Scarth," she said softly, "dean't go on! In your heart you know varry well as that's all poppy-cock. You're just talking and arguing and you know there's not a bit o' truth in what your saying and thinking. It's all wrong. It's a wicked thing as you're doing to father Leister's bairn on to Will'um. But— you're caught, caught in a trap you made yersen, an' it's ovver laate to get out now. Don't grizzle and whine—dean't pity yersen —you've made yer bed an' yer mun lie on it. No, have done!"

That night, when William having disposed of some cold potato pie, and half an apple tart made on a flat dish, having twisted round in his chair, lit his pipe, and poured the remainder of the pint of draught ale into his glass, Sally told him.

"Well, Will'um, I doubt I'm going to have a bairn," she said.

He looked up from the pipe which he was filling, and she was struck with the look of satisfaction on his pleasant, rather stupid face. He smiled and nodded.

"Noo then," he said, "luke at that!"

He inflated his chest, as if conscious that he had achieved something praiseworthy, his glance at Sally made her feel that he rated her intelligence only very little lower than his own. His eyes were full of approval and self-satisfaction.

"An' when d'yer reckon as it 'ul be, Sally luv?" he asked.

"I thought"—for a moment she hesitated—"why—April, I'd say."

He made a mental calculation, then smiled, shaking his head. "Naay, tha's getten it wrang," he said. "Naay—nine munths—saame as a coo, it is. Why, we've lost noa time, have we ? Ah hope it 'ul be a little lad. Gals can cum afther, eh ?"

"Whichever it is, it 'ul bring its luv wi' it," she said.

He finished his beer, wiped his mouth with the back of his hand and rose. "Ah'll just shut oop t' hens," he said, and as he passed her chair he stooped and kissed her cheek, saying, "Aye—Ah reckon as we've lost noa time, eh ? And what for need we, eether ?"

She did not move, then suddenly leant forward, her chin on her hand, staring at nothing. Somewhere she could hear a voice speaking, a quick, hurried voice, in which the laughter came as an accompaniment to the words, a voice which broke off, leaving sentences half finished. 'Sally, darling Sally—it's not true. How wonderful, nothing so wonderful has ever happened in the world. Clever, marvellous Sally—my Sally. When, tell me when—April, when the flowers begin to come out—no, surely—not April—oh, I'm so stupid, you know and I don't. Anyhow, what do months matter—the better the month the better the baby ! What rubbish I'm talking—I can't help it. I'm slightly crazy, crazy with happiness. A boy, do you want a boy ? I'll say that I want a girl, so that one of us will be pleased either way, and when one of us is pleased—automatically, we're both pleased ! Or"—and she could hear the little gurgle of laughter—"twins, Sally. Please, clever, miracle-working Sally—twins, a boy twin and a girl twin, then we'll both be quite satisfied !"

She sat upright, blinking her eyes, then rose and began to clear away the supper dishes. Those dreams were not possible any longer, they even made her afraid. She might think too much, talk in her sleep—not that William would ever hear her, nothing disturbed him.

ii

William was kind, she believed that he tried to be thoughtful, but he was accustomed to women taking childbearing as a matter of course. It was the natural outcome of a healthy marriage. Nothing to make a fuss and bother over. Gentry might lay up on sofas and such like, guard against this and that, and as like their bairns were weakly little runts. His old mother boasted that she'd had nine children, that their father had never earned

more than eight shillings a week, and that she had never missed a
day's washing before or after the birth of any of her bairns.
True, only three had survived, but that was just the will of God.
True, too, for years his mother had suffered with "bad legs" and
pains in the back, but these things were the heritage of women.
Vaguely he hoped that Sally wouldn't develop bad legs! Sally
had a nice little house, plenty of good food, and she'd do wonderfully well.

He was proud that he was to be a father, he even swaggered
about it a little. Talked to the housekeeper down at Wittingly
about "T'missus being a bit dowly—as is ondly reit at sooch a
time", and received various pieces of information regarding the
diet of expectant mothers. These ranged from stout which had
been stirred with a red-hot poker, "fur sitha, t' iron gets inter
t' stout, an' iron's good as all t'world knaws"—to a live toad
wrapped in fine, old linen and tied stomach downwards on the
pregnant woman's chest.

William returning home made his first announcement,
"Mrs. Wilki'son tells ma as tha should sup a lot o' stout, Sally."

Sally turned from the fire where she was stirring some gravy,
and her face suddenly scarlet, demanded, "Me—sup stout!
Nasty stuff—whatever for?"

"Why, seein' as tha's that waay."

To his astonishment, she flared up. "You've bin gossiping
about me to that lot down at Wittingly! Can't you hold your
silly tongue, Will'um? What's it gotten ter do wi' them? It's
ma business an' not theers. Kindly mind what tha says and ter
whom tha says it concerning me."

"Boot—it's nowt ter be 'shamed on! They weer all varry
seet oop abart it."

"All!" she retorted. "Lot of cackling old fules! Tell 'em
when Ah want advice Ah'll ax it fra' me own, not all an' sundry."

She resented that anyone should know. She wanted to keep
the child—to herself. William had been obliged to know, but
there she hoped the knowledge might have ended. The woman in
the next cottage, talking over the low hedge, looked wise and
said, "Ah dean't think sumehow tha's luking soa varry bright,
Mrs. Scarth." Sally retorted, "Ah can't mind t'time when Ah
felt better, Mrs. Watson." Old "Mother" Hebblethwaite, who
could charm away warts, cure gathered fingers and make cows
let down their milk, eyed Sally curiously when she passed her in
the village.

" 'Marnin', Mrs. Scarth."

"Good morning, Mrs. Hebblethwaite."

"Hoos things wi' yew ?   Ah did heard a whisper as theer might be summat——"

"Aye ?   Whispers are daft things, Mrs. Hebblethwaite, Ah'd advise yer not to listen ovver mooch ter them."

William grumbled a little.   "Ah see nowt ter mak' sooch a secret on.   It's nattural, afther all."

"Not natural ter me, onny road," Sally told him.   "I like ter keep things ter mesen."

When November had nearly run its course, Sally went over to Stallingford to see her aunt.   She had refused all previous invitations, and could not have said clearly why she accepted this one.   All the way there, while she drove through the lanes in the trap which her ladyship had sent over, Sally knew that her whole body was tense.   To visit Stallingford again was inevitably to suffer, to be reminded of all that had been once, and could never be again.   Yet the moment she saw the house, with its belt of tall trees—those elms which stood on the fringe of the park— she felt that she had—come home.   She wasn't Mrs. William Scarth any longer, she was Sally Hardcastle coming back after a visit to London or some such place with the Family.   The clock in the tower was striking three.   There was his lordship pacing slowly along the terrace with Agamemnon stalking along at his heels.   Agamemnon who had betrayed her—betrayed—them ! Poor old beast, he wasn't to blame.

George, who was driving, looked down from the high driving-seat and said, "It must be a'most like coming home, eh, Sally—or ought I to say Mrs. Scarth ?"

She laughed.   "Nay, Sally 'ul do all right, George."

"You're looking right bonny, if I may say so."

"*May* say so !"   She laughed.   "And why not ?   There's no woman doesn't like to be told that she looks nice."

He nodded.   "Aye, and why for not ?   It's their due, that's how I luke at it."

"A very good way to look at it."

The long flagged passage to Aunt Hardcastle's room, the room itself with the red chenille table-cloth, the canary in its gilt cage, the photographs—for a moment Sally thought that her heart missed a beat—there was a new one of Leister.   How tall he looked !   He wasn't really so very tall, Sally remembered.   Just the right height.   Aunt Hardcastle rising and enfolding her, the

K

faint scent of lavender and dried rose leaves which emanated from her.

"Oh, dear, it's nice to see you again, Sally. You'll have to slip up and see Mrs. Bishop. I doubt we shan't have her long, poor old lady. Just slipping away—that's it, slipping into Life Eternal, as the Rector said when he came last to see her. And Mr. Blachlet will want to see you, oh—and her ladyship wants to see you—particlar. 'Let me see Sally when she comes, Hard-castle, if you please,' she said to me, said it twice over."

Pleasant to be back, though she found it so difficult to keep her eyes from turning again and again towards that photograph, had to bite her lips to prevent herself asking how he was, and where he was. Aunt Hardcastle chattered on about the Family. Lady Gwendoline was, she lowered her voice to a discreet whisper, "expecting". She was very happy, her letters to her ladyship were full of her husband. His kindness, his generosity. They might come over this year if all went well, to show off the prospective baby. Sally, clenching her hands tightly, thought, 'It's coming nearer and nearer—in a minute she'll speak about him ! I don't think that I can bear it.'

She broke in, "Well, Aunt—I might as well tell you. I'm expecting a baby in April."

"Never ! Now that is nice ! I hope that William is pleased." Her voice implied that William being of lesser clay might not appreciate his good fortune. "He might well be ! And you're well, Sally—now whatever you want, my dear, ask for it, and it's yours." The kind woman wiped her eyes, sniffing a little, murmuring, "Just think of that !"

Blachlet came in, and Lingley and Mamzel, looking older and more yellow, Sally thought. Blachlet was fatherly and kindly, Lingley was amusing and trying to make jokes about how badly Sally must cook for William, asking if William beat her often, and if she retaliated with the frying-pan. Mamzel was affectionate, and inclined to recall old times. Sally listened, answered and laughed, and wondered when someone would mention Leister's name. Then she was escorted to her ladyship, and for a moment experienced all her old difficulty in understanding what she said.

"Ah—Sallie—howah very pleasantah to see yah and looking ah so well." Then as suddenly as if someone had wound up a blind and let daylight into a dusky room, Sally could understand perfectly. "You're looking very well. I hope that you are very happy. One day you must let me come and have a cup of tea

and see your nice home. Yes, indeed. Take back some fruit
and flowers with you, please. Though I'm sure that Scarth
brings back all you need from Wittingly. Sir George is very
pleased with him, very pleased indeed. There, I mustn't keep
you from your friends. Ah, yes—you must see Bishop. Poor
old lady ! I'm afraid that we shan't have her much longer—a
good woman, a really good woman. Good-bye, Sally."

A visit to Mrs. Bishop, who mouthed a little, and for a moment
did not seem to know who Sally was, then—again as if someone
had drawn up a blind, she realized quite suddenly who it was
speaking to her.

"It's Sally—little Sally Hardcastle—a good little girl, m'lord,
does her very best always. That's right, Sally—small, even
stitches. Count the threads—count 'em. I'm not so well,
Sally—no, no. Poorly—me breathing's badly—the nights is
dreadful. Yes, y'r' ladyship, I slept better'n what I have been
doing. Nice to see Sally, oh, very nice. I've thought of you, Sally—
no relations, I've not got. Thought of her, Sally Hardcastle."

The old wheezing voice droned on, and while she was still
talking the old lady fell asleep.

Downstairs again Aunt Hardcastle talked more freely, while
Mr. Blachlet sipped his tea and then excused himself. "I know
that ladies like their own private chats."

"Poor old Mrs. Bishop. They're good, Sally, letting her stay
here. Oh, they're good. Her ladyship looks well, doesn't she ?
His lordship as handsome as ever. They're very happy about
Lady Gwendoline. Wonderful place Mr. Vanderholt has in
America. It's like a kingdom, it's so large. Fancy, he took trees
over from England to plant in his park. Oh yes, money's no
object, none at all. His young lordship . . ." Sally thought, 'It's
come now ! I'm afraid and yet I want to hear. Oh, go on—go
on—tell me—quickly.'

"His young lordship—have another cup, Sally ? No ? A
bit more cake then ? What was I saying ?"

Sally licked her lips. "You said, 'His young lordship——' "

"Oh yes. He's home now. I don't know for how long.
Looks thin, I think. Less—what shall I say—less larky than
what he was ? Growing more serious. They say—mind, I don't
know how true it is—that he's very attracted by The Hon. Millicent Crompson. So we shall see what we shall see. They say that
one wedding makes many, and now her young ladyship's settled—
come in, what is it ?"

The door opened and Leister entered. He seemed not to see Sally, but spoke directly to Mrs. Hardcastle. He was thinner, paler too, and Sally thought that his voice had lost some of its youthful quality, it was heavier, deeper.

"Oh, Hardcastle—a message from my mother——" Then : "I say, this is very pleasant, Sally ! How are you ? I haven't seen you since before your wedding, have I ? You look very well. Yes, Hardcastle—the message. My mother wants you to look out for me—a silver-stoppered hunting-flask. She thinks that Blachlet may have it, and if not perhaps it's among your things—I mean some of our things that you look after. I'd like it as soon as possible. It's a shame to interrupt when you're entertaining your niece. Oh, and one other thing—my mother wants Sally to have some fruit, and cake and—oh, you know the kinds of things. She said something about some birds—dead ones, of course. Would you see to that for her ? Thank you so much. I say, can I have a cup of tea ? It looks so nice with the firelight dancing on the china. I used to have tea here when I was a small boy. You don't invite me now, Hardcastle. Why don't you ?"

"Oh, m'lord, as if you couldn't come without inviting ! I'll have them bring some fresh tea, that 'ul perhaps be a little stewed. I think that I know where the flask is. I seem to remember that you gave it to me yourself last back end, to have the hinge repaired. I'll see to it immediately."

But his lordship didn't want fresh tea, he loved his tea very strong he said, and if his mother had a fault, which sometimes he doubted, it was that she liked hers weak, and made from that dreadful wishy-washy China stuff. His lordship said give him Indian every day in the week. He was standing on the hearth-rug, his hands in his pockets, tipping backwards and forwards on his heels as he spoke, smiling and laughing.

Sally, he said, would pour out the tea for him. And—oh yes, another cup ? Well, couldn't he have one out of Hardcastle's cabinet, the one with the roses on it ? He'd really enjoy his tea out of that particular cup. Wash it ! Not at all ! Didn't he know Hardcastle's passion for cleanliness Very well, wipe it on a clean napkin if she must, only be quick—he wanted it so badly.

Then when Hardcastle bustled out, laughing and smiling with pleasure, he didn't seem to want the tea which Sally poured out for him. He put it down, then took her hand in his, saying,

"Sally, I had to see you. I couldn't help myself. My mother said that you were here. I made excuses to get rid of your aunt. Tell me, how are you? You've not changed, except to get dearer, sweeter, lovelier. Do you still love me, Sally?"

For the first time she spoke. "I shall always do that, m'lord."

"Will you? Do you mean that, or do you say so to sound— consistent, constant or polite? Oh, I've missed you so. I ought not to have come here today, it will bring back all the damnable misery. I couldn't help it, I had to see you. Do you understand, Sally, *I had to see you.*"

Watching him, wondering how she could endure the pain at her heart, she said, "Yes—you had to see me."

"You're happy? Really happy? Sally, not so happy as we should have been. No one could have made you so happy— could they?"

"No—no one."

He lifted her hand and pressed it to his lips, then stared at it a little ruefully.

"Sally—your pretty hands!"

"Aye, they're different from—what they once were."

"But you're not, not really, not deep in your heart. You can't be, say that you can't be. Tell me about yourself, Sally. I'm hungry to hear about you."

She drew a deep breath, then said, "Sit down, my dear," and hearing him draw a quick breath, she excused herself, "I always think of you as that—my dear."

"It's wonderful to hear it, Sally."

She smiled, her old wise, tolerant smile. "Is it? I don't know that I ought to talk to you, I ought to be brave and shut things up in my heart. Not tell anyone. It's difficult to keep secrets. They're a kind of weight. They press hard—here." She laid her hands on her bosom. "Somehow it's worst at nights."

He nodded. "Dearest, don't I know——"

"I'm going to have a baby, my dear."

She watched the muscles of his throat move almost convulsively. "You are—when, Sally?"

She answered slowly, breathing harder with the effort she was making to remain calm.

"Why, people think in May—but—I doubt that it will be in March or April."

He stared, looking stupid, as if someone had hit him in the

face. "In April or March . . ." he said, then : "Sally—then—then it's . . ."

She nodded.   "Aye, I don't doubt it.   It's ours, my love. . . ."

"Then—but people will know—Scarth—they'll all know. Sally, this is when you must come with me.   Ours—I've a right to be with you, it's not possible that——"

"Nay, that can't happen," she said gently.   "If you love me—and I believe as you do love me, the same as I love you—it's hard.   It's terribly hard, but—there isn't any going back now. I must go on with it.   Never fear that it 'ul have love."   She laughed shakily.   "A'most as much as I give you, my dear love—never quite as much.   Only, one day if your influence could help him—I've a sort of feeling it will be a boy—I wanted you to know that he had a right to ask you.   Not that he'll ever know—he won't.   No one will—except us.   There, do you want that tea ?   You don't, nay, I never thought you did."   She took the cup and carried it to one of her aunt's precious plants, pouring the tea on to the soil, leaving only a little at the bottom of the cup.   Then returning to where he stood, she laid her hand on his arm.   "It's been—been heaven itself to see you.   But you're over thin.   Take care of yourself, my luv."

He looked at her wildly.   "Sally, I can't bear it——"

"My dear, we've got to bear it.   Beggars can't be choosers."

"Kiss me, Sally—please—once, darling."

She shook her head, as if she were chiding a greedy child. "Nay, Ah ought not to—but—Ah never could refuse you aught, my dear."   Taking his face between her hands she kissed him, then said, "Now, go—I'll tell Aunt as you couldn't wait.   Oh—go, please go—quickly."

CHAPTER TWO

SHE was to see him once again, before the centre of passionate intensity of love seemed to change from Leister to the child she carried. He sent his servant over from Stallingford to ask if it would be convenient for his lordship to call with a message from her ladyship. Sally, dressed in her morning print frock, stood at the door listening to the smooth voice of a well-trained servant, with its spattering of "his lordship—this" and "m'lord said—that". There had been a time when she would have delivered such a message in just such a fashion, speaking correctly, evenly, with a slight hint of subservience when she rolled titles round her lips. Now she was Will'um Scarth's wife, apart from lords and ladies, servants' halls, butlers and ladies' maids. The man seemed—almost—to be speaking a foreign language, clipped and precise.

She said, "His lordship wants ter cum here this afternoon? Why, Ah sure—Ah'll be honoured."

"Her ladyship wished to come," the man assured her, "but she has, it appears, contracted a slight chill, and his lordship—who is leaving for Paris tomorrow, I believe—said that he would come in her place. I understood that her ladyship is sending you some personal message."

How queer it was, Sally thought, that these people, these dignified servants, never appeared to hold definite beliefs and opinions It was always, "I understand", or "I believe", or "It appears". As if they safeguarded themselves against having said too much or too little, as if they disclaimed any personality of their own, and took their colouring from their masters and mistresses.

"All right," she nodded, "somewheer about fower."

"I should imagine so. Good morning."

Once he was gone, she changed. She became a creature of tremendous energy, an excited troubled thing. Her calmness left her, she stood in the kitchen, her hand pressed against her heart, she could feel it beating heavily and fast. Her cheeks were flushed, her eyes shining. Then she flung herself into her work. What would shine must shine, what would take on a

higher polish must be polished until she could see the reflection of
her face in the object as she bent over it.   She examined the neat
white window curtains, regretting that she had hung them there
only two days ago.   She would have liked to tear them down,
wash and iron them   She remembered William's dinner, and in
the miraculous way possessed by women contrived to do not two
things but half a dozen things at once.   William's potatoes were
peeled and ready to put on to boil, William's rice pudding, with a
handful of currants flung into the milk, was placed in the oven.
She sieved flour, she kneaded paste and cake mixture.   In the
short time which lay before her she had achieved much, and all
done well and to her satisfaction.   William came in to his dinner,
to find the cottage filled with the smell of baking.   He went
through to the scullery to wash, calling out, "Tha's had a baakin'
daay seemly, lass."

Thankful that she was in one room and he in another, she
called back, "Aye, his lordship—Leister—sent his man round to
say that he was calling with a message fra' her laadyship.   Seemly
she's i' bed wi' a chill, an' she's sending him.   Ah can't boot offer
him summat ter eat and drink.   Ah'd not like to put on a poor
faace before onny o' them."

William, rubbing his arms with a rough towel, came back into
the kitchen.

"Luke at that !" he said.   "Sending his lordship wi' a message !   Naay, tha's reit—mak' a nice show."   He chuckled.   "Eh,
neebours 'ul be peering and wagging theer tongues, Ah'll lay !"

A queer wave of friendliness for William swept over her, she
laughed back at him, as if she said, 'Leave it to me, I'll show them
what we can do'.   He seemed to sense her feeling, and chuckled.

"Get oot t'best, Sally lass—talk well put on, my girl—tha's
diff'rent to what maist on 'em is, choose how.   Noa one knaws it
better'n what Ah do."   Again he laughed, and as he walked back
to hang up the towel, called over his shoulder, "Ah ofttimes think
if Ah dean't watch ooot, tha'll be making a reit gentleman o'
me !"

"That'ud be a full time job, Will'um," she answered, "Ah've
ovver mooch ter do i' t' house."

As she watched him eating his chop, mashing up potatoes
with a lump of butter, and later cramming spoonful after spoonful
of rice pudding into his mouth, she thought that, after all, things
were never so bad but they might be worse.   William was fond
of her, and she—liked and respected him.   They might both

have done worse, and she'd make up to him for this deception which she was practising on him now. Once that was over—she'd settle down to be the ideal wife—or what passed for the ideal wife in William's eyes. Now—this visit of Leister's, and all connected with it, was the last of her youth. She wanted to live every moment, she wanted to laugh, to be kind, motherly, everything he wanted—now. Once he was gone, she might never see him again, and she would face a new life with equanimity.

William wiped his mouth, looked expectantly towards the fireplace, and said, "Tha's not gotten sic' a thing as a coop o' tea, hast'a, lass? Ah could do wi' yan."

Good-temperedly, she rose and went to make the tea. "Nay, Ah niver knew t' time when tha couldn't do wi' a coop," she said.

"Why, it's cauld i' t' gardens this weather! Lil' Joe Gallus weer fair grizzling wi' t' cauld this marnin'. A'd ter send him in ter hot-house ter get his hands warmed on t' pipes."

As she poured out his tea, black and hot as he liked it, she said, "Better gie t' lad a pair o' mittens. Hot pipes 'ul gie him nothing but chilblains. I'll see if I can't get him a pair knitted. His mother oughter think shame not making the lad some."

His tea finished he rose, pulled on his coat, wound his muffler round his neck, and patting her shoulder as he passed her said, "Theer, have a nice time w' t' gentry, lass." The moment the door was closed Sally began her work. Moving quickly and neatly, never fumbling or dropping anything, she cleared away the dinner, washed dishes, looking at intervals to see how her cakes were cooking. By two o'clock everything was "sided away", the cakes were cooling off, and she had a moment when she might sit down and try to collect her thoughts a little.

Until now it had scarcely seemed true. Now she realized that she had polished, cleaned, baked, because Leister was coming to see her. In such a short time, she would hear his knock on the door, hurry to meet him. She might even let herself imagine, as he walked into the house, that it was *their* house, that he had come home from work, and that the long evening and a long succession of wonderful days lay before them. Then her practicality asserted itself again, and rising she began to lay the table. Bread-and-butter—to be covered with a plate and set aside in the pantry—seed-cake—he had always said to Mrs. Bishop when he visited the nursery, "Got any seed-cake, Bish dear? My favourite cake"—fat rascals, and her own speciality— a sand-cake made from a recipe which Mongsewer had given her in London. He had called it by some fancy name, but when she told Mrs. Rogers about it, she had looked at the recipe and said, "Oh, it's right enough, Sally, but it's nothing more nor less than a nice sand-cake—let Mongsewer call it what fancy French name he chooses!" Still—it was a lovely cake, Sally had never tasted any like them. There was just a touch of something that made them different from Mrs. Rogers', let her say what she liked. How nice that china looked—a wedding present—"A loving gift from Hannah Bishop". The teaspoons, real silver. Mr. Blachlet's present to her. She stood back and surveyed the table with a sense of pleasure. There seemed nothing incongruous to Sally that she should prepare a meal for her lover, it did not strike her as being almost fantastically unsentimental to have cooked and baked for him—on this—probably the only visit he would pay her. She was glad that her cloth was fine and shining with much ironing, happy that she should have prepared food for him, have set out her best to do him honour.

"Aye," she said briskly, "that 'ul do. That vase of flowers looks nice there. He likes flowers a'most as much as what Will'um does."

Upstairs she hesitated as to what she should wear. Her wedding dress—no, that was all wrong somehow, nice though it was! She took down various dresses, and finally selected one which she had worn while still at Stallingford, dark and neat, a little prim with its white frilling showing in a narrow line above the dark collar. And—another moment's hesitation—the locket which Mrs. Bishop had given her.

ii

She heard the knock, she knew that Mrs. Watson, and Mrs. Brewer, that Martha Hutchison over the road, and old "Grandfather" Peacock would all be craning their necks, watching and whispering. Squaring her shoulders, Sally walked to the door and threw it open. Leister stood there, with young Matson, the groom, behind him, holding parcels.

"Good afternoon, m'lord. I was sorry to hear that her ladyship was poorly."

"Nothing very serious, Sally! A chill—no wonder, for it's terribly cold. That's right, Matson, give the parcels to me. Come back—oh, when? Come back in an hour." He turned back to Sally. "For you're going to give me tea, I hope, and I have so many messages from my mother. If you're tired of me—well, you must just tell me to go ! Yes, in an hour, Matson."

"Very good, m'lord."

He came in, and she closed the door behind him, then stood leaning against it, watching him while he laid down his parcels and struggled out of his heavy driving-coat. She made no attempt to help him, just stood there—watching.

He held out his hands. "Are you glad to see me, Sally ?"

"I couldn't tell you just how glad. I suppose I ought not to be—but I'm past thinking of what's right and wrong."

He took her hands, drew her to him and kissed her, then said, "Come and sit down, I want to talk to you. I go tomorrow." Seated opposite to her, he spoke quietly, and with restraint. "Sally, I had begun to imagine that—I'd got over it. Then yesterday when I heard that you were in the house, I knew that the very thought of you set my blood racing again, made my heart hammer. Nothing was changed. I saw you—no, don't interrupt me—and you told me about the child. Sally, if it's my child as well as yours then I have a right to have a say in this. I have a right to take you away, to marry you the moment marriage is possible. Four months ago you refused, my father used his influence, and—now I come back to ask you again. Will you come away with me—not only for my sake, or for your own, but for this child's ? Think, Sally, think."

"I have thought," she said, "I've thought about very little else—but you, an' me—an' the baby. The answer's the same, my dear, as it was at Stallingford those months back. It's not possible."

He sprang to his feet, and laid his hand on her shoulder. "Listen, Sally—you admit that this is my child. You've no right to rob me of my child, or deny my child a father."

She smiled, twisting her head so that she could look up into his face.

"Nay," she said, "bastard bairns only have one parent—that's their mother. He shan't know he hasn't a father—i' t' eyes of the law."

"But I want to give him a father—I don't want him—or her—to carry any stigma !"

She rose and lifted the kettle from the fire on to the hob. "It's ovver late to think about that, my dear," she said, "we mum just do our best to—make things as right for t' little bairn as we can."

"Sally, Sally—can't I use any arguments, can't I influence you on my behalf as my father once influenced you against me ?" He stood, his hands hanging at his sides, his face drawn and wretched. "Sally, listen to me. No one will ever love you as I do. No one can. Are you going to fling it all away ?"

"Listen to me," she said, "sit down my dear love, and listen, and try ter see my side. I've given my promise to your father, I owe him a lot, he brought me 'out o' the land of Egypt and out o' the house of Bondage'—I'll never forget that. I won't break my word to him. I've done Will'um a great wrong, leastways that is what I know I ought to feel I've done, and I must pay for it. I've used him for my own safety, and my bairn's safety. I'll pay what I owe, in full so far as lies in my power. You've given me more'n you'll ever know. You've taught me the beauty of everything. There's nothing in the world that's beautiful that won't remind me always of you. Thoughts o' you 'ul be in the sunrise ovver the tree-tops out there, they'll be in the flaming of the sunset—ovver that way"—she lifted her hand and pointed towards the west. "In spring, in summer, all the year round when each month brings its own extra little bit o' loveliness— you'll be, somehow, part of it. The scent o' violets i' t' hedgerows, the smell o' roses, honeysuckle, meadowsweet, lad's love—'ul all carry something of you. Those things are what no one can tak' away from me. That's why"—she smiled suddenly—"I shall always want to thank you, that's why I shan't ever be able to stop loving you."

He stared at her, his eyes filled with tears, his mouth—which might have been stronger—quivering a little. He looked young, unprotected, and Sally longed to take him in her arms and comfort him, as she would one day comfort his child when the world treated it harshly.

"Nay, nay," she said, "I can't bear to see you do that. It breaks my heart."

"I think that mine is broken," Leister said.

She did not speak, but began to make the tea, warming the pot, and carrying it into the scullery to empty, putting in the exact amount of tea—one for each person and one for the pot, pouring on the boiling water with a hand which did not shake. Then she turned to him. "Tea's ready, my dear," she said.

He shook his head. "I couldn't eat, Sally."

"Luke," she said, and consciously she spoke broadly, feeling that in some queer inexplicable way the comfortable, slow speech might soothe him, "Ah've spent maist o' t' marnin' baking fur thee. This 'ul mebbe be t' fust an' last time as tha'll eat at same table wi' me. Ah'm not having thee cummen here while Ah'm this road. It's reit enoof noo, but i' anuther three-fower months it 'ul not be. Ah couldn't bear it. Let's have summat nice, summat happy tergether ter think on while we're apart, my dear. Noo, draw oop, do what tha Sally axes o' thee."

He blinked his eyes, set his lips more firmly, then said, "Oh, Sally, Sally."

But he drank his tea as if he were thirsty for it, and asked for more. He smiled because she had made seed-cake, and asked if she remembered.

"Aye, Ah mind well," she said, "your favourite caake. That's why it's here."

She told him about Mongsewer and the sand-cake, and what Mrs. Rogers had said, and he laughed and said that if the worst came to the worst they would open a cake shop in Bond Street and make a fortune with "Sally's Sand-Cake".

She said, "That's a th'out, only t' worst isn't coming to the worst; t' best's coming to the best, that's the way of it."

The room was warm and comfortable. Looking round, Sally thought, 'I shall remember this all my life. The shining black of the grate, the brass ornaments, the red raddle on the hearth, the bits of bright colour in the hearthrug. The smell of newly baked cake, the queer tangy scent of the tea, and—him sitting there, smiling like a bairn that's cried and can't quite forget its tears even though they've stopped.'

Leister said, "I feel that this is where I belong, Sally. If only I'd been born someone different from what I am, you and I might have lived here together. Queer woman you are, aren't you? Quite content to sit and pour out tea for me. Other women—when their lover came to see them——"

She laughed softly. "Aye, but because other women are dirty nastinesses, that's not to say that I am. I don't think of you as—my lover—ondly as—my love."

"Wouldn't you—let me make love to you—now?"

"Here? In Will'um's house, and me married to him? Nay, I've not played too straight a game, love, but I'm not going to make it more crooked nor what it is already. Don't let's talk about it, let's just think that we're both here, and—that's something."

"But, Sally"—his eyes were very bright, he was breathing quickly, leaning forward he took her hand and pressed it against his chest—"Sally—can't you feel my heart ?"

"Ha' done !" she chid him gently. "Nay, don't try me too hard, it's not reit, it's not fair. Tell me about them messages from her ladyship."

He sulked a little, as a child might have done who had been denied sweets or toys. She watched him, fondly, with a little smile twitching the corner of her mouth, and her eyes very tender. He crumbled his cake, he asked for more tea, and stirred it violently so that the liquid slopped into the saucer. She made a clicking sound with her tongue, brought him a fresh cup and poured the tea into it, saying, "There—drink it oop."

He shoved it away and said, "I didn't really want it !"

Sally laughed very softly, saying, "Nay, Ah'd be shamed going on yon road, so I would."

Leister looked up and met her dancing grey eyes. She was watching him, so kindly, with such understanding, without the slightest trace of annoyance that he felt suddenly ashamed. Her patience, her determination to do nothing to add to those deceits which she had already practised, her independence, and her courage, her refusal to whine or try to throw the onus of blame on him touched him deeply and sincerely.

He said, "I'm sorry, darling, darling David—your troublesome and unpleasant Saul is recovered. Let me give you my mother's messages."

Kindly messages, assurances that they—and to Sally Scarth "they" meant only one thing—the Family—wished her to have every care and attention. Her ladyship had sent clothes, would send more, his lordship had wished to send money, it appeared, but—and when she looked at Leister she saw that he scowled again. . . .

"But—what ?" Sally asked.

"But I refused to let them. They know, Sally, I'll swear that they know ! If anyone gives you money, it must be me. You'll take it from me, won't you ?"

"Aye, later I will—when it's needed, not for me, but for the bairn. I won't have him go short of anything." She glanced at the clock, and he saw her face lose some of its brightness. "The hour's up," she said, all the strength gone from her voice. "Matson 'ul be waiting, and all the neighbours staring to watch Lord Leister drive away. Good-bye, my dear love, I'll not see you agean for a long while. Don't worry, I shall be all right, and I'll find some road to—let you know."

"But money—money, Sally"—he spoke wildly—"I have it here. Take it now—you might want it. Look—there"—he pushed a roll of notes into her hand—"keep it and use it. Don't give it back to me—it's all you'll let me do. Hide it somewhere— anywhere—it's my right, Sally—darling."

"Very well." She took it, speaking quietly, her face devoid of expression. "Very well. Good-bye, my dear—be happy. Kiss me once." He caught her in his arms and kissed her again and again, very gently she pushed him away. "Nay, I said once, didn't I? No, not agean. I'm only flesh and blood—not stane. Let me oppen t' door for you. Now !"

He had pulled on his coat, and as he walked past her, the listening neighbours heard him say, "Thank you for a most wonderful tea, Sally ! I shan't forget that seed-cake in a hurry ! I'll give my mother your messages. Good-bye, Sally."

She stood very erect, framed in the opening of the door. Mrs. Watson whispered to Mrs. Brewer, "Why, she scarcelins lukes like a servant, does she ? Standing like sum laady saying farewell ter a visiter !"

"Good-bye, m'lord, and please thank her ladyship kindly."

iii

Early in January Mrs. Bishop died in her sleep. She left Sally Scarth the savings of forty years, amounting to some seven hundred pounds. Aunt Hardcastle said that it would make a nest-egg, and reminded Sally that one day "whatever I have to leave, when it pleases the kind Lord to call me, 'ul be yours, my dear". The actual money meant very little to Sally, she saw it translated immediately into education fees, paid tailors' bills and so forth for—her son. She had never counted the money which Leister gave her, she had rolled it in a clean handkerchief, and placed the handkerchief in a little tin box which had once held cough-drops. The box she had placed in her horsehair-covered trunk, under the linen, which, like all right-minded north-country women, she had laid away in case of death and burial. She would have "thought shame" not to have provided everything which might be needed for a laying-out—sheets, pillow-cases, even a nightgown and long white stockings. Above these things came her extra household linen, and the clothes for the coming baby.

From London had come a box full of infant's clothes, clothes so fine, so beautifully made and embroidered that Sally laughed when she handled them.

"Nay, Ah'll not be able to use them for any bairn of mine," she mused. "They'd cause ovver mooch talk. Why, Ah doubt if Lady Gwendoline has better for hers. How like him to order just—the best, never thinking of cost, or about them being suitable or anything. It's as well t' postman brought them when Ah was alone i' t' house."

February slipped into March, the trees in the woods were bent under the force of the gales, March was going out like a lion. Sally was well enough, growing a little tired of feeling clumsy and heavy, but her health was good. She had spoken to her aunt about engaging the midwife, but Aunt Hardcastle exclaimed in horror, "That old Mother Gamp! I've seen her, and—smelt her. Gin! Poof! Nasty old baggage. No, my luv, go and see Dr. Drummond, though since the mess he made of Annie's whitlow I don't know that I think so much of him. Still—he's the best to be got round here, and—go to him."

William stared. "A doctor! Why, Sally, there's nowt wrang is theer? Nay, ma muther never had nowt but a midwife, and not allus yan of them. Neebers was allus ready an' willing ter lend a hand, Ahm sure. What-t'ever 'ul a doctor cost, lass?"

"A guinea, I think."

"Eh—yon's a goodish bit o' money! Ah've heard as doctors want all sorts, an' all. Towels, an' hot water and goodness all knaws what else. A reit set oot, Ah've heard."

Speaking sharply, her face flushed with anger, Sally said, "Leave over, Will'um. Ah've money saved afore Ah married you. Onnyroads, Aunt Hardcastle wants to pay. As fur towels, well, we've enough and plenty o' them! If it's hot water as is needed, what's wrang wi' keeping t' boiler at t' side of the grate filled oop? Have done about it."

She was worrying, worry was making her irritable, painting dark shadows under her eyes, giving her severe headaches, making her generally feel that life under its present conditions was too much for her. Here it was March, and her child would be born in April. Already the women were staring, hinting that she "was nearly at t' end of her time".

Will'um, staring at her, said, "It's Maay, bean't it?"

"Of course it's May," she returned sharply. "When else would it be!"

"Nay, don't get vexed, lass. Ah was just thinking as mebbe it's twins. Wi' just about two months still ter goa, and you——"

Sally sprang to her feet. "Hold your tongue," she shouted. "You know that I hate that talk. Gie' ovver! Ah've not telled you yance but a hunnerd times! Ter hear you talk, Will'um Scarth, onnyone 'ud think Ah was a brood mare! Mebbe you'd rather Ah had t' farrier or t' vet fra ovver Maudesley way an' not t' doctor at all."

William was tired, he was worried over his gardens. The spring was late, everything was behindhand, and the old-fashioned hot-houses at Wittingly were difficult to manage. Sir George expected a lot with very little outlay. He expected things to spring up in a night, only this morning he had been round, grumbling a little.

"Damme, Scarth, everything's damned backward this year. First of April next week, and not much to show for it. I don't know, the more you fellows get the less you have to show for it. I swear that my father's gardener, old Harris, had all sorts and kinds of things ready for the table by the first of April!"

That had rankled. William knew all about old Harris, he had heard tales of him in the village, a cunning old Isaac if ever there'd been one, crafty as a fox. And Matt Hewitt who'd followed him had been as bad. Everyone said that the gardens at Wittingly had never looked as they did now, he worked early and late, and this was all the thanks he got. Now, here was Sally raging and shouting, and handing out a lot of nasty talk about mares and ver'er'nary and such like. Small wonder that a chap lost his wool a bit.

"Shut tha faace!" he shouted back "Ah'll not have oony female talk ter me yon road! Snacking at me, joost becos Ah show a bit o' interest in t' brat. Nastiness—Ah like that, an' you yattering on aboot mares an' sicklike. Mucky Ah call it. Shut oop!"

"Nay," Sally retorted, "it's not first time as you've spoke that road. Ah might as well tell you anuther thing, while this is ovver, an' bairn's born, Ah'm sleeping alone, i' t'other room. It's better fur me and joost as comfortable fur you."

He stared at her, his mouth slack. "W'at! Tha's gannen ter lig alane! Nay, but tha's deening nowt o' t' sort. Bidoot thoo ligs wi' ma, tha' can lig ootside i' gardin, sitha. Ah'll hae nane o' this i' ma hoose!" he said, his voice a little thick.

Sally looked at him, for a moment she hated him, hated his

coarse hands, his unshaven cheeks, the slight smell of the earth which clung to him. She shivered when she thought of his body touching hers, she wanted peace, darkness where she might lie alone and think. She was frightened and she knew it. Suppose that William found out, realized that the child was not his, and disowned it—and her ! After all she'd planned, and faced ! "Good night," she said, "Ah'm away ter ma bed—an' ma bedroom."

He made a movement to catch her arm, she stepped quickly to one side, caught her foot in the thick hearthrug and fell.

William, frightened, and because of his fear trying to brave it out, said, "That 'ul teach yer not ter polish that floor, wastin' good beeswax ! Git oop."

Her voice reached him queerly muffled. "Help me up an' Ah will. Gie me your hand."

Every vestige of colour had left his face, he was on his knees beside her, crying, "Nay, Ah niver meant ter harm thee. Nay, Sally luv, tha's arl reit. Dean't tak' on. Ah'll let tha lig whersomeiver tha likes. Theer—theer—Ah gotten thee. Help thee sen a bit, Sally luv—aye, that's better beer ! Theer !"

She sat in the big chair, leaning back, breathing queerly, he thought. She looked ghastly, and her head tilted a little to one side.

"I'm badly," she said, "help me up the stairs, an' gie Mrs. Watson a call, while you gan for the doctor. Gently, Will'um, Ah can't move ovver quick."

Mrs. Watson, the mother of eleven children—seven still above ground, while the other four occupied small graves in the churchyard—came willingly enough. She liked Sally, though she regarded her as having ideas above her station. She had seen Sally's nightgowns and underclothes hanging on the line in the garden and thought them "far ovver fancy fur a gardener's wife". She thought her "finicky" because she had said quite openly that though she kept hens, she was quite incapable of wringing their necks when the time came for them to provide meals for her and Scarth. Not that she didn't keep her house spotless, which was more than you could say for some of them that had been servants in big houses. That girl Willie Farmer married, that had been sewing-maid at Colford, why, she kept his place like a piggery, and the poor lad never had a button to his shirts. So when William Scarth, with a face like a peeled turnip, came rapping on the door, calling that his wife was took bad, carrying on as if the bairn might be in the world within the next five

minutes, Mrs. Watson took out a clean apron, and warning her
husband that if "Ower Henry screams i' bed all he wants is a
good hiding", hurried to be of what assistance she could.

She'd never seen a quieter, better-behaved woman than Sally
Scarth, never seen a better kept bedroom neither. Sally lay
with her eyes closed, the shadows beneath them making it look
as if her cheeks were bruised. She kept saying, "I'm sure it's
more'n kind of you, Mrs. Watson", and "Thank you kindly,
Mrs. Watson" for every single thing that was done for her. The
doctor didn't come for hours, and when he came Mrs. Watson
sniffed with a certain suspicion. Everyone knew Drummond's
failing. He talked roughly, more like a peasant than a man of
education, and it was known that the Earl had referred to him,
over at Stallingford, as "the disreputable old savage". Still, he
was the only doctor for fifteen miles, and so Wittingly, Stallingford, Maudesley, Murklethwaite, and Sowersly made the best of a
bad bargain. The Earl, Sir George Cope, and the rest of them
always sent for Dr. Halliday from Lockton.

He talked to Sally as if, she thought, he had a grudge against
her; firing off questions, and making grunting noises in reply
more like an animal than a man. "Thought you said April or
May—end o' one, start o' t'other? Fell—how d'yer mean—
fell? Trying to get rid of it, eh?"

She said, "Don't talk like a fule! Do you want my husband
to throw you out? Speak like that agean an' I'll send for Dr.
Halliday."

He gaped at her. Most of the country women treated him as
a creature possessing some special gift, they credited him with
the power of life and death. He said what he liked, and not one
of them dared to check him. Yet here was this girl, with a face
like chalk, and eyes like saucers, speaking to him of "sending for
Halliday".

"Why"—he stood up, his hands, palms turned inwards, in the
small of his back—"it'ul not be yet, I can tell yer that. I'll go
back and get to bed. Come round i' t' marning."

Sally said, "Is that all you're going to do?"

He grinned. "Why, what d'yer expect, young woman?
Nature 'ul do all that's necessary."

She closed her eyes. "When you come back," she said,
"remember I hate to have brandy puffed at me, will you?"

Downstairs, Drummond said to William, "Yon wife o'
your'n's a caution! Who does she think she is?"

William blinked his eyes. "Ah reckon she thinks as she's ma wife," he said.

"Bean't she?"

"Aye—what else 'ud she be?"

Drummond, his hands under the tails of his wide-skirted coat, scowled. "What's yer idea? Trying to smoke me—trying to be funny?"

"Noa," William said heavily, "it's not i' ma line of country—being funny. Goo' neit."

Sally's son was born forty-eight hours later. Mrs. Watson said, "Nay, it were a reit shame," and even Drummond, who obviously disliked his patient, admitted that she had "guts".

He shouted at her, "It's a little lad—that suit yer?"

"Aye," Sally whispered, "gie him here to me."

His little pig eyes twinkled, did 'em no harm to tease 'em a bit, brought them round a bit, made 'em laugh as often as not.

"What if Ah want ter keep him fur a bit? I might tak' a fancy ter him."

Her voice startled him, he thought that from a woman after forty-eight hours' hell, he had never heard such concentrated hate.

"Gie him here to me, I said—don't have any silly games, or I'll kill you when I'm about agean!"

He laid the baby down beside her. "Nay, Ah dean't want yer brat, missus. Got enoof o' me own—reit an' wrong side o' t' blanket."

CHAPTER THREE

SALLY lay in bed with the baby at her side. Her eyes were tranquil, her face looked soft and touched with some new sensibility which made it finer and gentler. That queer grim expression which had so often hovered round her mouth during the past months had gone. Strange, she reflected, as she lay there, while the pale spring sun sent long, wavering shafts of light across the white scrubbed boards, touching the white quilt of the bed lightly, as if it hesitated to disturb her thoughts, how she had changed. Ever since she left Stallingford she had experienced a mental hunger for Leister, a hunger which had at times reached a fierce intensity. She had ached for the touch of his hands, for the pressure of his lips, for the sound of his voice and his laughter. She could recall days when a sense of desolation swept over her, when she had felt that she was utterly lonely, abandoned, when she had thought of the life which stretched before her, and shivered, because it all seemed so grey, arid and purposeless.

Now, everything was changed. She had achieved something —she had given birth to the child which was hers, and the man's she loved. With the birth of that child had come reassurance. No one could take from her this baby which she had borne, this baby which was a proof of their love for each other. If she never saw Leister again, she would still look back on her knowledge of him with delight, for that knowledge had made this atom of humanity possible.

Leister, she faced the fact, belonged to the past. The child belonged to the future. Leister must marry, she had no illusions about that necessity. It was his duty—to his family, to his land, to the people who lived on that land. She might never even see him again, it was improbable that she would ever be held in his arms. The thought did not trouble her as it had done at one time. She could even shrug her shoulders, and accept it, with a little sigh, because Leister had belonged to her youth. He had been part of her childhood ; as a girl he had filled her thoughts, she had woven romances concerning him, he had been the first man to enjoy her womanhood. He had talked easily, and in her heart, she believed sincerely, saying that he was hers, as she was his.

True, she had been his entirely. She had lived, and slept and had her being, she felt, through him and because of him. Every action had been directed towards him, everything she had done had been with the idea that it might please him. She had taken additional care of her hands, so that he might be pleased with their softness. She had brushed her hair until it shone softly, because he had once praised it, and said that it looked as if the light had become tangled in it. She had been glad that her skin was soft, that her voice was pleasant and low for his sake. Leister had permeated her whole life, her whole being.

Lying there, she thought of him again and again, and always as someone whose place in her life had been filled with another love, another and greater interest. There was no feeling of bitterness towards him, she loved him as she had always done, as she would always do ; but the quality of her love had changed. Once he had been her lover—her dear love—now he was her child's father. Leister had developed without her help. His life had been planned for him by others. He might love her, might want to spend every possible moment with her, but his actual life was something in which she had never had, could never have had, any real part.

The child was different. From the moment of his birth he would look to her for everything. He was her responsibility. Her—dear love.

She looked down at his small puckered face, moved the shawl which enveloped him so that she could see his tiny clenched fist, with the nails which looked like minute scraps of pink shell, touched the dun-coloured down on his head very softly with the tip of her finger.

"Mine," she whispered, "he's mine ! Not a soul in the world can tak' him from me."

William had been enchanted with him. He had stood looking down at them both, his reddish-brown face twisted as if he were trying not to cry. She had watched the muscles of his throat working, seen how his whole body stiffened in an attempt to restrain his emotion.

"It's a little lad, eh ?" William said.

"Aye—Mrs. Watson says she's never seen a bonnier."

"Ah'll lay she's not neither." There was a long pause, then

William, licking his lips, said, "Eh, Sally—Ah'm reit oopset ! If aught had happened thee, Ah'd 'ad killed mesen. Ah'm axin' yer pardon, luv, humbly an' trewly. Ah'd not have had aught happen ter thee, not was it ever soa."

She smiled. "Nay, say no more about it, Will'um."

She had felt mean and small, knowing that William's sudden catching at her arm and her own fall had come as salvation to her, and as a solution to her problems. For a second she longed to tell him the truth, then prudence prevailed, and she made a mental promise to herself that she'd make up to William—for everything.

Curiously, since the baby's birth she felt more kindly towards him. The thought of his rough hands, his big, rather clumsy body, his little carelessnesses did not trouble her. She saw him for what he was—just William Scarth, gardener to Sir George Cope and content to live as his father, and his father before him, had lived. She had been setting standards for him which were too difficult, more—which were unnecessarily high. She had been taking Leister for a model and resenting the fact that while William did his best, according to his lights, he could never behave, speak, think or move as did the son of the Earl ot Stallingford.

She remembered a hymn which they had sung when she was a little girl in the House.

> ". . . with a pure, clear light,
> Like a little candle shining in the night,
> In this world of darkness, so we all must shine,
> You in your small corner, and I in mine."

That was right, different corners, different lights, different candles. William's light burnt brightly and clearly enough, though it might not be set in a silver candlestick. She remembered that once last summer she had grumbled to William about some stocks in the garden, saying that they were doing only poorly.

"I'd root them up, if I was you, Will'um, they're no good !"

He had stooped down and prodded about with his big earth-grimed finger, touching the plants gently, then saying, "Nay, poor things—they're not doing so badly. They're doing their best wi' what they've gotten. T' chap as had this plaace last weer no but a blood squeeser. Gie'en nout an' wantin' all. Let 'em bide, Ah'll mak' summat on 'em yet."

William had never had the chance to be anything but what
he was—and what he was, after all, Sally mused, was as good as
most and a deal better 'n many.

Again she looked at the sleeping baby. "It's chances that
folks want, chucky. That's what I'll see you get. Chances!
I'll not let myself get lazy, and talk broad because it's easier.
I'll speak pro'ply, so's you will, when you begin to talk, my little
love. I'll just remember enough broad talk to mak' you laugh,
like it used to make yer Da laugh."

ii

Sally was young and strong, and up and about again in just
over a week. At first, for it was the only time she had ever been
kept in bed in her life, she was frightened to find that her legs
were "wibbly-wobbly". She felt light-headed, and strange, but
these things passed, and she felt better than she had done for
months. It was wonderful to feel light, and free again, to be
able to move about easily, and never to have an ache or a pain.
The child was good, as Aunt Hardcastle assured Sally, all healthy
bairns were. He fed and slept, and woke to feed again. Nothing
appeared to upset or worry him, he gave no trouble during the
night, and would lie in his perambulator for hours, never making a
sound. William would stand staring down at him, not daring to
touch him, content to look intently, sigh gustily, and return to
the house to tell Sally that, "Lil' lad's a miracle, that's what he is,
a reit miracle."

The question of his name arose. Sally realized that she had
never given the matter a thought, the child was sufficient. She
had thought of him only as, "my dear love".

William said, "Ah dean't hold wi' callin' lads afther theer
Da's. Mak' it John William if yer like, boot not joost—William."

Sally said, "I don't care much for two names—John Willie
would be what he'd get, and to my mind that sounds daft-like."

Meditating, and with the air of one who proposes a world-
shattering idea, William said, "Ah've allus thout' as Percy
was a nice-ish naame—or r'arold."

"Oh no!" Sally exclaimed in protest, and knew that she
wanted—what did she want him to be called?—one of the names
written beneath the portraits in the long gallery at Stallingford.
Victor—that was impossible—Rollo—Anthony—Horatio. . . .

It was Aunt Hardcastle who settled it. Coming over to see the child, she brought word that his lordship, the Earl himself, would be glad to stand godfather, and that if Sally cared to choose one of his names for the child, he was quite willing. Aunt Hardcastle beamed at Sally, and declared that she'd rarely known his lordship more affable.

"One of his names," Sally said, thinking, 'he's afraid that I might choose Victor, if he didn't send that message'. She asked, "What are his names, Aunt?"

Looking like a stout herald, Aunt Hardcastle rolled out the names of the Earl.

"Charles—William—" she interpolated, "out of compliment to the late King—Anthony—Sixth Earl of Stallingford. Now, take your choice."

Sally said, "Anthony—I've always liked it."

Later Mrs. Watson talked with Sally, observing that the christening had been a great success, and having been told on good authority that the child shouted and screamed when the Vicar touched him with the water.

"I never heard anything like it!" Sally laughed. "I'd never heard him make a din like that before."

"It's good—varry good," Mrs. Watson declared, wagging her head. "It's t' devil being torn oot o' t' poor bairns. We're all born i' sin, an' habitations o' t' devil while we're christened, we all knaw that."

"Get along with you! How's the devil concerned with little bairns!" Sally laughed.

"Someone did tell me," Mrs. Watson continued more stiffly, for she distrusted any hints which inferred that the powers of the devil were limited, "that t' Earl weer his godfather. Ah could scarcelins credit it, Mrs. Scarth."

"It's true enough. His lordship's always been vary kind to me, and he sent the message with my aunt. That's why the boy's called—Anthony. After his lordship. My aunt's the god-mother."

"Noo, Ah niver did! Eh, that's a lucky thing for him, Ah sure."

But her eyes had narrowed, and her memory gone back to the night when Anthony was born, when Sally had said, "T' things are all i' t' kist, there—reit on t' top." She had opened the box and sure enough there were the baby's clothes, nicely made, good stuff, and plenty of them. Again Sally had said, "Aye, that's them!" Mrs. Watson had sharp eyes, and she had seen other clothes, lying below the first pile, clothes which "took her eye" and left her amazed. Such clothes—the finest lawn, lace which was assuredly real, tucks which were hand made and so small they scarcely looked like tucks at all. The next day, when Sally slept, she had gone back to the trunk, and quietly opened it. With hands that trembled with excitement, she turned over the clothes. On the top—good, and suitable things for the baby of Sally Scarth—underneath—almost hidden, as you might say, things which were fit for the children of Royalty. "Not the Princess of Wales' own bairns could have had finer," Mrs. Watson told Mrs. Brewer.

Mrs. Brewer wagged her head. "An' noo'—t' bairn's ter be named for t' Earl. Mrs. Watson, Ah can see as far threw a stane wall as maist folks wi' eyes i' theer heids. Mind ho' ondly doctor weer good enoof? Mind hoo yer told ma she opp an' spoake ter t' doctor? Saying as she'd send fur Halliday fur tuppence! Naay, Ah misdoot ma as theer's mair i' this than meets t' eye!"

"Ah've allus thout as yon Earl weer a reit gaston!" Mrs. Watson ventured. "Wi' yon gert yaller beard, an' yon masher glass dangling on t' end of a ribbin."

Together they spoke of their sorrow for William Scarth, of their doubts as to Sally's integrity ever since she first came to Wittingly. "Not bad, mind yer," they agreed, "boot summat strange aboot her, that Ah've allus thout, an' allus shall!"

William heard none of these tales, he had never been so happy in his life. Sally was better, the baby was strong and healthy, and had already shown signs of recognizing bright articles from dark ones. William hoped in his heart that the child's first articulate word might be, "Father" or its infant equivalent. Sally heard nothing and would not have cared if she had. She was interested, happy, amused by the baby, ready to work all day if by doing so she could make him more comfortable, make him grow stronger and bigger.

May came and went, June—and with June the roses which climbed over the walls of the cottage bloomed and sent their perfume in great gusts through the windows. The sun shone day after day, clumsy bumble-bees lumbered heavily through the air, sometimes getting into the cottage and banging themselves helplessly and stupidly against the window-panes. Sally would catch them and fling them out to freedom once more, saying, "Nay—what's wrong with you, great stupid! Outside's where you belong."

At night the "flittermice" whirled and swooped, by day the cuckoo—his song changed, grown harsh and less melodious, was heard in the woods. Young Anthony, lying in his cot in the garden, stared at the blue sky, where the great white clouds went sailing. His mother, watching him, standing beside him for a moment each time she came out of the cottage to hang washing on the line, to feed hens, or pull a bit of parsley, thought that he grew more lovely every day.

And Aunt Hardcastle came to tea. She praised Sally's cakes, praised the cleanliness of the cottage, noticed with pleasure, and said so, that Sally "spoke nicer than what you did a while back", and declared that Anthony was the best and most beautiful child she had ever seen.

Then, with the string of her bonnet untied, with a fresh cup of tea at her elbow, she had time to collect her thoughts, and deliver her news.

"I knew that there was something! We're all delighted at Stallingford, Sally, m'dear. At last, I said to Mr. Blachlet, at last! His lordship's going to be married! Now then!"

Sally jumped to her feet. "Really! Just a second, Aunt—I heard someone rapping at the door." She opened the door, looked out, up and down the road, then came back to the table. "No, I'm imagining things seemly. Going to be married—who to, Aunt?"

"The Hon. Millicent Crompson. Did you never see her, m'dear? Oh, elegant, very elegant. Just a leetle over-thin for my fancy, but—very elegant. They live—her family—at Crompson Mallard in—where is it, now—Bedfordshire or Dorset? I forget which at the moment. Her father is first cousin—or is it second cousin?—to the Duke of Norminster. Almost royalty you might say, yes, almost royalty. Her mother was a Miss Torrington from over Cumberland way. Liberals—or her father is—Lord Wayfleet. That's not what one would have wished, but no doubt she'll not bother her head with politics. They're not what you'd call a—political family."

"Oh, not a political family," Sally said.

"No, m'dear—not like the Devonshires or the Salisburys—but a good family. Good. Money, too—coal, Blachlet heard, in Cumberland—that 'ul be the mother's money, I don't doubt. Yes. Well, it appears that his lordship got engaged all in a hurry—about two months ago, but it wasn't announced until this week. It's in *The Times*—or it was. Of course everyone's delighted."

"Of course—they would be."

"So there we are! Waiting for a visit from the bride-to-be and his lordship. Oh, her ladyship told me that she'd told him about the boy here—about his lordship being godfather, and he'd written back to say that he was very pleased and—now what was it?—just a real bit of his fun—he hoped that all the good fairies had been at the christening to bring him—Anthony that is—presents. Just like him, full of fun."

Sally nodded. "Just like him."

"Tired, Sally?" her aunt asked.

"I've got a bit of a—headache. Nothing much."

"It's the sun—I get them sometimes, and as you know, when I've one of my really nasty heads, I'm good for nothing."

When she had gone, Sally picked the baby up, and carried him down to the end of the garden. It was queer how many of her problems she had hammered out standing there, with her eyes looking over the tree-tops towards the hills in the distance. Now, she thought mechanically, 'Those hills are too clear, we'll have rain within twenty-four hours.' He was going to be married—that was the end! Then the other Sally returned, 'Aye, and why not? You always knew that he must marry, always expected it, what's the matter wi' you?' She didn't know. Of course she had expected it, of course she had known that it must happen, but now that it had come—she winced as if a sudden stab of pain hurt her. 'It makes no difference to you! You never thought that he'd come back to you. He can't go on asking you to go away with him for ever. He asked you twice—how many men would have done that? He didn't even get engaged until—he knew that Anthony was born.' That was, queerly enough, some comfort, vague and indefinite, but a comfort just the same. Had he really waited, or had it only chanced that way? What did it matter? The child in her arms stirred, pucked up his face and whimpered.

"Nay, don't cry, my precious," Sally cried, rocking him gently, so that his face became calm again, his eyelids flicked and drooped over his eyes and once more he slept. Nothing mattered—she had known that it was all over—finished and done with—and what right had she to whine now over this piece of news—news which she had been expecting? She turned and walked back to the house, her head erect, her whole carriage telling of courage and triumph over the pain which she had suffered.

iii

In July she told William that she was going to have another
child ; he smiled with satisfaction, and said, "Nay, that's nice
ter hear. Ah dean't think it's reit fur onny bairn not ter have
sisters and bruthers." Then he chuckled. "We dean't waste
mooch time, do we ? An' afther all—why sh'ud we ? Nay,
Ah'm reit set oop aboot this noos, Sally."

She was glad too. She felt that in having this child—
William's child—she was, in part, wiping out the debt which she
owed him. The prospect did not dismay her, she knew her own
strength, was conscious of her own vitality. All through the
autumn she thought that she had never felt so well. She walked,
either carrying Anthony or pushing him in his perambulator.
Through the woods, gathering brambles, looking for sloes, and
later when in the early mornings the mists hung lightly over the
fields, only to be dispelled by the sun, which still shone with some
heat, looking carefully for mushrooms.

William said, "Eh, yer a gert walker, ower Sally."

She replied, "It's good for the boy, an' it's good for me."

"Nay—Ah'm glad as yer do," her husband assured her. "Ah
ondly wish as Ah could cum wi' yer. Naething as Ah like better'n
picking bumilkites along wi' yer."

"You and your funny old-fashioned names !" She laughed.
"What's the matter with calling them brambles ?"

"Ah dean't knaw—Ah've called 'em that naame since Ah can
mind—saame as moudiwarps, and pricky-back urchins—what
you call moles an' hedgehogs."

He eyed her affectionately. "Eh, it's nice ter be wi' yer, Sally.
Ah reckon"—he spoke more slowly—"as we get along better'n
what we did—maybe you like me more'n what yer did, eh ?"

"I like you very well, William," she said, "I'm fond of you.
I think that I've sort of settled down, got rid of a lot of my silly
ideas."

"If you've settled down," he said, "happen as Ah've pulled
mesen oop a bit, gotten a bit more'n yer levil, eh, Sally ?"

"Get along with you !" She laughed. "Old muddle-head !
My level indeed !"

William went back to work, she washed the dinner things,
tidied the house, then took Anthony, asleep in his perambulator,
to walk through the woods. She loved the quietness, the shade

broken by sudden splashes of sunlight through the spaces between the trees. Her eyes were quick, as are those of most country people, and she saw a thousand things which a townswoman would have missed. The white scud of a rabbit disappearing into the bracken, the sudden flash of a jay's blue among the green leaves, a patch of yellow water buttercups—bobblekins the country folk called them—growing where the ground was marshy, the quick fluster of a covey of young partridges, cheepers, William would have said, making a dash for the undergrowth—twenty sights and sounds which pleased and satisfied her.

She began to sing softly some old North-country song, sung by mothers to soothe their bairns to sleep for hundreds of years. One of those old songs, never printed, but passed down from mother to daughter down the years. A little song, with few notes in the tune, about babies and rabbits, about mothers who loved their bairns and fathers who worked for them, about cold winds and wild storms and children lying safe in their mother's arms. A comfortable little song, calculated to ease the fears of little children. Once Anthony opened his eyes and stared at her, and leaning forward she cried, "Aye, ma chucky, Ah'm singing ter thee—my bonnie lil' lad !"

As she stood upright again, she realized that Leister was within a yard of her, and the thought flashed through her mind, 'Nay, I don't want to be hurt ! It's over ! What's he want with me, why can't he leave me be ?'

He drew level with her, looked at her gravely, and said, "Well, Sally."

She answered, "Good afternoon, m'lord."

"My lord," he repeated. "You used to call me something else, once upon a time."

"Aye, a long time ago. That's all over."

"I don't matter any more ?"

"Isn't that best ?"

He looked at the sleeping child. "This is—the boy, eh ?"

"That's my son," she answered half defiantly. "My son, Anthony."

"You're fond of him, Sally ?"

With queer suppressed passion, she said, "He's everything in the world to me ! He's the sun and the stars, the spring and the summer. He's—the light of my eyes—that's what he is. That's how fond of him I am. Fond ! It's a poorish kind of word—fond !"

He nodded, and stood watching the child, absorbed, and she fancied unhappy. He had grown thinner, his face had lost its roundness, and much of its colour. Once she remembered she had told him that his cheeks were like the roses which grew on the wall by the entrance to the stable yard—"a kind o' warm rose colour," she'd said. She couldn't have said that now. Then he had said, "Those are the roses of the Lancastrians, Sally. I'm a Yorkshire man—the white roses are ours—Yorkshire's." He had shown her the white "York" roses and told her about the Civil War.

She had said, "Eh, history would be easy if it could be taught that way, wouldn't it ? With roses and gardens and words like pictures."

Now, abruptly, without turning to her, he said, "I'm going to be married—next week."

"I hope that you'll be happy, m'dear."

That had slipped out, she hadn't meant to say it ; only he looked old and unhappy, and her heart had gone out to him.

"No harm in hoping," he said. "It's nice to be called— m'dear again, Sally."

With a little spurt of jealousy leaping up in her heart she said, "There'll be others who'll call you—my dear."

He shrugged his shoulders. "I doubt it. 'Leister'—or in moments of wild affection—should they ever occur—'Victor'. Pah ! Why am I talking like that ? God knows. I'd have married you, Sally, stuck to you, loved you, been happy with you. Only now—you don't care for me any longer, do you ?"

"Not—in that way," she admitted. "I'll always be grateful to you. You gave me so much, you taught me so much. More'n anyone else ever will. I'd not wish that anyone else ever should. I must turn back—it's time the boy was home again. He'll be hungry, poor lamb."

"Yes," Leister said, "yes, of course. I shan't see you again. I go south tomorrow. This is just a last retrospective wander— closing the book. I go to Berlin ! You see, I'm developing into the hard worker you wanted me to be. Under-secretary, and a round of social stuff ! In reality I'm as much good as that child would be. But I shall be the Earl of Stallingford one day, and must be given pleasant work to do. My German is atrocious. I'm not even clever." He paused and looked at her intently. "You're growing very lovely, Sally. God, you'd have been some use at an embassy, with your sound common sense, and good heart! One day the nation will recognize that people—real people like you—are one of England's assets. Be happy, Sally—and thank you, because you were always kind—or at least always tried to be kind."

"Good-bye, m'dear," she said, "and God bless you."

"If ever I can do anything for—the boy—come to me and tell me."

"I should—of course I should."

"Will you kiss me good-bye?"

She hesitated, then said, "I'd rather not, it makes it all difficult somehow." Then her face cleared, and she said, almost eagerly, "I'd like you to kiss—the boy."

Leister frowned. "I don't know that I want to—I'm not sure that I'm not jealous of him. He's the reigning sovereign, I'm the deposed monarch. If it will please you, Sally." He stooped and brushed the child's cheek with his lips, then stood upright and smiled for the first time.

"Oh, Sally—how like you to make me do that. You've a great sense of the fitness of things, haven't you? If you hadn't possessed it to such an extent—I shouldn't be going south to my wedding! Good-bye, dear, darling Sally. Stupid, lovable, delightful, infuriating Sally." He took her hand, lifted it to his lips, then turned and walked away down the path, the way he had come.

Sally watched him. He did not turn, and presently she began to make her way home again. She felt curiously unmoved. Sorry, of course, that he had been sad, still more sorry that he sounded bitter and disillusioned. She wondered if she were to blame. He hadn't said that he admired Anthony—hadn't asked any questions regarding him. But he had kissed him. She whispered softly, "That 'ul be the only time your Da will kiss you, luvey."

As she made her way home, through the woods where the sun sent long, slanting rays, touching the tree-trunks and making them gleam like gold, she knew that Leister had lost his power to hurt her. She loved him—she would always love him—but it was a temperate love, utterly divorced from the wild passion she had once felt. Once he had been her dear love—now he was—"my dear". There was a world of difference, the two were poles apart.

As she wheeled the perambulator round to the back gate, she stopped suddenly, and laughed. William, coming to the back door, looked out and saw her.

"Why, Sally—tha's latish. But Ah've mashed t' tea soon as Ah heard t' gaate click. Ah were waiting on hearing that. What's t' joke, luv?"

She pushed the perambulator down the neat, narrow flagged path, still smiling.

"The woods were so nice," she said, "I saw this and that—flowers and birds, and one thing and another—and I've forgotten to get any brambles! That's what I set out to get."

He followed her into the house. The tea was laid, and the place looked homely and comfortable.

"Why, many a time folks sets oot ter get yan thing, an' cums back wi' anuther," he said. "An' oft times yan as good as t'other! Ah done it mesen, ganned oot ter get mushrooms, an' cum back wi' sloes or summat o' t' sort."

Sally nodded. "That's right, William. Pour out the tea while I feed the boy, will you? Eh, it's nice to walk out, but it's nice to come back to tea all laid. You're a good husband, William. You spoil me."

He poured out the tea, carefully and yet clumsily. "If Ah weer rich, Ah'd spoil thee reit enoof. Ah'd gie thee gold an' diamon's, carriage an' pair—a fine house——"

"Much I should care for any of them! Nay—only one lump—thank you."

CHAPTER FOUR

SALLY'S second child—a girl—was born almost exactly a year after Anthony. She was, as William said, "A nice lil' lass." Within a few months it was clear that she "took after" her father, with her rather indeterminate fair hair, and eyes which were blue only because they just missed being grey. William adored her, and would have been content to look after her all day long. He never felt quite at ease with Anthony, and found his large grey eyes disconcerting.

"Yon lad fair stares one oot of countenance," he told Sally. "Ah niver seen such a bairn fur staring! Ah allus wunder what he's thinkin' aboot."

"Maybe he'll tell us one day," Sally returned.

When Elsie was two months old, Aunt Hardcastle brought the news over to her niece that Leister's wife had produced an heir. Sally listened, surprised that the news left her so unmoved. Leister seemed to belong to another world, she felt that she scarcely remembered how he looked, that she could only recall the tones of his voice with difficulty. She thought that Anthony was like his father, but she had always felt that children were really not like anyone in particular, except that they might be fair or dark, and so claim a likeness to one or other of their parents. It was through William that she first realized how marked the child's looks were to those of his father.

William was standing beside the chest of drawers which served as a dressing-table, fiddling about with Sally's little boxes, while he discussed a new type of dahlia which Sir George had brought from London. He picked up the locket which old Mrs. Bishop had given Sally for her wedding day. He turned the locket over in his big hand, and murmured that it was a pretty thing.

"Aye, it's nice, isn't it?" Sally agreed.

Then she heard an exclamation, and found that William had turned it over and was staring at the little photograph inset into the back.

"When did'st tha have this done?" he asked.

Sally, taken aback at the question, said, "Have what done?"

"T' photer o' t' lad? Aye, it's good, reg'lar spit on him."

For a second she hesitated, then said, "Nay, that's not Anthony! It was in the locket when poor old Mrs. Bishop gave it to me. I asked her who it was, and it appears that it's some little nephew of hers, taken years and years back. Let me see it." She looked at the picture closely, astonished to find how exact the likeness was. "Nay, I don't see that it's so like him," she said, handing the locket back to William. "Most babies are something alike, that's all. It's just a photo of a bonny little bairn, same as what ours is."

William shook his head. When he got an idea fixed in his head, he clung to it with a tenacity which was astonishing.

"Why, Ah can see t' likeness, choose how," he insisted. "It's a reit likeness an all."

She laughed. "Get along with you. Once you make up your mind about anything, one can't shake it. You're always the same."

She put the locket away, half afraid to look at it again. The likeness was astonishing. Anthony at a year old was unmistakably like the picture of Leister at two years old. That night, when she bathed the child, she thought how different his slim legs and arms, his delicate wrists and ankles were to Elsie's sturdy limbs, sturdy even at a few months old. She noticed his, Anthony's, hair grew into a little peak at the back, very soft and smooth, but with a faint tendency to wave. His eyes were dark like her own, large and well shaped. He was admittedly a beautiful child, almost too beautiful, she thought. The kind of child that everyone would take notice of, wish to speak to, feel an interest in. She rebelled at the idea that living in a little village it was inevitable that people would speculate about him, some might even notice that he was like Leister. If only they lived miles away, where no one knew "the Family", and where no comparisons could be made! But William was sufficiently content at Wittingly, he got on well enough with Sir George, and gardener's jobs were none too easy to get. It wasn't likely that he would consent to try for another place further afield. She must just make the best of things, and be ready to laugh at any suggestions that her son was like the gentry. One thing was certain, as soon as Anthony was old enough he should go

away to school—even if by doing that she caused comment.
Gardeners' children did not go to boarding-schools.

Not that she allowed her thoughts to disturb her unduly.
The boy was still too young for his features to be particularly
definite. She could see the likeness ; William had only noticed
it because he happened to hold the photograph of Leister in his
hand ; it wasn't likely that other folks would see anything—not
for years anyway.

During the three years which followed, Sally Scarth was
remarkably happy. Life flowed on at an even pace, her children
grew, they were strong and healthy, rarely ailing, and therefore
good-tempered and tractable. When Anthony was four years
old, her second son was born, and named Thomas. He promised
to be like his sister—robust, heavily built and fair.

He had just begun to crawl about, getting under everyone's
feet, pulling things over, and generally proving a thorough
nuisance, when Aunt Hardcastle was taken ill, and, after a
short illness, died. Sally had been over at Stallingford for some
days before her death. Again she experienced that queer sensa-
tion of having returned home after a long absence. There
were changes in the servants' hall : Mr. Blachlet had gone to
live in retirement at Torquay, where he opened a small and very
exclusive private hotel. Mamzel too had gone, and returned to
Paris to live with a widowed sister. Mrs. Rogers, stouter and
redder than ever, was still at Stallingford, and Lingley still
attended on his lordship. The rest of the servants were strangers
to Sally.

Her ladyship was kind, declaring that Hardcastle must have
everything she needed. She talked to Sally about Leister,
about his wife and their son, Athol.

"A dear little boy, Sally, but—very delicate. His lordship
worries about him a great deal. You're lucky, your children
are strong, poor Hardcastle told me."

"All very strong, m'lady, thank you."

"What a blessing !"

The Earl came up to ask after her aunt, and stood talking in
the old nursery, one foot resting on the steel bar of the fender.
His golden beard was streaked with grey, Sally noticed ; there
was a network of wrinkles round his eyes. A new dog followed
him about now, Agamemnon was dead.

"I'm grieved about your aunt, Sally," his lordship said.
"One grows very fond of people—she's been with us for many

years. Done her duty always. Great thing—duty. Fine thing, noble thing. How did Halliday find her this morning?"

"She's sinking, m'lord. He said there was nothing to be done."

"Bad—bad. Deeply sorry, Sally."

She felt that he was trying to speak more intimately to her. He stood there, staring down at the fire, his lips pursed a little, his fingers beating a tattoo on the mantelshelf.

"Your only relative, eh, Sally?"

"Yes, m'lord."

"Ah—but you've got a good husband, I'm sure."

"I couldn't wish for a better, m'lord."

"Splendid! And the children——" She thought, 'This is what he has been wanting to say!' He continued, "Yes, the children. The eldest boy—called after me. My godson, eh?"

"Yes, m'lord, your godson. Anthony."

"Good boy, eh? Strong, healthy, well set-up, yes?"

"I'm thankful to say that he never ails anything, m'lord. Excepting measles and a cold now and then. Nothing."

He nodded. "Ah—different from poor Leister's boy. Nice little boy, but delicate—very delicate. Always something wrong with him. He's three, yes, three. I must come and see your boy one day, Sally. As a good churchman, I ought to know something of my godson, eh? Well, I'm glad—" he paused, "that everything's turned out so well. Yes, indeed—very glad. Good night, Sally."

"Good night, m'lord, and thank you."

It wasn't what he said, Sally reflected afterwards, it was what she felt he had wanted to say. "Ah—different from poor Leister's boy"—was there a hint of regret somewhere? She regretted nothing, except that one fact, that she had deceived William, that she was still deceiving him, if it came to that. They were happy together, it was very seldom that she lost her temper in these days. She had grown more tolerant; perhaps she understood William better. Perhaps she had come to understand that she had no right to try to make him conform to her ideas. He was hard-working, honest, kind to her and to the children, and what more could she, need she ask?

Aunt Hardcastle died in her sleep that night, and Sally found that she had left everything to her. She had been at Stallingford for over thirty years, she had saved, been careful of her money, and from time to time his lordship had given her advice regarding certain gilt-edged investments. She left more than four thousand pounds. His lordship, grave and sympathetic, advised Sally to "leave the money where it is—so far as investments go. They'll improve, slowly—but there's no doubt improve they certainly will."

After the funeral Sally packed her aunt's things and returned to Wittingly.

ii

William said, "Nay, tha's right, Sally luv. What wi' t' brass as Mrs. Bishop left tha, an' noo this. Happen we might move inter a bit bigger house, eh ?"

"Nay, this is right enough," Sally returned. "It's handy for your work, and I couldn't abide one of those nasty little red brick hutches on the Claverly Road. Like things bairns build with toy bricks and about as solid !"

So they stayed in the cottage, which Sally had come to love. She liked the red-brick floors, the wide open grate, the low roofs, and deep-set windows. The walls were thick ; the place was cool in summer and warm in winter. She loved the porch, with its stone seat on either side, and the flagged path which led to the gate, bordered with lavender which she picked and tied in bundles to lay among her linen. She had become a good housewife, and her herb teas, her cough mixtures, jams and pickles were justly renowned. Every season of the year brought its particular work, and with the years Sally found that she looked forward with pleasurable expectation to her various brewings and bakings.

At twenty-eight, she had broadened a little, her figure had become more full, but her movements were as quick and exact as ever. She boasted that she could do the work of two women and never feel tired. Men and women spoke of her as "that bonny wife o' Scarth's", and even old Sir George had said to William on more than one occasion, "Good-looking woman, your wife, Scarth. Keeps her children nice—credit to the village."

She was intolerant of incompetence, she hated "scuffing through work" and "slummocky women". She had forced herself to speak with barely a trace of dialect, yet when she grew impatient she could slip back into the old-fashioned words, which in moments of irritation seemed to her so much more expressive than the more conventional phrases.

"Sha werrits an' natters on an' grummels fra morn while neet," she would say of some woman who was never content, but when there was actual trouble, or when someone lay sick, Sally Scarth was willing to "lend a hand" and would contrive to do the work of her own house and the sick woman's as well.

"Tha's a champion," William said more than once, "tha never seems ter be scratting or ovver thrang, boot tha gets things done as no ither body does as Ah iver saw. Ah weer talking wi' Chuck Little t'other day. He tell'd ma as theer's niver no comfort i' t' house, allus washing henging aboot, or bairns scrabbling and wingeing on, or summat o' t' sort."

To which Sally would return with that superb intolerance of the successful housewife, "Why, what do you expect. Ellen Little's nobbut a poor shiftless thing ! No method, never has had. That kind are never done, for they've never learnt to make their heads save their heels."

She was respected and admired in the village, but she never gained the real affection of her neighbours. She was too reticent concerning her affairs, she disliked gossip, and confided in no one. She displayed no interest in the fact that "it was said" that John Moore was running after Joe Blenkinsop's wife, or that Alice, down at the mill had got herself in the family way to a lad from Bradford. Her only comments to such pieces of news were that if Joe Blenkinsop spent more time at home and less in the "Prince Charlie", he'd be able to keep an eye on his wife and her doings ; that if Charlotte Moore kept her house a bit sweeter, her husband would find it sufficiently attractive to sit at home. As for the misfortunes of Alice Carter and her lad from Bradford, Sally surprised and horrified everyone by saying, "Poor lass—I only hope that it's not true."

When Mrs. Brewer told Mrs. Watson that she was going to give Sally Scarth the rough side of her tongue for giving to every tramp on the roads, Mrs. Watson agreed that she had reason enough to speak.

"Living next door, like what Ah do," she said, "Ah knaw if onny one does. Not a day goes by boot sum mucky old tramp, some Egyptian or other, comes scawling oop Scarth's path. Every time it's, 'Nay, Muther' or 'Nay, Dad, Ah've not mooch brass, boot yer welcome ter a bit bread-an'-butter, an' a lump of cheese.' Ah get fair sickened wi' it."

Meeting outside Scarth's gate, Mrs. Brewer spoke. "Ah

surprised at yer, missus, for ever gieing ter them good-fur-nouts, Ah am reely."

Sally turned her wide grey eyes on the indignant Mrs. Brewer. "Are you ? Look at that now."

"Aye, it's all tergether all wrang, missus."

"Is it ? Who says so ?"

"Why—Ah do, and neebours do. We all do, all on uz."

"Then go on saying it ! Leave me to mind my own business."

"It's encouraging 'em ter cum threw Wittingly——"

"Aye, well, they can do wi' a bit of encouragement, missus, let me tell you that ! It's miserable work—cold work, dry work, walking and tramping on an empty stomach." Then with sudden irritation, "Have done, woman, and mind your own business and leave me to mind mine ! I'll give to who I've a mind, when I've a mind."

Mrs. Brewer, her mouth sagging open in astonishment, murmured, "Eh, luke at that noo", and returned to retail the story to Mrs. Watson.

The two gossiped with energy, they recalled the story of the baby clothes, which Mrs. Watson had seen at the time of Anthony's birth, they noted that Anthony bore not the slightest resemblance to either Elsie or Thomas, who might, so they stated, "ha' bin spat oot o' Will'um Scarth's very mooth". They remembered that the Earl was Anthony's godfather, and that her ladyship—"or soa Sally Scarth gie oot"—had sent presents, and sent them by no one less then her son and heir.

"Ef yer ax ma, missus," the irate Mrs. Brewer said, "theer's summat varry queer aboot t' hale thing !"

"She keeps' t' lil' lad dressed oop ter t' nines ! Lukes like some gentlemen's bairn."

"On Will'um Scarth's money ! Nay, niver i' this world, niver !"

"An' Elsie an' t' youngest are allus neat as nip !"

Both Mrs. Brewer and Mrs. Watson were partial to their glass—and even more partial to a succession of glasses—and their tongues wagged freely. The story began to circulate through the village. Finally it reached the ears of William Scarth, who having to dismiss one of the under-gardeners, had words with the man as to the cause of his dismissal. The man lost his temper, accused William, quite unjustly, of only keeping his own job because he had influence in high places, and ending his statement with the words, "An' ef yer content ter father anuther man's bairn an' ter hev a wife as is nout but a leet skets—so's yer can hould doown yer job—why, Ah hopes yer satisfied."

William said, "Here—what's awe this here? Other chap's bairn—leet skets—my wife! Ah'll show yer, yer gret good-fur-nout. Ah'll knock thee teeth doon yer throat!" Which William Scarth—who weighed nearly sixteen stone—proceeded to do, and do very effectively.

Sir George Cope, pottering round the gardens, came upon them, when William was administering the knock-out blow. He stood and watched the under-gardener sag gently at the knees, and sink ungracefully to the earth, before he spoke.

"Now, Scarth, what's this about? I don't allow this sort o' thing, y'know."

William licked his bleeding knuckles before he answered. "Nay, an' Ah dean't like it no mower nor what you do, Sir Garge, boot when things like this here"—he pointed to the recumbent under-gardener with the square toe of his boot—"speaks agean ma wife an' ma bairns, summat's got ter be done. Ah be lesser'n a man ef Ah didn't tak' steps."

George Cope was a gossip, he had few interests in life beyond his neighbours' business; he had still, at sixty-five, an eye for a good-looking woman, and Sally Scarth had struck him as being decidedly good-looking. His small, dark eyes shone with pleasure.

"Tut, tut, never heard such a tale! Of course you were right. Get up, my man, d'you hear me. Get up and take yourself off! Just give me a straight answer to a straight question. What's this you've said to Scarth here? Come on now, out with it!"

The man rose, and with hanging head mumbled that he had only repeated what he had heard. The story, he said, was all over the village, that one o' Scarth's bairns wasn't Scarth's at all, in a manner of speaking.

"And if it wasn't Scarth's—whose was it?" Cope demanded with a fierceness which concealed his curiosity.

"They do saay as it's his lordship's—Stallingford's."

"Good God!" Sir George ejaculated piously. "What a damned disgraceful thing to say! I never heard anything more abominable in my life. Stallingford! 'Pon my soul! You deserve a damned good horsewhipping! You—you—lout!"

"Ah ondly said w'at Ah'd heard i' t' pooblic!"

"By Gad, don't answer me back! D'you hear? Don't give

me any back answers ! Take your money and go, and let me catch you round here again and, by Jove, I'll set the dogs on you. Off you go ! Good-for-nothing blackguard ! Stallingford, well—upon my word !''

At tea-time, William found it impossible not to scan the features of his eldest son. Anthony sat munching bread and home-made jam, his small face intent on extracting every atom of enjoyment out of the process. He was growing tall, William reflected. Tall and well made. His hands were well shaped, his wrists were slender. His smile—for at intervals he looked up from his munching and met William's eyes–was delightful. Thomas, a solid child, never looked up from his food to smile and yet he scarcely seemed to derive the satisfaction from his meal that his elder brother did. Elsie, who was seven, drank her milk from a mug with a broad blue band round the top, and gurgled a little as she did so.

Sally said, "Drink nicely, Elsie luv.''

Elsie was understood to say that it was exceedingly difficult to drink without noise.

"That's because you've got your mouth full, my ducky,'' Sally returned. "Empty it before you drink.''

Thomas said, "It gie's it a luvely taaste ter swill milk aboot i' yer mouth wi' bread an' jam.''

His brother ceased eating and grinned at him. "Only pigs have swill,'' he said, "not boys.''

Sally said, sharply, "Get on with your tea, Anthony, and don't talk about pigs in that way.''

Thomas, who adored him, and who had the temper of a saint, said, "Muvver—An'nony ondly meant as——''

"Get on with your tea.''

No, William reflected, no one could say that she favoured one more than the other. They were all treated alike, given the same amount of clothes, the same treats, the same weekly pennies. She never made fish of one and flesh of another. But Anthony was unlike the other two, there was no getting away from that. Sally had always said that she loved his lordship, revered him, was grateful to him. It had been a distinct mark of favour when he stood godfather. He'd never offered to do it again. That was natural enough—there was always more fuss made over the firstborn. Might she not have been led astray by the attention of a man like that ? 'The wicked bastard !' William thought, adding mentally, 'Allus supposin' it's trew !''

After tea, when the children went out to play before bedtime, William still sat at the head of the table, his big heavy face clouded, his great shoulders slack, his whole attitude despondent. Sally watched him, then said, "What's to do, William?"

He looked up, frowning. "Luke here, Sally, Ah might as well get it off of ma chest. Hast tha heard onny taales gannen round t' village?"

"Plenty," she said easily. "I've never known such a place for old wives and wagging tongues. What is it now?"

"It's aboot—thee an' me," he said heavily.

She was busy at the fireplace, and turned to face him; for one moment a shade of anxiety crossed her face, but when she spoke her voice was still light and even amused.

"What have they to say? That you drink and beat me, or that I've gone off with old 'Fondie' Baker?"

"Nay, it's no matter fur joking, Sally. Ah gie'd a fellow a reit lammacing this marning fur saaying—what he did."

"Which was—?"

"That one o' t' bairns wasn't mine! That's what the dirty b—— said, aye, the low-down, mucky-tongued b——! Ah bloody well gie'd him summat an' it 'ull tak' more'n soap ter rub oot. Ah said——"

She came forward and laid her hand on his shoulder. "Nay, have done," she said, "I don't like dirty talk and you know it. No need to ask which of the bairns it was—though they'd say anything, these nasty old women!—for Elsie and Thomas are as like you as peas in a pod. It's Anthony, eh? And if he's not yours, whose is he, tell me!"

With his face purple with rage and emotion, but in some measure reassured by her apparent unconcern, William almost shouted, "Stallingford's!"

"Stallingford's—the Earl's!" Sally's relief was such that laughter came easily. She threw back her head, and William heard her laughter with gratitude. "I never heard such an old wives' tale in my life. The Earl! The man who found me in the House! I shouldn't think that he's ever so much as looked at anyone except her ladyship. Him—with that bright yellow hair, and Anthony's is a sort of pale brown. Him—with the brightest blue eyes I ever saw, and Anthony's are almost as grey as mine." Then, her voice changed, it was colder than William had ever heard it. "How dare they! How dare they say such a thing of him! Go and tell them, William, that you told me, tell them that I laughed, tell them, too, that if we hear any more of it, if it costs me every penny I've got—I'll go to law about it !''

She did not ask if he had believed the story, she did not want to be forced to tell him more lies ; she had hoped that the whole affair was over and done with. She had her son, her "dear lil' love", and that was sufficient. Dimly she wondered where and how the story had started, vaguely she speculated as to who was the originator of it all.

William sighed gustily. "Ah—that's good as Ah told thee, Sally. Ah weer reit down oopset. Eh—Ah didn't half paste t' chap as said it ! Ah gie'd him saame as what bottom o' peggy tub gotten ! Ah'll laay as he'll not oppen his mooth soa wide agean, choose how. Noo, Ah'll get me down t' garden an' redd oop t' hens a bit.''

He was satisfied, reassured, content. Sally watched his broad heavy figure as he made his way down the garden, and thought how pleasantly solid William was. Like a rock. You could depend on William—depend too that he would react in certain ways to certain suggestions. She sighed, wishing that she could be frank and above-board with him. Always when he had shown himself particularly kind, thoughtful or loyal she had these little qualms of conscience. She might work for him, she knew that no man had a better home, better food, greater comfort ; she hoped that she had repaid him—for all that he—unwittingly—had done for her, but there were times when doubts assailed her.

"All very well to say that I've paid him back, but a bargain's a bargain, and t' kind of coin's got to be agreed on by both parties. Will'um doesn't realize that I am—paying back.''

She had avoided catastrophe, she had apparently taken the story so lightly that William's fears, his suspicions, had been dispelled, but as she went to the door to call the children in, as she washed them and got them ready for bed, she felt queerly ashamed. She was a proud woman, and to feel mean and small not only hurt, but disgusted her.

'Not that it's any use crying over spilt milk,' she decided. 'I've myself to blame, not another soul. Maybe I was in a difficult position, but I'd no call to squirm out of it the road I did. There's no turning back now—look at it how you like. I must make the best of it. Hold my head high, and look them all in the face, and—laugh at them !'

iii

Sir George Cope, entertaining Sir Harry Cormick and Mr. Hebburn from Rastingly, recounted, and recounted he felt pretty smartly, the story of the morning's encounter with the gardeners. Cormick said that he'd dealt with it very well, 'Damned well', and that it reflected credit upon Sir George's loyalty. Mr. Hebburn said that, after all, such things were not unknown, and in his day, at least, had not been considered such a blot on a man's character. They agreed that people were getting damned narrow-minded, Puritanical, and that when all was said and done, men were men and women were women.

"Partic'ly pre'ry ones," Hebburn, who had enjoyed Cope's port, said.

Sir George, his face assuming that immense gravity of a man who is not quite certain that his tongue will obey the dictates of his brain, said, "Zackkerley—'s wharr I always shay."

Harry Cormick, whose head was reputed to be the strongest in the county, and was indeed the strongest in the Riding, listened attentively, and decided that he would not only recount the story when opportunity offered, but also give admirable imitations of both Cope and Hebburn.

William went that night to the "Prince Charlie" and when asked if it were true that he had half killed Noah Blessing, replied, "Summat damned near! Yon feller weer wrongly naamed—Blessing. *Pest* 'ud ha' bin a better naame fur him!" He then ordered a pint in a pewter tankard with an air of truculence, and receiving it banged the tankard on the counter so that the beer splashed all over his hand, and announced, "An' if soa be as any other b—— wants a bloody good hiding, so's he find not ondly his faace boot his backside sore fur a munth, kindly—one an' all—gie'd t' b—— me address."

The landlord, while applauding the sentiment, felt himself in duty bound to expostulate.

"Nay, nay, William, Ah didn't luke ter heard talk like that fra' thee, lad."

William replied darkly that he himself never looked to say or do a good many things that he might be called on to say and do, if he were bothered much longer by the kind of crawling reptile which called itself—Blessing.

The remarks, particularly the ability to call Blessing "out

of his name", went round the village, and was greeted as a piece of ready wit.

Harry Gledhill, the landlord, gave it as his considered opinion that "Ah allus knew as William Scarth weer a good man, Ah allus knew as he weer a respectable man, boot—Ah never knew as he weer a clever man. That saying of his concerning Noah Blessing—well, fur ready wit it 'ud tak' some beating, say what yer will!'"

And Sally walked through the village with her head held even higher than usual, and in the village shop, met the women's eyes steadily and coldly. One woman ventured to remark upon William's damaged hand, adding, "Ah did hear as he'd had words wi' Noah Blessing."

Sally replied, "That's right, missus, and if you've time to go and ask him, I don't doubt as he'll tell you what they were. Happen some of them might be useful to you when next you're weary of waiting for your husband to come home from 'the Prince'. Good morning, all."

Mrs. Hughes, stout and easy-going, folded her arms on the counter, and addressed her customers. "If onny on thee thinks ter git oopsides wi' Sally Scarth, Ah doot yer'll have ter be oop afore t' dew's off of t' grass. Happen she scrapes her tongue a bit, but she's a reit lass is yon."

Walking briskly back to her own house, Sally muttered viciously, "I'll learn 'em."

CHAPTER FIVE

SALLY always thought of 1890 as a black year, a twelve months filled with difficulties and trouble. A new and mysterious disease called "influenza" attacked the district. It came to rich and poor alike, the strong were as liable to succumb to it as the weak. At first everyone said, "Aye—it's a newish thing—boot Ah doot it's nobbut a bad cold wi' a fancy naame. Mak's doctors seem mower important like." Then one morning in February William came home to tell her that there was trouble over at the Manor at Stallingford.

For a second she held her breath, waiting to hear that Leister was ill, but William, who could never tell a straight tale in a straight way, lumbered on slowly.

"It weer Sir Garge as told ma," he said. "Cum along this marning an' tell't ma. He said as he'd met t' Earl—Stallingford —at railway station——"

Sally said, "Nay, William, get on wi' t' news. Don't hiver and haver!"

He blinked his eyes mildly in surprise. "Aye—Ah'm telling thee. Stallingford said as he weer theer ter meet sum gert Lunnon doctor—Sir Somethink Somebody—Ah dean't mind t' naame—ter tak' him ovver t' t' Manor. Seemly . . ."

Sally thought, 'It's coming now! Leister's ill!'

". . . Her laadyship's took wi' this noo complaint—'fluenzer. Noa, not Laady Stallingford, her young laadyship. Aye, baddish she is an' all."

Four days later, she heard that Leister's wife was dead, and stood at the gate—while the baker, who had given her the news, chattered on about the family, and the two children who were left—thinking about Leister. Wondering if he had loved her deeply, if he would miss her badly, and feel that his world was suddenly desolate and he himself terribly lonely. Elsie and Thomas walked over to Stallingford to see the funeral, and returned home with long stories of immense wreaths, and the length of the procession, and how pale Lord Leister had looked, walking with a little child on either side of him.

Elsie said, "Muther, the boy's just about my age, but he

lukes a lot young'n what I do. Right thin an' pale he is. The little girl—oh, she's bonnie! But she weer sobbing terribly. Lots o' people cried an' all when they saw her."

Sally clicked her tongue, and said, "I wish I'd not let you go. I don't hold wi' prying on other folks' grief!"

Thomas sniffed; he was tender-hearted and tears came easily to him. "Ah wished Ah'd not gone, Muther. It weer reet heartbreaking, soa it weer."

"Then drink up your tea, Thomas luv, and you'll feel better."

She watched them eating and drinking, thinking that she was glad that Anthony was away, somehow she felt that she would have hated for Anthony to go to the funeral. Like his brother, he was sensitive to other people's grief, and the sight of a funeral such as the others had witnessed would have upset him for days. Not that he was a molly-coddle. He could hold his own with any boy of his own age, but he was inclined to brood over things, to let them colour his imagination, and he suffered in consequence.

At fourteen, he was at school in the Midlands. She had been determined that he should obtain his education in a place where his antecedents were not known, where there would be fewer comments, and less questioning. William had looked doubtful, scratched his chin and given it as his opinion that it was "no use o' eddicating a lad above his station i' life"; but Sally had replied smartly that Anthony's station would be what he could make it, and that she saw no reason why he shouldn't make something of his life. William was fond of his children, but he left all decisions to Sally, and after his one small protest accepted her ruling that Anthony should go to a boarding-school.

"Mind you," she said, "Elsie and Thomas can go and all, if they show signs of caring for books and such like. From what I can make out they'd both rather run a mile than open a lesson buke. Anthony's never happy without books or papers, he's for ever reading something. The money's there—Mrs. Bishop's and Aunt Hardcastle's—and it's going to be used for the bairns. Give them the chances we never had, William."

Elsie at thirteen was tall and solidly built. She looked what she was—a healthy, pleasant country chiid. She hated lessons in any form and confessed to Sally that she wanted to be a dressmaker.

"If that's what you've set your mind on," Sally said, "that's what you shall be, my dear, only you must be a good dressmaker. I'll not have you spending your life making Sunday clothes for village lasses. You can go to Jane Baxter for a year to learn to baste and gather and so forth, but after that you'll have to be apprenticed to someone good. I'll maybe speak to her ladyship about it. She'd know the best places—sure to."

Thomas, snuggling up against his mother, rubbed his untidy fair head against her shoulder, and said, "Mum—can I be a gardener like what my Da is ? That's what I'd like. Can I, Mum ? When can I leave school, Mum ? I hate it—I won't plant things no better for learning sums an' grammar, will I ? I'm ten, Mum—when can I leave school ? Soon, eh ?"

"When you've passed into the sixth standard and not a minute before, my lad. I'll have no ignoramus for a son, choose how !"

Thomas pouted his full lips, slanted a glance at his father, who shook his head.

"Nay, tha' muther's reit, saame as what she allus is. Ah'd 'a bin a lot better off if Ah'd had a bit mower schooling. It's a handicap ter a chap not ter be able ter spell all t' fancy naames o' flowers when he's writing oot list fur t' seedsman."

"What kind o' names, Da ?"

"Why—" William hesitated, "theer's auricula—hardy perennial. You'd think as it started wi' a 'o'. Boot it's a 'a'. Theer's calliopsis—Ah allus thout as it weer—c—a—lly—hops— sis. It's nout like it ! Dahlia—that's no soa easy as tha'd think. No mower is gypsophila. How'd tha spell that, Thomas lad ?"

Thomas, puckering his forehead, gave it as his opinion that there was only one way, and that was, "G-i-p—s-o-ff—o—l-a-h."

"Ah—Ah'll lay as thee muther knaws different ! Tha's wrang, Thomas ! Nay, tha mun study a bit mower yet, eh, Muther ?"

Sally watched him, talking to the children, listened to his slow, deep voice, with its broad comfortable accent. Noticed how he smiled and how his eyes crinkled at the corners. Saw his huge capable hands, planted on his knees, and thought—as she had done so often—how solid and dependable he was. He had put on weight very much, his movements had become clumsy, but when he came to handle plants, rose bushes, and seedlings those big hands of his were as gentle as a woman's when she handles her baby. He had never given her a moment's anxiety. He loved his work, his home and his children. She

N

knew, too, that he gave her absolute devotion. He still found his greatest pleasure in walking with her on Sunday afternoons, when he would lumber along through the woods, talking of the country sights and sounds, completely content, asking nothing more of life than to be with her and the children.

That night, when they were alone, sitting in the "houseplace" after the children had gone to bed, she looked up to find his eyes watching her intently.

"A penny for your thoughts!" she challenged.

He smiled, that slow, wide smile of his. "Nay, Ah'll mak' noa charge, Sally lass. Ah was thinkin' as it weer a varry good life as we'd gotten tergether. A nice lil' home, t' best bairns i' t' world, enoof brass ter get along wi, an' as fur ma—why, Ah reckon as Ah've fahnd t' finest wife not i' t' three Ridings, boot i' all England. Ah'm a varry contented chap—an' reitly! That's what Ah weer thinking."

She gave him back his smile, and leaning forward laid her hand on his knee.

"Change that bit about the finest wife—to the finest husband, and I could say all that and a lot more. I'm a very happy woman, my dear."

"Eh—it's varry nice ter hear tha saay that, Sally luv. Ah have it i' ma heart ter believe as tha means it, an all."

"Every word of it!"

He nodded. "Aye—well, Ah'll awaay ter ma bed. Cuming, m' dear?"

"I'll just lay things for breakfast, then I'll come."

ii

Two days later, Sally observed at breakfast that March had come in like a lion, and looked like going out like one. William said that after all a peck of March dust was worth a king's ransom, whatever that might be worth, for he'd never heard a sum named. Thomas repeated in a high sing-song voice, "March brings breezes loud and chill, Stirs the dancing daffodil."

His mother said, "Aye, loud and chill. Wrap a scarf round your neck, William, and see that you get Cook to give you something hot for your elevenses."

After he had gone she found that he had left the knitted scarf hanging in the back kitchen. She sent Thomas flying

after him with it, but William—who hated "feeling muffled"—
sent it back, saying that he didn't want it, and that "muffled
cats made bad hunters".

Exasperated, Sally cried, "Drat the man! I'm not asking
him to wrap it round his hands, the great gormless thing!"

He came home that night, complaining that he felt chilly.
Sally scolded him, told him that he was more bother than the
bairns all rolled into one, and proceeded to dose him with treacle
possets, and later with whisky and hot milk. In the morning
he declared that he was better, "reit as rain, barring a bit o'
headache," he said. At midday he came home and announced
that he was taking the rest of the day off from work. He ached
all over, he said, felt hot and cold at once, and admitted that he
would be glad to lie down, with a hot brick to his feet. The
next morning Sally sent for Dr. Halliday.

William laughed breathlessly, coughed and managed to say
that she was making a lot of fuss about nothing and that Halliday
would only mock at her for an old wife.

Instead, Halliday shook his head, saying, "Ah, I wish you'd
sent for me sooner!" and admitted that William had congestion
of the lungs.

Sally nursed him with a kind of passionate intensity for four
days. She never slept, never took off her clothes, and felt that
she would gladly have given the last drop of her blood to ease
the pain which seemed to tear his chest when he coughed.

It was on the evening of the fourth day, when Halliday came
for the third time, that he told her William was dying. She
stood clutching the edge of the table, swaying a little, her face
white and haggard.

"Is there nothing can be done?" she whispered.

"My dear, you've done everything," Halliday said. "No man
ever had a more devoted nurse. His weight is against him. All
that fat. You've done all and more than one could have
expected."

"How long has he?"

"It's difficult to say—six hours, ten, twelve—even twenty-
four. If you want to send for the eldest boy—I should telegraph
immediately. I'll send it off for you, if you like, as I go past the
post office."

Sally nodded. "Aye—William's been a good friend to
Anthony——" Then correcting herself, because caution had
become automatic, "Friend—father, I mean. I can't speak

straight ! If you'd send it, Doctor—that's the address. Thank
you kindly."

William lay very quiet, only his difficult breathing seemed to
fill the room. As Sally entered, his eyes met hers. She came to
the bed and took his hand in hers, feeling that if she held it tightly
she might pass some of her own strength to him.

He said hoarsely, "Ah'm baddish, seemingly, ma lass."

"Nay, we'll soon have you right," she assured him. "The
worst's over, you only want feeding up. And"—she managed to
smile—"trust your Sally to do that, eh ?"

"Ah'd trust ma Sally wi' aut an' everything," he said.

Anthony came the next morning He raced from the station,
arriving panting and breathless, demanding, "How's Father ?
How's Father ?"

Sally laid her arm round his shoulders. "Go up, my dear—
say good-bye to him."

"He's—not—dead ?" The boy's face was white.

"No, no—but he'll not be here so long now."

When Anthony came downstairs again, to stand with his
face buried in his arm, leaning against the mantelpiece, she
went up to William. As she mounted the stairs she could hear
her son's sobs, until they seemed to become merged into William's
short tearing breaths.

William said "Hod' ma hand, luv. Ah've seen t' lad. Good
lad yon."

She felt her whole body stiffen. She couldn't deceive him
any longer. It was almost too late, but she must make the best
of what time she had.

"William, my dear," she said, "I've gotten something to tell
you, something I ought to have told you years ago, but I was
cowardly—I didn't trust you enough——"

"Nay—h' done !" William said. "Ah knaw, luv. Ah think
as Ah allus knew. No call ter get oopset. Tha's made a reit
do on ower marriage, m'dear. A reit do. Yon's a good lad—Ah
luv him as if he weer—my son."

She bent over him. "Tha's ovver good, William, ovver
good. How didst tha knaw ?"

For a second she fancied that his eyes twinkled. "Ah've
eyes i' ma heid, luv. Boot t' cháp weren't—Stallingford !
Niver mind who—still tongues mak' glad hearts. Ah'm a varry
contented, loocky chap—dear luv. Go' bless thee." He closed
his eyes, and she thought that he slept. Once he opened them

and said, "Dean't leave go of ma hand, luv." He did not speak again, and soon after midday he died.

She had never known that grief could be so devastating. She felt that it was a physical thing, something which tore and twisted her, which battered and bruised her. She resented his death passionately. Why should William, only thirty-nine, have died and left her ? Why should he, who had never harmed anyone, who asked only to be allowed to work for her and his children, be taken when wasters and runagates like Mitchell, and Matt Gibson, were left ? Why had William to die, in the prime of life, when poor creatures like "Fondie" Baker dragged out a miserable existence, and lived lives which helped no one ?

Standing at the back door, the morning after William died, she realized that she had been wrong. March was going out like a lamb. 'Aye,' Sally thought bitterly, 'it's done all the damage now, William's killed—through that bitter wind, and now it's changed its mind seemly.' She felt that she hated the sunshine, the blue sky where the white clouds sailed so serenely. She hated the distant hills, the tall trees, the bright patches of ling. Gorse, William had called it sometimes, chuckling and saying, "When t' gorse is oot o' bloom, then is kissing oot o' fashion." How often had he said that, invariably ending with, "Why, lass —as t' gorse bean't oot of bloom, so seemly kissing's not on-fashionable. Reckon as Ah might ax fur one, Sally ?"

The children were miserable—but, curiously enough, it seemed that Anthony felt William's death more acutely than either of them. He was useful, she didn't know what she'd have done without him. He was only fourteen, but he had the ways of a grown man. She had heard him talking to the undertaker, listened with a queer little thrill of pride to him giving his orders. There was nothing subservient in his tone, no—"Just what you think, Mr. Bowman," or "You'd know better than I should, Mr. Bowman."

"The best, please," he had said, "the very best for my father, Mr. Bowman."

A man wearing a bowler hat and a coat with a rather greasy velvet collar came to see about William's insurance. It was Anthony who brought out the policy, and sitting at the table with the man listened and gave his assent. Not that he wasn't suffering ; there were times when Sally wished that he would sit still and not bother himself. He looked white and drawn, she thought that he didn't eat enough, and there were dark-bluish marks under his eyes. Not that he wasn't a help and a comfort, not that he didn't try to comfort his brother and sister, but she felt that he was showing too markedly the difference between them. Already several women had said, "Yon eldest boy of yours has a reit way wi' him", and "Eh, your Anthony—talks as if he'd bin uster gie orders all his life. Not rude nor cheeky, mind ye, but—well, measter o' things, as you might saay."

When the Vicar called, it was Anthony who talked to him, while Sally sat by the fire wiping her eyes, wishing that the man—kind enough though he was—would go away.

"You must be relieved, my boy, that you were home in time to speak to your father."

Anthony replied, "I was, sir. He was always simply splendid to me—to all of us."

"I was speaking to Sir George Cope only this morning. It will comfort you to know that he tells me your father always did his duty, performed his work to the very best of his ability." The tone was kindly, but faintly pompous. Sally saw Anthony's chin go up a little, heard a queer cold note in his voice, which reminded her suddenly of Leister.

"Thank you, sir—but it would have been impossible for Sir George—or anyone else—not to admit these things. We—my mother and I—have always known them."

Not "Sir George Cope", simply "Sir George", Sally thought. Not disrespectful, but not occurring to Anthony to say anything else.

"You've sent this boy to boarding-school, Mrs. Scarth, I hear. I'm afraid now that he'll have to buckle down and forget his—er—lesson books. Be a prop and stay for you, eh?"

It was her turn to stand on her dignity a little. "That's as may be, sir. It depends on what Anthony wants to do."

The Vicar wagged his head gently. "Beggars can't be choosers, Mrs. Scarth."

"We're far from being that, thank you, sir."

"Really!" Sally thought that he sounded faintly disappointed. "Really! Has Scarth saved money then?"

"We've not been into my husband's affairs as yet——"

"I should have thought that with a wife and three children— well, I don't wish to discourage you, Mrs. Scarth, but I don't think that you can rely on Scarth having left you——"

That was when Anthony rose to his feet. He looked so slim and tall in his black jacket and striped grey trousers, with his wide white collar ; his head was thrown back a little, and a faint colour tinged his cheeks.

"Forgive me, sir, but might I respectfully suggest that my mother is tired, and unhappy. My father told me to take care of her. I don't think that she wishes to discuss our affairs at the moment. Might I suggest—sir—that my mother would like to rest ?"

The Vicar stared. He was a mild enough mannered man, possessed of an astonishing curiosity regarding other folks' affairs. He had "heard things" regarding Sally Scarth, regarding this boy who stood there talking to him as if they were equals !

He said, "Well—really—I don't know—I'm not usually——"

"No, but my mother isn't like—other people. She is—unusual, sir."

"Then," suddenly regaining his composure, and becoming huffy, "I will wish you a good evening."

"Good evening, sir. I'll open the door, the latch is a little stiff."

Yet to the landlord from the "Prince Charlie", to old Harry Somersgill, to Jack Tinker when they came to "see t' last o' William", the boy was kindness personified. Not only did he escort these old country men to the death chamber, standing by them while they made their queer, apparently blunt remarks which in reality hid such a wealth of genuine affection, but later he offered them his mother's famous cordials with an air which could not have been bettered. On the day of the funeral, which was attended by Sir George Cope and the agent from Stallingford —"representing the Earl"—Sally, despite her grief, could not prevent herself indulging in a sense of pride. Anthony, though obviously suppressing his emotion, attended to everything. Little Thomas, in his stiff new black suit, whispered to Sally, "Bean't ower Anthony wunnerful, Muther ?" ; and Elsie— through her sobs, for she possessed little restraint—watched her elder brother with eyes filled with admiration. It was queer, Sally thought, how the pomp of even such a modest funeral as that of William Scarth helped to "hold you up". It was impossible for her to give way completely while people were watching, and so from the cottage to the church, from the church to the graveside, she walked with head erect, Anthony on one side, Thomas and Elsie on the other. Only when it was all over, when everyone had been regaled with those good things which are part of a traditional Yorkshire funeral "spread", did she feel

that someone had cut the invisible string which held her upright,
and that she longed to sit down, relax, and talk quietly to her
children. Her children——! In her heart she knew that what
she really wished for was to talk to Anthony about the future,
and what it might hold for them all.

It seemed that, despite all their affection for their father,
the end of the funeral ceremonies had come as a relief to Elsie
and Thomas. Sally knew that they felt happier, less restrained,
that their tongues were loosened now that their father was
buried 'It's right, too,' she thought. 'Why should bairns be
made miserable and depressed ? For them to have a corpse in
the house is too much. They don't rightly understand what it
all means—it's hard for them. I'm glad they've managed to
laugh a bit, poor little souls.'

She knew that she herself was stunned, that her lack of any
acute feeling of desolation was chiefly due to the fact that she
had not yet fully realized what William's death meant to her.
That would come later. There would be those hours when she
must look through his clothes, fold them and put them away ;
when she must decide what her future life was to be, come to
decisions regarding the children. Not that William had ever
interfered with her plans or suggestions, but it had been a
comforting thing to know that she could talk, while he listened.
His comments had never been remarkable for their imagination
or their profundity, they had been in the nature of an accompaniment to her thoughts, they had served sometimes as a
brake when she was apt to be too impulsive. She could still
hear his slow speech, "Nay, Sally, Ah'd not be ovver sharp, if
Ah weer i' thy shooes", or "Nay, lass, gan slow, it 'ul paay thee
i' t' end." There had been, too, his endless selection of queer
Yorkshire sayings, proverbs and the like, which he always uttered
as if he had only that moment evolved them from his inner
consciousness.

"Ah'll tell thee what," he would say, gravely considering the
bowl of his pipe, which he held in the hollow of his hand. "Yon
chap's as friendly as a bram'l bush—Ah can't saay no fairer" ;
or, "Ah've nout good ter saay fur yon lass—she's as common as
a deear snek—onny chap can handle her !"

Now, with Thomas and Elsie safely in bed, with Anthony
sitting opposite to her in William's chair—he had said tentatively,
"Do you mind if I sit in this chair, Mother ?"—she felt relaxed,
and able to think clearly for the first time since her husband

died. Until now she had scarcely remembered that she had tried
to tell him about Anthony, and now she thought that she could
hear again his hoarse whisper as he assured her that he knew.
Vaguely she wondered how he had found out, and with that
speculation came comfort that he had said that he had been
content and happy.

He had borne her no grudge, he had said nothing which could
hurt or wound her ; there had been no recriminations—that
wouldn't have been in keeping with his character. She did not
concern herself deeply with the question of how he had known
about Anthony. What did that matter ? Somehow, somewhere
he had gained the knowledge—and he had never allowed it to
influence him in the least.

She said to Anthony, "We've lost one of the grandest men
that God ever gave breath to."

He nodded. "Yes, I think so too. He said to me, when I
went up to see him"—for a moment she saw that the boy's lips
worked and that he was hard put to it to keep back his tears—"he
said that I was the firstborn, that I'd always to look after you,
and behave well. He said that you were the finest woman in
the world."

She sighed. "Aye, poor William, he thought that. I've my
doubts, Anthony."

"I've not," he returned stoutly.

Sally smiled ; it was good to hear her son praise her. She
began to speak to him of their future, forgetting that she spoke
to a boy of fourteen, treating him as she might have treated a
man of her own age. She told him of Thomas's wish to be a
gardener, and he interrupted to say that if Thomas wanted that,
then he ought to learn something about the scientific side.

"It's all right, Mother," he said ; "but in these days everyone's got to—specialize. The old rule of thumb days are over.
He ought to go to a proper college and learn about patent manures
and all kind of—well, fancy things. Then he'll be able to demand
good wages."

"Aye, I expect that you're right, only Thomas is no scholar."

"Then he must be apprenticed to some good man," Anthony
insisted. "Some big market gardener, who'll teach him properly.
No use going to Sir George as a garden boy."

She talked of Elsie, and of her determination that she should
learn under a first-class dressmaker, and finally she spoke to
Anthony of his own future.

"You've all got to have chances," she said. "I've gotten a bit of money, and Da left us something—about a hundred pounds with his insurance and clubs. We're all right for money. What ideas have you, son ?"

"If it's possible," he said, "mind, only if it's possible, I'd like to stay at school until I'm sixteen—another two years. I think that I might get a scholarship—drawing. I don't want to be an artist, Mother—I mean not to paint pictures, I want to do things like you see in *Punch* and papers like that. What's called—a black-and-white artist. I could work that in with journalistic work, if I've enough education. There is money in it, and—a future, Mother. Is it possible ?"

"Why, it sounds a queerish way of earning a living," Sally said, "but—how'd you get a start, Anthony luv ? I mean, you'd have to get work on a paper, wouldn't you ?"

"That's it !" he said eagerly. "That's it ! There's a boy at school, his name's John Clifton, his father has a paper called the *Warningshire Herald*. That's only a—sideline. He's really interested in a big London paper—the *Comet*. He's—important."

"Aye, I've heard of the *Comet*," Sally said.

"John is a friend of mine ; he's clever, Mother. He showed his father some drawings that I did. Funny ones—to illustrate jokes, y'know. His father came down to see him, and John took me to have tea with him. He said that when I was sixteen, unless I'd gone backwards instead of forwards, he'd find a place for me. First on the *Herald* and then—later on the *Comet*. What a chance, Mother, eh ? It's—astonishing, isn't it ? If I can work and perhaps if I got a scholarship, he'd let me work that out, and then take me on. You see, if I had a scholarship I shouldn't cost much to keep, should I ?"

He was leaning forward, his hands clasped round his knees, his eyes shining, his whole face alight with expectancy and excitement. She sensed that this was the first time that he had really voiced his hopes to anyone, and her heart filled with affection for him. She had always loved him, sometimes so much that she was afraid that she might—unconsciously—make a distinction between him and her other two children. Sometimes it had been difficult. She had always feared a little that William might notice not only a difference in her treatment of Anthony, but in Anthony himself. He might have seen, as she didn't doubt that others had seen, that Anthony was built in a finer mould. Well, now William knew—he had said so, and assured her that his knowledge had brought no bitterness with it. He had been content—and now, on the evening of his funeral, Sally Scarth felt nearer to William than she had ever done. It was as if for the first time they clasped hands, conscious that there was no barrier between them. All barriers were down. and understanding had come with knowledge.

She said, "If that's what you want—that's what you shall have, my dear. It will be hard work, I don't doubt, but hard work never hurt no one. There 'ul be enough for us all, I don't fear that, and even if there wasn't, I'm still able to work—until"—she laughed with the pleasure that the words brought her as she spoke them—"until you can keep me, when you begin to make money."

The next day he went back to school, and Sally felt lonely, 'lost' she said to herself. There seemed so little to do in the cottage, without William. The two children were out at school all day, they went to bed early, and the long evenings stretched before her, to be spent alone in the houseplace. She had never been a great reader, at most she did little more than read the weekly local paper to William, while he sat and smoked, making his comments at intervals. She had never made any particular friends, women had never "dropped in" to gossip over the fire with her. She felt no particular interest in her neighbours and their little affairs.

The spring came, the evenings lengthened, days became warmer, and Thomas—who loved working in the garden—kept her table supplied with bright flowers. She knew that she looked forward to Anthony's holidays, when she would have someone with whom she could talk, and exchange ideas. Thomas and Elsie were good children, but Elsie cared only for making clothes, and Thomas promised to be a silent fellow, as his father had been. During the three months which followed William's death, Sally felt like someone marooned on a desert island, trying vainly to find sufficient to occupy her during the long days, and the interminable evenings.

Once Lady Stallingford drove over, and spoke kindly concerning William's death. She looked old and tired, Sally thought, and her voice had grown monotonous in tone. Leister, she said, broken by the death of his wife, had taken a trip round the world. Later he might take up politics, they were not certain. He had felt attracted to land improvement, but there had been difficulties. It all sounded vague and rather unsatisfactory,

Sally thought. It wasn't good for a man, and a young man, to be without work. William would have said, "Satan 'ul find sum badness fur them wi' idle hands, mark ma words."

'I'll watch that my lad isn't idle,' she decided, while she answered, "Yes, m'lady, well, that 'ul be very nice, to see his lordship in Parliament, I'm sure."

"I worry a good deal about the children, Sally," Lady Stallingford continued. "Such dear little children—well, Athol isn't very little now—twelve. Muriel's only ten. He's far too delicate to go to school, and tutors give so much trouble! Or they seem to at the Manor. If only we had our dear old Bishop with us still—ah, dear! You've never thought of—taking a place again, Sally?"

Sally drew a deep breath. To live again in a big house, with gardens and no prying neighbours. To have plenty of work, to know that if you were lonely there would always be someone to talk to. To have charge of linen, and china and silver—the special bits of silver, like christening cups and so on—to make clothes, mend, darn.

"Why, no, m'lady. Of course not—while my husband was alive—and the children still too young. Thomas is only ten, y' see, and Elsie—thirteen. One day—I don't know——"

Her ladyship rose. "One day—yes, well, we might talk about it again, Sally. One day——"

CHAPTER SIX

In 1893, the Earl of Stallingford, travelling to the United States to visit his daughter, Lady Gwendoline Vanderholt, was drowned in the sinking of the *Eastern Star*, when she came into collision with an iceberg and went down with all hands. To Sally Scarth his death came as a real and personal loss. She had not seen him for several years, except on one occasion when riding to the meet at Wittingly Hall, he passed, magnificent in pink coat and white buckskins, through the village. He had seen her, and raised his crop to his hatbrim in greeting, calling, "Good morning, Sally! Good morning."

He looked older than his years warranted, Sally thought. The famous beard, beloved of caricaturists, was more grey than gold, and his shoulders were a little bowed. When she heard of his death, it was not as the elderly man on a raking chestnut horse that she saw him, but as the Chairman of the "Board", who had asked questions of a small pauper child, and laughed because he could speak dialect almost as broadly as she could. She remembered every word that he had spoken, could have reproduced every inflection, as she had done more than once for her aunt and Blachlet in the sitting-room at Stallingford.

The light had caught his eye-glass, she remembered, as he had turned, smiling, to speak to the other gentlemen—Sir Trafford Motley, Mr. Cormick and Sir John Wittersley. Others, too, she could not remember. She recalled the cold eyes of the matron, and the smell which always hung about her black bombazine dress.

Thomas said, "Was he nice, Mum—the Earl?"

She replied, "He was good, Thomas. He was all that a great gentleman ought to be. Never so taken up with his own grand position that he'd not time for the poor, and weak and down-trodden."

Elsie asked, "Is that him who's Anthony's godfather?"

"Anthony's named for him."

Sally thought that she felt as women must feel when their fathers die. She had never known a father, and Stallingford had filled her childish heart with all the reverence and love she would have given to one. She thought, scarcely formulating the idea, that but for him she might now be the Countess of Stallingford. The thought brought no sense of injury. Things were better as they were—she had her children, she had known the love of a good husband, and, Sally told herself, 'A pretty countess I'd have made !' As the years had passed, she had come to think more often of the Earl than she had done of Leister. Stallingford had made his mark, he had organized improvements, he had drawn up schemes, his estate was famed for its excellence and the comfort of its cottages. Other landowners had copied him, but he had been one of the pioneers. He had boasted that beyond voting according to the dictates of his party, he had never concerned himself to any great extent with matters political. Sally had heard it said that he often quoted lines from some play, which Mr. Blachlet had said would be hard to beat.

"So far as memory serves me," Blachlet said, "they run something like this :

"While the House of Peers withholds its legislative hand,
And noble statesmen do not itch
To interfere in matters which
They do not understand,
As bright will shine Great Britain's bays . .

And the rest has escaped me."

She attended the memorial service at Stallingford, and let her eyes rest on Leister as he stood there, at his mother's side, looking aloof and sad in his deep mourning. The day was fine, and the sun slanted through the stained-glass windows, making splashes of colour on the old stone flags. Those windows—she knew them all—knew why and when they had been given to the church. The one by the font—"In memory of Caroline, wife of Hubert, fifth Earl of Stallingford"—that was his lordship's mother ; the one of David slaying the giant Goliath was in memory of his lordship's younger brother, who had died in the Crimean War. She had heard old "Gaffer" Watkins explain to visitors, "The faace o' yoong Daavid is tak'n fra a portrait o' t' Honourable Capting hiss'en." The raising of the widow's son at Nain, over the tablet in memory of Victor, third Earl, was "given as a thankoffering for the recovery of His Royal Highness, Albert Edward, Prince of Wales. February, 1872." The Prince had been quite young then, Sally thought ; now he had grown-up sons and daughters. The east window, with its harsh colours

typical of the period, was more recent, put in on the occasion of
the Earl's silver wedding "as a thanksgiving to Almighty God".
The tablets, the tombs, the bronzes, she knew them all—each
one in memory of some dead-and-gone Stallingford who had done
his duty, and done it without ostentation. It was like reading
history, Sally thought—the wars against Napoleon, fights at
sea, the Indian Mutiny, the Crimea—back to those tablets
which were becoming smooth and illegible through time, so that
the rounded cheeks of the stout cupids were losing some of their
rotundity. The colours were fading from the tomb of Arthur
and Elizabeth Stallingforde praying with their thirteen children
kneeling behind them in two neat lines ; the detail of the armour
on the recumbent body of Sir John, who had been killed, Sally
remembered, in some wars called Crusades, was blurred.

'The past,' she thought, 'the Stallingfords of once upon a
time, and there—the present and the future. Leister and his
son Athol.'

Leister, tall, stooping a little, his brown hair thinning at the
temples, his sensitive face drawn round the mouth and nostrils.
Watching him, Sally thought that even he had not escaped the
touch of time. He was no longer the vivid young man she had
known, she felt that his outlines had become a little blurred
like those of Sir John, or of Arthur and Elizabeth. William
would have said that he looked "a bit waffley like", and as she
remembered the words she felt a spasm of disloyalty. This was
no time to judge a man, when he was attending a service in
memory of his father, who had died so tragically.

He was still young, thirty-nine was nothing of an age. His
life lay before him, and there was plenty of time for him to make
his mark and leave an honoured name behind him. His son
stood beside him, Anthony's half-brother, and as she watched,
he turned and glanced down the church. He was sixteen, a
year younger than her own son, and the likeness was disturbingly
apparent. He was Leister as she remembered him first, Leister
when he played against Harrow, when he bought her a workbox, when he used to come into the nursery and talk to old Mrs.
Bishop and little Sally Hardcastle. Like Leister as he had been
then—but with a difference. The same difference that there
was between the Leister of those days and the Earl of Stallingford
today. This boy was like a pale reproduction of the one she had
known. Slight, thin, and with queer nervous gestures as if it
irked him to stand still. Somehow, it hurt her to watch them—

father and son—standing there while the Vicar boomed words which were too difficult, and phrases which were too complicated to bring much comfort to ordinary folk.

' "I am the Resurrection and the Life",' Sally thought. 'All of us can understand that. It's St. Paul who's so difficult, somehow.'

She let her eyes go back to the pew where the Family stood and knelt. The little girl—the same age as Thomas—was a lovely little thing. Like a fairy, with long twisting curls and a small heart-shaped face, she stood very erect, scarcely moving, listening to what the Vicar said.

'She'd have made the better lad of the two,' came to Sally's mind.

The service ended, and the tenantry and villagers waited until the Family should have come down the aisle to their waiting carriages. Stallingford came down with his mother leaning heavily on his arm, his son and daughter followed behind. As he drew level with the pew at the back of the church, where Sally stood, he looked up and their eyes met. For a second his seemed to waver; she felt that he was not quite certain who she was; then they steadied and he gave the slightest possible inclination of his head, and passed on.

Two days later she was sent for to come to Stallingford.

ii

She went, wearing her decent black clothes which she had never discarded since William died. She was a big woman, straight and well made. She brought with her a feeling of confidence and security. She smiled readily, showing white, strong teeth, and her skin was as clear as a girl's.

The butler—Mr. Harrison—younger and less impressive than Blachlet, told her that his lordship and her ladyship were waiting for her in the library. Sally frowned. She had never wanted to enter that room again; it held too many memories for her.

"Very well. . . ."

"I'll tell her ladyship that you are here, Mrs. Scarth."

She waited in the big hall, with the Corinthian pillars, the two suits of armour which the men hated cleaning, she remembered; there were the same carved chests, the big chairs on either side of the great open fireplace, the same feeling of quietness and space.

"This way, if you please, Mrs. Scarth."

The library! Memories crowding back. "Will you do me the honour of becoming my wife." "Allow me to present you——" She wanted to turn tail and run away from them all. Lady Stallingford, seated in a large padded chair at one side of the tall fireplace, held out her hand and said, "Ah, Sally—it's very kind of you to have come."

Leister's voice—Stallingford's voice—repeated, "Very kind —yes—very kind."

"Oh no, m'lady, y' lordship."

Stallingford said, "Sit down—er—sit down, please."

"My son feels that he must go abroad again, Sally," Lady Stallingford said; then turning, rather wistfully, Sally thought, to her son, "I suppose you have quite decided?"

He frowned, like an irritated child. "Yes, yes—I must get away. I can't stand living in England. I want change—change of scenery, people."

His mother continued, "My son feels that he must get away, Sally. He is closing the Manor. The children will come and live here—since our terrible loss——"

"Indeed, yes, m'lady—I was grieved."

"I'm sure of it—quite sure of it."

Like a parrot Stallingford repeated, "Sure of it—dreadful, terrible."

"As you know, perhaps, Leister is delicate. School has always been impossible—quite impossible for him. He needs constant care."

Again the queer, querulous voice repeated, "Constant care—constant."

"He has had a succession of tutors, and my grand-daughter an equally long succession of governesses. I am too old, Sally, too—" for a moment her voice shook—"too broken to be able to exercise the control over the household as I once did. My doctor insists that I shall winter abroad. He wishes me to take a cure—immediately. I must go and see my poor daughter. The servants are good, very good—but—I tell you this in confidence—Mrs. Collins, the housekeeper—she's good, Sally—she's honest, but she has never been able to—to——"

Irritably Stallingford said, "To make the wheels run smoothly. That's the trouble. Never smooth running. Can't manage the servants. Harrison's all right. Quite all right. The men don't give trouble. The women—give nothing else."

Sally Scarth, her hands folded on her knee, looked from one
to the other. She saw her ladyship, incredibly thin, as she had
said, "broken"—she seemed so fragile, so unable to face difficulties ; she saw Stallingford, his fingers for ever twisting his tie,
or drumming on the edge of the desk, a frown showing between
his eyebrows, his whole body seemed to be too tightly strung.

She said, and her calm voice with its broad accent seemed
comfortable and reassuring after the voices of Lady Stallingford
and her son—the one weak and inclined to quaver, the other
indecisive and irritable : "M'lady—m'lord—I take it that you'd
like me to come back here. To take the place my aunt once
held."

She looked from one to the other. That was why they had
sent for her, that was what they wished her to do. To come
back to Stallingford as housekeeper. Sally Scarth, who for the
last sixteen years had lived in a small cottage, cooking, washing,
mending for her husband, the gardener to Sir George Cope.

Lady Stallingford bowed her head. "That was what we had
in mind, Sally. Oh, I know that it is asking a great deal, but
we've known you for so long, you learnt everything from dear
Hardcastle—there never was a better servant—and——"

Her son, leaving the table against which he had been leaning,
began to pace up and down the room. "That's what we want—
it seems a wonderful idea—wonderful . . ."

'She's almost too tired to talk,' the idea came to Sally, 'and
he's wearing himself out !'

She hesitated. It would be wonderful to come back to Stallingford—to feel that she had come home for good. True she
liked her cottage, but it had never been to her what Stallingford
was, never could be. It wasn't only the grandeur, the big rooms,
the many servants, the comfort—it was the sense that here she
belonged. That was the word for which she sought—*belonged*.
Elsie, at sixteen, was going next week to Madame Moore at
Harrogate. Sally had paid sixty-five pounds for her to be
apprenticed ; she had spent quite a lot of money in buying her
everything she could need. Elsie would be able to compare
with the best of them so far as clothes went. Thomas, who
had been chafing for over a year at having to attend school,
was ready to go to Bingley Castle, where he would be a pupil
of Mr. Alexander MacIntosh, the man who had introduced the
"Elspeth MacIntosh" sweet pea to the gardening world, and
whose small but efficient text book on the Delphinium had

been acclaimed as the last word in horticultural erudition. Thomas, excited and thrilled, already saw himself producing a new flower of some sort or another, and calling it "Sally Scarth". And—Anthony—that was where Sally's mind shied as a nervous mare might shy at a piece of fluttering paper. Anthony, who was seventeen, in London working hard at design, figure drawing, and being so good, living in his cheap boarding-house—which certainly wasn't as nice as his own home—never saying a word, never asking for anything but the most obvious necessities. How could she bring him here—when the likeness between him and Stallingford's son was so evident?

Stallingford said, "Well—what d'you think of it, eh? Yes?"

She hesitated. "M'lord, there's a lot to be said for it—and believe me, m'lady, I do feel that it's an honour that you've asked me—but there's things to be said against it. My children —they're out in the world, but they'll be coming back for holidays and the like, I shouldn't wish them not to have a home to come to, as it were."

"Surely that is a detail, Sally—we could find some way of dealing with that . . ." Her voice trailed off, as if it were too much of an effort to continue to concentrate on the matter.

"The house is big enough in all conscience," Stallingford said, "far too big——"

The door opened and he spun round, ready to be angry at the interruption. "Yes—what is it, Harrison? I'm busy!"

"It was for her ladyship, m'lord." Harrison came nearer to Lady Stallingford, bending over her, speaking quietly. "The Honourable Mrs. Hugh Glover has driven over. She wished me to say that she is only in the neighbourhood for a few days, staying with Lady Haslock at Worford—she hoped that your ladyship could spare a moment to see her."

"Constance Glover? Of course . . ." She rose. "Sally, I shall be back as soon as possible. Talk it all over with his lordship"—she laid her fine hand with its blue veins on Sally's arm. "I hope so sincerely that it can be settled. Such a relief . . ."

Stallingford watched the door close, then turned back to Sally. Suddenly, she felt, he had changed, or rather he was trying to change It was as if he had put on the clothes of the young man she had once known—and they didn't quite fit. His old eagerness had lost its impulsiveness, it was studied and forced. He was like an actor who longs to play a part which he played twenty years ago, in which he made a great success.

"Sally, you must come !" he said. "You once said that you'd never deny me anything I wanted."

She smiled tolerantly. "That was a long time ago, m'lord."

"But—we're the same people, Sally. I can still trust you, deep in my heart I love you. Oh, not as I once did—that's over, the romance is dead, but the deep, well-founded love is still there. I can trust you—believe in you. I can see in you —salvation for those children of mine. Oh, Sally, come back. I shan't be here—or very seldom, and then for very brief periods. I've grown to hate the country. I must get away—I'm going to America, and then to the Fiji Islands. Sunshine, I want sunshine. I wasn't very happy with my poor wife. . . ." He sighed, and Sally felt that he blamed her for his unhappiness, never considering that he might have contributed to hers. "My father's death has been a great shock to me. Athol is difficult ; I don't understand Muriel. Your children—well, we can arrange something about that. They could have some of the old nurseries when they were at home. Oh, that would be easy enough. My mother and I—we should never make difficulties. It's all so simple—so obvious. . . ."

Sally, watching and listening, realized that he was thinking solely about himself. He wanted to get away, he found life difficult, he didn't understand his children—he saw in her a means of escape. He was prepared to become petulant and irritated over the discussion and arrangements.

"Sit down, m'lord, you'll weary yourself out walking about." He stared at her, then came and sat down near her. "Listen," she said. "It's all over and done with—between you and me— but—how much does her ladyship, your mother, know, m'lord ?"

"Nothing—nothing. She's always been devoted to you, because of the way in which you behaved over Gwendoline and that fearful fellow—I've forgotten his name—who wanted to run away with her. My father assured me that—for the rest— she knew nothing. I swear that's true—absolutely true."

"I see. . . ." She frowned, thinking deeply. How difficult it was to put everything into words. And here was Stallingford growing impatient again, tapping his feet on the floor, twisting his fingers. "There's one other thing," Sally said, speaking slowly, "my son—Anthony—he might be Lord Leister's twin brother. He might be you, m'lord, when you were seventeen."

He stared at her, his mouth slack, his eyes bewildered. "Good Lord—is that true ? Is he really—so like ?"

"Exactly, m'lord."

The bewilderment gave way to something almost approaching pleasure. "Like me, eh ? Is he ? Like Athol ? Well—'pon my word. Sally—it's queer how things happen, isn't it ? Poor Sally, I didn't behave very well, did I ? My father never quite forgave me. But I'd have married you, Sally—imagine it, you might have been Athol's mother. Whew—it would have saved us all a packet of trouble ! And he's like me, is he ? I'd like to see him one day. Like to do something for him—my son. My son and yours. . . . Ah, Sally——"

She cut him short. The sentiment jarred on her. These things belonged to the past, she had put them behind her. She wanted to come to some conclusion, to know what arrangements could be made for her children, if she took this situation.

"M'lord, those things are all done with," she said. "If you can swear to me that her ladyship knows nothing—about us, about my son, if some arrangement can be made whereby my children can stop here when they've got holidays, or so that I can go to meet them somewhere—I'll consider it. I'll do my best to look after your children—so far as lies in my power. I shall have to be given authority—mind. I can't be neither nout nor summat in the house, with you and her ladyship away."

For the first time Stallingford laughed. "Oh, how delightful to hear you speaking dialect again ! It's like a drink of fresh, clear water ! Of course it can all be arranged. I'll talk it over with my mother. Your son"—she saw his eyes change, become sentimental and regretful—"our son, Sally—must come whenever Athol is away, or you must go to some pleasant place to meet him, spend holidays with him."

She sighed, she knew that he was prepared to accept anything which she said, to alternate between selfish satisfaction because he had been given his own way, and sentimental retrospect. She would have to work out all the details, and submit them to her ladyship. Anthony mustn't come to Stallingford—that was quite certain. She would go to London to see him. Maybe it might be better so. Anthony was going to make a success of his life, he was going to reach great heights, no need for everyone to know that his mother was housekeeper at Stallingford.

"I'll come, m'lord."

"When, Sally, when will you come ?"

"That 'ul be for her ladyship to decide, m'lord."

"Yes—yes. No need for me to wait to see you—er—installed,

is there? You see, I want to get away—no one knows how necessary it is for me to get away. This place gets me down, makes me depressed—unhappy."

"Yes, m'lord—you'll be able to get away. I promise that I'll come."

He held out his hand and she took it, half surprised that to touch him again made so little impression upon her. It was a thin, over-sensitive hand, without much grip, she thought. It kind of slid in and out of yours again, you scarcely felt it. William's word—"waffley" came into her mind again.

iii

That night she sat in her cottage and thought matters over. They wanted her, over at Stallingford. His lordship was gone, and instinctively she felt that he had held things together, that he had dealt with tutors and governesses, with housekeepers and general upsets and confusions. Her ladyship had never been one for holding the reins, as it were. His lordship, on the other hand, had always known all about everything. Every tenant, every servant, even tradesman—that had been part of his scheme of life, to have knowledge which might become useful. She had heard him herself stop and speak to some frightened new under-housemaid, who tried to slide past him, pressing against the wall, hoping to pass unseen.

"Ah, you're new here, I think. What's your name? Annie Smithson. Let's see—isn't your father Harry Smithson who works for Dr. Halliday? I thought so. I must tell your father that I've seen you." Or to some scarlet-eared gardener's boy, trundling a barrow down the avenue. "Hello, my boy—I've not seen you before! What d'they call you? Tom Potter—what, Jim Potter's son? I thought so. Ah, see that you're a credit to your father, that's right, that's right."

He never forgot, either; his memory for names and faces was phenomenal. Not only names and faces, but little incidents, such as, "You're the boy who made thirty-two against Wittingly, eh? I thought so!" or "Wasn't it your mother who walked off with the first prize for home-made bread at the show? Ah, I never forget."

Proud, even a little boastful, of his memory he had been. Just as he had been conceited over his splendid beard, his ability to make folks laugh, to get on good terms with them, and to gain their trust. Now, all that he had worked for, all that he had done was to be jeopardized because his son cared nothing for them. His grandson, delicate, weak, and difficult, was to be left to the care of tutors who were here today and gone tomorrow. In another twenty or thirty years he would rule Stallingford! She had heard of "absentee landlords" in Ireland, and she had felt that there was something very wrong about any man who left his land and his people to the care of agents—however good they might be—and merely took rents and revenue to spend on pleasure. Here was Stallingford preparing to be an absentee landlord, allowing his son to grow up with no proper training

"Duty's a fine thing, Sally," the Earl had once said to her, "a fine thing, a noble thing."

As if he had been there facing her, Sally said softly, "Aye, you did more'n your duty to me, m'lord. The dear God only knows where I'd have been but for you. Maybe I made a mistake, I don't want to make excuses for myself. I was young and head-strong, I didn't think what I was doing. That was my mistake —and I've tried to pay for it, all I could. I shall go on paying for it to the end of my life. And rightly, I don't doubt. But I have got a duty to you—and yours. I've duty to my own bairns, but I don't see that in doing mine for the Family, I shall be neglecting what I owe to my own. I'll come to Stallingford, I'll do what I can—I swear that. My best and only my best."

She took Elsie to Harrogate, and felt faintly abashed before the elegant Madame Moore, who interviewed Sally in her office, where the carpet was so thick that your feet fairly sank into it. The shop—well, it was scarcely like a shop at all—no counters, only drawers and fittings, long glasses and little curtained-off cubicles. Madame, tall, a lady with a presence, wearing gold-rimmed eyeglasses which seemed to enhance her elegance, shook hands in a slightly aloof manner.

"Mrs. Scarth—ah—and this is your daughter, Elsie—ah!"

Sally said, "Yes, madam, and I hope she'll make the best use of her time, and be a credit to us all."

"I hope so—hope so sincerely, Mrs. Scarth. How old are you, Elsie?"

Elsie shuffled her feet and mumbled, "Ah shall be seventeen come next spring, m'um."

For the first time Madame Moore showed real interest. "Oh,

dear—we shall have to correct that accent, if you please, Elsie. That—will—never—do! Aye—not Ah! Say it—say—Aye shell be——"

Obediently Elsie repeated, "Aye shell be——"

Sally thought what a shame it was to make the girl talk so daft!

"Much better—oh, much better. We shall soon have you speaking—quate nicely, Elsie." Elsie was content enough, she was to live in the house of another apprentice's mother. Sally paid her board and lodgings for a month in advance, explained that she was subject to a bilious attack now and then, and that she was to visit the dentist every three months.

"I'll send a pound of butter and some fresh eggs over every week," Sally announced.

Mrs. Lessing said mildly that Harrogate butter and eggs were really excellent.

Sally sniffed. "Maybe they are, I'd never doubt it, but Stallingford eggs an' butter are famous all England over. But, perhaps"—with a tinge of sympathetic pity—"you'd not know that? No? Oh, they are—and the cheese-cakes as well. I'll see that you have some."

Two days later she took Thomas over to Bingley Castle, in Derbyshire. Thomas, almost sick with excitement, sat opposite to her in the train, asking from time to time if she were certain that his new box would be quite safe in the guard's van. He was a cheerful-looking lad, with yellow hair which refused to remain neatly plastered to his head.

"You're pleased to be going, Thomas?" Sally asked.

"Why—Ah'm pleased ter be going to learn summat," he returned. "Ah'm grieved ter leave you, Mum. But, one day Ah'll grow a noo' flower—Ah'll call it afther you. See if Ah dean't. Eh—Ah'll work reit hard."

MacIntosh met them at the door of the neat little house where he lived with his wife, situated at the edge of the gardens. Sally took to him and his wife immediately. They spoke without giving themselves airs, they were direct and simple, and the house was as clean as her own. Where with Madame Moore she had been stiff and constrained, with the elderly Scot and his wife she was her natural pleasant self.

"I hope that my boy 'ul do well with you, Mr. MacIntosh," she ventured.

"Ye're boy will dea weel, or ye're boy wull go, Mistress

Scarth," he returned. "Ah deemand a lairge preemium forr the reason that Ah'm prepared tae gie value in the metter o' teaching them as arre wulling tae be taught. Ye tell me that ye're late husband was a gairdener, Mistress Scarth——"

Thomas, forgetting to be shy, burst in with, "Aye, he weer a grand hand wi' them flowers ye're soa stuck on, mister—delphiniums. Time an' agean he tuke t' fust prize at show. Ah weer ondly a little 'un when he died, boot Ah mind a lot o' tricks an' dodges he had wi' 'em. Ah tell yer anuther thing, he weer fust raate wi' pansies! Aye, gert big 'un like coloured plaates——"

Sally said, "Thomas—Thomas, mind your manners, luv."

MacIntosh shook his head ; to Thomas he seemed like a kind of benevolent god. "Nay, Ah like tae hear the laddie so in-terested i' the worrk. A guid gairdener mun' hae his hairt i' his wark, mun' be fully conscious o' the beauties which arre spread beforre hum." He leant back in his chair, and tilting his head so that he apparently spoke to the ceiling, recited in a deep voice, heavily charged with emotion and expression :

> "Noo' Nature hangs her mantle green
> On every bloomin' tree,
> An' spreads her sheets o' daisies white
> Out-owre the grassy lea."

Returning to a more usual position, he spoke to Thomas. "That, my mannie, was written bi' a mon who—whativer might hae bin his faults—tae change one o' his ain verses—'True it is, he had one failing, Had a mon ever less ?'—he was a lover o' nature. Naething else will mak' a man a first-class gairdner. Mistress Scarth, Ah hae it in ma mind tae believe that this lad o' yours, Thamas, will be baith happy an' useful here."

Sally, a little overcome by the poetry, for to hear people reciting poetry at three in the afternoon made her distinctly uncomfortable, said, "Well, I'm sure I hope that he will be. It's very kind of you and Mrs. MacIntosh to allow him to lodge with you, I'm sure."

MacIntosh leant forward and tapped her gently on the knee with the stem of his pipe.

"Mistress," he said with immense gravity, "hae nae fears—Ah've taken a liking tae the lad—an' what Ah like, it wad ill become ma guid wumman tae not fancy. Nay, nay, he'll dae fine !"

She returned to Wittingly, to sleep for the first and last time alone in the cottage where she and William had lived. Tomorrow, Jepson's cart was coming to take her belongings over to Stallingford. Her last thought that night was, 'I shall use the same table-cloth that Aunt Hardcastle used—the red one—and maybe —I might get a bird.'

BOOK FOUR

CHAPTER ONE

LADY STALLINGFORD departed for Aix ; his lordship had already left when Sally and her belongings arrived, and she was left in charge of the huge house and its staff. Before she left, Adelaide Stallingford had called the servants together and explained to them that Sally was "almost as much part of Stallingford as the house itself". In her own sitting-room, Sally, talking matters over with Mr. Harrison, had listened with some pleasure to his statement.

"Her ladyship, Mrs. Scarth, could not have spoken in a more complimentary manner. The last housekeeper, and believe me, I have nothing—as you might say—concrete to speak against that lady—was weak. More, she was highly nervous, and disinclined to risk black looks or tempers for the sake of the work." He sighed. "As a result—the work suffered."

She said, "I may tell you, Mr. Harrison, that black looks mean very little to me. I'm here to see that the work's done, and done it will be whether or no."

"A spirit," he said, "which I applaud, Mrs. Scarth."

She set about arranging her room, first spreading Aunt Hardcastle's red tablecloth, and, standing back, Sally knew that her eyes filled suddenly and unexpectedly with tears. She was—home. The years had been swept away, and she was back where she belonged. For the first time she realized fully how much she had missed Stallingford and all that went with it. It had—although she had never known it—irked her to know that another woman sat in her aunt's room. It irked her to know that another woman—who did not know Aunt Hardcastle's ways, methods and rules—should be in charge of the staff. Only that afternoon she had noted a trace of dust here, a badly polished tap there, peering at a flower-vase, she had frowned. 'That water was never changed this morning, nor that vase properly washed before fresh flowers were put in !' There were signs that authority had been lax, that maids had scamped their work, and that whoever had been at their head had lacked the power to enforce discipline.

As she set out her photograpns she planned her campaign.

She must start as she meant to go on. She must be firm, strong in the knowledge that the Family trusted her. There must be no nervousness that this under-housemaid or that parlourmaid might give notice. There were as good fish in the registries as ever came out of them. Those who didn't like to conform to her way of thinking—as regards work—could go, and go as quickly as they liked !

She was neither deeply religious in a conventional sense, nor was she over-sentimental, but at that moment she wished with all her heart that one day the Family might say, "Well done, thou good and faithful servant." It was not only for the praise from the people she loved and respected that she wished to make a success of her work, there was in her—as in so many North country women—a sense of "fitness". There was, she felt, only one way in which to do anything to give satisfaction. The right way ! To use the wrong method, to leave corners untended, angles undusted, carpets improperly swept, was wasteful, because it meant—doing work twice.

She smiled. 'Leastways, it means doing work twice when Sally Scarth finds any dust !'

That evening, with her sitting-room set in order, with William's photograph—in which he looked so stolid that he might have been carved out of a block of wood—and the late Earl's— the one which she had seen long ago, when she was a little girl, first come to Stallingford—standing on each side of the mantelpiece ; with the present Earl's picture taken when he was seventeen, and Lady Gwendoline's—at her presentation—she stood back and surveyed everything.

"Lovely," she said softly, "lovely. Only one thing I'd like —a nice little bird." And later, "Mebbe, a bonnie tabbie cat. They're a great comfort when they sit before the fire there— thrumming away."

She called the maids into her room. They came, inclined to giggle and crowd near the door. Their inquisitive eyes stared at the tall, rather heavily built woman with the smooth hair and calm manner. They did not realize that Sally Scarth at that moment suffered agonies of nervousness. Her steady eyes watched them all, for a moment she did not speak. Alice—a kitchen-maid—giggled suddenly.

"What's your name, my dear ? Alice—where do you work ? The kitchen. Ah, then you're nothing to do with me, you come under Mrs. Rogers, and couldn't learn your work under a better nor a finer cook. Mrs. Rogers' cooking has been known and praised by half the nobility and gentry of England. To say nothing—" Sally paused, "to say nothing of His Royal Highness himself. No, I've nothing to say to any of you girls from the kitchen. Good night."

She addressed herself to the others, wishing that her heart beat a little less heavily.

"I came here when I was twelve," she said, "and now, when I'm thirty-seven, his lordship and her ladyship have asked me to come back again. I know every cranny and corner in the house. I know how the work should be done, because there's very little here that I've not done, one time and another. You can either do work the right way—or the wrong way. I like the right way, it's easier and quicker. Things will have to be done my way from now on. If there is any blame attached to anything—I am willing to shoulder it, if it's been through my orders. I want obedience from everyone—cheerful and quick obedience. If I have to speak sharp—no sulks. No back answers. I know her ladyship's wish is that everyone should be happy and comfortable, but they must earn that happiness and that comfort —they must show themselves worthy of enjoying it. If you have any complaints—bring them to me, I'll always listen. And don't think that I don't know my work as I expect you to know yours. I can scrub and polish and clean with the best of you! Now, good night, and tomorrow I'll inspect everything."

Later Mrs. Rogers, immense and unwieldy, came to sit and talk with her. She wheezed a little as she talked, she breathed heavily, and so great was her bulk that she found it impossible to sit on a chair, she merely rested against it.

"Nice to have you back, Sally—ugh, ugh—the place wants someone with a strong hand—ugh, ugh. That last woman was no good. Weak, silly thing! Believe me, Sally—asking Mr. Hughes, the agent, to come in here and drink sherry! Giggling and laughing with him like any girl! Ugh, ugh. Smarming round the maids, saying that she was sure they meant to do their best, but they must have *forgotten* this or that! Forgotten! Nice road to talk, eh? You'll have your work cut out, m'dear. Oh, dear me, yes. You ought to have a chat wi' Mr. Haviland, the tutor. Dear me, I'm ofttimes sorry for that young man! His young lordship—Sally—eh, my dear, what a handful! So's her young ladyship, only in a different way. Ugh, ugh—my breathing's bad tonight, always is when I've been making pastry. Pastry and curry. They're too much for me really i' these days. Jugged hare, that's another thing that makes my breathing bad. Still, one mustn't grumble. I'll help you in any way I can, Sally. Don't lose heart at first, it's bound to be difficult. There, I'll get away to my bed. Good night, m'dear —ugh, ugh—it's nice to have you back."

It was about half past nine when someone knocked on her door, and when she called out, "Come in," his young lordship entered. He lounged into the room, and for the first time Sally saw that he limped a little. He was tall for his age, and might have passed for her own Anthony's twin brother. A twin brother who—lacked something. A replica of her own son, but it seemed that the outlines were blurred, as if some inferior artist had made a copy of Anthony Scarth and labelled it, "Athol, Lord Leister".

He said, "Oh, hello—Mrs. Scarth. My grandmama told me to come and make your acquaintance."

"It's very kind of you, m'lord. Won't you sit down?"

"Eh?" He stared at her, and she felt that his mind had wandered away, for he recovered himself with a little start. "Oh yes—rather, thanks. I hope that you're comfortable."

"Very, m'lord. Of course I'm not really—settled yet. That's bound to take a day or two."

"If there's anything you want, my grandmama asks that you'll tell me."

"Thank you, m'lord."

He crossed his long legs and settled himself more easily in his chair, his eyes wandering round the room, his fingers—intertwined—moving nervously.

"You've got a family portrait gallery here," he said. "M' grandfather—did you know him well, Mrs. Scarth?" Then without waiting for her to answer, "And—hello!—that's my father. At Eton then, wasn't he? Lord, I wish that I'd gone to Eton. I hate having to stay at home, with a tutor. They're all frightful saps—tutors, Mrs. Scarth. I had one who was just a Bible-puncher, another who believed that Homer was the beginning and end of everything. Then there was old Brownsmith—he drank." Leister chuckled, and Sally made a noise which she trusted indicated that she was deeply shocked. "The best of the lot was Turner—George Alderton Turner." He whistled. "Whew! He was a—dog, Mrs. Scarth. Ran after

the maids ;   your predecessor caught him one night coming out
of one of the housemaid's——"

Sally said, "I don't think we'd better discuss them, m'lord.
They're gone and they must have been unsatisfactory or his
lordship would never have dismissed them."

Leister stared at her, he frowned, then laughed. "I see—
you're shutting me up, are you ?"

"Not that, m'lord ; but I don't like talking about—nasty
people when there's so many nice ones to talk about."

He scowled frankly this time, his eyes narrowed, and he sat
stiffly upright.

"I see—I suppose that you've been given orders to hand me
out a whole lot of pi-jaw at every opportunity, that's it, eh ?
My father—'Do what you can with Leister', and my esteemed
grandmama, 'Try to make Leister a better boy'. Oh, I know it
all. They're always trying to make me do something I don't
want to do, trying to make me into someone I don't want to
be ! I'm damned sick of the whole thing. My grandfather
always talked about 'Duty', my grandmama always harks back
to, 'Remember that you've got to fill a great place in the world'.
My father—oh, with him it's just 'don't do this' and 'for God's
sake don't say that !' the whole blessed time. They treat me as
if I were a great silly kid."

She looked at him ; there was something almost pathetic in
his outburst. It was so obvious that he was weak—mentally
and physically. Obvious, too, that he hated restraint and
supervision. She thought of her own boy, working hard in
London, writing her long letters about his progress, about his
determination to make a success. Anthony was only a year
older than this boy. She knew that she wished to obtain Leister's
confidence, to make him feel that while she sympathized, she
still felt and saw the justice of his elders' feeling regarding him.
If she spoke frankly the chances were that she would offend
him, set up a sense of antagonism. She knew these weak, rather
violent characters. It was a risk to speak plainly—but Sally
took it.

"Show them they're wrong to treat you that way, m'lord,"
she said.

"Oh ! Show them ! Rather—that's all right—but how ?
Tell me that, will you ? How ?"

"Prove to them"—she smiled her slow, easy smile—"that
you're not—a great silly kid."

"Well—I'm not, I'm sixteen!" He was indignant.

"I think it's a matter of showing that you understand—responsibility, m'lord, if I may say so. My husband used to say—he spoke very broad Yorkshire—'Show me t' chap as can knaw t' value o' a penny, an' Ah show thee t' chap as knaws t' value o' a pound.' There's a lot in it, m'lord."

"Oh. . . ." His frown died away, and his lips curved upwards at the corners. In an instant he looked years younger. "I see—you mean do this rotten old Homer and the other classic Johnnies, and maths and all the rest of it—and soothe the family that way, eh? Though, I don't know—Haviland—that's my tutor—he's a bit of a beast. Says he sets a high standard for me. What's the use of that—my brain isn't in the high standard class! Still, I might try—until I get sick of it. I get sick of things pretty easily." He rose, and holding out his hand said, "Good night, Mrs. Scarth. I'd like to come down again some time and hear some more about the things your husband said. He sounds a sensible fellow, eh? Oh, and I say, Mrs. Scarth, don't let my sister put you against me, will you? She's an awful little beast sometimes, and she hates me like poison."

"Nay, I can't believe that anyone could do that, m'lord!" She meant it, for the lad, with his queer changes from nervous anger to almost childish frankness, made an appeal to her. He wanted looking after, not driving but leading. He was more of a woman's job than a man's, she felt. Somehow, he seemed more like a girl than a boy, with his queer spurts of nervous irritation, and his obvious belief that everyone was against him.

He grinned back at her. "Can't you? It's true! Most people hate me. I don't play any games—one leg's shorter than the other, not a lot, but enough to make it difficult to play games. Besides"—with another of those bursts of self-revelation—"I don't like games. They bore me." Then, half defiantly, "Now tell me that my father played in the Eton eleven at Lord's, and that my grandfather was a fine horseman!"

Sally said, "If I did, m'lord, it's only what's true."

"That's no reason why I should like cricket and rowing and riding and all the other beastly things called—sport! It's only a tradition—that's all. A conventional attitude of mind. There's no merit in playing cricket."

"You know, if I were clever," Sally said slowly, "I believe that I could show you that there is, m'lord. It's being in—a team, and everyone doing his best. Something like that, only I haven't got the wits to say it all."

"I'm jolly glad that you haven't, Mrs. Scarth. I'm sick of hearing it. Good night, and I'll come and see you again soon." He stood at the door, swinging it backwards and forwards. Sally was to learn that he always found it insuperably difficult to go. He would hang about, repeating that he was going, and yet seemingly incapable of getting out of a room. "It's not a bad room, is it ? I say—you want a bird in that window. A canary in a gilt cage. Y'know, hopping up and down all day long. I'll get you one, shall I ?"

He went at last, and she felt queerly saddened by his visit. He was so obviously restless, unhappy and dissatisfied. At sixteen he was still at home, working—or not, as the case might be—with a tutor who evidently had little influence over him. She compared him again with Anthony, and thought, 'Aye, well, money's not everything.'

His sister was quite different. She came into Sally's room the next morning. Strikingly pretty, and as decisive and clearcut in her speech and movements as her brother was indefinite. She spoke in short, rather abrupt sentences, and stood with her hands behind her back, her chin well up, her steady eyes never wavering for a second.

"How d'you do, Mrs. Scarth. I'm Muriel Leister. I hope that you'll like being here. Grandmama says that you were here when you were younger than I am. What I want to know is why weren't you at school ?"

"Why, m'lady, children—poor children left school early in those days."

"Oh, I see. You've got some children, haven't you ?"

"Three, m'lady. One boy almost the same age as you are."

"Where is he ? What is he doing ? Is he at school ?"

"He's in Derbyshire, learning to be a gardener, at Bingley Castle."

"Bingley ! I've been there. That's where the Groves live. They're sort of cousins of ours. A lot of times removed. I'm looking out for something to do—a career. I might be a gardener. I could go to the Groves and we could learn together, couldn't we ? Or I might be a—don't tell anyone, will you ?— a doctor. Oh yes, there are going to be women doctors. They'll have awful rows first, I expect, but they're—determined ! It's a great thing to be determined, isn't it, Mrs. Scarth ?"

"It is indeed, m'lady."

"Leister says that he's going to give you a canary. What can I give you? Oh, do let me, I'd like to. A cat? That's easy—only what colour shall it be? Tabby? I'll see Jim in the stables. He's awfully clever. He can tell if kittens are boys or girls. Which would you like? Boys are less bother, because they don't have so many kittens, but girls are nicer, I think. I'll see about it."

ii

Sally settled down. There were difficulties, there were moments when she longed to box the ears of some maid who gave herself airs. As on the morning when she found Agatha cleaning a bedroom in what Sally stigmatized as a "left-handed fashion".

"It's my way of doing it, Mrs. Scarth," Agatha replied, when corrected.

"It's not mine—and I don't like it."

"It looks just the same when it's finished!"

Sally bit her lip, her fingers, as she told Mrs. Rogers later, "fairly itched". "That's neither here nor there. If it's done your way—you'll have it to do over again in mine."

The amount of stores demanded astonished and distressed her.

"You had soap yesterday, Jane."

"It's all used up, Mrs. Scarth."

"You shouldn't leave it in the water——"

"Mrs. Collins never grumbled at the amount of soap we used. She liked to have the place clean!"

"So do I!" Sally snapped. "That's why you're leaving at the end of the month!"

There was far too much: "It's not my work, Mrs. Scarth— that's Annie's work", or "I've never been asked to do that, Mrs. Scarth." She knew that she spoke sharply, "I don't care who's work it is, get it done", or "Never been asked to do that? You're not being *asked* now—you're being *told* to do it!" It was months before she felt that her orders were obeyed, before she felt satisfied that her staff realized that she held the reins and was determined that they should work as she wished. Slowly the references to what "poor Mrs. Collins" had said or done ceased, and Sally felt that the first part of her work was accomplished.

"I think we may congratulate you, Mrs. Scarth," Harrison said, "in having asserted yourself, once and for all."

Sally nodded. "Yes, the worst's over, but it's been a job, really."

There were other minor disturbances. Harold Haviland, Leister's tutor, a tall, thin young man with glasses and an earnest manner, was evidently attracted by Muriel's quick intelligence. Muriel wanted to learn Latin and Greek, and Haviland agreed to give her lessons. He confided to Sally that he felt that sense of competition might be good for Leister, "might spur him on, Mrs. Scarth". The effect was entirely contrary. Leister resented his sister's presence, realized that her intelligence was obviously keener than his own, sulked and finally declared that he refused to "learn lessons with a kid who is three years younger than I am !" Muriel cried, confided to Sally that Latin and Greek were necessities to her if she wished to be a doctor, and added that if her career were ruined the blame could only be laid at her brother's door.

Her own governess complained that Lady Muriel cared nothing for embroidery and sewing, she scorned the idea of learning to paint in water-colours, and that she made such strides with her arithmetic that Miss Willis was hard put to it to keep even one lesson ahead of her pupil. Muriel grumbled that her education was "going to pot", that she was sick of being taught by an inefficient old woman, even if she had been governess to the daughters of a duchess. "And look at them," Muriel Leister demanded, "look at them ! The two biggest idiots in England."

Miss Willis burst into tears because Muriel told her that she knew nothing about cube root except the name, and that her ideas on algebra were as hazy as a misty morning. Haviland declared that Leister was intolerable, that he slacked consistently, and when rebuked grew insolent. Haviland, exasperated beyond bearing, declared that what Athol Leister needed was a damned good hiding, it might put a little energy into his blue blood.

Leister replied, "Hiding, eh ? Perhaps you'd like to give it to me !"

"Nothing," Haviland retorted, "could give me greater pleasure."

"You daren't ! What's the good of talking like that ! Just damn' silly ! Showing off !"

Haviland gave the boy a smart smack on the cheek with his

open hand ; Leister screamed with rage and probably a certain amount of pain, and finally had some kind of nervous attack which necessitated his remaining in bed for a week.

His sister said, "Serve him right. Now, Mr. Haviland, we'll be able to really get down to that Greek without Leister's potty interruptions and sulks."

Stallingford returned shortly before Christmas, and to Sally's relief took both the children to London, where they remained for a fortnight. He came back to Stallingford with them, and on the first evening visited Sally's room.

He looked old and tired, there were pouches under his eyes, and his voice sounded more querulous than ever. He complained that no man ever possessed such tiresome children— Leister was a waster, and Muriel was a pig-headed little fool. On the other hand, at thirteen she knew twice as much as her brother, her intelligence was greater, and she definitely had application.

"I can find nothing—nothing," Stallingford said, "to give me the slightest hope—not the slightest hope—that my son will ever be of the least use in the world. None whatever. Too old for the Navy—besides, he says that he'd loathe the idea. The same applies to the Army. Admitted, he's not strong—not at all strong. Too highly strung. Makes the most of his physical disabilities too. Church—he's too big a fool to pass any examination. Diplomacy ! He can't speak English—to say nothing of any other language. Law—with an eye to politics in the future ! Pah ! I'm at my wits' end."

"It's difficult, m'lord."

"Difficult !" He glared at her as if furious that she so underestimated his worries. "It's infernally difficult ! Incredibly. It seems a little hard, when all that I ask is peace and quiet, that I should be worried to death by a pair of inconsiderate brats."

Sally said, "The thing is, m'lord, to find out what they both want—isn't it ?"

"Want ! What they want ! No one ever considered what I wanted when I was that age, did they ? I did as I was told, and did it without question. I don't know what children are coming to. Do your children give you much trouble, Sally ?"

"I can't say that they do, m'lord. They're all liking their work. Elsie sends me very good reports from Madame, and I saw her when she had her holiday this year at Scarborough. I went over for three days. She's a nice girl. Thomas—Mr. MacIntosh writes that he's pleased with him, he's interested and he's steady. Fourteen now. Mr. MacIntosh wants to take him over to Italy, m'lord. He goes every year, it seems, to get some rare plants for Bingley. Mrs. Groves, it appears, is very interested in foreign flowers. Oh, I'm quite satisfied with them both."

He grunted, almost as if he resented the success which her children were making, then said abruptly, "And—the eldest boy?"

She tried hard to keep too much pride out of her voice, endeavouring to speak as if Anthony's attainments were nothing out of the ordinary. Anthony, who at eighteen had been given a place on the *Comet*—John Clifton's paper. True, she explained, it was only a junior position, but Mr. Clifton had seen one of Anthony's drawings—a caricature of Mr. Gladstone and Mr. Joseph Chamberlain playing cricket. She didn't really know what it meant exactly, but Mr. Clifton had had it printed in the paper, and allowed Anthony to sign it—not A.S.—but "The Ass"—that was what Anthony had chosen. Again Sally admitted that it sounded rather silly, but she thought the drawing very good.

His lordship was sitting up very straight in his chair. "He did that? I saw it. Remember someone speaking about it at the Club. So he did that, eh? At eighteen—ah, well. Sally, bring him to lunch with me when you have to go up to town next. At the Cecil or the Savoy—will you? I'd like to see him. When are you going up?"

She hesitated. She did not really want Anthony to meet Stallingford. She didn't trust the Earl's reaction to a meeting with his son. He might be gloomy, he might allow himself to be sentimental. He might even commit the error of comparing Anthony's small success to Leister's inability to find a niche for himself. On the other hand, it was a temptation to show off her son, to hear him talk—speaking so well—to this head of a great house.

"Her ladyship did want me to go up to get new linen, m'lord. Linen and curtains. I know exactly what she wants—for the guest rooms. I thought of—next week."

He rose from his chair. He looked faintly excited. That was like him, Sally thought. With him one nail always knocked out another.

"Splendid! Send me a note which day you're coming, and

I'll send a telegram to the house in town. No, no, I shan't stay there—mausoleum ! I'll be at my Club—the Bellingham. We'll give the fellow luncheon, a real slap-up luncheon that a boy will like."

He had forgotten about the original reason for his visit, to discuss the future of his two children, he was completely absorbed in the idea of meeting Anthony. Sally looked at him a little doubtfully. Anthony was a handsome fellow, and he would, she knew, present a contrast to Leister. Would the Earl be able to resist some hint, some note of personal pride, from creeping into his voice ?

She said, tentatively, "Yes, it's most kind of you, m'lord, but—forgive me—you'll be very careful, won't you ? You see, Anthony knows nothing—I mean, he has no idea."

"My dear Sally !" Stallingford's tone was tolerantly amused. "Of course. You don't suppose that I should be guilty of a gaffe of that kind ! It's merely a natural interest in your son who is doing so well. I like young people—" he paused, and his face clouded, "except my own two, confound them."

He stayed at Stallingford another three days, wandering about, indulging in futile arguments with his son, and rebuking his daughter for being impertinent one minute, then shouting with laughter at her the next. Then, on the day when his mother returned, he decided that the place was getting on his nerves, and after a brief interview with her, in which he told her that whatever arrangements she made for the children would meet with his approval, he went back to London. The two children were present at the interview, and half an hour later they both entered Sally's sitting-room.

Leister said, "Hello, how's the bird, Mrs. Scarth ?"

"Very well, m'lord. He sings most beautifully."

Muriel said, "How's the cat, Mrs. Scarth ? Is he growing ? Oh, rather !"

"Growing beautifully, m'lady, only I'm afraid we shall have to find another name. 'Percival' won't do for a lady cat, will it ?"

"So your wretched pet stable boy was wrong," Leister said. "I always knew that he was just a little faker ! 'Percival'—and it's a she !"

"Oh, shut up ! Anyone can make a mistake once, can't they, Mrs. Scarth ?"

"Indeed they can, and lucky if they only make one. Most of us make hundreds, m'lady. What was it you wanted ?"

They sat down, Muriel curling her feet round the leg of the chair, Leister sprawling on the sofa. They spoke in chorus as a rule, and Sally had to disentangle their sentences as best she could. Leister apparently wanted to travel   Other fellows travelled, particularly when they weren't very strong, and it did them no end of good. Enlarged the mind, showed them new places, gave them new interests. He didn't mind going with a tutor—no, he barred Haviland. No fellow could travel about happily with another fellow who had smacked him on the face, it wasn't possible. If he could go away for six months—even a year. Africa, India, China—"Jolly interesting place, China, Mrs. Scarth—they eat bird's nests and all kinds of killing things" —he would come back with his ideas for the future crystallized. Would she tell his grandmother, would she explain that he really was dead keen, and that he honestly felt it would do him no end of good ? He'd be eternally grateful, never forget it.

Sally said, ."Well, it might be a good idea, m'lord. If her ladyship should mention it to me, I'll tell her what you said. But why not tell her yourself ?"

He wriggled. "Oh, I don't know—I can never talk to either my grandmama or my father. They look at me as if I were—a disappointment. Kind of—grieved and sorry. It's awful. I'd rather they shouted at me any day !"

Muriel's petition, which had been poured out at the same time as her brother's, when disentangled appeared to be that Miss Willis must go ; she didn't know as much as Muriel herself. She'd like a first-rate modern governess, one of the women who had got a degree at the University. Someone who really understood "maths" and wasn't stumped unless they had the book of answers at their elbow. And Mr. Haviland. She wanted him to stay to teach her Latin and Greek. Other subjects, too— with names which Sally did not even try to remember.

"But couldn't the young lady—always supposing that your grandmama will allow you to have her—do all that, without keeping Mr. Haviland here ?"

Muriel shook her head. "I want them to be—fresh," she explained. "To come to teach me in relays. I should wear one person out in no time. You have no idea"—confidentially—"of the energy I've got. I'm just bursting with it ! I'm thirteen— no nearly fourteen, and in lots of ways I'm miles—simply miles behind. It comes of only having that fool, old Willis, to teach me !"'

Mechanically Sally said, "Oh, for shame, m'lady. I'd never speak that way!"

"You would if she'd ever tried to teach you," Muriel returned.

That night, after dinner, Lady Stallingford sent for her. Sally listened to her long story of how difficult the children were, of some strange plans which they appeared to have evolved, and how young people had changed since her ladyship was young, "when we had the same dear governess—Miss Charteris —for years, and she remained with us until my youngest sister— Mrs. Carrington, you remember, Sally—was married. I don't know really what is the matter with young people today. They're never denied anything, and yet they're never satisfied."

'Never denied anything,' Sally mused, 'except what would have done most of them a world of good, a well-smacked bottom now and then!' Carefully she repeated what the children had said to her, while Lady Stallingford lay back in her chair, smiling a little, only listening, Sally believed, to half she said, and at last giving it as her opinion that "they evidently are really fond of you, Sally. I can see that you're going to be our dear Hardcastle over again."

"Do you think that it might be a good idea, m'lady? It's what they both want, anyway."

Vaguely Lady Stallingford shook her head. "I don't really know. It's so difficult for me to say. I never had to decide anything for myself. It might be good—but, of course, it might not be. One can scarcely tell. I really think that Stallingford must decide for me. You're going up to town about the linen, Sally. I'll arrange for you to see him, and you can take a letter from me. I think that he'd better leave it to Mr. Gregson—after all, he has managed our business for years. Poor Miss Willis—I always liked her so much. She might come with me as a companion. Her father was Colonel Willis—of the 23rd—or was it the 32nd?—I forget. I think that might be quite good, she's a kind creature. Muriel dislikes her because she knows nothing about—cubes. What are cubes?"

"Something to do with sugar, I believe, m'lady——"

"Ah, then of course, why should she know anything about them! I think that everything can be arranged quite nicely, Sally. You'll take my letter to his lordship, tell him what I have said—make it quite clear, of course—and then he can pass it all on to Mr. Gregson. It's all rather silly—this education that Muriel talks of such a lot. She'll marry, of course, and then what good will it be to her ? Still, if it makes the dear child happy. Education is quite a harmless thing, after all ! And dear Leister —he isn't strong, and doctors always recommend sea voyages. I wonder no one has suggested it before for him, poor boy. How delightful it will be to see him come back—well and strong, and able to settle down to something. As no doubt he will. Well, good night, Sally—you're a great help to me."

CHAPTER TWO

SALLY called for Anthony at an address which he gave her in the West End. He came hurrying out, looking this way and that, his eyes searching for her.

"There you are! I'm so sorry I had to keep you waiting a few minutes. I came here to look at some new machine which they claim can reproduce the human voice." He laughed. "I've heard it! It's like a voice—but I shouldn't like to say that it was a human one. Now, Mother dear, what's all this about lunching with the Earl? You mustn't give me ideas above my station! I hope that he won't recognize his son's suit, which is what I'm wearing at the moment. I must say he's awfully kind about giving you stuff for me. And what a godsend, too! On my pay I can't afford dress suits, and yet they're sort of stock-in-trade." He slipped his hand through her arm, and pressed it closely. "Nicest mother in the world. Where are we going? I say, you look terribly nice. Handsome, that's the word. The handsome Mrs. Scarth and her to-be-one-day famous son."

She turned her head and looked at him. Queer to think that she was taking him to see his father; queer, too, that she felt so little personal interest in the meeting. She could scarcely remember that Leister had once been her lover, the whole incident was so remote and had begun to assume the air of improbability, which made her wonder sometimes if she had not dreamt it all. Yet when she looked at Anthony, when she listened to his quick speech, his light voice, when she watched his movement, so quick and energetic, she knew that he was indeed Stallingford's son. Walking with him now, while he chattered away to her of his work, his chances of success, of his drawing, she might have been walking with the Victor Leister she had once known. Those short sentences, often terminating in a quick, brief laugh, that decisive manner of speech, that ability never to fumble for a word, that capacity for laughing at himself—these had all belonged to Stallingford, as she had once known him.

They were to meet him at the Cecil. He would be waiting.

Sally showed not the slightest apprehension, to her the glories of a London restaurant could show nothing finer than the big dining-room at Stallingford, the cooking could be no more elaborate than that which was produced in the kitchens at Stallingford. The people lunching there could not be more important or higher in the social scale. As for her own appearance, that troubled her not at all. She knew that her clothes were plain, simply and essentially good.

That morning, when she dressed at Belgrave Square, she had turned and twisted before her looking-glass, noting the admirable fit of her short black jacket with its heavy braiding, and she had thought, 'My word, John Jackson's nothing to be ashamed of in his dressmaking department. Nothing better ever came from Leeds or York !' Her long dark skirt was well hung. "Mind that it doesn't dip at the back, nor ride up in the front, if you please, Miss Carter," she had told Jackson's head dressmaker.

"Not likely, Mrs. Scarth ; we all know how particular you are !" Miss Carter had replied.

Her hat—that had been a difficulty. She had talked for twenty minutes to Mrs. Jackson, who ran the millinery. "I sometimes think that I ought to wear a bonnet, Mrs. Jackson."

"Never in the world !" Mrs. Jackson replied. "That's entirely gone out ! Not that the old Princess bonnets weren't smart to a degree, as I always said. But old-fashioned they are now and there's no denying it, Mrs. Scarth. No, it's hats now—and hats it 'ul be when both you and me are past wearing them ! Black —well, you'd not fancy something lighter ?"

But Sally had refused, and said that it must be black or nothing, and hat though it might be, it must look as nearly like a bonnet as possible. The result had pleased her. It was simple, comfortable, and not over-trimmed. Some of the hats she had seen in London looked like nothing so much as a bunch of flowers just picked and stuck on the women's heads. Just real silly !

They walked slowly down Regent Street, Anthony making her laugh with his comments on everything. The carriages, the footmen waiting for their mistresses outside the smart shops, their arms folded, their faces assuming an expression of dignified aloofness. The paper-boys rushing about shouting some particular line of news, the constant stream of well-dressed people, and once one of the Royal carriages bowling along so smoothly on its excellent springs.

"London's a good place," Anthony said.

"The country's better, my dear. I'm always glad to get back."

"One day I'll have a house in the country for you, and a flat in London—at the Albany for myself—and you, when you like to come to stay, eh ?"

"You'll have a wife by that time !"

"I doubt it—until I can find a girl as nice as you are."

"I'm not a girl, luv."

He piloted her over the road, and into the portals of the Cecil. "Queer that so many famous restaurants are in the Strand," he said, "and yet it's not London's finest street by any means."

"Which would you call the finest street ?" Sally asked.

"Regent Street—it's the only one with a definite style. That lovely curve . . ."

Stallingford was lounging in a chair in the entrance hall, his long legs outstretched, his face heavy and uninterested. From time to time someone passed who spoke to him, he nodded, gave a brief greeting and relapsed again into his attitude of complete boredom. He had asked Sally to bring her boy to luncheon. In Heaven's name, what for ? He'd never seen the lad, who would in all probability be either a young hobbledehoy or some self-sufficient young puppy of a reporter. Far too sure of himself, or else heavy in hand, lumpy and dull. He ought to know better than to give way to these senseless impulses. Life was sufficiently boring without actually seeking boredom.

Sally was all right. Wonderful how she had taken hold of things at Stallingford. The children, tedious young brats, talked a good deal about her, seemed fond of her. So much the better ; she could possibly influence them. Make them less bother to everyone. Not that she was really clever—she possessed a certain common sense and astuteness. He'd not wonder if she'd scarcely ever read a book in her life !

That had been a queer business, his falling in love with her. He'd been sincere enough, too. One of the few times when anyone but himself had really meant anything to him. She'd just caught hold of his heart in some strange way. After his father smashed the whole business he'd felt that life wasn't worth living. He remembered how he'd wandered about Paris, unable to settle to anything. His work had gone to pieces, the Ambassador had sent for him and spoken sharply. He hadn't cared.

What was his work compared with the loss of Sally Hardcastle !
She'd married—by Jove, if ever any woman played straight by
him and his family, that woman was Sally Scarth. Kept her
mouth shut, asked no favours. Only one—when he met her in
the woods, just before his marriage, she'd asked him to kiss the
boy. She might have made capital out of it all—she'd never
asked for a penny. He doubted if she'd have accepted it had it
been offered. Independent spirit—good spirit !

Then—"Bring me another sherry—light—yes, very dry !"
—he'd met Millicent, and the family had talked for the twentieth
time about marriage, and the necessity of providing an heir.
Millicent—poor soul—had been charming to look at. Dull as
ditchwater. Delicate too. Leister inherited that delicacy. One
leg a bit shorter than the other. Millicent had been through a
bad time when the boy was born, nearly died. Sir Howard
Pritchard had stayed in the house for three days. Gosh, what
days they were too ! Millicent had never been really strong
afterwards, and yet queerly enough Muriel was as fit as a fiddle,
while Leister never seemed to gather any superfluous strength.
Clever child, Muriel. Too damn' clever sometimes. She'd got
the making of a blue-stocking in her if they didn't look out.
Then Millicent died, and he had wondered vaguely whether he
should not go home and try to get on the right side of Sally.
Of course, prudence had prevailed, only the impulse had been
there. He'd heard that her husband died, and again thought,
'By the Lord, I could go and ask her to marry me. I've done
my duty, provided an heir.' But when he had listened to his
mother, heard her suggestions that after his father's death they
might get "Sally Hardcastle to come back—these wretched,
inefficient women are so tiresome, Victor", he had known that
he didn't really want to marry Sally. He didn't want to marry
anyone. He wanted to live his own life, to travel, to chase the
sun round the world, to collect old china, Eastern carpets—he
had some of the finest in England—and most of all he wanted
to be free of responsibility.

Men shook their heads, he knew that—said that he had not
fulfilled the promise of his youth. They had imagined that a
great future was waiting for him. Well, what of it ? He didn't
want a future spent in long arguments, his life cluttered up with
documents and red leather despatch-cases, messengers and
complications. Once upon a time he felt the stirrings of ambition ;
if they'd let him marry Sally Hardcastle—he might have done

something good, just to show them all that his marriage hadn't spoilt him or his chances. They hadn't, and she had joined hands with his father—and here he was, at forty-one, doing nothing except wander about, and get damned lonely, and bored to death.

He drained his sherry, looked up to find a tall, slim lad standing before him.

"I'm Anthony Scarth, m'lord. My mother is here."

"Ah!" Stallingford got out of his chair, and stared at the boy. "So you're young Scarth, eh? Where's your mother? Better bring her here. We'll give her a sherry before luncheon."

"Yes, m'lord."

Stallingford stood, his hands plunged deep into his pockets, staring after the figure of the boy. The likeness was unmistakable. He might be taken for Athol, except that he was more robust, walked without a limp, and held his shoulders well back. Better-looking than Leister, if it came to looks. More vital, better colouring, skin clearer. Good-looking fellow. Well turned out, too.

He was coming back with his mother. Stallingford smiled. He was doing the unconventional thing. Lunching with his housekeeper and her son—and his. The idea pleased him, it seemed to prove that he had courage, that he followed his own line and cared for no one. He went forward, holding out his hand. She looked well, not handsome but comely, and healthy. There was something essentially comforting about Sally Scarth.

"Ah, Sally, nice to see you. Let me give you a sherry? Yes—and you, young fellow?"

They sat down, for a moment conversation was difficult. Sally stared about her and gave it as her opinion that it was a big place. Stallingford said that it was too big.

"I got the linen and chintzes, m'lord. The linen in Bond Street—as usual, the chintzes at Debenham and Freebody's. Very beautiful they are, I think."

"Ah—you did, eh? Good."

"Her ladyship wished me to give you a letter, and to tell you about the ideas that his lordship and his sister had about the—well, about their education."

"Did she? I'm sick of them and their education, Sally. Sick! Let 'em do as they like. Don't bother me." Then, turning to Anthony, "You give your mother much trouble with your education, eh?"

"I don't think so, sir—m'lord—I wanted to do something definite, and I made up my mind that I'd do it. It must be much more difficult for people like your son."

"Difficult! I don't see that at all. In Heaven's name why—difficult?"

Anthony smiled. "Well, you see, when you can buy anything in the shop, it's difficult to make up your mind what you really want. When you've only got a certain sum, you think pretty hard before you set out to buy anything. You see, if you make a mistake—well, you have to stand by it. I think that's how it is."

"Ugh! I'd be satisfied if I believed that my son ever thought at all! Come and have luncheon."

Over luncheon Stallingford watched the boy closely. The fellow had good enough manners, he spoke when spoken to and otherwise kept his mouth shut. Sally was bent on putting the case for Leister and Muriel. Their father listened, twisted the stem of his wine-glass in his fingers, protested that he had no time to look for tutors or governesses, no time to arrange tours round the world, and that he had it in his heart to pity the unfortunate fellow who was in charge of Leister for six or eight months abroad.

"Her ladyship suggested that Mr. Gregson should arrange matters, m'lord," Sally said.

Stallingford's face cleared. "That's right—talk to Gregson. No need to bother me. He'll do everything admirably. Yes, that's right—let Gregson do it." Then abruptly, "How'd you like to tour round the world, eh, young fellow?"

"I hope to—one day, m'lord. It's one of my ambitions."

"Ah, you've got ambitions, then?"

"Too many, I expect. I was telling my mother some of them this morning."

"Well"—impatiently—"what are they, eh? Thousand a year, money to fling away on horses—what else?"

"I only got as far as a flat in the Albany this morning."

"Only, eh? See who that is—man with an eyeglass? Henry Chaplin. Let's see who else is there—fat fellow, curly hair—dreadful chap—know him? The playwright—Wilde. Dreadful fellow!"

Anthony said, "He wrote the play that's running at the Haymarket—*A Woman of No Importance*. I saw it the other night. Oh, the tickets were given to me from the office. I went in the stalls and felt no end of a swell." He laughed. "Thanks to your son, m'lord."

"How's that ? How's that ?"

"I wore the dress suit he gave my mother to send to me."

"Done any more drawings lately ?"

"One or two. It's terribly difficult—but it's great fun all the same. Mr. Clifton is very good, gives me a chance whenever it's possible. Of course, I'm only learning my job at the moment. I want to get some books to illustrate if I can. Like Paget and Pegram, y'know."

"How old are you ? Wait a minute, I'll tell you. Eighteen —in—what is it ?—March ?"

"That's right, sir." He had forgotten to say "m'lord", Sally noticed.

They continued to talk, and slowly Stallingford lost some of his heaviness, spoke less jerkily, and his questions covered a wider ground. They were speaking of the return of Mr. Gladstone in the previous year, of the Labour members—Anthony called them ; his lordship ticketed them "Socialists". They'd not last, Stallingford asserted ; their entry into politics was only a flash in the pan, then they'd sink into the oblivion which was their rightful place. Anthony said nothing.

"You don't think so, eh ?"

"Respectfully—no, sir. They can't, and if they could they mustn't be allowed to."

"Ah ! You like what you're pleased to call—reforms, do you ?"

"It's not a question of liking or disliking, sir. Reforms come—you can't stop them."

"Like to see England run by a lot of brick labourers and plumbers."

"Only if they were the best men to run England, sir. Soldiers have run the country, the clergy have done the same ; it's not a question of what a man's profession happens to be, is it ? It's how much he has the good of his country at heart."

"I see ! And Ireland ought to have Home Rule, you think that ?"

"If the people of Ireland want it sufficiently, yes, sir."

"And these delightful ladies who want to vote, what about them ?"

"The same would apply, sir. If they want it sufficiently, they'll get it."

Stallingford raised his eyes in protest, but Sally thought that she had not seen him so interested for months. He was smiling ; he looked younger, more vital.

"Don't be a parrot, my boy. What does his—wanting it sufficiently—mean ?"

Anthony frowned, thought for a moment, then said, "Want it sufficiently to suffer in order to obtain it, sir. That sounds dreadfully priggish, but I believe that it's true."

"I see—and would you be prepared to suffer in order to get something you wanted ?"

"I hope so, sir."

The big restaurant was crowded. Men passed their table, nodded to Stallingford ; women bowed ; he was known, so it seemed, to everyone. Rather bitterly, Sally thought, 'And down the village he'd not know mor'n half his tenants, or where or how they lived !'

A tall man with a large untidy moustache passed, giving a " 'Morning, Lord Stallingford."

Stallingford held up his hand. "Oh, Crawshaw, just a minute. I've got a young friend of mine here. Draws—did a cartoon in the *Comet* a few weeks ago. Good work ! Wants to do illustrations for books. Let him come and see you, will you ? Personal favour to me, eh ?"

The other man turned a bloodshot eye on Anthony. "Illustrate books, eh ? Line or wash ?"

"Both, sir."

"Come and see me—wait, I'll give you my card. Come—let's see—day after tomorrow. At eleven. Good morning, Stallingford. Hope you've not sold me a pup."

When he was out of earshot, the Earl leant across the table a little. "Worst-mannered man in town. But he's important, he's Sir George Crawshaw, of the—well, possibly you know about him. Ah, you do. Wait, I've not done yet. Waiter, go and ask Mr. Givvens if he'll do me the favour of coming to speak to me. I shan't keep him a moment."

Frederick Givvens of the Givvens Press came over. Stallingford told the same story. Givvens stared at Anthony—he was inclined to squint a little, the boy noticed—told him that he held out very small hopes. "I only take the best, Lord Stallingford."

"That's why you need this fellow," Stallingford returned.

"I hope so. . . ." Givvens drifted away.

Stallingford again explained that he was an ugly devil. "Always cross my thumbs when he speaks to me—nothing so unlucky as a squint! But not a bad chap. They tell me," he said, "that he's clever. Let's see, who else is there? Ah, there's old Luke Jennings. I think that we go over to him, eh? Come along."

Sally watched them go, noticed how easily Anthony slipped between the tables, in some way never colliding with anyone, and yet moving very swiftly. She sighed. Stallingford had behaved admirably, never by word or look given the slightest hint of their relationship, yet he evidently liked the boy, felt drawn to him, found him amusing or interesting, perhaps both. Was that fact going to make difficulties? She almost wished that she hadn't consented to bring Anthony to this luncheon. They were coming back, and she saw the Earl slip his hand through Anthony's arm. She heard a man say at the next table, "Yes—Stallingford—the boy, his son, I suppose. They're awfully alike."

"Well, Sally"—the Earl sat down—"we've done a good morning's work. Not every day young fellers can get an appointment to see old Luke Jennings. Isn't he called the Father of Journalism or Fleet Street or something of the kind? Now—listen, my boy, if my son goes on this voyage, how'd you like to go with him? Great chance, see the world, get new ideas. Company for both of you—what d'you say?"

She watched her son's face, saw the light which shone in his eyes, noticed how his mouth softened and curved with pleasure, and held her breath. He mustn't go—abroad, where Leister would have introductions to everyone of importance, where it was inevitable that the likeness would be noticed and commented upon. Yet she must not be the person to oppose the idea, must not make it possible for Anthony to say in years to come, "If only you had allowed me to take that chance." She sat silent, her hands clasped tightly.

Slowly the smile on Anthony's face died, his eyes lost their dancing light and became serious and intent.

Stallingford said, "Well—what about the idea, eh?"

"It's most awfully kind of you, sir, of course it's a wonderful chance—but you've been giving me wonderful chances all the morning. To lunch here with you, to meet all these important people, to have introductions that men twice my age would give their ears for. It wouldn't be much use using those introductions if I were to be leaving town very soon after using them, would it, sir ? I'm in this game, and no one can afford to lose opportunities such as you've given me this morning."

Stallingford grunted. "Have it your own way—all you young people know your own business best. When I was your age I was told what I'd got to do and——"

Anthony laughed. "Did you do it, sir ?"

"More or less, I suppose."

"I wonder which predominated ?"

The Earl's eyes caught and held Sally's for a brief second. "Ah—that's too long a story to tell you now. Come and have luncheon with me again one day. I mean that, remember."

Driving back to Belgrave Square, Anthony was excited, and full of questions. He talked of the stupendous luck which was his—"meeting men like this—Givvens, Crawshaw and old Luke Jennings" ; he wanted to know what the Earl did, why had he left the Diplomatic ? Somewhere in a book of memoirs he had found a reference to him as a young man. "This man who wrote the book, Mother, praised him, said that he had a great future."

Sally Scarth had a sudden mental picture of a young man riding in Rotten Row, beside an old man with a scarlet face ; someone had whispered that he had the ability to make the careers of young and promising diplomats. She remembered how Stallingford's eyes had found her that morning, how he had swung off his hat, and the people standing near had speculated as to whom he bowed. In those days he had been regarded as full of promise. He had told her that he was not particularly clever, had that been modesty or conviction, she wondered ? He'd changed—she sighed—and not for the better. A poor life, doing nothing, wandering about collecting china and rugs, which came to Stallingford and were scarcely looked at again.

Anthony said, "Mother, you're not listening ! Day-dreaming, that's what you're doing, a most pernicious habit for you young women ! Here you are, at your exalted residence. You're off tomorrow ? I'll say 'Good-bye' now. Come to London again soon, it's so nice to see you, talk to you, listen to you—your voice is the most reassuring sound I know."

"Just a minute—I want to give you some money." She fumbled with her purse.

"I don't honestly need it. I'm a plutocrat in these days. Thirty-five shillings a week, to say nothing of odds and ends.

No clothes to buy, thanks to your young lord—I'm always glad that he has such admirable taste ! Oh, well—bless you ! Sure that you can spare it ? It's awfully dear of you. Good-bye, dearest Mother."

Back at Stallingford, she compared him with his half-brother. Leister was waiting for her, anxious to know what his father had said, and how soon it might be possible for him to get away. He was pleased with what she told him, but his pleasure seemed cool and half-hearted, there was no flash of real excitement. He lounged in her arm-chair, his legs swinging over the arm, his whole body looking slack and languid. His tone was friendly, and she believed that in his heart he had a queer sort of affection for her, but from time to time she heard a new note of patronage. One moment he spoke as he might have spoken to any elderly woman, the next as he would only have addressed a servant.

"You saw my father—oh, that's good !" Then in the next breath, "Well, what did he say ? I hope you remembered what I'd said. And Gregson, did you see him ?" Yet a moment later he would be saying, "I don't know what we'd do without you, Mrs. Scarth—you're the greatest piece of luck that ever came our way !"

In a month everything was settled. Leister went off for his six months' trip in company with a new tutor, who Sally described as "beef to the heels". A large, lumbering young man, with a pink face, and a powdering of freckles on his snub nose. His references, so Mr. Gregson assured them, were admirable.

"Possibly a better sportsman than he is a scholar," he explained, "but a young man of the highest character."

Old Lady Stallingford sighed. "I hope for the sake of everyone concerned that he won't wear those dreadful knickerbockers very often ! And that really terrible tie."

Gregson chuckled softly. "That's his greatest pride, that grubby-looking tie carries the colours of the most famous Rugby team, amateurs, of course, in the world."

"I cannot see that is the slightest excuse ! Still, Leister appears to have taken kindly to him. And my grand-daughter's governess ! I admit that she terrified me."

"She is, I agree," Gregson admitted, "cast in a Junoesque mould."

"Junoesque ! She's larger than life size ! Miss Helen Meade —there again, Muriel seems to regard her as a paragon of all the virtues. Poor Mr. Haviland looks as if she frightened him as she did me." Lady Stallingford shook her head. "I cannot see—I never shall see, why girls want this higher education, and if they must have it, why—apparently quite automatically —any taste they ever had leaves them. Miss Meade's blouse— dark-red flannel—and a belt of leather which reminded one of the navvies who work in the streets. She said to me, 'I've had a little chat with Mr. Haviland. I fancy that we shall make a good coaching team for your grand-daughter. That's an intelligent girl! But she's got a lot of leeway to make up, a lot of leeway. Another year with the old lady who has been so successfully wasting her time and she'd have—lost the tide!' Mr. Gregson, she didn't talk to me, she *boomed* at me."

"Again I can assure you that Miss Meade's credentials are of the highest. She has a first——"

"Don't tell me! It's all a lot of very stupid nonsense, and we might as well admit that both my son and myself are only allowing this—new idea to be put into practice because I am too old and too tired, and he is too lazy and indifferent to make alternative plans."

Muriel bloomed and blossomed under the new state of things. She was obviously delighted to see the back of her brother, whom she detested. She liked the ordered life, the knowledge that she had two people devoting their energies to teaching her those things which she longed to know. The girl had a good brain, and she had chafed continually at the old-fashioned methods of the excellent Miss Willis. Within a week she developed a passionate admiration for Helen Meade, and would have gone without sleep or food to gain her approbation. She liked young Haviland well enough, but Helen Meade's vigour, her energy, her somewhat masculine method of attack on all problems from equations to Home Rule for Ireland, appealed to Muriel instantly. From having been forced to seek for additional knowledge in the Stallingford library, where she knew many of the books were old and out of date, she could now demand explanations, and realize that her continual questions were regarded as a distinct sign of grace.

"I've never been so happy in my life," Muriel told Sally. "It's like a new world! I'm not so far behind as I feared I might be. Of course, Miss Meade's wonderful. She wants me to matriculate, and then—" she whistled—"then there'll be the tug of war, when they know that I want to go to Oxford! Grannie will have a fit, my father will storm for five minutes and then

relapse into somnolence again—and, of course, Helen will win!
As she says, 'We've got to be fighters, Muriel—keeping our
swords bright always!' That stirs you, doesn't it, Mrs. Scarth
—words like those.''

Sally replied doubtfully, "Why, m'lady, I don't know that I
care a great deal for fighting and swords. What is there you've
got to fight?"

Muriel, well primed by her beloved Helen, answered immediately, "What? Oh, Mrs. Scarth, ignorance, prejudice, malice,
jealousy—the Deadlock family, and the Circumlocution Office!"

"The Deadlocks? Which Deadlocks might those be?" Sally
asked. "Did you mean the Blacklocks? Over at Mallingly
Court?"

"Mrs. Scarth, you're wonderful! I must tell Miss Meade
that. Do you know, she says that I can call her Helen if I
like. *If I like!* But it seems almost like blasphemy."

"Take my advice, m'lady, and never rush into Christian
names. Once started they're hard to leave off. Don't work too
hard; and I think that I'd better send to London for some of
that lotion your grandmama likes you to use for your hands.
They look a bit on the rough side to me."

Muriel held out a pair of hands, red and ink-stained. "They
look less rough when they're clean," she admitted, "they do
really."

"Then we might try soap and water first, and the lotion
afterwards," Sally said dryly.

CHAPTER THREE

SALLY sat by her fire, while the big tabby cat purred firmly on the hearthrug and the canary chirped at intervals as if to attract her attention. She folded her hands and stared into the depths of the bright fire. She was entirely content, she told herself. Last week, she had been in London, she had seen Anthony, heard his news, listened to his statements that Stallingford had been a brick to him, and that if things went on well he ought to be earning not only a living, but "a jolly good living, Mother, by the time I'm twenty-five". He had taken his first holiday abroad, doing a walking tour in the Black Forest, and his note-books were filled with sketches which seemed to Sally to be little short of masterpieces.

Elsie had been moved to London, to Madame Moore's shop in Knightsbridge. She was growing very pretty in what her mother called "a perky way". She was fair, and smart, her figure was good, her energy boundless, and Madame assured Sally her taste was exceptional.

"For her age, Mrs. Scarth, she possesses a remarkable sense of line, if you understand me."

Sally didn't, but she replied that she was glad to hear it, and hoped that Elsie would do well.

"Unless she changes in a most remarkable and unforeseen way, Mrs. Scarth, there is no doubt, in my mind at least, that she will do very well."

Elsie had listened to her mother's account of the interview, shrugged her shoulders and laughed her queer, rather shrill laugh, so different from Sally's deeper tone.

"Oh, Madame's not a bad old thing, reely," she said. "Knows how many beans make five, and who's worth their keep and who isn't ! Once I'm out of my time—another two years, Mum—we shall know what she *reely* thinks of me. I don't cost anything yet—except my food !"

"You've lost your North country accent, luv," Sally said.

"You've got to, Mum ! Our ladies 'ud think nothing of you if you talked like a clodhopper, reely they'd not. I've worked hard to learn to talk nice."

249

"That's a good girl." But in her heart she thought that Elsie talked dreadfully "well, put on", and scraped her tongue far more than was necessary. Truth to tell, she was a little ill at ease with this smartly dressed girl of eighteen, with her certainty, her knowledge of life in London. Elsie chattered of the people she had seen, of Madame's clients and their bills, she knew who paid, who did not pay, and who was—paid for.

Sally said, "Nay, luv, I don't much like to hear you talk that road. It's not nice."

"It's true !" Elsie objected. "Everyone knows that it's true. Old Sir Sholto Mauvern hasn't a penny, everyone knows that ! Lady Mauvern buys six and seven dresses at a time from us. We all know that Mr. Percy Samuel pays for them."

"Even if you do, there's no call to talk about it !"

"Mum ! Reely ! You'd think these people were different to what we are."

"So they are," Sally said stubbornly. "Maybe not your Mr. Samuel, I've never heard of him ; but the Mauverns are a fine family, and Lady Mauvern was a—let's see ?—a Miss Anersley— they come from the south somewhere—Dorset, I think. Of course they're different, Elsie, and I should be sorry to think otherwise."

Again Elsie's queer shrill little laugh. "Mum, you *are* old-fashioned, reely !"

"Then if being old-fashioned means having a proper respect for your betters, my dear, I'm glad to be old-fashioned."

Thomas was easier. He came over to Stallingford to spend his week's holiday, and slept at the cottage of one of the under-gardeners. He had grown and broadened. He was going to take after William, Sally thought. His movements were slow, so was his speech. He wore heavy clothes and an unobtrusive tie, his boots were immensely thick and yet he contrived to look—what indeed he was—a pleasant, well-set-up young man.

It appeared that MacIntosh was as a god to him, and his name appeared as often in the conversations as Helen Meade's did when Muriel talked to Sally.

"Muther, we went to It'ly. It was wunn'erful. The plaaces we saw ! You've noa idea how in-ter-esting Mr. MacIntosh is when he's abroad. What he knows ! Why, he's forgotten mor'n most chaps ever do know ! He's letting me help him wi' some experiments wi' sweet peas. Oo—it's in-ter-esting ! He's gotten a little room, 's'pechully heated, it's like a doctor's room, where he'd do operations. Scales—that 'ul weigh the tiniest, weeniest lil' grains o' polin. Bukes—for records is kept of everything. He lets me do some o' the figgering. Says that I'm sooch a neat writer. I was allus a neat writer, Mum, wasn't I? He says that fur fifteen there's very few lads knows what I do. He says I've got a reit gift f'r it. Theer's a new dahlia—oo—I'd like you to see it. It's striped—red and white. Even stripes like as if they'd been drawn wi' a ruler. Oo—it's a treat!"

He heard quite a lot from Anthony. "He sent me a drooring, Muther. Like a kind o' comic drooring—of some of these Lunnon coster chaps talking while they push their barrers. I've got it framed, hanging in my room at Mr. MacIntosh's. He says that it's one of the best things he's ever seen of its kind. I wrote and told m' bruther that, I thout it 'ud give him heart to know that a man like what Mr. MacIntosh is tuke that mooch notice of his drooring, eh? Mr. MacIntosh says that if he gets on, he might get him the chance to do some flowers—fur illustrating a seed catalogue—a friend of his has a big seed place outside Lunnon. Carter's the name. That 'ud be a chance for our Anthony, eh?"

A good boy, Thomas, and able to talk sensibly with Mr. Wilson, the head gardener at Stallingford. He told Sally afterwards that the boy showed intelligence, and a grasp of essentials. Wilson was a change from the old type, Sally thought. A gentlemanly man, who spoke as well as his lordship, and never soiled his hands. He only really worked, as she had seen gardeners work, when he was arranging plants and flowers for the house, or sending up things to show at the big exhibitions in London. There was a story that the Princess of Wales had seen an exhibit of his, and said that she would be glad to have cuttings for her own garden at Sandringham. Someone had taken a photograph of Mr. Wilson standing talking to the Princess, not looking a bit abashed either.

People were changing, Sally thought. In the old days they seemed to have known a lot less, but the work had been done just the same, the gardens had looked just as well under a man who could barely read and write. Thomas said that everyone had to be a specialist in these days, and that the man who didn't specialize was left behind. People wanted more clothes, more amusement, they liked to go about—why, last summer even Mr. Harrison had taken his holidays abroad. She couldn't have imagined Mr. Blachlet doing that! Then there was Lady

Muriel wanting to learn this and that, and getting all excited over some examination that she was going in for. Try as she would, Sally could not imagine her ladyship—Lady Stallingford —ever wanting to enter for an examination.

She said to Lady Muriel, "Why, that is nice, I'm sure, and what will the prize be, if you win it?"

The girl had laughed, and said that there was no prize, but the examination was the key which opened the door for you. Miss Meade said that it would take three years to make that key so that it would work smoothly, and didn't Sally think that Miss Meade had most beautiful and original thoughts.

Sally replied that indeed she didn't doubt that she had, and privately wondered what on earth it all meant, and what was the good of going in for examinations if there were no prize at the end of it.

Two days after Christmas, when both Lady Stallingford and his lordship had been at home, Leister returned from abroad with his tutor. Leister was sulky, and looked white and drawn; the young tutor was scarlet in the face, and his ears looked as if they had been scalded and polished. They arrived late one evening, and Sally heard of it from Mr. Harrison, who looked into her room, and said, "A surprise for you, Mrs. Scarth—his young lordship's back. Something's wrong, of that I'm certain. He and the tutor are both in the library with his lordship at the moment."

Sally said, "Oh, dear me, I do hope not!"

She heard nothing, except that once the sound of the Earl's voice raised in anger reached her ears as she sat in her room. The next morning Muriel came in to see her. Her face was flushed, and Sally felt that she was not altogether dissatisfied that Leister should be in trouble, while she only asked to be left in peace to pursue her studies. She sat on the arm of a chair, swinging her legs, and demanded, "I say, Mrs. Scarth, what's wrong?"

"I didn't know that anything was wrong, m'dear."

"Whew!" the girl whistled. "I should just say that there was! Athol's come home, and Mr. Blackett's going, and Athol's got to go to a crammer's in town. My father was raving like a lunatic last night——"

Sally said, "Well, I think we'd better wait until his lordship tells us himself, don't you? It's really not our business at all."

"You're awfully strait-laced, Mrs. Scarth, aren't you?"

"I've always found that it paid to mind my own business, m'lady."

The story, disjointed, filtered through to her later from the Earl and from her ladyship. Mr. Harrison told her something, how Mr. Blackett had said, "Nothing will induce me to stay!" Leister had stood, white and silent, only muttering at intervals, saying that Blackett was "all wrong".

His lordship, leaning his head on his hand, had spoken to Sally in the library.

"Most unfortunate—most. Blackett, and I believe him to be a good fellow, won't stay. Some rumpus or other with Leister. As always, Leister can't behave himself. Now we've got him at home again, until I can send him to a crammer's in town—or the country. I don't know which way to turn. No man ever had such worries, no man. Must be somewhere where they will be sufficiently strict, that's what's necessary, firmness. Apparently he was too much for Blackett, no sense of obedience. A nice kettle of fish!"

She said soothingly, "He'll grow out of it, m'lord," not knowing in the least what Leister should grow out of. "He's still very young. Not eighteen yet."

"Very little short of it! Look at your own son, Sally! Earning his living. He lunched with me in town last week. Pleasure to talk to him. Got sense!"

Again she felt that little quiver of fear, that sense of danger. The Earl liked him, the Earl compared him to his own son, to Leister's disadvantage. One day he would blurt out the whole story! What would Anthony say, think, do?

Then her ladyship talked, vaguely and uncertainly. "How upsetting it all is, and we felt that everything was going so well with Mr. Blackett, a nice young man, even if his clothes were dreadful. Now it appears that Leister has been really naughty. Giving trouble. Yes—very naughty. Leister says that Mr. Blackett is making mountains out of molehills. It's difficult to understand. My son thinks that he must go to a crammer's, and that a military career might be good for him. I don't know—I get bewildered. You know, Sally, that I have never been used to worry—the Earl never allowed worry to come near me. Yes, give me a handkerchief—in that top drawer, Sally—no, not a lace-edged one. Thank you."

Leister himself lounged about the house and grounds, moody and sulky. He looked ill, Sally thought, and wondered if study were really a good thing for him. She had never seen the Earl so galvanized into life. He went to London, and returned saying that he had interviewed various crammers, and that as soon as Sally could arrange for Leister's clothes to be packed, he was to go off to Henley.

"Far enough from London, let's hope, to keep him out of mischief," Stallingford said.

That night Leister came into her room, and asked, "Is it true that I'm going to Henley? My God, what a place to send a fellow! Just because of that sneaking Blackett. Rotten prig, that's what he was! I'll tell you this, Mrs. Scarth. I'm not going to addle my brains with a lot of books and study. Why the hell should I? The Army—can you see me in the Army? I'd hate it. I swear that I won't work—I'll show them all."

Sally, watching his pale face, with the little nerve twitching at the corner of his mouth, thought how different he was from Anthony; and thanked God for the difference. He looked spineless, somehow, with his inability to keep his shoulders squared, and his trick of twisting his fingers together.

She thought, 'It's as though a rot had set in—his late lordship, strong and straight, mentally and physically. The Earl—he's a lot weaker nor what his father was, and it's as if Leister had no strength at all. Just a waffley fellow, as like as not he's got the makings of a proper waster in him. Ah—it's a bad look-out. Pity Muriel hadn't been the boy, with all her book-learning.' She spoke to Leister, trying to make him feel less vindictive. "Nay, if you do your best, m'lord, it will please the Earl mor'n anything. It wouldn't be for so long you'd have to study, and they say that the Army's a lovely life. Make the best of it!"

"How can you make the best of anything," he asked, "when every damn' thing's all wrong? You might be able to, I couldn't."

Leister departed, and his father followed him as quickly as possible. Lady Stallingford said that her doctor refused to allow her to winter in England, and she too left for Monte Carlo, where her son had promised to join her. Stallingford settled down again, quiet, dignified, and only peopled by the servants, and Muriel and her governess and tutor.

ii

February had been, and showed every intention of being, a bad month. Sitting in her room, Sally could hear the water

rushing down the pipe outside the window, and only that morning
Mr. Roysten, the agent, had said, "We shall have to watch
those gutters, Mrs. Scarth, with all this rain."

"Indeed, yes," she returned. "They always say, 'February
fill dyke', and it looks as if February was going to live up to its
name."

He nodded. "I've never had such a difficulty in keeping dry !
It gets through the thickest mackintosh, this rain. Well, good
morning, Mrs. Scarth ; it can't last for ever."

She sat there beside the bright fire, working at some household accounts, thinking that money didn't buy what it used to
when she was a girl. She was thirty-nine this year ; she felt
that she had never lived anywhere except Stallingford. The
time when she was married to William seemed almost vague,
misty, like a dream which had been pleasant while it lasted.
William remained as a memory of someone who had been kind,
and essentially good. As she thought of him, she looked up at
his photograph. It wasn't like him, really. She had said at the
time that he was looking too fixedly at the camera. "Look a
bit natural, William, for any favour," she'd said. But William
had suddenly turned sulky, and said that having photographs
taken any road was a lot of daftness, and that the chap could
get on with taking it as quick as he liked. "Nay, Ah can't sit
here grinning like a Cheshire cat ! Ah wean't, neether !" he
grumbled.

Her eyes wandered round the comfortable room, resting on
the various photographs. That was what people seemed to be
now, she thought, pictures. William was dead, and what she
had left to remind her of him, well, it wasn't like William at all.
His lordship—the late Earl—handsome, dignified, but—only a
photograph left. And Stallingford—who had once been her
"dear love"—there he stood, with his head thrown back a little,
as if he flung out a challenge to the world. That was what she
remembered. That picture was more real to her than Stallingford
was now. That handsome lad, with the wide-apart eyes and the
brave expression and attitude, had nothing in common with the
discontented, grumbling man she knew now. She listened to
him speaking, in his queer, querulous tones, she noticed his
frown, the way in which he allowed his mouth to twist with
sudden annoyance, and again and again she had thought, 'Eh
you do little but grizzle i' these days.'

'Yet it's not to be wondered at,' she thought. 'Nothing stays

still. That fire has changed in the last minute; that pot of
hyacinths isn't the same as it was yesterday, and it 'ul be
different tomorrow. Nothing's really mine—except the minute
I'm living in. Yesterday's gone, tomorrow's not here, only
this minute, when I can say 'Now', is mine. You lose folks as
you lose time. They just move along—upwards or downwards
according to your way of thinking. You don't walk along
exactly the same path, there's not room. It's like a view, you
see different things from whatever place you stand, and even the
matter of a couple of inches one way or the other 'ul make a
world of difference. The shadow thrown by a tree, the light on
a river, the church tower in the distance—just depends where
you stand—what you see. It's the same with minds, I suppose.'

She let her thoughts run on, and sat with her hands folded
in her lap, her work forgotten. People were always talking
about what young folks should "make" of their lives. Did you
have to "make" something of it? Couldn't you just be—what
you were? She didn't suppose that people would think she'd
made much of her life, if all came to all. True, she had a good
salary, she lived comfortably, she was trusted, but she was just
the housekeeper at Stallingford. Queer to think that if she died
scarcely anyone in the world would know about it, but if she'd
married Victor Leister, and been Countess of Stallingford, then
hundreds of people would have opened *The Times* and the
Morning Post and said, "Oh, look, there's the Countess of
Stallingford dead!" Yet she would have been the same Sally
Hardcastle—or would she? Yes, she thought that she'd have
been just the same as what she was now, because she'd have
stepped out of her right place into another. They were different,
these great families—they had different ideas, they regarded
some things as terribly important, while others—that might
matter a lot to Sally Scarth—scarcely troubled them. There
was more to it than that, Sally mused. They were something
more than just ladies and gentlemen—they belonged to the
land. They belonged to the land, and the land belonged to
them. True, some of them forgot their duty—she sighed, thinking of the Earl, away in Monte Carlo, with Mr. Roysten wanting
his authority to put a new roof on the cottages at Hallows End.
But that was their fault, their—yes, no good mincing matters—
their sin. It wasn't the fault of the system that had put them
where they were. System—better call it Providence, and be
done with it.

Anthony had laughed at her, saying that she was a snob, that she loved her lords and ladies, her great houses and gardens, picture galleries and state-rooms. Well, so she did ! Where'd you find houses like Stallingford and Chatsworth and Windsor, like Markenfield and Fountains Hall ? It took England to make houses like that. England, that was right, for these places weren't just the work of one set of builders, they were the result of time, and labour and—aye—love.

'Now I'm getting at it,' Sally thought. 'I'm slow, but I do get there if I'll give myself time. These houses, these castles belong to England, not to Lord This or the Duke of the other. They've been made while history was being made ! So have the families that live in them, and they belong to England too. That's what hurts me when I see Stallingford going on like a grizzling bairn, or Leister slumping about, never willing to do a hand's turn or use his brains. They're lacking in duty ! They've a right to make the best of the brains as God has given them ; they've a right to use them to help others weaker and poorer than themselves—and if they don't, well—they'll sink down and be lost !' She frowned, picked up the poker and attacked the glowing coals as if she had a personal grievance against them. 'Aye, they'll be lost—and no one but theirselves to blame—but —England 'ul be the poorer. Not the poorer for losing some of them for what they are now, but for losing what they might have been—like his late lordship. Here, it's like watching a losing fight, and I know it. Stallingford's got little interest in anything, his son will have less, but that's no business of mine. It's my business to do the best I can for them all, because I remember what they were, and what they could have been. Maybe it's even partly my fault. If I'd never loved Stallingford, or if, having loved him, I'd married him, he might have been different. It's all a puzzle. If one person chucks a stone into a still pond, you can see the pattern, the circles all right ; but if ten folks start flinging in stones, the pattern's lost and it's difficult to sort out the circles at all. I thought that I did what was right—and as like as not I did what was wrong. Eh, it's very difficult to know.'

She turned back to her books, and had already become absorbed in them when little Annie Bennings, who had only been at Stallingford for a week and still regarded Sally with awe, knocked and said, "If you please, m'um, there's a gentleman here to see you."

"Where is he?"

"He cum ter the side entrance, m'um. He didn't give no name. Just said Ah was ter ax if you'd see him."

"Show him in, then. Only always make people give their names, Annie."

"Yes, m'um."

A moment later Anthony entered. He stood at the door. Little Annie slipped away as if she had been detected in some crime, and Sally cried, "Anthony, whatever are you doing here?"

He laughed. "And that's a nice welcome, Mother! I was at York, there's a conference there, I was reporting it and making sketches of the Church dignitaries. Finished sooner than I expected, and I came along here. You don't mind, do you?"

"Mind—nay, I'm glad to see you, but——" She hesitated. She knew that she had not wanted him to come to Stallingford, that she was afraid that some of the servants might notice the likeness and draw conclusions. And as she admitted that, she wondered a little why she should mind so much. Likenesses were common enough. The Duke of York was like the Czar; everyone said that the Prince of Wales had a double; she had heard it said that everyone in the world had a twin so far as looks went. "Mind, no," she repeated, as if to reassure herself; "only I don't often have people here—Thomas stays in one of the cottages and so does Elsie. But it's lovely to see you. And let me take that wet coat, and come near the fire, and Annie shall bring you some tea." She let her hand rest on his shoulder. "Aye, it's nice to see you, Anthony m'dear."

He stretched his feet out before the fire, and sighed with content.

"I wish that we had a home of our own, Mother. You and me—it would be so nice."

"Maybe we will have one day."

He laughed. "Not you, you'll live and die at your beloved Stallingford! Among your aristocrats!"

"Now! They've been very good to me," she protested, "very good."

"And you—haven't you been good to them, and won't you go on being good to the end of your days?"

"I hope so," Sally said simply. "Now, tell me about what's to do in London."

"In London—well, some people admire Sir William Harcourt

very much and some dislike him intensely. Some people say
that the French have made a huge mistake in condemning
Dreyfus, and others say that it is merely a demonstration against
the Jews; others, again, say that the man is a hero. Some
very foolish people are being very clever, and some very clever
people are being quite remarkably foolish. Sir Henry Irving has
produced *King Arthur* at the Lyceum, and many people think
that the play is not good enough for him. Now, what else is
there? Incidentally, where is your young sprig of aristocracy
in these days? Didn't you tell me that they'd sent him to—
where was it?—Maidenhead?"

"Henley, dear. Why?"

"Well—Heaven forbid that I should come to you with tales,
but I saw him in the Haymarket a few nights ago—at least
someone told me who it was—he wasn't behaving too prettily.
I was on one side of the road, he was on the other, but—he
was not too sober, and his friends—were distinctly unlikable.
Perhaps you could give him a hint, Mother."

He watched her smiling face change, saw the look of anxiety
which crossed it, and said quickly, "There's no need to worry;
probably if I got a bit tight, and played the fool, no one would
notice. But Lord Leister's a different proposition, isn't he?"

"Aye," she said, suddenly emphatic; "thank the Lord he
is too!"

"I didn't mean to upset you——"

"You haven't upset me. There, drink up your tea. It 'ul
warm you. Are you going to stay the night, my dear? They
could find you a room down at the lodge, I don't doubt."

"You're talking to a hard-working man, a gentleman of the
Press," he said. "I've told the dog-cart from the 'Horse and
Wagon' to come for me at seven o'clock. I must catch the night
train up to town. This is just a flying visit."

"Did they know who you were at the 'Horse and Wagon'?"
She didn't know why she asked the question or why his reply
gave her a sense of satisfaction.

"No, why should they? Queer that you ask, though. I
meant to tell you, I heard the landlord——"

"Aye, Joe Runnings——"

"Fattish fellow, wearing a scarlet waistcoat—well, I heard
him telling a fellow in the bar—yes, I admit that I had a very
good half-pint of 'old and mild'—that I was Lord Leister!
Needless to say that I tried to look the part, and probably added

a couple of bob to the price of the dog-cart ! Am I so very like him ?"

Sally nodded. "Aye—like enough. I can't see that anyone could take you for him, but Joe Runnings would see a lot clearer if he didn't see everything through a mist of beer ! Yes, what is it ? Come in !"

Anthony had his back to the door and did not turn. The younger of the footmen entered.

A goodish fellow, though Sally and Harrison had been doubtful about engaging him because he wore glasses, and was entirely unable to see without them. He had proved to be a good servant, and only a few days previously they had congratulated themselves on having engaged him.

"Yes, Henry ?"

"Two gentlemen are here, Mrs. Scarth. They asked for his lordship—when I said that he was away they asked for someone in authority——"

"Well, tell Mr. Harrison then."

"He's away for the day, Mrs. Scarth. Gone to Ripon to see his married sister, he said."

"Very well, Henry, I'll come. Where are they ?"

"In the little office, Mrs. Scarth."

"Tell them that I'm coming." She turned to her son as the door closed, conscious that she was filled suddenly with that queer realization of things as yet belonging to the future, which comes at times to people of the Broad Acres. Not that she could have said in words what she realized, she only knew that she had reached a momentous point in her life, and that again she might be asked to make sacrifices. She had no idea what that sacrifice might be, but the premonition was so strong that it became almost a physical thing. She laid her hands on her body, and sighed.

Anthony said, "What's wrong, dear ? Indigestion ?"

"No, it might be, but it's not. Stay there. I'll be back in a minute."

"I'm very comfortable, don't mind me," he said.

In the little office, a room which was reserved for such business people as did not warrant or demand the grandeur of the library, Sally found two men waiting. They might have been turned out of the same mould, she thought, except that one wore a heavy brown moustache and the other was clean-shaven, with little clipped side-whiskers. Their overcoats were heavy, with velvet collars, their collars were high and stiff, their ties undistinguished. They carried bowler hats in their hands.

"Good afternoon." Sally glanced from one to the other, making the one greeting serve for them both. Ordinary people, she rated them, of no particular importance, and yet they filled her with a sense of dismay. "And what can I do for you?"

"You are Mrs. Sarah Scarth? The housekeeper? The Earl is away, we're told."

"That is correct. Sit down, won't you?"

The moustached man said, "And the Countess of Stallingford —where is she?"

"Her ladyship is in Monte Carlo."

"And Lord Leister——?"

Something in his tone startled her. They had been leading up to this. The Earl, his mother—and lastly—Lord Leister. As a wild creature in the woods shies away from something which it cannot understand, so Sally's mind seemed to shy away from these men.

"Did you want his lordship?" Then with sudden change of tone "Suppose you tell me what your business is, and why you're here. Is it business?"

The whiskered man said stiffly, "We prefer to conduct our business in our own way, Mrs. Scarth."

"Business?" Sally said, suddenly testy. "But what business? I don't want to sit here and just answer questions that don't seem to lead anywhere. I've a visitor in my room, and I should like to get back. What is this business, please?"

She saw them exchange glances; they were obviously not used to a housekeeper who spoke with authority, who gave orders, and asked more questions than they did themselves.

"Well?" she said sharply, pressing her advantage.

"Lord Leister is at a crammer's at Henley, I believe?" He raised his eyebrows, making the statement a question.

"Well?" Sally said again. "Go on."

"For some time Mr. Trotter has been anxious concerning his lordship——"

"Then Mr. Trotter should have communicated with the Earl!" Sally flung out.

"Lord Leister's movements—he has been in London a good deal——"

"And why not? His great-aunt lives there, she's devoted to him—Mrs. Powers."

The man frowned. "Mrs. Scarth, if you persist in making these interruptions you make it very difficult for us. As I said——"

She nodded. "Yes, I know what you said, but before we go any further, I want to know by what right you come here, by what right you ask these questions, and what gives you the right to suppose that I've got to answer them. Let's get that straight first of all, shall we?"

Again that quick exchange of glances, and the taller of the two spoke.

"We are police officials," he said, "and I have our authority here." He tapped his breast pocket. "Do you wish to see it?"

With an immense effort she kept her expression unchanged. "Nay, so long as I know it's there. Now perhaps you'll tell me *why* it's there?"

"You read the papers?"

"No more than I can help." She felt her heart beating, her mind rushing back to that sudden return of Leister's from abroad, when that red-faced young tutor 'had said, "Nothing would induce me to remain here—with him!" She thought, 'Whatever it is, I can't see a way out yet—I must keep talking until it comes to me! I'll manage something—somehow.'

"You've read of a certain case—a notorious case?"

"Why, I've read and heard of it. I've no patience with it all—people who are gentry as Lord Queensberry is, look at it how you like, behaving in this way. Postcards and nose-pullings! A nice way to go on. As for this court case everyone's read so anxiously—why, I said to Mr. Harrison, 'What a lot of time wasted! And a pretty crew, all of them. One man's a great bully, the other's a dandified piece of affectation! A lot of mud stirred up, and to what good purpose?' That's what I said to Mr. Harrison."

"It may interest you to know that the police are taking a—certain interest in quite a number of young men—among them Lord Leister. Now you see the reason for our questions, Mrs. Scarth."

She thought that she felt the blow—that it struck her just below her heart. This was where the Family, her beloved Family, had got to, was it? Every generation dropping down the ladder—a rung or two at a time.

"I've never heard such a piece of rubbishy impudence in my life!" Sally said.

The man with the side-whiskers, his eyes narrowed a little, smiled, and when he spoke Sally felt that his veneer of civility had gone ; he was prepared to bully.

"Very high-handed, Mrs. Scarth ? The fact remains that Lord Leister has been missing from Henley for two nights ; he spent last night at a house which bears the worst possible reputation, and left for the North, we are informed, at midday." He looked at a large silver watch. "He ought to arrive here any moment now, and we shall wait to hear what he has to say. Now you have it !"

Sally Scarth, the workhouse girl, flung back her head and laughed, a noisy, rather rough laugh, with her mouth open showing her very good white teeth. She stopped short, stared at the two men, then—as if the sight were too much for her—threw back her head and laughed again.

"Nay," she said, after a moment, wiping her eyes, "forgive me. You're a poor lot, after all, you policemen ! You think you're very bright. By rights, I ought to send for his lordship's agent, and the solicitor over from Stallingford, they'd deal with it"—her voice changed, became hard and resentful—"as it ought to be dealt with ! Lord Leister in a house with a bad reputation indeed ! Lord Leister mixing with young men who, if their parents dealt right with them, would get their bottoms smacked and be kept at home on bread and water ! Lord Leister leaving London at midday ! Would either on you know him if you saw him, I wonder ? Oh, you've got a photograph—let me see it. Aye, I remember when it was taken, about six months ago. The first suit he had made with those long fronts to the jacket. Not as smart, as I said at the time, as the old kind. However, that's neither here nor there. We'll ask his lordship to come and tell you where he was last night, and how he's spent the day. Because he's here, and has been for the last hour or so —sitting in my room—as he's always liked to do—bless him ! —drinking tea and eating bread and home-made jam."

CHAPTER FOUR

SHE rose, walked slowly to the door, opened it with every appearance of control, but when it closed behind her she almost flew back to her own room. Anthony was lying back in the big chair, his eyes were closed ; she thought that he was asleep, but as she entered he sat upright and said, "Have your friends gone ?"

"No," she told him, and was surprised to find herself breathless. "No, Anthony, you've got to help me, help—the Family. Leister's in some kind of trouble . . ."

He nodded. "Which does not surprise me. He's been riding for a fall."

She laid her hand on his shoulder. "You've got to be Leister," she said. "You were at York last night, seeing a friend—he's leaving for America shortly. You know that you'd no right to leave Henley—you've always hated being tied—been disobedient—and that's all. I can't tell you any more—they'll wonder why we're not coming. Anthony, you will do it, won't you ?"

He smiled, and shook his head. "Your beloved Family again ! Why should I help your nasty little Leister out of his furtive little scrapes ?"

"Because if it hadn't been for his grandfather I should have been a workhouse brat and you'd maybe have been the same. That's why, Anthony."

"You have a positive genius for gratitude," he said ; but he smiled and, leaning forward, kissed her. "All right—I'll play-act for you. Though I should doubt if the likeness will stand the strain. You yourself say that it's not so marked."

"I can't see it," she lied, "but Joe down at the 'Horse' did, and I can get him to come up later if necessary. Wait—your room at York—was it booked in your name ?"

"No, by Jove ! Wilson was coming up, and I was sent instead at the last minute. I say, Mother, the fates are on your side ! Come on, I'm almost longing to 'strut' on the stage and play the aristocrat."

Anthony walked down the passage with her, she threw open

the door and said, "Lord Leister," feeling that she had cut away
the last bridge which could lead her to safety.

Anthony stood, his hands in his pockets, looking from one
detective to the other.

"Well, gentlemen," he said, "and what is all this ?"

The Brown Moustache said, "You are Lord Leister ?"

Anthony laughed. "It looks like it, doesn't it ?"

They were both staring at the photograph, looking up from
time to time as if to verify what they saw on the printed card.

Anthony laughed. "I suppose that you have some authority
for this preposterous game, warrants or permits or something
of the kind ? Otherwise, I think"—he turned to Sally—"Mrs.
Scarth, that a couple of grooms might spend a happy five minutes
throwing these people out."

The whiskered officer said, "We've every authority, my
lord—if you care to see——"

Anthony waved his hand, as if to consign the official papers
to the realms of unimportant things. "I don't want to see
them—it's enough that you've got them. Have you finished
with that photograph of mine ? Let me see it, will you ? Now
I wonder where you got this ? If Ellis sold you one, I shall
make myself remarkably unpleasant ! Did he sell you one ?
Oh, he didn't—good. I say"—again he turned to Sally—"I'm
wearing this very suit—the one you've never liked. That's queer."

She said primly, "I never liked it. It's very shabby now,
m'lord."

As if he had forgotten the existence of the two men, he
pulled open the inside pocket, showing the tailor's label. "It's
not so old—— Oh, well—what's the date ? I can't read upside
down."

She read, "Lord Leister—January 8, 1894."

"Only just over a year. Don't encourage me to be extrava-
gant, Mrs. Scarth."

Tolerantly, with the air of an old servant who takes a conscious
liberty, she said, "Nay, you need no encouragement from me,
m'lord."

"Might we ask where you were last night, m'lord ?"

"Eh ?" He spoke as if he had forgotten their presence.
"Me ? Last night ? Playing truant. Mrs. Scarth here knows
all my misdeeds. Don't you, Mrs. Scarth ? I've had my lecture
in her room. I suppose old Trotter's sent you, eh ? Well, he
ought to feed us better, be a bit more sympathetic, understand

that one's friends—damn it—are one's friends. But—no ! Ask for leave—and—what ho ! She bumps ! So I took French leave. Two days ago——'' Sally had heard him hesitate for the first time, and blamed herself for not having primed him better.

"Two days ago——"

"Well—damn it—two days, three days—what does it matter ? Ask old Trotter. I came up to York—to see Freddie Collet— you remember him, Mrs. Scarth ?—and—frankly, I'm afraid that time didn't exist, at least not clearly, for either of us. Go to York, gentlemen, and you'll find it painted a bright and cheerful shade of red ! I stayed at the—hanged if I remember the name of the place—'Red Lion', 'Black Lion'—'Drunken Duck'—some animal, I know that—but my friend drove me out to see some friends of his—there again, don't ask me what they're called or where they live. Tall, darkish man, and a stoutish—but still pretty, mark you !—woman. Mr. and Mrs.——'' He shrugged his shoulders. "There again it might have been Sir and Lady, Earl and Countess—then when my friend departed for Liverpool —he's going to America——"

Black Moustache said, "Not France, my lord ?"

"France ? Why the devil should he go to France ? Oh, you mean Paris, gay time and so forth—no, he's off to New York. That's why we were singing 'Off to Philadelphia in the Morning' all yesterday. York rang with it ! Where was I ? Oh yes, when he had gone, I was overcome with remorse and came home to tell my woes and confess my sins to Mrs. Scarth here."

"Did anyone see you arrive here ?"

He stared blankly. "See me arrive ? Well, of course people saw me arrive. I went into the 'Horse and Wagon'—and had a word with old Joe—what's his name ?—Runnings. I've got a marvellous memory for names ! We had half a pint of old and mild together. And now, Mrs. Scarth, don't we think that we're a little bored with this business, and don't you think that you might send these people in something to drink and send them on their way ? Remember"—his voice was suddenly cold—"Mr. Trotter will have himself to blame if he finds this piece of impertinence reacts on him—as I shall see that it will. I have been very patient, and answered your questions, but don't imagine for one moment that I have not resented it. Don't think that I don't know what you were hoping to find— and you've failed ! Shall I tell you why ? Because there was nothing to find out, never has been and—never will be ! I wish you a very good afternoon !''

He turned, said, "Come along, Mrs. Scarth," and was prepared to leave the room when the man with the side-whiskers said :

"Excuse me, my lord, I always heard that you limped a little—went, as it were, a little short on one leg.''

For a moment Sally felt her heart miss a beat, they were given away, that one small detail ! To her surprise and relief, Anthony spun round on them, his eyes blazing.

"Confound you, and what if I do ? Have you never heard of cures ? If old Trotter had been more sympathetic, as sympathetic as my—relations, he might have discovered that I went to London for treatment, a treatment which has been successful. Or almost so. I've had enough of your questions and prying—get out of here as soon as you like, or, by God, I'll have you flung out. Mr. Trotter will hear what I think of this stupendous piece of impertinence—tonight. Come, Mrs. Scarth—tell one of the footmen, if you please, to see these people off the premises.''

Back in her room, he flung himself down in the chair and wiped his forehead.

"Whew—two awful minutes—when they asked how long I'd been away from town, and that wretched limp ! The rest—not difficult. Oh, Mother darling, I'm very much afraid that your lordling is what is technically known as—a bad hat. And do you realize the temptation which you have put in your hard-working son's way—to make a story out of it all. To rush back to town and find it the best bit of copy for weeks ?''

"Anthony, you'd not do that !''

He laughed. "Of course I shouldn't. I was joking, and you ought to have known it. People are never tired of telling you that all's fish that comes to the newspaperman's net, but we're not such bad chaps as all that. Well, Mother dear, that's given a spice to our time together. I must think about getting on, we shall have the dog-cart here in no time. Be rather a lark to offer those two bungling idiots a lift to the station. Confound it, if they're on the train that means I must travel in a pluto-cratic first-class carriage ! Lend me a couple of pounds, will you ? No good spoiling the ship for a ha'porth of tar.''

"Why, my dear, whatever you want——''

He faced her and laid his hands on her shoulders, looking into her eyes very steadily and without wavering. "Whatever I want . . .'' he said. "You'd give me whatever I wanted ?''

Sally caught her breath, she had heard almost the same words before, spoken by a man who looked so like her son did now. She said, "I'd give you anything you wanted, my dear love."

"Then one day—" he said, "one day, not now, there's too much to be done, and"—he laughed—"it seems that you have infected me with this conviction that one must bolster up this family of yours—but one day, Mother dear, I want to know the truth of all this."

"The truth?" she said, stammering a little.

He nodded. "Yes, my dear, the truth. There—I can see the dog-cart waiting and——" He spun round; the door had opened and Leister, untidy and dirty, almost fell into the room. "For heaven's sake—what's this?"

Leister dropped into the big chair. Sally sprang to his side. "M'lord, what are you doing here? Did you drive up from the 'Horse and Wagon'?"

Leister shook his head. "Me? No. I dropped off the train as it slowed up at Calford Halt, they were picking up some country people. I came over the fields. Scarth—I'm half dead. I'm in a mess. There's a mistake, of course. The police have some crazy idea in their heads—I don't know what. If only my father didn't rush off and leave me to shoulder everything alone. I've no one to turn to. I've done nothing wrong. Nothing! Someone persuaded me to go with them to someone else's house—there was some kind of a row. They saw me, and, of course, knew who I was. Damn it, I'm cursed unlucky! I want to get to—France."

Anthony Scarth, standing with his back to the fire, said, "Ah—France!"

Leister stared at him. "Who the devil are you?"

"I was Lord Leister five minutes ago," Anthony said. "Now you can resume your own identity." He turned smiling to his mother. "It's saved you the price of a first-class ticket!"

"Nay, I'm moidered," Sally said. "I don't know what to think, I'm sure."

Leister, almost sobbing, beat his clenched fists on the arms of the chair. "I must get away. I've got to get away—tomorrow morning early. To France—that's where I must go."

Anthony was staring at his reflection in the glass which stood above the mantelpiece.

"Yes, there is a likeness," he said, as if he spoke his thoughts aloud, "it's distinct. What would you say, Mother, two peas in a pod?" He turned and faced Leister. "Stop snivelling; let's know what's the truth of all this. They *can* get you, I suppose?"

"Get me?" Leister's face was pallid and blank; the question did not seem to have penetrated into his brain. "Get me?"

"You've been mucking about—mucking about for no reason except curiosity, nasty curiosity. There's no mentality at the back of it, there was no driving impulse, no! Just that you've a dirty little brain in a dirty little body. And you've made a mess of your copy-book, and put yourself in the power of the cops! You know what a cop is? A rozzer, a beak, a Robert! You don't want to get to France for your health's sake, you want to get there because you don't think that you'd appreciate free board and lodging and a diet of skilly. That's right, is it? You're a nit-wit, you haven't even the sense to keep on the right side of the law. Never learnt the eleventh commandment? Learn it."

Laying her hand on his arm, Sally said, "Anthony, my dear, don't be hard."

"Hard! God, I'm not hard, Mother! It's the unfairness of it all. His chances—and he's flung them away, for nothing except a—new excitement. Now what's to be done? Our two charming friends—the police——"

Leister almost screamed. "They're here? The police are here?"

"They're just going," Anthony said grimly, "and only because I make such a damn' sight better lord than you do! Lord Leister is returning to London tonight. Then he must go in one of the family carriages, crests and coats of arms and all the rest of it. Mother, send a man on a bicycle to the station, tell the stationmaster that a carriage must be kept for his lordship. Do that now. Now, m'lord, change into the clothes that I'm wearing—no, only the suit and tie. We'll do that while you're sending the fellow on the bike, Mother."

Sally returned to find that they had changed clothes, and Leister stood pulling the tie straight before the glass, his face sulky and overcast.

He turned as Sally entered. "Look here," he said, "if this is your son, he's been most infernally——"

Smiling, Anthony said, "And you shut up, because when you talk you only talk rubbish! Mother, he's got no money. How much can you let him have ? Ten—fifteen ? That's good, get it out for him. Now, m'lord, out you go and tell the driver of that dog-cart that it's a mistake, you didn't want him to come back. Why should you, when your stables and coach-houses are filled with magnificent stuff ! Here's five bob—that's enough ; and do your level best not to limp."

Leister said, "You give orders pretty easily, don't you ?"

"It's a gift," Anthony assured him ; "go and carry them out, and be quick about it. Mother—his train goes direct to York. Can I get another that means a change somewhere ? It will make me late getting in, but I want to get on another road if I can. Cover his tracks."

She pinched her lower lip between her finger and thumb. She was white, shaken, incredibly distressed, but she trusted him implicitly. "One of the men could drive you over to Otley," she said. "There's a slow train for the south—mind, it means a lot of changes—about half past six. I could send young Charlie, he's none too bright, if you muffled your face up a bit, and— could you talk a little broad, Anthony ?"

"Me ?" he queried. "Me talk broad—aye, luv, theer's nout easier for ma."

She laughed. It was a relief to hear him speaking the dialect, to see his dancing eyes, his mouth which smiled so easily. Leister sat huddled in the chair, twisting his hands, drawing long sobbing breaths. Sally looked at him, and thought a little sadly, 'Nay, he's nobbut a poor thing ! You can't be over hard on him.' She looked back at her own son, who stood, hands deep in his trouser pockets, rising and falling gently on his heels.

He said, "That's all clear then. He'll want a bag, Mother. If you have one that is positively covered with crests and coats of arms, so much the better ! Those chaps are almost certain to be on the train. I'll get along in a dog-cart to Otley, and— we'll hope for the best. Only, Lord Leister, let me advise you to get down to Dover or Folkestone just as quickly as a train will carry you. Now, Mother, that bag, my dear."

"I'll get it ready."

Leister lifted a haggard face and stared resentfully at Anthony. "You're a cocky, self-righteous bastard, aren't you ?"

For one brief second Anthony's expression changed, then his smile returned.

"Bastard—I can't say—cocky and self-righteous I certainly am not. But, God, look at your chances, and look how you chucked them away! You're not *real*, there's nothing *sincere* about you. That poor devil who was sentenced at the Old Bailey the other day—well, as I see it, the dice had been loaded against him since he was born. But you—you're just a damned sensation-monger! You want to be—in the swim! And you've got into a damned muddly kind of river. You're a muddler. Why come back here—when you might have gone direct to France? Some clever idea of covering your tracks! Been reading *Sherlock Holmes* and *The Mystery of a Hansom Cab*, eh?"

Leister moaned. "You don't understand—it wasn't my fault at all—if Frank——"

Anthony nodded. "Yes—as my mother would say, 'If pigs had flown——!' Oh, shut up, and don't whine! Look here, if you see those fellows on the road, offer them a lift. Don't talk, be cold and very much—the lord! Ah, everything ready, Mother?"

Sally nodded. "His lordship's bag has gone down to the carriage, everything's ready. Mrs. Rawlings has packed a basket, m'lord, with a bottle of wine—thought that you might be hungry. There, you'd best be off."

"The money—oh, thanks so much, Mrs. Scarth, you are a brick. And"—suddenly clutching Anthony's arm—"you don't think that they'll be waiting for me at Dover, do you?"

"Not if you keep your mouth shut, and leave your little friends alone for the few hours you'll be in London."

"Go to Mrs. Powers', m'lord," Sally begged. "That's where you ought to go."

"She's about the only person who has ever understood me! Good-bye, Mrs. Scarth. Good-bye—I suppose you're Scarth too."

Sally watched the little smile touch Anthony's lips. "I think you're safe in assuming that. Just make something of an exit, won't you? Head up, and—don't limp. That is important."

He went out, and Anthony heard Sally saying, "The bags are in, Henry? Mr. Harrison will be sorry, m'lord—yes, over to Ripon. My kind respects to her ladyship, and to his lordship. It's a pity that Lady Muriel's away—yes, gone to stay with Mrs. Franklin over at Runswick for the week-end, she and Miss Meade."

She returned to her room. Anthony held out his hand and drew her to her chair.

"Sit down," he said, "you're all in. Won't you let me get you a drink of some kind?"

"Well, I don't know . . ." She was "all in"—white and shaken, with beads of sweat standing on her temples. "Well, there's some sloe gin in that cupboard, Anthony. I might take a sip of that. And you ?"

"I'm having a whisky-and-soda," he said. When his hands were busy with the bottles and the glasses, he said, without turning back to meet her eyes, "And—that might have been me, or t'other way round ? Funny thought, isn't it ?"

She gasped. "Anthony—what d'you mean ?"

He came back to his original place before the fire, glass in hand. "I mean—I'm the Earl's son. That's it, eh ? No, no, don't get worried—of course I'd like to know—lots of things. That he didn't treat you too badly, that you didn't have too bad a time——"

"He wanted to marry me, Anthony."

"Did he ? By Jove, and I don't blame him ! But . . ." He stood, his glass in his hand, looking at her speculatively. She felt that this knowledge came to him, bringing with it a sense of amusement. "But . . . ?" he asked again.

"But . . ." his mother repeated. "Do you mean—why didn't I ? Well, it wouldn't have done, my dear. Could you imagine me—Countess of Stallingford ? These things happen in books, Anthony, they don't really happen."

"No ?" His eyebrows were lifted quizzically, as if he were teasing her. "Lavinia Fenton—Belle Bilton—there are others—their names have escaped me."

"Who married earls, love ?"

He nodded. "Earls and—that type of person, yes."

"They weren't servants, my dear, were they ?"

"Ladies of the theatre, Mother."

"Oh, that's different, Anthony. They're clever people, they've learnt how to talk, and dress well—oh, they're quite different, and yet I don't know that even with them it answers so very well, marrying into the gentry. No, I've never regretted that I didn't marry his lordship." She paused and sighed. "I was very fond of William."

Anthony nodded. "A great fellow, William. He knew, Mother ?"

"Yes, he knew," Sally said slowly. "He knew without my telling him. And he loved you the same as he loved Elsie and Thomas."

Anthony sat down, stretching out his long legs, staring into the fire. "What a field of speculation it all opens up, doesn't it ? If you had married him—what would he have been like now, or you—or me ? A stronger man than he is now, of that I'm certain. And me ? I might have been like that poor fish we've just sent on his way to France. I wonder how many of us have the incentive to work—for work's sake ? Less people than we generally suppose, I fancy. Then blood must grow a bit thin, down the years. Undiluted blue blood—might be, will be, the better for a little dilution with the ordinary red variety. One's knowledge of work and what it really means must be somewhat dim after years and years of easy living " He drank his whisky-and-soda, set down his glass and sprang to his feet. "I must get along," he said. "I'm a chap what has to live bi t' sweat o' me brow !" He laid his hands on Sally's shoulders, and looking at her very tenderly, said, "Yes—the Earl would have been different—better, stronger ; me—Heaven only knows ; but you—whether you'd been Sally Scarth or Sally, Countess of Stallingford—you'd never have changed. You'd have been the same straight-dealing, warm-hearted, adorable thing that you are now, even"—he laughed—"though you are the world's greatest snob !"

"Nay, you do nothing but make fun," she said. "Anthony— tell me, it hasn't come as a blow to you, my dear ?"

He frowned. "I think that I knew," he said. "How I knew, or when I first knew, I can't tell you. It sort of *seeped* into my consciousness. At first it seemed rather romantic, it made lunching with the Earl additionally—what ?—not amusing, that's not the word I want. It added—spice to it, as it were. I didn't know anything, I merely speculated. It was so obvious that you didn't really care for his asking me to lunch with him ! You didn't really hide your feelings awfully well, Mother dear ! Once or twice, when he'd had his second brandy, he grew a little sentimental. Hinted that as a son I might have given him less trouble than Leister. Spoke of you with a definite tenderness. Oh, very nicely. I liked him best when he spoke of you when you were young. I like him, y'know. He's really very simple and kindly. When he forgets himself for a moment. I'm glad that he did want to marry you, darling. He was very fond of you ?"

Sally sighed. "Aye—I do believe that he was fonder of me than he's ever been of anyone. I believe that truly, Anthony. Never think of him as a bad man, my dear. He's never bin that

T

in his life. He's not the *same* man as I knew then. He's changed, grown peevish and petted, grizzly and queer-tempered. I don't think of him now as—the man I used to know. And in a way I'm glad. It makes it so easy for me to stay here, and—keep an eye on things. It's the place that matters to me now—Stallingford. Aye, and that's changed !"

"The old Earl ?" Anthony queried, and watched her face change, grow younger, it seemed to him, her eyes shining with a new light.

"The old Earl—ah ! He was different. It was him that stopped us marrying. He *knew*, he was wise, wise and good, my dear."

"I don't want to go," Anthony said impetuously. "I want to stay here and listen to you. I want to hear your story right from the very beginning. About your recollections—the first things you remember. . . ."

His mother laughed softly. "Eh—the first thing I remember's—sleeping rough."

"Sleeping rough ?"

"Sleeping under a haystack in a field, one summer night, and lying awake, trying to count the stars. That's the first thing I remember—cuddling close against my mother."

"Oh, it's too tantalizing !" he cried. "I don't know anything about you, and I want to know everything. Promise that you'll tell me. Promise that next time you come to town we'll have a whole day, and you'll talk and talk and talk. I want to know ! I want to know what's made you what you are, what's given you the ideas and standards that are yours. And I have to go—when I want to stay !"

"Aye, you must go. I'll tell Henry to order the trap."

As she went, leaving him struggling into his raincoat, turning up the collar, and grumbling softly, she thought, 'And I've been afraid that if he knew he'd not love me so well. He seems to love me more, it's not separated us, it's drawn us closer ! And it's me he wants to hear about, me when I was little, and slept rough, and the workhouse and everything. He'll understand, there'll be parts he'll hate, but there'll be bits that 'ul make him laugh. Bits that 'ul bring tears to his eyes. That's where he's different from Thomas and Elsie. They'd never want to know, and if they did hear that I was a workhouse brat they'd feel 'shamed. Anthony 'ul only feel—angry, the same as the Earl did—all those years ago. Angry and only ashamed because a great rich country like this of ours lets bairns be unhappy and treated badly.'

She gave her order, and went back to Anthony. "He'll be round in five minutes to drive you to Otley. Better ask where you change, my dear. I'm afraid it's a bad train. You'd better let me wrap some cake up for you, and fill a flask. I've got one in my drawer."

She bustled about, while he stood watching her.

"You're happy tonight," he said.

She glanced up at him, and he saw how bright her eyes were. "Aye," she said, "I'm happy—content's maybe a better word."

"We're very fond of each other, aren't we?"

Her North country aversion to demonstrations of affection asserted itself. "Why, most mothers and sons are fond of each other, aren't they?"

"Now come!" he teased her. "Don't get all difficult and Yorkshire! We do love each other."

"Oh, give over!" she retorted, her face flushing. "It's down t' South you've learnt this way of talking! I've told you that I love you, that's enough, don't harp on, lad! There, put that flask in your pocket, and the packet in the other. It 'ul help out while you get to London. The trap's there. Turn up your coat collar, and just slip out quickly. I don't want anyone asking questions and making remarks. Be a good boy, and God bless you!"

He slipped his arm round her, and kissed her. "Good-bye— and even though you hate it, even though it's a proof that I'm growing soft and Southern—I don't believe there's another woman in the world like you! You're a wonder!"

She pushed him gently away. "Nay, give over!" she chided. "I shall have you missing that train, and that 'ul be a bonnie set-to! Get along now, like a good boy. There—off you go. It's been nice to see you."

He climbed into the tall dog-cart and drove away into the night. The young groom who drove uttered half a dozen sentences and relapsed into silence, and Anthony Scarth, his chin buried in the upturned collar of his coat, let his thoughts run on, un-checked. Queer to think that he might have been Lord Leister— that Stallingford might have been his home, his heritage. Queer, too, to remember that the Earl, that pale-faced, thin-haired old-young man was his father; that once he had been in love, passionate, devoted and possessed of a longing to make Sally

Hardcastle his wife. With that thought came a sense of satisfaction, that she would have "filled the bill" as a Countess, as
well as she had filled it in every other capacity which had come
to her. He chuckled when he thought of the blunt common
sense, the intolerance of what was false or unreal which his mother
would have brought to the position of Countess of Stallingford!
Yet she had always possessed a great sense of the fitness of
things. Anthony remembered once when she was telling him of
the early unpopularity of the Prince Consort. Aunt Hardcastle
had retailed stories to her niece, and Sally, like many people to
whom reading does not come easily, had a memory which was
astonishingly retentive. What was the old story which was at
the back of his mind now? Something about the amount of
candles which were used at Buckingham Palace. Some tradition
attached to it all? The Prince had discovered the waste, insisted
upon it being checked. Anthony remembered how, as a lad, he
had chuckled and said, "Good for him, eh, Mother?"

"Well, I don't know," Sally had retorted doubtfully. "I
don't know that I think it's a very proper thing for a gentleman
like the Prince Consort to be bothering himself about candles.
Seems to me that if he'd any doubts there were other people to
satisfy him. No, if I'd been the Queen—bless her!—I'd not
have been best pleased, as I don't doubt for a minute as she was
either! A nice thing if her ladyship came bothering into the
pantry to see if the salt-cellars were properly filled!"

"Masters and mistresses, be they just plain folk or gentry,"
she often said, "have their places to keep the same as servants
have, and *gentry* never step out of their right places, let me
tell you."

He loved to tease her, to call her a snob, but her snobbishness
had nothing to do with the mere admiration for wealth or position. Again and again he had heard her speak of the Earl as
"Stallingford"—as indeed so many Yorkshire tenants did of
their lord of the manor; but nothing would have induced her
to refer to Mr. Soloman Woolfe, who bought Cardingly from the
impoverished Sir Grant Manders, without the prefix to his name.
No, she was a great woman, with courage, determination and the
ability to stand alone.

For himself, the knowledge that he was a bastard affected
him not at all. He could see no shame attaching to himself, that
had always appeared to him to be one of the least reasonable
conventions. A child of shame! How could the child be held

responsible, and why on earth should any stigma attach to it for something which was outside its power to prevent? He smiled, a little grimly, as he remembered that to be a bastard—always supposing that your father was lower in the social scale than a royal duke—was supposed to inflict a permanent injury on the character, to say nothing of the prospects of anyone!

The realization that Stallingford was his father had come so gradually that now he felt little or no shock. His affection and his regret for William Scarth were unimpaired. He had loved William before this realization came, and he would continue to love him. He wondered what would have been William's comments had anyone told him that he had done a noble thing in "fathering another man's child"? Not that plenty of countrymen didn't do it, but they expected to be paid for doing so. When had William known—had he known from the day he married his wife? Anthony felt his cheeks flush in the darkness, these speculations were no business of his! The facts were all that concerned him, such facts as affected him.

He had grown to know the Earl pretty well. Stallingford, lonely and disappointed in his own son, had found it pleasant and amusing to lunch occasionally with this very much awake young journalist. It had pleased him to know that he could still "pull strings", pleased him still more to discover that Anthony did not expect to have those strings pulled on his behalf. He was confident that success would come to him, and content to work for it. The lad was neither a prig nor a budding rake. He admitted that he liked reading, he admitted that he liked pretty girls. He had ideas—some of them sounded fantastic to Stallingford—about the future of the Labour Party, Socialists and the like. Only once had the Earl felt that Anthony made a remark which was in obvious bad taste.

"Tell me—" he said, "tell me as briefly as you can, what are the ideals—if you can call them ideals—the aims, objects and so forth of these Socialists?"

"I think, sir," Anthony said, speaking slowly, as if he were trying to choose his words with fastidious care, "to put the teachings of Jesus Christ into ordinary everyday politics."

Stallingford knew that he was shocked, knew too that he showed it.

"Good God, my boy!" he cried. "You mustn't say things like that!"

"It's what I think, sir, and you'll admit that a finer set of ethical rules would be difficult to find."

"Tut, tut ! Very likely, very likely ; but—you can't talk about Our Lord over a luncheon table ! That won't do at all !"

Yet when Stallingford, enjoying playing the role of playing "father" even though he played it incognito, had made some careful and discreet mention of women, Anthony had flushed, looked uncomfortable, and crumbled his bread nervously.

Stallingford said, "My dear boy, don't be nervous. I want to—er—safeguard you—er—forearmed—er—or rather I mean —forewarned is—well, you understand me."

Scarlet-faced, Anthony had stammered, "I'm sure, sir, only —well, I do like girls, but I'm not keen on—I mean I've never— that is—my work is frightfully absorbing, and I do want to get on."

Queer, interested in politics, could say astounding things without turning a hair, and yet got red-eared when women were mentioned and it was suggested—well—were young men changing ? Didn't they think that a good time meant champagne suppers, and ladies of the chorus, drinking toasts out of slippers, going home with the milk ?

Anthony Scarth, sitting beside the silent young groom in the high dog-cart, contemplating his long and probably cold journey to London, would have admitted to anyone that going home with the milk did not attract him in the least. He had always known that his mother's money supported him, that he had been given every possible advantage, and that it was his duty to make good, to repay his mother for what she had done. Added to this, he was possessed of a genuine ambition, and an unaffected joy in his work. There were certain things which he wanted, hoped for and intended to have ; things which money could obtain for him. He was ready to live simply, to endure a certain amount of discomfort, to wear Leister's cast-off clothes, because he believed that by doing all these things he would be able to save money and gain his objectives more quickly. He longed for a comfortable flat, for sufficient money to buy the books he wanted, the good clothes for which he longed.

He wanted to be able to leave journalism alone and devote himself entirely to drawings and cartoons. He would never write well, and he knew it—even to himself, and he admitted that he tried to read his own efforts with all possible leniency—

his reports were dull, stiff and unimaginative. "If only they'd let me draw 'em," he sighed to his friend, Bill Thorpe.

"You can't draw a fire or a street accident, you fathead !"

"Can't I ? I can—and make 'em both funny !" Anthony retorted, and proceeded to do so, even Thorpe admitting that he could "squeeze a laugh out of nothing".

"Otla' Station," the groom said.

Anthony fumbled for half a crown, scrambled down, gave the tip, and with a "Good night" entered the station.

"Lunnon train ?" the porter repeated. "Why, in a manner o' speaking theer is noa Lunnon train, not fra here. Yer ought not ter have cum here at all, bi reits. Theer is a train—aye, i' seven minutes—allus perviding she's not laate, which she moastly is—an' yer mun change at Leeds, an' agean at York—nay, will it be York ?—nay, Ah doot not. York—noa ! Nor nout like it ! Nay, ye'd better ax at Leeds, mister. Aye, that 'ul be best, ax at Leeds. Aye. . . ."

As he was carried towards London by a succession of slow trains, all cold and all lacking in comfort, Anthony, trying to keep warm by wrapping his overcoat round his knees, smiled a little grimly. Leister was being carried south in an express train, he was seated in a first-class carriage ; at every stop the guard would appear at his carriage door, solicitous and attentive.

"Perhaps," Anthony mused, his lips curving into a smile, "I have underrated the benefits attached to legitimacy."

CHAPTER FIVE

THE storm burst over Stallingford three weeks later, when the Earl returned. He arrived late one evening, muffled in a fur coat, ready to snap and snarl at everyone. Mr. Harrison reported that he was in a "rare temper, worse, believe me, than anything to which his lordship has previously treated us". He went directly to his room, and appeared to spend the next two hours ringing bells and demanding first one thing and then another.

What kind of wood was being burnt in the grate ? Had he not always insisted that apple wood and only apple wood was to be used ? Did his orders mean anything or did they not ? Was he of the slightest importance in Stallingford or not ? Why was the light so bad ? Why was the bath water not sufficiently hot ? Harrison and footmen were kept busy tearing up and down stairs trying to rectify the faults which were apparent to his lordship and to no one else.

Sally, in her own room, listened and thought, 'Eh, it's a pity that you never had anything to grumble about ! Life's been over easy for you, I doubt.'

In the morning he sent for her, and she was shocked at the change in his appearance. He had always been thin, but now he had grown even more fragile. His eyes were sunk deep in his head ; on his hands the blue veins showed too plainly. His voice sounded colourless and mechanical. His hair, so sparse over the temples, looked almost damp, and lay lifeless against his skull. Sally remembered that he was only forty-two. He looked ten years older.

She stood waiting in his big sitting-room, and heard him moving about the bedroom, talking to his valet in that queer, querulous voice, as if everything gave him ground for complaint. Finally he entered the sitting-room. He was dressed, except for his coat, and was wearing a dressing-gown of dark purple silk with a padded collar and cuffs. He was smoking a cigarette, and Sally noticed that his fingers were stained with nicotine. The valet followed him.

"You can go," Stallingford snapped. "I'll ring when I want you. Good morning, Mrs. Scarth—sit down."

"Good morning, m'lord. I hope that you had a good journey."

"I had a foul journey," he retorted. "Perfectly foul. You know why I've come, Sally. Leister arrived at Menton, in a state of dither which I have never seen equalled. He had several stories—none of which held water. Apparently you saw him—can you tell me the truth?"

"Well, m'lord, he came here one evening. He wanted some things just before leaving for France——"

"Why did he want to come to France at all?"

"That I couldn't say, m'lord——"

"Oh, Sally, have done! Don't fence with me. It's all too serious. You know the truth, and I want to know it too. I'm finished with him. He's no damned good, he's weak and he's a liar—I suspect"—slowly—"that he's several other unpleasant things as well. Now, let me have the truth!"

She watched him with steady eyes, her face was perfectly calm, nothing went to indicate that her brain was in a turmoil. She only knew the truth vaguely herself. The whole thing had been like a nightmare. Of course she had heard of the scandal, listened to comments and speculations in the servants' hall, and, as often as might be, she had checked them, because she hated "that kind of talk".

"Why, there was some mistake," she said. "Some idea that his lordship had been in Lunnon, in bad company, and two—well, police officers they were, I suppose, came here. Just a lot of impudence and meddling with what didn't concern them—as I told them. It was partly that Mr. Trotter to blame, m'lord. Getting into a panic because his lordship had been away from the school for a couple of nights. Oh, that was naughty, I will admit, but he'd been to York to see a friend. This young gentleman was going to America, it seems. Oh, his lordship—who was here when they came—he spoke up and told them just what he thought of their impertinence. Very crestfallen they were too. That was all, and his lordship left by the night train to town. That's the story, m'lord."

For a second the old Victor looked at her from Stallingford's eyes. The one-time alert young man she had known, with the queer little trick of narrowing his eyes when he was concentrating. He ceased at that moment to be an elderly, irritable man with thinning hair, with a cigarette dangling at the corner of his weak mouth, wearing a preposterously gorgeous dressing-gown : he

was the Leister she had known in the old days. His head thrust
a little forward, his eyes alight, even his mouth seemed to have
taken on a sudden firmness.

"And that, Sally, is the truth, eh ? You'd not lie to me,
would you, Sally ? That's the truth, eh ?"

She hesitated, his eyes never wavered, then she said slowly,
"It's the truth, m'lord, as far as anyone need know it. It's all
the truth that anyone except three people 'ul ever know."

"Ah ! And those three people—are . . . ?"

"His lordship—myself, and—my son."

Stallingford threw back his head. "So ! Tony's in this,
is he ?"

Strange to hear him speak of their son as "Tony" ! The
diminutive came with a kind of affectionate ease. She did not
speak, and Stallingford said again, "So Tony's in this, eh ?"

"He was here at the time, m'lord. He was here before his
lordship came, he saw the—the police officers."

Stallingford sat down ; he rubbed out his cigarette, and placed
his hands on his knees, leaning slightly forward, looking eager
and interested. Queer how once anything caught his attention
the years fell from him, Sally thought.

"Look here, Sally," he said, "I want the whole story. No
embroidery now. The truth. It's between us. You won't make
things worse for Leister. I'm done with Leister. He can take
which road he likes. I want to know what happened. Now—
from the beginning."

Slowly and carefully she told the story, making light of
nothing, even admitting her fear of discovery. She retailed what
Anthony had said to the detectives, what they had said to him,
how he had turned on them coldly furious, and how finally
Leister had driven to the station in one of the Stallingford
carriages, and Anthony had left for London by Otley.

Stallingford leant back and drew a deep breath. "So that's
the tale, eh ? He's got your resource, Sally. Remember,
years ago—Dover and the 'Lord Warden' ? You got the family
out of a mess then. Tony's making history repeat itself." Then
more slowly, almost reflectively, "And they accepted him as
Leister, eh ? No doubts about it, eh ? That's interesting. I
wonder—if he ever—suspects anything, Sally ?"

The room was very quiet ; once a piece of burning wood,
crackling suddenly, seemed to Sally to fill the place with an
unbearable noise. Stallingford sat watching her, his face intent,

his hands pressing on his knees so that the blood was driven from the finger-tips, leaving them white. It was a strange scene, the great room, with its heavy hangings of old red brocade, its long windows, the carved furniture, and the great mantelpiece ; the man with his white thin face, and his gorgeous gown ; the woman heavy, deep-bosomed, and wearing a dress so plain that it almost amounted to uniform, and over all the sense of expectancy.

"Does he—suspect anything, Sally ?"

"He knows, m'lord."

Sally did not know what effect she expected the words to have on Stallingford, but he sprang to his feet with an exclamation, and began to pace up and down the long room, his hands plunged deep into the pockets of his dressing-gown. She watched him, taking short quick steps, his whole figure seeming to be charged with sudden energy. At last he came back to the fireplace and stood before her.

"He knows, eh ? He wasn't horrified ? He likes me, I think. Might like me more if he had the chance to know me better. Stallingford's entailed, but Versley isn't, neither is Scranton Moor—there's enough money to keep them both up and do it well. Let Leister have Stallingford—let him have what money must go with it. What do I care ? I've never liked the place. Versley and Scranton shall go to Tony. He'll know what to do with 'em. He'll fill the bill. There's something in the boy ! He's not thread paper and cotton wool like Leister. Sally, I'll do it ! I'll go and see my lawyers when I get back to town. It's been done before. Why not again ? Old Hector Brisley acknowledged his son—Maurice. Damn' good fellow he is too. Tony ! Nineteen and earning his own living ! Time for him to go in for anything he wants ! Make a mark in the world. By God, what a difference it will make to me !"

Sally Scarth squared her shoulders, she stood there apparently unmoved, and when she spoke her voice was steady and even. Only her heart thundered and pounded against her ribs.

"Nay, m'lord, you'll not do it," she said, "for I won't allow it. It's the law of the land that a bastard child has one parent only—its mother. Anthony's only nineteen, and until he comes of age I'm his guardian and I'll have a say in what he does or in what's done for him. I'll not have him taken and pampered and petted. I'll not have every road smoothed out for him. He'll come to no harm working. Already people say that he has talent. He's got plenty of work to do, and he can do it, and do it well. You'll say nothing to him of what we've spoken this morning. Nothing!"

Suddenly sulky, Stallingford said, "And who'll stop me, pray?"

"I will! Anthony's mother. I've always been against this meeting, m'lord. I've never liked his lunching and dining with you. I've always had my doubts that you might let something drop. I mean more to him than anyone! Oh yes, I know that as I know that tomorrow morning's sun 'ul rise. If I tell him that I don't want him to see you again, I've no doubt that he'll do what I say. He maybe is your son, but he's my son too. I've plenty of faults, the dear Lord knows, but weakness isn't one of them. Leave my son be, Stallingford! Leave him be to work out his own ways of living. If not—I go from here tonight, and you've seen Anthony for the last time. I mean it!"

Stallingford listened, and as he listened Sally felt that she watched his energy, his enthusiasm vanish, leaving him again slack and bored, irritable and ill-tempered.

"Tush! What a fuss about nothing!" he exploded. " 'Pon my word, you positively hector me, Sally. No other man would stand it. Another man would tell you to go, and you know it."

"No one's stopping you saying it, Stallingford, if so be as you wish to."

"Ugh! Rubbish! I make a suggestion, a suggestion which any other woman would embrace with gratitude—yes, that's right—gratitude! Instead, I'm treated to a tirade about son and mothers! There are times when you forget your place, and forget it badly!"

She asked quietly, "What is my place, m'lord—housekeeper or—caretaker of your son's safety?"

He flung his hands above his head, the gesture reminded Sally of a hysterical woman rather than a man. "Oh, for God's sake," he almost screamed, "don't nag! I hate being nagged! Let the thing alone. It's always the same, has been all my life. And you know it. The moment I saw a chance to be happy, the moment I found a real interest, something which meant something in my life—someone stepped in and said, 'No!'! My whole life's been a disappointment. No one knows that better than you do. As a young man—after I married—then my children—I detest the pair of them! Now—Tony! Oh, I ought to be used to it by now."

Again he slumped down in the big chair, staring at the fire miserably, his face a mask of desolation. For a brief moment Sally had the impulse to put her arm round his shoulders, to draw him close to her and try to talk him out of his despondency. Not that she loved him as she had once done, but there was something so childishly unreasonable, so hopelessly wretched in his outlook. Perhaps he had longed to have Anthony for a companion, perhaps his pride in the boy had been real and sound. She daren't risk it. Anthony was hers, he belonged to her as neither Elsie nor Thomas did, and she hoped passionately that his future might hold nothing but what was good. The momentary impulse passed, she sighed, and realized that the past was too far away to be dragged into the present.

"If that's all, m'lord," she said, "I'll get back to my work."

He looked up, his eyes miserable, his mouth bitter. "God, you've grown hard, Sally."

"I'm sorry, m'lord."

ii

He left three days later. Stallingford settled down again into its accustomed round. Muriel worked harder than ever. Miss Meade and Mr. Haviland were delighted with her. To Sally they seemed to regard her as trainers might regard a promising colt. Later in the spring she departed for France, with the indefatigable Miss Meade, to improve her accent and take extra lessons in some subject or other—names meant little to Sally. With July Lady Stallingford came home, and the house was filled with people. The old lady was growing very frail, but she admitted to Sally that she was determined that her grand-daughter should meet "the right people".

"This young woman, and a very clever young woman, Miss Meade, I'm sure, must not imagine that she can entirely rule my grand-daughter's life. There is such a thing as marriage, and Muriel won't always be sixteen," she told Sally.

So again the house was filled with young people, and Lady Muriel sulked a little and complained that they interfered terribly with her work, that they thought of nothing but playing games, and enjoying themselves. She appeared to dislike them all except one tall pale boy, called Hugh Thursby, who stammered a little, wore glasses, and spent most of his time in the library, sitting on the top of the library steps reading books.

Later, Lady Gwendoline Vanderholt came over with her little stout husband and her three beautiful and precocious children from America. She had grown very lovely and met Sally without the faintest sign that but for her she might not now be married to this pleasant American who so obviously adored her.

"That's how people ought to behave," Sally decided. "That's what breeding does!"

They came and went, these people, the house filled and emptied again ; Thomas came to spend part of his holiday with his mother, grown out of all knowledge, and Sally spent five days in London to see Elsie and Anthony. Thomas was broadening, growing more and more solid, more and more absorbed in his work, his plants and flowers. Elsie's elegance was almost frightening, and her voice was so refined that Sally could scarcely understand what she said. Her clothes were beautiful, and she wore them well, there was no gainsaying that. She spoke several times of some man called André Heyse, who, it appeared, was a French dressmaker of great repute.

Sally said, "You seem to think a lot of this gentleman, Elsie."

Elsie laughed and patted her elaborately dressed hair self-consciously. "Well, Mama, if I said thet he thought a lot abaout me, Aye might be speaking moah correctly."

"Good gracious ! You don't mean that he's in love with you, Elsie ! My dear, and you not eighteen yet !"

Elsie simpered a little and then with a sudden air of worldly wisdom explained that French gentlemen did not take age into account as did Englishmen. Mr. Heyse had not actually begun to pay court to her, but his intentions were unmistakable. Oh yes, Madame Moore knew about it, and thought that it would be a fine thing for Elsie. Mr. Heyse, it appeared, had a wonderful business, not a shop at all, in the rue de la Paix. "One of the best streets in Paris," Elsie explained.

Sally, disturbed and distressed, spoke to Madame Moore. Madame laughed, smiled and nodded. Mr. Heyse was undoubtedly attracted. Rich ! Madame flung her hands heavenwards. Successful ! Words appeared to fail her. She called to one of the young ladies who, smooth and slim in black satin, paraded up and down the long salon.

"Miss Travers, bring me the brown Heyse, if you please."

Miss Travers came, carrying a dress composed of what appeared to Sally to be twists of brown tulle, the whole thing looked ordinary enough.

"Just hold it out for madam, if you please."

Sally looked, wondered what all the fuss was about.

Madame breathed, "A masterpiece! Yes, take it away, Miss Travers. That," she said, "is a Heyse! Not shown as yet. My clients will fight for it!"

Sally thought privately that it looked as if they had done so already. She nodded. "I see. And you think this—gentleman is—well—a good match for Elsie?"

"One of the finest dressmakers in Paris—in the world."

"Seems queer to me, men being dressmakers, madam, I'm sure."

Madame shrugged. "What—when you think of Worth?"

"And he's got a really good position?"

Madame laid a plump hand on Sally's arm. "If Elsie were my daughter and were marrying into the aristocracy, I should not feel the same sense of pride that I do when I contemplate one of my young ladies marrying Monsieur André Heyse."

'And that,' Sally thought, as she walked away from the elegant shop, 'just shows what rubbish people can talk when they give their minds to it. The man's a shopkeeper, and no more and no less! Still, if Elsie likes him! Eh, dear, it's a puzzle, I'm sure.'

She told Anthony about it, and it was pleasant to listen to him explaining what these big French men dressmakers really were, how they actually held positions of great importance, dictated fashions and evolved designs. She felt better about Elsie after Anthony had explained it to her. He had a trick, had Anthony, of taking all her worries and straightening them out for her, all the things which seemed dim and confused he could clear in a few words. He had a chance to go to America, he told her. No, not for good, but to make sketches for some big advertising firm. Interesting, and it would pay well.

"Besides—" he hesitated, "I think it might be a good thing for me to get away for a bit, Mother. Don't think that I'm unkind, don't think that I don't appreciate all that he does and wants to do for me, but—the Earl—is in town such a lot, and he is so lavish with his invitations. I hate to refuse. He's lonely, I think, and disappointed. By the way, he told me that Leister has gone to South Africa for a trip, if he likes it he may do some farming there—but . . ." His voice trailed off and he sat crumbling his bread.

"But what, luv?" Sally asked.

"But—it's queer, Mother, that—his being my father means so little to me. I always imagined that automatically people loved their fathers and mothers. I find that they don't. I like him, I'm sorry for him—desperately sorry—but love just doesn't come into it. Is that all wrong, do you think ?"

She frowned, longing to find the words to clothe her thoughts. "Nay, it's hard to say," she admitted. "I don't know that I believe in—this automatical love for parents. Like a machine that's wound up and is bound to run smoothly. Babies are different, so's little children. They're like kittens and puppies and such-like. But when children grow up—well, parents, to my mind, have to earn love and affection. If it was just something that came willynilly, then children ought to be able to recognize their parents wherever they met them. A child that never remembered seeing its father ought to be able to say if it met him in the street—'Eh, that's my dad !' Instinct ought to tell them. Instinct doesn't tell them, and so seemingly love doesn't come by instinct neither. Now—and I don't know that really this is a very nice way for me to talk to you, Anthony luv——"

He patted her hand. "It's all right, Mother. Don't worry ; we're living in 1895—nearly 1896 ! Besides, you and I—we're different from other mothers and other sons. Go on."

"Well, maybe there's something of God's justice in it. If fathers or mothers don't do their duty, then they must pay by losing the love of their bairns. I'd blame a child for not loving its parents who had been good and kind to it, who had loved it, and tried to be—yes, tried to be *friends* with it ; but I'd not blame no one for not loving bad parents. For look at it how you may, I don't see that there's any call to. Your—" she hesitated, then went on steadily, "your father's had things made difficult for him. Circumstances were against him. He's never been able to stand up against circumstances, though I don't see what he could have done, not i' this case, I don't really, Anthony. Now, you're grown, you're clever, you're nice-looking—oh yes, you are !—and he wants your company. He wants to make things smooth for you. And that's what I don't want ! I'm able to make them sufficiently smooth. You'll not need to go short of anything, my dear, not that's necessary, but I don't want Stallingford coddling and making much of you until you're weak as water."

"I don't want that either," he said eagerly, "I don't honestly,

Mother. You see, I do *like* him, but I don't love him—as, for instance, I loved William Scarth."

"Aye, I understand that," Sally said; "but William was a very different pair of sleeves."

Anthony went to America; and with the New Year came the news that Elsie was going to marry her André Heyse, and Sally went up to town to meet him. He was short and stout, and his clothes were beautiful, and he was going bald. He wore patent leather boots and immaculately creased trousers, and had a trick of bunching the tips of his fingers together and kissing them whenever he saw anything which seemed to demand his admiration. He spoke excellent English, and was lavish in his praises of Elsie's cleverness.

Sally, big, stout and plainly if well dressed, was the type of woman he had never met before. He watched her, his head cocked a little on one side, looking like a speculative robin, and told Elsie later that if her mother would allow him to dress her he could make her look positively distinguished.

"For the distinction ees there, my Elsie !" Heyse maintained. "Yore mother hez height, 'er form is good though 'eavy. I can imagine that eef I was to mak' 'er a dress of——"

Elsie squeezed his arm and laughed. "Get on with you ! Mother'd never let anyone make dresses for her that didn't live in Yorkshire !"

The wedding took place in London, Thomas, in the absence of Anthony, gave his sister away. A more ill-assorted group of people could scarcely have been found. Thomas, with his fair hair refusing, as it always did, to lie down on his head, wearing a good if obviously country-made suit of blue serge. Sally—looking somehow larger than usual, in a dress of black silk, which Mr. Jackson declared "would stand alone, Mrs. Scarth", and a bonnet which she felt was so small as to look ridiculous on her mass of brown hair. Madame Moore, elegant, rustling and scented, with a spray of orchids which Thomas whispered to his mother cost "every penny o' two pounds" ! The bridegroom, who looked as if he had been poured into his clothes and polished, accompanied by his brother Louis, who wore a pointed beard which caused Thomas's face to assume a strange and strained expression every time he looked at it, and Elsie in a costume with immense sleeves designed by the bridegroom, and a hat which he informed Sally was the greatest masterpiece ever evolved by his brother Louis.

The luncheon followed at the Savoy, and Sally insisted she should pay for it. She handed Thomas her purse, and watched his face turn slowly purple as he saw the sum which had been charged. It was a strained and difficult business. Louis Heyse spoke very little English, and was immensely proud of what he did speak. From time to time he fired off inapposite remarks at Sally or Thomas, both of whom looked at him blankly.

"Lon-don," he announced, "ees a grreat ceety !"

"Aye, it's that all reit," Thomas replied.

"Par-eess ees a ver' beau-ti'ful ceety !"

"So I've heard," Sally agreed.

Spurred on to fresh efforts, he announced firmly, "Zee Preence grrows ver' fat !"

Thomas said, "Prince—what prince, mister ?"

"Preence off Valis."

"I don't think we'll discuss His Highness like that, if you don't mind," Sally said coldly.

It was a relief when the newly married couple departed, taking the bowing and smiling Louis with them, and Madame Moore drove off in a hansom to Knightsbridge. Sally, left alone with Thomas, sighed. She was tired ; she had found the whole day trying and uncomfortable. Her son-in-law irritated her with his compliments, his brother, she decided, was little short of a fool—a man milliner, of all things in the world ! Madame Moore was all very well, but she gave herself a lot of airs, and what was she after all ?—a shopkeeper.

"I'm glad that's over," she said to Thomas.

"Aye, so'm I, Muther. It weer fairly getting on my nerves that woman leaning forward ovver t' table crushing them orchids ter nout ! Ah'll tell yer what, we'll goa an' get a wash an' brush oop at yon smart 'otel o' yourn, and we'll goa somewheer wheer we can get a reit good laugh. How'll that meet the bill ?"

He took her to the Tivoli, and though it was not quite the same as going out with Anthony, who took almost too much care of her, yet it did her good to listen to Thomas roaring with laughter at the jokes and clapping his big hands together, giving all and sundry whole-hearted applause. He was big, she thought, for fifteen, big and strong, comely and healthy. She'd have no trouble with Thomas. Not, she reflected, that she'd had any trouble with her children—good bairns if ever there were any. Only she sighed again when she remembered that Elsie had married a foreigner—a man who made dresses for women.

1895 slid past. Leister remained abroad, and when Stallingford came to the North he never mentioned him. Once when
Sally ventured to ask, the Earl scowled and said, "If you want
any information concerning Leister, ask his grandmother. I
have no interest whatever in him."

Old Lady Stallingford, more frail than ever, returned to Stallingford for good in 1896. She was too old, she said, to travel any
more, she wanted her own home and her own friends round her.
Her presence in the big house made little or no difference. She
kept very much to her own suite of rooms which overlooked the
park, and as time went on her appearances downstairs became
more and more rare. She was seventy-five, and had never,
Sally felt, fully recovered the loss of her husband. She lived
more and more in the past, and only when she talked to Sally
of bygone days did she seem to regain something of her grip
upon life.

She missed Leister, she admitted. Muriel was of little interest
to her. "Too absorbed, too occupied with this study, and—
what good will it do her, Sally ? Tell me that. I ought to have
people here, she ought to visit—but I'm too old, too tired. She
hates going away. The only young person she seems to like is
Hugh Thursby—Arthur Thursby's son from Tancaster. I wish
Leister were home. I wish my daughter would come over from
America to see me again. It's dreadful to grow old—and
lonely, Sally."

At last Sally wrote to Stallingford, told him that his mother
was fretting, and that to fret was bad for old people, and wouldn't
he come down to Stallingford and see what could be done. He
came, wandering about the house, bored and uninterested. He
sat in his mother's room and scarcely spoke ; he walked beside
her bath-chair, trailing his stick behind him, dutiful and dull.
He sent for his daughter, and asked questions about her work.
Was it true that she wanted to go to Girton ? If she wanted to,
he supposed that she could—she'd do as she wished ; they all
did, he was never consulted.

"Mind, you won't find a husband at Girton," he warned her.

Swinging her long plaits, Muriel replied, "There are things I
want more."

"When you go you might advise me of your departure," he
said, formally polite.

"It won't be for two years at least. I'll let you know, of
course. There'll be papers for you to sign."

"And bills to pay, I don't doubt. My only use in the world."

"I wonder how much longer I'm expected to stay here?" he said to Sally one day.

"Her ladyship enjoys having you here, m'lord."

"That seems incredible to me. I contribute nothing to the general gaiety."

"It's someone for her to talk to, m'lord."

He stared at her, then laughed suddenly. "Never gild the bitter pill, do you, Sally?"

"I don't know what you mean, m'lord."

The Vanderholts came over from America, and Stallingford's gloom deepened. They were a devoted family; the youngsters appeared to find their mother the best company in the world, and their father the most amusing of companions. They admitted that they were "just crazy" about Stallingford. Victor, who at seventeen was head and shoulders taller than the Earl, spent his days out of doors, riding round the estate with Mr. Roysten, asking questions, making notes.

"A serious young man," Roysten told Sally. "Tells me that he wants a model ranch of his own. He'll do well, intelligent, keen, interested in everything. The difference between Leister and this lad must strike his lordship pretty forcibly."

The younger girl and boy, Ann and Henry, were tireless. From morning until night they wanted to be going here, visiting that old abbey, or the other old manor house. Everything thrilled them, the cottages with their thatched roofs, the queer dialect of the country folk, the town with its weekly market and the stalls set out with produce. Their rather high voices could be heard everywhere, recounting their exploits and their impressions.

Muriel said, "Of course, they belong to a new country. They come of a young nation. That's why they've got such curiosity. Such vitality. It seems to me, Mrs. Scarth, that in America the education is in advance of ours here. Miss Meade says that at present the Americans are strictly utilitarian. They've produced nothing worth recording in art, literature or music, but they are willing to adopt the art of other nations with real appreciation."

Sally said, "Look at that now! Well, that's pleasant to hear, I'm sure," and wondered what it all meant.

Lady Gwendoline came to Sally's room and talked to her, talked in a very friendly way.

"It's nice to think that you're here, Sally. We owe you a great deal, you know. Oh yes, I've not forgotten. What a little fool I was, a wicked little fool into the bargain ! Why, I just dare not think what my life would have been if I hadn't married that angel of a husband of mine ! And my children, Sally, they're darlings, aren't they ? My brother glowers at them, but my mother adores them. Muriel's going to be a regular blue-stocking ! So stupid. Far better send her out to me in another couple of years and let her marry some nice American. Have you heard, Leister's coming home, and my husband wants to take him back with us. If anyone can make a man of him, Mr. Vanderholt can ! I hope Leister will realize that. It's time that he *did* something. My sons won't drift about, playing at work. They've got to make good, and they will ! You just can't allow boys to drift about as Leister has done. It's asking for trouble. Sally, I must go—I'll come and see you again.''

Nice to think how well that marriage had turned out ! It seemed so long ago since Dover, and the "Lord Warden''—and —everything.

CHAPTER SIX

LEISTER came home, and left again for America. The Earl—obviously relieved that the width of the Atlantic was put between him and his son—departed for some foreign spa. Lady Stallingford gave up any attempt at entertaining on her grand-daughter's behalf, and retired to her own rooms, from which she scarcely stirred except to take dignified drives round the estate with her companion. Elsie wrote from Paris that life was filled with interest, that André was producing "confections" which would be the talk of London, and that Louis was a worthy assistant in the matter of millinery. Thomas sent his mother short and excessively limited letters, dealing only with the latest developments in the flower world; and Anthony sent brief, amusing notes telling of how hard he was working, and what small success was coming to him.

Sally, living quietly at Stallingford, felt that her life had flowed into a backwater. Nothing would ever happen again except the ordinary routine, and she knew that she experienced a certain relief at the realization. She was tired of worries, of scenes, weary of Stallingford's irritability, of Leister's weakness, of Lady Muriel's self-assertiveness, of Lady Stallingford's self-pity. She felt that she had lived so long that her life had been filled with difficulties and worries, and now she was thankful to remain quietly at Stallingford, doing her work, running the big house efficiently, capable of making the machinery move on oiled wheels.

She was only forty-one, but like many women of her class, and particularly women who have worked since they were children, she looked older than her years. For twenty-nine years Sally Scarth had worked, shouldered responsibilities, planned and contrived, and the early years of middle age found her an elderly woman. She was tall and held herself erect, her hair was scarcely touched with grey, her skin was smooth and soft, but her movements were those of a woman past her prime —slow and heavy.

The servants liked and respected her. She was just without being harsh, she was always willing to listen to explanations,

to weigh up reasons, and to make allowances. The young servants went to her confident that her advice would be worth
having, the older ones were glad to confide in her. Sally Scarth,
housekeeper of Stallingford Manor, was something of a personality, ladies of the county coming to call on Lady Stallingford,
their visits ended, would say to Mr. Harrison, "I should like to
have a word with Mrs. Scarth, if she is in her room."

They had grown to like her, these ladies ; it was a pleasure
to them to sit in her comfortable room and listen to her sharp
comments on the affairs of the day. She never pretended to
know more than she actually did, and she relied on her sound
common sense for her opinions. She knew nothing of matters
political, and cared less. When Mr. Harrison discussed the
spoken word of Lord Salisbury and Mr. Joseph Chamberlain in
the servants' hall, Sally listened, and said nothing.

When Stallingford, on one of his rare visits, spoke of Salisbury's statement that the Great Powers were liable to grow weary
of the plaints of suffering Christians oppressed by Turkish rule,
Sally nodded.

"He's right, of course," Stallingford said. "Even our patience
wears a little thin."

"I don't doubt it, m'lord," she agreed ; "but it wears thin
no quicker because it's Christians that are suffering. England's
only patient when it suits her."

When she went to London to see Anthony, and replenish the
linen cupboards of Stallingford, she experienced her first sense
of fear for what the future might hold. She was so completely
without preconceived opinions, so utterly without ideas which
had been formed for her through the medium of the Press, that
her mind was entirely open and receptive.

Anthony, looking thinner and taller, his face losing its boyish
lines and growing older and more mature, talked to her of things
apart from his work or her own.

"Things are brewing, Mother," he said. "This Jameson
Raid is a pointer. They might haul them up at Bow Street, but
the people were with them and everyone knew it. Oh, they'll
be used as scapegoats, but they'll be heroes just the same !
Expansion's in the air, and not only that, but—and Chamberlain
used the word—predominance. We're growing too rich, too
powerful, too arrogant. 'Africa was created to be the plague of
the Foreign Office'—no one but an Englishman could have said
that. Oh, whatever we tackle we shall come through, that goes

without saying, but whether we shall come through with hands which have remained moderately clean—that's another matter."

Sally, listening, said, "But what do you mean, my dear? War? Who's to make war against us? Africa? I thought we'd beaten all the natives and taken them to work in the gold and diamond mines."

She never knew why Anthony threw back his head and laughed.

"All the same, Mother, watch a gentleman called Paul Kruger and his friends the Boers."

"In Africa? I thought Mr. Cecil Rhodes ruled South Africa."

"An opinion shared, I don't doubt, by Mr. Cecil Rhodes," Anthony said.

In 1898 old Lady Stallingford died, she slipped away quietly in her sleep, and so her maid found her. Sally, looking down on the still face, which might have been carved out of fine ivory, thought, 'And you're the last of them, m'lady. Now there's no one left who knew Stallingford as you did, who remembers what life was like in those days. Poor dear soul, you were very tired of it all, you'll be glad to get back to his lordship.'

Strange to think that here was the last person who remembered the coming of the little workhouse child, Sally Hardcastle, to Stallingford. Sally had never known her well, she had always remained a little in awe of the old lady, always felt that a curtain separated her from her mistress. There had been moments when Lady Stallingford had drawn that curtain aside, and for a brief interval they had been two women speaking together. Those moments had always been short, and Sally never regretted the fact. To her it was right that the gentry should keep a little aloof, when they spoke in a friendly, even intimate fashion she felt that theirs was a gracious condescension. There was no question in her mind of Jack being as good as his master—in Sally Scarth's world, Jack and his master lived on different planes, and what was right for Jack was by no means necessarily right for his master, or vice versa. As she read in her Bible, "Male and female created He them", so she held that "gentry and common folks created He them". Her interpretation of that word "common" was the old and correct one, not the modern meaning assigned to it, signifying cheap or without merit.

As she watched the funeral procession move away from the house, noting the carriages with their coats and crests emblazoned on the panels, as she saw the representatives of the great families who had come to pay their respects to the dead Countess, she thought, 'Aye, you're saying good-bye to mor'n the Countess of Stallingford, you're saying good-bye to a bit of hist'ry. The days are over when to be an Earl meant that you were something like a little king, with the duties of a king. Stallingford's sorry that his mother's dead, but he's itching to be off again. He'll only listen with half an ear when Mr. Roysten talks to him tomorrow about the Long Wall, or Culver's Cottages. Lady Muriel 'ul be glad to be back at her Greek verbs and her Latin stories—Leister's not here at all. Nay, the gentry, as I used to know it, is done with. More's the pity.'

Within twelve months she felt that Fate conspired to prove that she was wrong. Those Boers of whom Anthony had spoken grew, so it seemed, over puffed up. Mr. Harrison said that they wanted a lesson and England would have to give it to them. Sally listened, tried to understand, and grasped only that they were farmers who didn't want to give too many rights to Englishmen.

The new cook, who had replaced Mrs. Rogers—now living with her daughter outside Northampton—said, "But surely, Mr. Harrison, a crowd of farmers 'ul never dare to fight England !"

Mr. Harrison, with his eyeglasses placed on his nose, looked up from the evening paper which he was reading. This "evening paper business" was another thing which Sally never understood. In the old days *The Times* and the *Morning Post* came to Stallingford, there were various Sunday papers delivered for the servants' hall—*Lloyd's*, *Reynold's* and the like—but evening papers every day of the week—never !

Mr. Harrison said, "Mrs. Duchers, when dogs grow impudent, there's no saying what they'll dare, and they must be taught their lesson. They will be taught it, believe me."

Suddenly it seemed that Stallingford was galvanized into life. The Earl came back, looking younger than he had looked for years. He was going to raise his own troop of horsemen, yeomanry, from the estates of the Earl of Stallingford, from every village young men, farmers, yeomen, doctors and the like were to be asked to join.

Stallingford's Horse !

"We're going to show them, Sally ! Leister's on his way back from America. And—listen—Tony's joining me. That's right ! You can't hold them back. They're all the same. Furious at this insult to England !"

"But, m'lord, what insult ?"

"Tut, tut, Sally ! The way they've treated the English colonists."

She went to London to see Anthony. He talked as if the whole thing were something rather unpleasant, as if it tasted nasty in his mouth. She felt that when he spoke of the reasons for the war that he was gently mocking, not only her, but himself.

"Predominance, what did I tell you ?" he said. "The greatest nation in the world must be predominant ! We always believed that trade would follow the flag, but here—South Africa, y'know —we realize that the flag must follow trade ! Of course in a poor country there'd be precious little trade, and so the wretched inhabitants would have to forgo the inestimable privilege of having the flag. It's all quite simple when you know the rules of the game."

She shook her head. "I don't understand it all," she said.

He leant forward and touched her fingers lightly with his own. "If people were honest that's what ninety-eight per cent. of the population would admit."

"And what makes you want to go and fight, Anthony luv ?"

He raised his eyebrows, and again she felt that he was making fun—this time of himself.

"Me ? Heaven knows ! Something deep down inside me makes me want to go and prove that we're the best people in the world, that we can do the job better than anyone else. That where the Union Jack flies 'the slave is free'. It's got nothing to do with reason, nothing to do with logic or conviction. It's something that I can help as little as I can help having brown hair or a fair skin. There's a war—and I want to be in it ! There, that's the truth ! 'Cook's son, duke's son, son of a belted earl, son of a Lambeth publican—you're all the same today.' That's inspired verse, Mother ! Not true, because the cook's son won't get the same consideration as the son of a belted earl ! But it's going to send men out like children running to a sweet shop or flies gathering round a honeypot. Anyway"—with a queer tilt of his chin—"I wouldn't let Leister go and stay at home myself ! And you'd not wish me to."

"Wish," Sally said. "I don't wish no one to go, why should I ? What are all these clever gentlemen for if they can't settle quarrels like this without having to get boys like you and Lord

Leister to go and fight ? They're paid to do it—Mr. Chamberlain and Mr. Balfour—I mind him once coming to stay at Stallingford and I thought then he looked properly dreepy !"

Anthony said, "They didn't find him dreepy in Ireland. 'Bloody Balfour' they called him there !".

"S-sh," Sally said. "No need to repeat what the Irish say ; they say some very queer things one way and another ! Nay, I never thought a lot of Mr. Gladstone—not after that business with poor General Gordon—but he'd never have let it come to this ! Eh, my dear, take care of yourself, and don't take risks." Then with sudden irritation because she was nervous and worried, and the thought of Anthony—her dear love—going out to fight, almost drove her frantic with worry : "What's Mr. Rhodes doing ? I thought that he had all South Africa in his pocket ? A nice set-to. . . . My word, I'll lay that the Queen's prop'ly put out over it all. I can't bear to think of it. There's his lordship, never taken any interest in anything for years, he's like a boy again, and what for ? Because he's getting lads like you, and Leister, and Mr. Thursby and young Mr. Marston and Mr. Roysten's son and a whole lot more to go out and shoot farmers ! I don't know what the world's coming to ! Say what you like, it's all wrong and no good 'ul come of it. Nay, luv, I wish you'd stay home."

Again he laughed. "There are times when I wish that I could," he said ; "in the still, small hours of the morning somehow the glory and the glamour don't seem quite so obvious. Then at midday I smack my chest and tell myself that I'm lucky to be going. Do you know that Thomas is coming too ?"

"No ! Thomas ! What's he meddling wi' this for ? It's nothing to do wi' him !"

But it appeared that Thomas was going, and his lordship was delighted and said that there wasn't a troop in England to match Stallingford's Horse. He spent money like water, and equipped them as no other volunteers were equipped in the country. A Royal Duke came down to Stallingford to review them, and gave it as his opinion that the Boers would rue the day they'd imagined that they could oppose the might of Britain, to say nothing of Stallingford's Horse.

"'Pon my word, Stallingford," said the Royal Duke, "they look to me as if they could tackle the job single-handed ! Make Brother Boer turn tail and run without help from anyone."

The Earl, smiling and rubbing his hands, said, "It would ill become me to contradict you, sir ! I'm proud to have my own opinion backed by you !''

Sally never believed that they would go. The whole business seemed so fantastic. That the Earl, Leister, Anthony, and the stolid Thomas should all turn themselves into soldiers to go out and fight some farmers in South Africa was incredible. They were in camp, training, then—quite suddenly they were gone, sailing on a ship called the *Dundee Castle*, with their horses. Anthony had rushed back as far as York to see her. He looked strange and unfamiliar in his uniform, with a slouch hat turned up at one side and a leather strap under his chin.

They sat in the lounge at the Station Hotel, and he held her hand, quite openly, not caring who saw, or what they said if they did see. He kept on repeating that she was not to worry, that he would be all right, he'd see that Thomas was all right too. The whole thing might well be over by the time they arrived, then it would have been a pleasure trip and nothing more.

"Aye," Sally said ; "and what if it's not ovver, what then ?''

"Then," he said, "we'll try to make a good show and not let Yorkshire down."

Not until the train carried him out of the station did she realize that she was shaking, that her knees trembled, and her heart felt as if it were a bird imprisoned in her breast. He'd gone, that was the last she'd see of him, he was going in this great ship—with horses—to South Africa to try to kill Boers—and she remembered that in return the Boers would try to kill him. Anthony, Leister, Thomas, Thursby, Roysten, Marston and the rest—all going out to run the chance of being killed ! Good Yorkshire lads—her own two lads—running risks, getting into danger—and for what ? Just because a lot of good-for-nouts in Parliament weren't worth their salt, and let things come to this pass ! They'd not gone out to fight ! They'd sit at home, safe and sound, warm and comfortable, and let the lads put right the mess they'd made.

She walked out of the station, her eyes smarting, with a pain at her heart, and her mind filled with anger. She was caught, they were all caught. This war was a machine, and once it was set in motion by these politicians ordinary people such as Sally Scarth and her sons could do nothing. Thomas had talked about "what was right" and "upholding the Empire", his round, fresh-coloured face serious and intent ; Anthony had talked too, with his eyes dancing, and his mouth smiling, as if the whole thing were a huge joke.

She had snapped at them both. "Aye, cantering off, and what's to happen to your work ? Tell me that, will you ?"

Thomas said that Mr. MacIntosh had promised to keep his job open for him, and that he hoped to find some interesting flowers and such-like in South Africa, which he might bring home. It was a great chance, he said.

"And it needs a war to make it possible for you to go out and pick wild flowers, eh ?" Sally asked. "What about your work, Anthony ?"

He laughed. "Dearest, how practical you are ! What is our work compared with—this adventure ?"

"Aye, it 'ul be an adventure all right," she said, "if you get that right hand of yours damaged, and can't draw any more ! Nay, have done, both of you ; I want to hear no more on it."

ii

At Stallingford half the great house was closed, windows shuttered, the place seemed asleep. Lady Muriel passed her examinations, whatever they were, and left for Girton. Miss Meade said that she had done brilliantly, that she was a credit to them all—meaning, of course, herself and Mr. Haviland. Mr. Haviland was going as tutor to Lord Mansfield's sons, and Miss Meade was going to open a school of her own at Bournemouth. Another chapter was ended, Sally felt, another door closed on the old days.

In the servants' hall, Mr. Harrison had a big map, with little flags which he moved about from day to day. He showed Sally where it seemed probable that Stallingford's Horse were. She looked, said, "Oh yes—I see", but it meant nothing to her. She read the papers, even those flimsy evening journals that came to the house, but they were difficult to understand ; the names, she felt, were heathenish.

Sieges—she thought that sort of thing ended in the days you read of in history, when towns had walls round them. Ladysmith, Mafeking, Kimberley—sieges at all of them. Names of the Generals—she remembered some of them—General Buller had once come down to visit at a neighbouring house and had driven over to Stallingford—a heavy, thick-set man with a strong plain face. Methuen, Gatacre, Carew, Plumer—and later

Roberts. Everyone knew Lord Roberts, they sang songs about him, called him "Bobs". More names—Modder River, Magersfontein, Tugela River—and then—British losses.

Her heart used almost to stop beating when she thought of it. British boys killed, Yorkshire boys—her boys !

Mr. Harrison shook his head as he read the papers. "Terrible —heavy losses."

"But, Mr. Harrison, I thought the Boers were just farmers, not soldiers at all ?" Sally asked, frowning in her effort to understand.

"They're cunning," Mr. Harrison said, "that's how they do it—by low cunning and treachery. That's how it's done !"

She had letters, written on odd scraps of paper. Thomas's jerky, and telling her nothing much ; Anthony's amusing—too amusing, Sally felt, he was trying to make it all sound like a picnic. She knew differently—she remembered those "heavy losses".

1900 came in, and Thomas was killed at Spion Kop. Sally got the telegram one morning when she was sorting linen. She opened it, read it, and shut her eyes for a minute because it seemed such rubbish. How could Thomas be killed ! It wasn't possible. Thomas had never done anything wrong to anyone, she didn't believe that he could have done anything wrong even to a Boer.

Alice, one of the linen-room maids, looked at her and said, "I hope as it's nothing wrong, Mrs. Scarth."

"Why, I don't know," Sally said slowly. "It says that my son Thomas is killed."

"Oh, Mrs. Scarth . . ."

"Mind you, I don't believe it," Sally said. "They say anything these days—anything."

"Would it be from the War Office ?"

Sally looked at the bit of pink paper again. "Aye, that's where it says it's from."

Then it dawned on her that, after all, it was true, and that Thomas was killed, that she would never see him again, never listen to his stories of new flowers, and never laugh at him because his hair would not lie down flat to his head. She felt her face twist, knew that she began to cry. Not like a grown person—quietly and with restraint, but like a great child. She heard the noise that she made with a kind of dismayed surprise and yet could do nothing to check it.

"Aye—it's me lad as is dead ! Ugh—ugh—my Thomas ! Nay, it's not reit—ugh—ugh—as dear an' good a lad as ever stepped—ugh—ugh . . ." on and on, repeating herself and unable to do anything to stop the noise which she made. "If he was here," she said, "he'd be t' first to say, 'Nay, Mother, give ovver do !' " Then she remembered that he would never be there again, and rocked herself backwards and forwards as if the pain was too much for her.

They were all very kind. Mr. Roysten came over to see her, and so did the Vicar ; and young Mr. Thursby wrote a beautiful letter from Africa to say how much they'd all liked Thomas and how they missed him. Anthony wrote too, not amusing this time, just angry and horrified.

I keep saying, "But why Thomas ?" [he wrote]. *Why not some- one less good and kindly ? Plenty of rotten fellows would never be missed. Twenty years is no time for a chap to have lived. Even I have had four years longer than he had. And nothing to show for it. Sitting there, talking, and then a bullet pinging through the air, and a little blue hole in his head—to let his soul get away out of this filthy business ! Oh, damn everything !*

Sally felt old, old and shaken. She was afraid. Before, it had seemed that even with those "heavy losses" her boys must be safe, nothing could touch them. Now Thomas had gone, and she felt that death was stalking closer to Anthony.

People said that it—and "it" meant the war—would be over any time now, but still it dragged on, gains on this side, gains on that. New stories of brutalities, of cruelties, of treachery and double-dealing. Generals sent out, other Generals brought home again. Stormberg—Colenso. Sally forgot which came first, they were names which struck dread in her heart. The C.I.V.s went out, and again the war "was as good as over". The Queen was ill, the Queen was dead ; she died, someone read in a paper, in the arms of the German Emperor. Mrs. Duchers said that the new king would be Albert the First. Mr. Harrison said, "That I should doubt very much, Mrs. Duchers. Not an English name, only by adoption." Again the war was over, and yet still fighting went on. The Boers were hiding, the Boers were hoarding ammunition, the Boers were always cropping up somewhere unexpectedly. Then, in June 1902, at some place with a name which Sally did not attempt to pronounce, peace was made, and the war really was over.

That night Sally sat in her room, her hands clasped, looking out over the park, listening to the faint sound of the little brook as it trickled over the stones. It was over, and they would be coming home—all except Thomas and poor young Mr. Thursby. Her "dear love" would be with her again.

Watching the tall trees, so dark against the evening sky, listening to the sounds of the countryside, the sudden chirp of a bird, the rustle as some little wild animal made its way homeward to hole or burrow, Sally sighed.

Thirty-four years she had lived with Stallingford as the centre of her world. Even when William was alive, she had felt that this was where she "belonged". She had worked here as a little girl, she had grown up under this roof. She had come back as a widow, and now—it had lost its meaning for her. It had ceased to be the hub of the universe, it was just a grand old house, splendid and magnificent, but it didn't mean anything to her any more. She wanted to get away, to live in a place of her own again, with Anthony to come and go as he pleased. She wanted to forget that she had once loved Stallingford, that Anthony was his son as well as hers. She wanted to be rid of responsibility; she longed to have no more orders to give to linen-room maids, still-room maids, housemaids, parlourmaids and the rest of them. She was weary of the endless questions : "Please, Mrs. Scarth, shall we . . ." or "Mrs. Scarth, would you tell me if you . . ."; she had lost interest in fine linen, and shining damask, in lace curtains and hangings of heavy silk brocade. The thought of the priceless carpets and rugs worried her, the great Venetian glass chandeliers which took so much washing and polishing had ceased to hold any real beauty for her. There were too many rooms, too much valuable furniture, too great a number of pictures of incredible value. She wanted simplicity and quiet. She had done her work, she had waited until the war was over, and now—she wanted to depart in peace, to live in peace, simply and easily. The war was done, ended— surely this would have taught the nations a lesson that what they began as a kind of "picnic" could develop into a wholesale slaughter.

She had listened to Mr. Harrison, to Mr. Roysten, even to the Vicar in church on Sundays, declaiming that war was necessary, that England must predominate, that wherever the Union Jack flew a great benefit was conferred on the people who lived under its shadow. Well, it might all be true, she didn't pretend to know. All she knew was that somewhere in Africa Thomas lay dead, her youngest child, who had never harmed anyone, who had loved his work and his flowers, and who had lived only a bare twenty years. Not only Thomas, he was, as you might say, a specimen. There were hundreds, thousands like him. Nice lads, good, clean-living lads who had gone rushing and tearing out to Africa—and for what ? Boers—well, she knew nothing about them, but she supposed that Boer lads had died the same as English boys had. Lads were lads all the world over—young and interested in their work, lads with fresh pink faces and hair which stuck up in a little drake's tail at the back of their heads.

She rarely expressed opinions ; but when Mr. Harrison said one evening at supper that they were living in a wonderful age, that they had seen the end of a glorious war, Sally Scarth rose to her feet and stood facing them all down the long table.

"Glorious war !" she said. "No war's glorious. What's it all for ? Tell me that ! Nay, I'll tell you. Gold mines and diamond mines. Will my lad come home a penny richer, or wiser, or happier ? O' course he won't. And listen to me, all of you—it's a bad thing when people begin to believe that they can get what they want through a war ! Wars are made by greedy folk with hands stretched out to gather gold and power. That's who makes wars. It's like as if them in power put some 'fluence on the lads, to make them think a lot of dreams—glory, patriotism. What is glory ? Tell me that. What's patriotism ? Loving your country. Then live for her, live for England, don't die for her. My poor Thomas 'ud have made England bonnier with flowers, growing them, watching them, loving them. Wouldn't that have been serving England better nor what he has done, lying dead in some grave in Africa wi'oot even an English rose tree blooming over him ? I've seen the map, Mr. Harrison, with a piece added that's got to be painted red—red for England. My God, red for blood ! The blood of our boys as ought to be working here, in their own land, making two blades of grass grow where at first there was only one." She stopped and stared at them all, as if they were strangers to her, then said in a queer, quiet voice, "I think that Jesus Christ must be the unhappiest soul that there is !" Then blinking her eyes, as if she had been suddenly blinded by a light, she said, "Nay, I don't know what made me talk that way. Good night, everyone ; I'm away to my bed."

She walked out of the servants' hall, leaving them all staring after her. Mr. Harrison said in his quiet voice, "I don't think this ought to be repeated. Mrs. Scarth has given one son to the Empire, and her other son is only now returning to England. She has suffered a great strain, but there isn't a more loyal soul living. A very fine woman, and—we must make allowances for the sufferings of a mother's heart."

Mrs. Duchers said, "I'm entirely with you, Mr. Harrison. I think we may rely on everyone here to regard what Mrs. Scarth's said as said in—confidence."

Mr. Harrison bowed. "Very properly said, Mrs. Duchers. Thank you."

The next thing she heard was that she was to go to Southampton. His lordship had arrived on the *Welbeck Castle*, with what remained of Stallingford's Horse. He wanted Sally to join him there immediately. She was to go direct to the "Star" —Mr. Harrison said that wasn't the name of the big station hotel at the docks, but probably his lordship wished to be quiet. To have been out there all this time—and "out there" to everyone meant South Africa—must have been a great strain.

She showed his telegram to no one :

Come immediately Star Hotel, Southampton. A. well.

The only thing she didn't understand was why Anthony had not sent her a telegram himself. She felt a vague uneasiness that Anthony should be with the Earl. Had Stallingford tried to gain influence over him ? Had he been making much of him, pampering him ? As she packed her bag, Sally Scarth thought, 'I'll have none of it. My boy's come through this and he's going to make his own way in the world. I'll not have Stallingford bolstering him up, making a softie of him, choose how.'

Stallingford hadn't mentioned Leister. That did not surprise her. He'd never liked the boy, and probably he liked him no better now than he'd ever done. She finished her packing and drove to the station in the high dog-cart and left for Southampton.

CHAPTER SEVEN

SALLY stood in the hall of the hotel. Vaguely she realized that she liked it. It was old, it had dignity. She was quietly glad that she was to meet Anthony again here. She spoke to the clerk in the reception desk.

"I—well, I really want my son—but perhaps it would be better if you told the Earl of Stallingford that Mrs. Scarth was here."

She was shaking, she knew that. Her hands were trembling, and again she experienced that queer feeling that someone had shut a bird up inside her breast, she could feel it fluttering. Not a bird really ; her heart, and she knew it, but that was how it felt. In a minute he would come down those shallow stairs ! Her son, after all this time she would catch him in her arms and know that he was safe. He had escaped from the Boers, he had come home to her again.

The clerk said, "Mrs.—er—Scarth—would you go up to the Earl's private sitting-room ? George, take this lady to the Earl of Stallingford."

That was when she began to grow frightened, when she knew that little beads of sweat were forming on her forehead and top lip, that her hands were growing moist and that her whole body was shaking with fear. Where was Anthony ? Why was she sent for to see the Earl ? She followed the waiter up the stairs, holding tightly to the banister rail, dragging herself up, step after step.

A landing, double doors, the waiter flinging one of them open, walking in before her, saying : "The lady to see you, sir." Instinctively Sally thought, 'If I'd the training of that fellow he'd learn how to announce people better'n that.' Then a long room, with two deep windows, and Stallingford coming towards her, with his hands outstretched. He was very thin, bronzed, but with deep pouches under his eyes. Old, he looked—impossible to believe that he was scarcely fifty. His shoulders were bent, his hands holding hers were brittle, as if they were made of paper. Only his eyes were very bright, alive, vital.

"Sally, Sally—it's all right. I've brought him home safely."

She licked her lips. Felt the floor more solid under her feet. Reassured—more secure. Her "dear love" was all right, then.

"That's good news for me, m'lord."

Stallingford said, "Come and sit down, Sally. I've got to talk to you. Changes, Sally, big changes. Poor Thomas—I was sorry. A good lad, first-rate lad. Died bravely."

'Died bravely,' she thought. What did he mean? Thomas had died because a bullet had hit him while he sat talking. Bravely—died bravely. That was the sort of plaster people learnt to use, to comfort you. As if it mattered. A lad died— bravely or not, he died.

"Thank you, m'lord. Yes, it was a bad blow to me, poor Thomas. A good boy."

"A good boy indeed. But, Sally, the other's left. I'm going to tell you. Listen to me. It's a long story—a difficult one. I've never been one to pretend, you know that. I've always said what I felt, believed. Anthony's ill—oh, he isn't going to die." For the first time Stallingford laughed. "Die—he won't die. He's mending every day. Lying sleeping quietly in a pleasant bedroom here in this hotel. You shall see him in a moment. Ill on the boat. Ill when we embarked. Taken on board on a stretcher, practically unconscious. I've tried to look after him. I swear to you, I have."

"That's very good of you, m'lord."

"Now—my story. Leister and Anthony—both ill. Fever. You know that I never cared for Leister. I don't know why— God forgive me!—but he was poor stuff. Nothing would change him. I was proud—out there—of Anthony, of Thomas—of young Thursby, of Roysten. Never of my own heir." He broke off suddenly, unexpectedly. "Let's have some tea, Sally. Yes—I'll order it." He sprang to his feet, rang the bell, waited until the waiter answered it. "Tea for two—at once—be quick about it, please." Then came and sat down again near Sally, took out his cigarette-case, tapped the cigarette on the table sixteen times—Sally counted the taps—lit it, drew a deep breath, and then rose and walked to the window and stared out.

The waiter entered with tea. Stallingford spun round. "On the table there! That's right. No, nothing else. Thank you. Now, pour out, Sally." She saw him pull out his handkerchief and wipe his forehead.

"Listen—no, I don't want sugar. Leister died in Cape Town—Anthony was ill. I took a chance. I was the only person who knew. Rest of the men who knew them were in billets, coming down by train. Leister died. I changed the papers. It's recorded that Anthony Scarth died and Athol Leister came home with me. Athol Leister's asleep in the bedroom in this hotel with a nurse watching him at this moment. Sally—the likeness—no one could tell. No distinguishing marks. I arranged everything. It's a chance—for him, for me, for the whole estate, Sally. He's got grit, guts, ideals and ideas. Back me up, Sally. Your son—and mine, one day Earl of Stallingford. Not defrauding anyone. It's all right. If I don't do this everything goes to a weak-kneed third cousin ! Unthinkable. No good to anyone. Anthony's good stuff. It's—it's ordained, Sally. You'll stand by me, won't you ?''

She stared at him, as he stood before her, his thin face touched with colour, his hands held out towards her, trembling, supplicating. He was almost pathetic in his intensity. She saw, as if it had been revealed to her in a vision, that he realized how he had failed to do his duty by the lands which were his, by the people who inhabited those acres, and how he saw in Anthony —young, energetic, interested—a saviour for those folk whom he had neglected. At the same time her own sentiments regarding the governing classes of England came rushing over her. She might have railed against the new order, she might have felt disillusionment and disappointment that the "old order" had changed so lamentably, but she was not going to be a party to a deception. She was not going to foist her son—Stallingford's son though he might be—on the gentry as one of their own !

She looked at him coldly. "And you pretended as Anthony Scarth died, m'lord ?''

"I did ! It was a chance, Sally. I'm proud of the boy. He's all I always hoped that my son might be—he's intelligent, he has ideas, he's strong and——''

"Then all I've got to say, m'lord, is that you took a very great liberty.''

The words seemed so inadequate that for a moment Stallingford smiled. She meant nothing, she was going to stand by him. Together they would make the most of this likeness, they would work together to make the world believe that Anthony Scarth was Athol, Lord Leister.

"Sally——''

"Nay," she said, suddenly lapsing into broad Yorkshire, "nay m'lord, I've worked for you and yours since I was twelve years, old. I've known what I owed to your family, I've tried my best to pay what I owed, but now—I'm done! I'll have none of it. Anthony's my son, and no gentleman, you know that. I'll not have him jockeyed into a position that isn't his, that the chances are ten to one he can't hold. You don't pick earls off the trees like as what you'd pick cherries! There's more to it nor that—an' if there isn't, then it's a poor look-out for England. You've done this, and you mun put it reit. How, I don't know, but having done it, you can undo it. You will—because you must!"

He watched her, his eyes narrowed, his weak jaw thrust forward. "It's my word against yours, Sally. If I say he's my son—if he agrees—what chance have you against the two of us? Tell me that. My God, I could have you certified with very little trouble, certified as crazy, as not knowing your own son."

She did not move, for a second her eyebrows lifted a little, then she smiled and shook her head, speaking as she might have spoken to a stupid child.

"Nay, Stallingford, it 'ud tak' mor'n you—Earl though you are—to certify a Yorkshire woman as crazy when she were nothing of the kind! We're hard-headed, and you should know it, you've lived wi' uz long enoof. I can't help what you thought you'd do, it's no business of mine what ideas you had, what plans you made. They're not my ideas, they're not my plans. You say—if he agrees! He won't, and if he wanted to, I'd not allow it. That poor boy that's gone—I know that you never cared a lot for him. He was weak, he was a poor waffley fellow. That's no reason why, because he's gone, you and me should try to deceive people. Anthony 'ul come home with me. I'm grateful to you for what you've done, I'm sure that you've been kind to him, treated him well. I'd have done the same for your son, if things had been the other way round." She met his eyes squarely, her voice was low but quite steady. "Years ago, when I was caught—aye, caught—I was 'flaid, and I made another man believe that Anthony was his. It was a sin, m'lord —I know that now. Luckily for me, my husband forgave me. But I'm doing no more of it. I've done with falsifying and lies, with pretence and tricks. No one 'ul make me do those things agean—not you, were you a thousand times an Earl. That's my last word!"

Stallingford pulled up a chair and sat down near her. He

leant forward, his thin brown hands clasped tightly, his whole figure tense, his voice hoarse with feeling.

He argued, he painted a picture for her of the life which might be Anthony's, he recounted the chances and opportunities which would be his. Power was his for the asking. Power for good. He admitted his own faults. "I know that I've never taken my work, my duties as I should, Sally. I've put myself first. I hated the estate ; the tenants bored me. I was wrong. I'm too old to change now. Anthony's young. He'll come to it fresh—eager—interested. He'll be like my father—his grand-father, don't forget that, Sally—wanting to do what's right, what's just to the people who are in his charge. Anthony's got a sense of responsibility. I never had ! If you refuse to help me in this—you're not only defrauding your son, you're robbing the people who are waiting for a decent landlord. The world's changing. New ideas are here ! Anthony 'ul put them into practice. Don't think only of yourself, of your son. Have a larger, wider vision, Sally. Think of the villages where he'd be welcomed, think of the good he could do—would do. You can't fling away a chance like this—it's wrong, wrong, wrong."

Very calmly, Sally said, "Nay, m'lord, what you say's just going in at one ear and out at the other. I'll have none of it. Right—wrong—duty—chances ! How can any good come of what's founded on a wrong ? The gentleman who's the heir, how do you know that he won't do well, won't work hard, won't make a good landlord ? He's got his rights, hasn't he ? He's next in the line ; very well, he must step into his rightful place. I've no more to say. My first and last word is—no !" She drank the last drops of her tea and set the cup down. "And now, m'lord, I should like to see my son."

Stallingford sprang to his feet, he stood before her, his hands catching at hers. He had flung pride to the winds, he was just a weak man, begging, praying to her to help him to carry out the plans which he had made.

"... And after making the statements which I have made —how the devil can I put it all right ?"

"That's your business, m'lord, not mine. You made the statements, I didn't."

"Sally, for the last time—think !"

"I have thought, m'lord—I've nothing fresh to think about."

"It's not fair to Tony—it's denying him a great chance, a stupendous chance."

"A chance to lie, to live a lie—no, thank you r"

"For the sake of others—because he can do so much."

"Oh, have done !" Sally exclaimed. "How do either of us know that he'd do anything ? And if he did, it's not his work. He wasn't born a lord—I won't have him acting a lie, and maybe one day giving himself away. I'll be no party to it all. That's my last word."

"Sally, I'm fond of him. He's the only person in the world I am fond of——"

She said, coldly, "That's not true, m'lord. You're fond of yourself, always have been, always will be."

"My God——"

"This is only a new kind of self-indulgence !" she retorted. "It's to please yourself. You've been disappointed in your own son—and now you want Anthony !"

"Damn it, isn't he—my son ?"

"No, m'lord—legally, he's only mine !"

They argued and wrangled. Stallingford growing more and more irritable, angry and conscious that nothing he said would move her ; Sally forcing herself to remain calm, speaking frankly and often hurtfully. As she spoke she felt that she was severing the last remaining ties which bound her to Stallingford, the old house which she had once loved, and all those memories which used to be so precious. She had allowed herself to be held bound, she had returned after William's death because she loved the place, loved her memories, loved the Family which had meant so much to her. Now, fighting down Stallingford's arguments, she knew that she was cutting loose from those anchors which had held her fast for so many years. As she spoke she was conscious of a pain which was almost physical. Her life, filled as it had been with admiration for the old Earl, with an appreciation of what his family with its traditions and beliefs meant, was shifting—suddenly—and the things which had been, to her, foundations were no longer real and solid, but ephemeral, fantastic, and existing only in her own imagination.

Here was Stallingford suggesting that they should band together to perpetrate a deception on the whole of England. He was asking her, begging her, threatening her if she refused to agree, to help him to foist her son on the tenants, the gentry, even the government, as one of the hereditary legislators of England. She had known that there were weak and indifferent legislators, she knew that there were members of the ruling classes who did less than their duty, but she had always believed that these people possessed something which was theirs by virtue of their birth, and their blood.

She knew now that her disillusionment was not a sudden thing. Here in this room in an hotel in Southampton it was crystallized, but it had been growing and forming in her heart for months. She could scarcely have said why. The Family had been generous enough to her, they had treated her well, they had been considerate and kindly, but she had felt this growing sense of dissatisfaction. The old order was not only changing, it had changed. She had watched Stallingford lose his grip, lose his interest in matters which belonged to his estate, she had seen his son—weak, lacking in resolution, and she had resented these things more than she had known.

It was as if now all her resentment, all her disappointment, was brought to the surface, shown to her plainly. Her realization hurt more than she could have believed it would. She felt that Stallingford himself was to blame for having robbed her of something in which she had believed for so long. She knew that her life at Stallingford was over. She could never go back. She wanted, now, only to get away, to take Anthony with her, to make a home for him, and to live her life quietly and shouldering her own responsibilities. Great rooms, splendid pictures, rich hangings, gold and silver plate, priceless carpets, meant nothing to her. She had felt a pride in them because they were part of Stallingford, and now her pride in the place—in the people who lived there—had died.

She watched the Earl, his face growing hot, his voice mounting so that it sounded high and thin in her ears, and felt that he was a stranger to her. He was asking her to become his accomplice in a fraud. Years ago she had been party to a fraud, and she still felt a sense of gratitude to some Power stronger than herself, Who had allowed William to know, and to be able to forgive. She had done her best to be a good wife to William, and a good mother to his children ; she had never allowed the thought to be definitely formulated in her mind that she was paying off a debt, but it had lain there nebulous and vague but existent.

Thomas was dead, Elsie married, living in Paris with her own interests, her own ambitions, and only Anthony was left to her. To allow Stallingford to carry out his plan was not only to take hands with him in what seemed to her a piece of dishonesty, it was to give up her son, the person she loved best in all the world.

He was to be the future Earl of Stallingford and she would remain Sally Scarth, the housekeeper. Any real intimacy between them would be at an end. They would be forced to watch their words, their looks, the very inflections of their speech.

"Nay," she said. "Save your breath, m'lord. I'll have nothing to do with it all. It's not right. It means giving up my son. It means losing everything that's mine. I'm going to see him, I've wasted overmuch time."

He flung up his hands, his face was quivering. "It's the worst blow I have ever had!"

"I'm sorry, m'lord."

"I don't know how I'm going to unravel the tangle——"

"A tangle of lies——"

"It's going to be terribly difficult."

"You should ha' thought of that before, m'lord."

"God! You're hard, Sally."

She rose. "I want to see my son, if you please."

ii

She was taken to his room. He lay there, brown-faced and incredibly thin. She thought, 'Nay, he lukes more like a skellington nor anything else.'

The nurse, rustling as she moved, rose and said, "The Earl told me to expect you, Mrs. Scarth."

Sally nodded, moved past her towards the bed, bent down and said softly, "So you're home, my dear love?"

Anthony licked his lips, his eyes smiled. "Yes, I'm home all right, Mother."

She bent lower, and he smelt the scent of lavender and thyme with which her clothes were impregnated. The perfume brought back to him everything that was—his mother. With her came the thought of clean cool sheets, of rooms with open windows, of newly baked bread, and flowers standing in a brightly coloured jar on a table spread with a checked cloth.

Sally said, "Don't weary yourself with talking, my dear. I'll talk—you listen. Get well. I'm leaving Stallingford. I'll find a little house for us somewhere. Quiet and with a lot of sunshine and a bit of garden. I've worked over-long. We've got enough money saved. Don't worry. Just get well and come home to me."

His weakness made his lips quiver suddenly, made his eyes fill with tears.

"Mother—I'm so grieved about Thomas."

"Aye—poor lad. Nay, don't cry, Anthony. Just get well and come home."

"I will—yes, I will. Do you have to go ?"

She bent and kissed him. "I've a lot to do, my dear. I'll come again before you come home."

"All right, Mother. Don't be too long."

She went back and talked again to Stallingford. He had overcome his hysterical anger ; he was cast down and sulky. He sat there, his shoulders lifted, his head lowered. He looked old and feeble, weak and without determination. Watching him, Sally wondered how she had ever loved him. He'd been different in those days—he must have been different. He had forgotten his desire to make Anthony a worthy successor to the old Earl, he sat there grumbling that she had made matters very difficult, that he scarcely knew how he was to get out of the mess and muddle.

"You got into it, m'lord. You never consulted me."

"No one stands by me, no one !"

She told him that she was leaving Stallingford, leaving in a month's time. Everything would be in order, whoever followed her would find everything ready to their hands.

He stared at her. "What will you live on ?"

"I've saved, m'lord ; my aunt left me money, so did old Mrs. Bishop, and so did your lordship's mother. And Anthony 'ul work. We'll do very well."

"Queer to think of Stallingford without you ! You've been tangled up in my life—Sally—right through it. Almost impossible to go back to the place and not find you there. Oh, if everything had only been different—eh, Sally ?"

"Things work out for the best, m'lord."

"Do they—I wonder ?" Then, frowning, his head lowered a little, his expression suddenly truculent, he said, "You've no faith in me, have you ? You don't believe that I can still get the reins in my own hands and make the place my chief interest ! Eh, answer me."

"No, I don't, m'lord. You've left it alone over-long. It's difficult to start again at fifty."

He jerked up his chin. "Ah ! I'll show you. I'll show you all. I know what I can do, and I'll do it."

"I'm very glad to hear it. No one 'ud be more glad than I would. Now, m'lord, I've told the nurse to let me know when Anthony's ready to come home. And—" she paused, "I'd like to pay the doctor's bill and the hotel bill and—everything."

Stallingford swung round at her. "Oh, for God's sake leave me something! You don't know how this has hurt me, Sally. You've smashed the last hopes I had—it means a hell of a lot to me. Let me do something for the fellow."

"Very well, m'lord, and thank you. Now, I'll get along. Good-bye, and—thank you again."

Almost stupidly, as if he scarcely comprehended what she said, Stallingford answered, "Good-bye—Sally—and thank you. Good-bye."

iii

She had found her house. One of those small yet dignified houses of grey stone, with good slate roofs which are still to be found in Yorkshire. There was a garden, full of homely flowers, there were cool rooms, and there was a good kitchen with a shining grate and oven. Sally Scarth stood outside in the small bright garden and looked at the place with satisfaction. She would be happy here. This was where Anthony would come when his work allowed, this was where she would prepare good meals, where beds would be kept well aired and where smooth, scented sheets would always be ready. There were alterations to be made, she wasn't going to be dependent on a well for her water supply. Pipes must be put in, she must have running water, she wanted a bathroom. The time was past when she could face a weekly bath in the washing-tub! She walked into the house and smiled as she visited every room in turn. Air, light, space. Not all the castles in the country could give her more. It would be strange to have only one young village girl at her beck and call, after Stallingford, where she had twenty people waiting on her orders.

"Maybe, having learnt how to give orders to twenty," Sally mused, "I shall know how to behave right to one!"

She sat down in the old Chippendale armchair at the side of the fireplace. Her hands rested folded in her lap, her lips were touched with a smile.

She had come home. She had begun by sleeping rough, by spending nights in the casual wards of workhouses, she had

trudged beside her mother during harvests and the time of
potato-picking. She had been cold and tired and hungry. She
had known the miseries of a workhouse child, unloved, unwanted.
She had realized the good fortune which came to her when
Stallingford's father "brought her out of the house of bondage".
From want she had gone to plenty, from harshness she had
moved to where she found nothing but warm kindliness. There
had been comfort, good food, and an orderly life waiting for her.
Like poor Joe—of whom she had never heard nor read—thinking
of the old Earl, she formulated the words, "He was very good
to me."

She had worked honestly, and with a single mind. She had
loved her employers, their well-being had been her first thought.
She would willingly have given her life for them. Then
Victor had come—Stallingford, when he was only Leister—and
he had taught her what a personal love meant. Her love for the
family had been one thing, her love for him had been another.

She might have been Countess of Stallingford, but she had
known it would have been wrong. Looking back, she knew that
for a year, two years, she might have made Leister happy, might
even have spurred him on to work and show an interest in the
lands and the people over which he had power. And after that
—no, the old Earl had been right.

She had been lucky, she thought. Life itself had been kind.
Leister flashing into her life like some bright light, and then—
almost before that light had died—William had come, good and
thoughtful, and—she thought—'as sweet as a nut, and as straight
as a bit of string'. Her children—Anthony held a place of his
own, but the others had been good bairns. She sighed. 'Poor
Thomas!'

Then, slowly the realization had come to her that she had
finished her term of usefulness at Stallingford. The Earl cared
nothing for the place, he never would, come what might. The
old Countess was dead, she had slipped away to join her husband.
Leister was dead, and Muriel thought of nothing except her books
and her learning. Sally Scarth had finished her work. There
was nothing to keep her, and she had gone her way.

In this little warm, friendly house she was going to begin
life all over again. Today Anthony was coming home. Sally
glanced up at the clock, then called, "Ellen, get the table laid.
Mr. Anthony 'ul be here in no time. Pop those fat rascals in the
oven for a minute, and open a pot of bramble jelly."

"Yes, Mrs. Scarth."

Sally rose, and walked down the flagged passage to the front door. There under the little porch she stood, her eyes turning towards the road up which Anthony must come. It would never have occurred to her to go to the railway station to meet him. She disliked meetings in public, with everyone staring, with everyone watching and commenting, saying later, "Eh, Mrs. Scarth didn't half cry when her lad come home !" In her own mind, she decided, 'Nay, keep such things for your own house. Let's be decent i' public, choose how.'

He was returning today. He wrote that the Earl had left Southampton, that he had been worried and disturbed, but unfailingly kind. Again Anthony had said, "I like him—really, you know." Somewhere Stallingford was wrestling with the muddle which he had made. Well, people like the Earl of Stallingford had ways and means of smoothing rough places. He'd get it straight somehow, Sally didn't doubt.

They might see him again—she didn't know. This house of hers was twenty-five miles south-west of Stallingford. He'd likely never come that far. Thinking of him, Sally knew that a queer tenderness, which had lain dead for so many years, stirred in her heart. She had a lot to thank him for—poor Stallingford. Love, romance, laughter—and Anthony. That was why Anthony meant so much to her. All those things had gone to the making of him. He was the result of whatever romance she had known in her life.

Stallingford was—the past, and Anthony was the future. She was not yet fifty, she was strong, she loved life, and she needed someone to be the centre of that life. Anthony was the pivot—the mainspring—the meaning of it all.

She looked down the quiet street, at the solid little houses with their gay gardens, their trim windows, and mathematically straight curtains. Once before she had come to live in a small house, she had found it cramping and restricted. Now—she had ceased to long for huge rooms, for dignity, for splendour, even if that grandeur were only reflected to her by a great family. She had—in her own way—shared all those things. The nobility, aristocrats, even princes of the blood royal, had slept under the same roof as Sally Scarth ; she had heard stories of their whims and fancies, their likes and dislikes so often that she had felt that she knew them, and she had been proud of her knowledge.

The last years had shown her the impermanence of such

things. Those farmers out in South Africa had done more than
they knew. They had opposed the might of England, they had
robbed her of the heads of her great houses, taken from her
those young lives in whom her hopes were centred. Athol, Lord
Leister had been a prey to them as had Thomas Scarth. War
levelled everything. War proved the instability of all that
people like Sally Scarth had believed lasting and enduring.

'Nay, it's a fool-like thing—this war-making,' Sally thought.
'I' twenty years' time it 'ul be as if it had never happened ; no
one better nor worse, except those poor lads lying out there wi'
their lives cut short.'

In the distance she heard the whistle as the train passed under
the railway arch outside the village. In a moment Anthony
would be getting out at the station, old George would take his
bags and put them on the old tumbledown hand-cart, and
together they would make their way down the long narrow street.
He was coming home.

All her life she had been concerned with the lives of other
folks, their comfort, the smooth running of their house, even
with William she had sunk her own individuality so that she
might make his home what he wished it to be—because she was
paying off the debt that she owed him. Now she was free ! Now
she could make a life with her son, together they would be
happy, and she would savour the full flavour of his success. He
would go back into the world, to London, to his drawing-boards
and pictures, but he would come here from time to time, and
his home would be waiting for him.

'A home,' she thought, 'that's what I'll make it ! A reit
home. A place where he can know that nout waits for him but
love and warmth and understanding. He's been out i' South
Africa, papers say that it's men like him that have been helping
build the Empire. Maybe they're reit. Maybe it's greatly
important.' She frowned. "An' maybe it's not!" she said
softly, forgetting that she was speaking her thoughts aloud.
"There's not so many of us vastly concerned wi' Empires, but
there's precious few on us as dean't want homes. We all want
that—English an' French and Germans and Roosians—even
Boers. Ah doot if we all ran our homes reit, if everyone had
enough money ter pay t' butcher an' baker—an' keep homes sweet
and clean and comfortable, if we'd bother our heads less about
making wars an' such-like. It's not richness as moast on us
wants—it's the knowledge as we've enoof coming in ter feed an'

clothe us. Security—aye, that's the word. Security ! Summat that's lasting, an' real an' good."

She blinked her eyes, as if they were dimmed a little, and she wished to see clearly. There was old George, with his hand-cart—it badly wanted a lick o' paint an' all—and beside him walked Anthony—thin, moving a little stiffly, talking very fast and intently. They came nearer, and she saw old George point out the house to Anthony. He was saying, she knew it as if she heard the very words, "Yon's thee mother's house—yon wi' t' porch."

Anthony looked, saw her and waved his hand, shouting, "I'm here, Mother—I'm here !"

Sally's eyes smarted ; she knew that her throat contracted and that she could so easily have begun to cry. Instead, she squared her shoulders, and walked down the little path. At the gate she waited, Anthony quickened his steps, and reached her, caught her hand in his. His eyes were very bright, his cheeks were touched with colour.

"I'm home," he said. "Home, Mother !"

She bent and kissed him. "Aye—an' just in time fur tea an' all."

He laughed. "That sounds good !"

"There's fat rascals an' tea-cakes," she said. "T' kettle's on the boil."

He slipped his arm through hers and together they went into the house.

"Fat rascals and tea-cakes, and the kettle on the boil," Anthony repeated. "I believe that you'd say the same if I'd been away for twenty years. If the whole world were shaken, rocked, become disintegrated—if nations had risen and fallen, kings lived and died—there'd be women like you standing firm, and making fat rascals and tea-cakes."

"Well, and why not ?" Sally said. "You've got to eat, haven't you ? Come your ways in, luv."

Sirmione,
  Italy.